*I*n the hour before dawn, ~~~~~~ ~~~~~ ~ish-erman had gone to the River ~~~~~ ~~a to ready his little boat for the day's work. There, busy about his morning routine of checking his nets and lines, he found something among the reeds at the water's edge to make horribly real the rumors he had heard throughout the summer.

What he'd found was no human thing, yet the fisherman could not give it a name. It had two arms and two legs, like his own Elvish kin or the Mannish folk. But there the resemblance stopped. Its hairless skull seemed, from the several protrusions on it, to be deformed. Judging from its prone length, it might stand as tall as a small child. One shoulder was hunched, drawn up even in stillness, again suggesting deformity.

It's face bore no touch of humanity at all. . . .

Other TSR™ Books

THE
JEWELS
— OF —
ELVISH

Nancy Varian Berberick

Cover Art
Clyde Caldwell

TSR, Inc.
PRODUCTS OF YOUR IMAGINATION™

To Bruce,
for the love and the friendship

THE JEWELS OF ELVISH

This book is protected under the copyright laws of the United States of America. Any reproduction or other unauthorized use of the material or artwork contained herein is prohibited without the express written permission of TSR, Inc.

Distributed to the book trade in the United States by Random House, Inc., and in Canada by Random House of Canada, Ltd.

Distributed in the United Kingdom by TSR UK Ltd.

Distributed to the toy and hobby trade by regional distributors.

DRAGONLANCE is a registered trademark owned by TSR, Inc. FORGOTTEN REALMS is a trademark owned by TSR, Inc. TM designates other trademarks owned by TSR, Inc.

First printing: April, 1989
Printed in the United States of America.
Library of Congress Catalog Card Number: 88-51278

9 8 7 6 5 4 3 2 1

All characters in this book are fictitious. Any resemblance to actual persons, living or dead, is purely coincidental.

TSR, Inc.
P.O. Box 756
Lake Geneva, WI 53147
U.S.A.

TSR Ltd.
120 Church End, Cherry Hinton
Cambridge CB1 3LB
United Kingdom

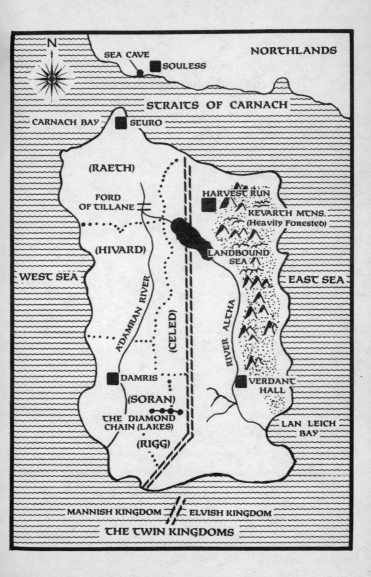

PROLOGUE

I am Islief of the First People. Once I was called the Wise, but now my people name me the Sinner, for indeed I have sinned.

None may deny she came to me in direst need, the Elvish warrior maid Aeylin. Her tears were for her people, and for a land ravaged by wizardry most foul, under the cruel hand of the Sorcerer. Aeylin begged me to save her people, and my pity gave birth to the sin for which I still suffer.

None save magical defenses can hope to prevail against sorcerous attacks, and I knew there was but one object powerful enough.

Unbeknownst to my people, we descended through the city that had been hewn from solid rock into the Crown Hold and gazed upon the pedestal of rare black diamond, atop which rested the powerful gift from the gods to my people. A band of silver-chased gold held each of four jewels at the crown's points, surrounding the glowing ruby at its center.

Emerald: Proud Ruler of Nature.

Sapphire: Gentle King of Air.

Diamond: Wild Prince of Water.

Topaz: Golden Thane of Fire.

Ruby: Fearsome Mistress of War.

I knew too well the fabled powers of the crown, and what its loss would mean to my people. Able to command the very elements themselves, the crown was Aeylin's only hope to save her people from the Sorcerer. And so I gave it to her freely, in order to restore balance to a world run mad with sorcery.

And now I pay the price the gods must exact for sending the crown out into a world where it was never meant to go. For that is the price of my sin: To await the dawn of a new age. . . .

PART ONE

Thou blossom bright with autumn dew,
And colored with the heaven's own blue,
That openest when the quiet light
Succeeds the keen and frosty night.

—William Cullen Bryant

For iron Winter held her firm;
Across her sky he laid his hand;
And bird he starved, he stiffened worm;
A sightless heaven, a shaven land.

—George Meredith

CHAPTER 1

In the autumn, a fisherman brought to the Elvish court at Verdant Hall a tale to throw the folk into a frenzy of speculation and fear. Reports of violent raids on the hunting camps in the northern mountains had flown about the Elvish king's hall all summer. Reports deteriorated into rumor, and the people began to recount tales of magic foul enough to be named sorcery used in those raids.

Wherever folk gathered, they repeated the rumors. Hunters, folk whispered, vanished from their camps, only to return vacant-eyed and soul-reft, as walking dead.

Soon Dekar began to hear a terrible name drifting through Verdant Hall. "The Sorcerer," folk would whisper, "it could only be the Sorcerer. Who else is capable of such violent magic?" Dekar's people knew their history and legends well. "He has been biding his time all these years, growing in strength and feeding on hatred. Was it not our Queen Aeylin who defeated him in ancient times? Where but here would he seek his long-awaited vengeance?"

It needed only the fisherman's story to change the shadowy whispers into solid fear. And though his people's voices—advisor, warrior, fisherman, and hunter alike—edged toward panic, Dekar strove to hold himself apart.

Still, the old king did fear, for the fisherman's story was the confirmation he needed to know that the Sorcerer walked again.

In the hour before dawn, the young fisherman had gone to the River Altha to ready his little boat for the day's work. There, busy about his morning routine of checking his nets and lines, he found something among the reeds at the water's edge to make horribly real the rumors he had heard throughout the summer.

What he'd found was no human thing, yet the fisherman could not give it a name. It had two arms and two legs, like his own Elvish kin or the Mannish folk. But there the resemblance stopped. Its hairless skull seemed, from the several protrusions on it, to be deformed. Judging from its prone length, it might stand as tall as a small child. One shoulder was hunched, drawn up even in stillness, again suggesting deformity.

Its face bore no touch of humanity at all.

The lips, the fisherman said, hung thick and pendulous over a mouth filled with sharp yellow fangs. The creature's hide was scaled, rough and of a flat, greenish color. Although the thing could not have been dead for more than a few hours when the fisherman stumbled on it, it stank as though it had been days rotting.

"Of swamps and dead things," the fisherman told his king. "It reeked of death."

The fisherman's tale was not the kind that could easily be suppressed. Dekar, in his wisdom, did not try. He knew his folk would better face that which they could see than that which, hidden, grows larger and more fearsome. Thus he let the story make its rounds of the court, only laying on his bards the charge of seeing that this tale grew no larger with the retelling than the frame of its truth. His were a people weary of war.

It is a bitter thing, the old king thought, that fear should bring about a truce between the Mannish king and me.

It was an age-old strife, the war between the Elvish and the Mannish. Almost it had become a tradition. How fine a thing to end it in his lifetime! Still, Dekar had never thought that a truce with his old enemies would come because of a new threat.

But so be it, he thought. Truce is truce, and it must be declared if Alain and I can hope that our peoples will survive the threat from the North.

He wondered how the earthy little magics of the Elvish would hold up against sorcery. Not well, he thought. And if by some chance they did, it would be difficult to use them. His new allies feared even the little magic skills of the Elvish as much as they dreaded the fell sorcery of the enemy to the north. And yet Dekar needed this alliance. The Elvish could not stand alone.

Standing apart from the group of his advisors who now gathered on the sweeping terrace of Verdant Hall, King Dekar braced his hands on the polished wood rail and gazed out over the broad width of the River Altha. "Lovely Ribbon of Silver," his bards called this river. Sourced in the rocky foothills of the Kevarth Mountains to the east, Altha ran boldly north, danced aside to feed the Landbound Sea, and coursed west and north again to wed the A'Damran and nourish the northern plains of the Mannish province of Raeth. Yet, beautiful as that water was, Dekar's thoughts were not with the river but with Nikia, his daughter, whom he had just summoned.

His news would not be a complete surprise to her. She had been told of his plans before this, and then she had displayed the dutiful acceptance of the things that he expected of her. Still, Dekar did not think that she was prepared to have her strange destiny meted out to her so soon as this.

Yet, he thought, she is a princess. She has been trained to this, and she has the heart for it. I shall miss her, but she will do as I command. In his mind, he hastily amended the last to "as I ask." He would indeed command his daughter, but it would be presented as a request.

She would obey the command, but graciously, as though granting a suit.

"Father?" Though Nikia's voice was light and soft, Dekar

heard an underlying note of doubt. Her wide eyes, silver as the light dancing now on the Altha's waters, were shadowed by lowered lashes, hidden as though she did not wish him to view, and perhaps pity, her fear. Her hands she held clasped tightly behind her, as a child would who knows that judgment is about to be handed down.

Dekar sighed. This was no child, no elfling, but a woman grown, for all that her summers only numbered seventeen. Her hair, a glorious skein of silver, had been recently unbound in the coming-of-age ceremony and cascaded freely about her shoulders, tumbling nearly to her hips. There was much, the old king thought, of her mother in her. Her tall grace, the firm set of her chin, the elegant tilt of her canted ears, all were gifts from his long dead queen. But the steel in her, he mused, that is the gift I have given her. May it please the gods that this steel stand her in good stead now!

"Join me here, Daughter." He turned his back to the river, glanced at his advisors gathered in a knot just beyond earshot, and took Nikia's hand.

"*Halthin*," he said to his advisors, using the formal address, "excuse us now. I will join you in the hall shortly."

Their murmuring ceased. They cast, each with his own degree of boldness, glances at the princess, then left.

Still holding his daughter's hand, Dekar turned back toward the river. "Nikia, it's time."

"Aye, Father." Her voice was heavy now, and her struggle to accept her duty showed clearly on her face.

Dekar was a man divided. His heart ached for her even as his mind rejoiced that no cajoling would be needed. The bards called it the Curse of Rulers: His soul stood aside to watch the rift grow between heart and mind, and his soul, given as it was to his obligation to rule, could do nothing to ease the struggle. It could only accept.

Gently Dekar took his daughter's hand. "I'll send word to the Mannish king with his ambassador."

Nikia did not speak but rested her head against her father's shoulder. Tears stung behind her eyes. She would have wept had Dekar not reached to stroke her hair gently. The trembling of his hand might not have been seen by an observer, but Nikia felt it. Lifting her face to his, she invited the familiar fatherly kiss that had always been her comfort. Though his hand trembled, Dekar's lips were firm on her forehead.

"Sweet child!" he sighed. "I'll miss you."

"And I you, Father. Oh, and I you!" Nikia drew a little away, placing a fraction of the distance between them that would soon grow larger. "But I am to be a wife."

"Aye, child, and you will be a good wife. He is fortunate, this Mannish prince. He's won my greatest treasure."

He's won Dekar's greatest treasure, Nikia thought, and my father will win the treaty. But I?

She dared not follow that thought further. Slipping her hand into Dekar's, she led him into the hall.

* * * * *

The tale of the tavern owner's wife ran through the Mannish capital city of Damris as though it were a fire raging in the meadows surrounding that stone-wrought city. King Alain's capital was a large one, but fear sped the tale. It ran from the winding maze of the Street of Taverns, to the cobbled marketplace, and down to the A'Damran's banks before dawn had become noon.

In the night, a loud clatter of hooves rang through the tavernkeeper's upper bedchamber. The squeal of the beast rent the night's silence as its rider pulled it roughly to a halt before the tavern. Slipping from her bed, the tavernkeeper's wife crept to the window of her chamber and unfastened shutters she had only an hour ago closed. She leaned over the sill to see who came to her tavern at so late an hour.

The moon, only two days after the full, shed a ghostly light, limning with silver the houses, the cobbled streets, and the dark, cloaked shape of the horseman. The rider, controlling his prancing mount with arrogant strength, turned his face up to the opened window. He met the woman's eyes and held them, laughing.

Gasping in horror, she flung herself away from the window and slammed the shutters. Trembling, she tumbled back into her bed and woke her man with a tale that he at first credited as a nightmare.

"Huge he was," she gasped, her hands unsteady on his arm. "Huge and black, cloaked and hooded. He looked up—aye, he looked up and he could see me. I know he could! His eyes were red, glowing like the embers in the hearth, but more than that! They were empty—aye, I will swear to it—they were empty of all but the promise of damnation, and he—he laughed."

She shivered and pressed herself closer to her man, as though seeking the warmth and reassurance of human presence. As she did, the clattering of hooves echoed through the night, and laughter hissed through the narrow streets.

It was such laughter as neither the woman nor her man had ever heard. Snake-voiced and soft, it was, and they wondered that it could have carried to their chamber high up over the inn. But it did carry—the voice of a dead thing, a dark and cursed thing, filled with the sighing of creatures who are damned.

* * * * *

Alain paused in the entrance to the Great Hall, stopping for a moment to watch his two sons. They had responded dutifully to his summons and waited now for his arrival. Fenyan, the older, stood near the brazier, warming a cup of what was assuredly wine. He was a tall young man, neatly made and neatly dressed. Thinner than his younger brother, he had long, clean limbs, the mark of his mother's kin. Slate-blue eyes were quick and keenly observant in a long and narrow face. He wore his reddish hair carefully groomed in short military fashion. Alain smiled. His older son, the commander of his armies, set the latest fashions, military or otherwise.

Garth, standing apart from his brother, was Fenyan's opposite. Dressed in old and faded riding leathers, the boy stood a handspan shorter than Fenyan and, at twenty years of age, could hope to attain no greater height than he now possessed. Like the king, Garth had the sturdy, well-muscled limbs of a veteran horseman. His hair, long, brown and unruly, tumbled over his collar in a fashion typical only of Garth. His dark, merry eyes even now laughed. Capable of the same seriousness of mind as Fenyan when the occasion commanded, Garth's was, nevertheless, the lighter heart of the two.

Alain loved them both.

Fenyan was the first to note Alain's arrival. He stood a moment longer at the brazier, holding the cup carefully over the coals, and then moved to meet the king. "Mulled wine, Father?"

Alain took the cup with nodded thanks. "I have had word from Darun, Garth. Dekar is ready."

Garth's smile faded, then returned with only a little less brightness than before. Fenyan, again, spoke first.

"You intend to proceed with this—this treaty, Father?"

"It's always been my intention. You know that."

Fenyan looked away, his eyes touching his brother only briefly.

Garth cleared his throat in the silence. "I understand, Father. Sooner, then."

"Aye, Garth, it will be sooner. You've both, no doubt, heard the story that has been running about the city?"

Garth snorted. "And here in the Citadel as well. Were I a bard, I would call it 'The Tale of the Tavernkeeper's Wife.' "

"There is little to make light of, Garth."

Chastened, Garth shrugged. "What do you make of it, Father?"

"I?" Alain smiled grimly. "Just what everyone else does, from the kitchen boys to my own council members. Danger is as close at hand as we thought. According to Darun, the Elvish king found, only a few days ago, some dead thing that was neither man nor elf at the river near his hall. It's clear to me that this thing found in Elvish lands and the creature that visited the tavernkeeper's wife here in Damris are Sorcerer-bred. The mage is bold now, letting his creatures venture into the capitals of our two kingdoms. Were they spies? I know not. Neither Dekar nor I will guess at their reasons for being so far south. By Darun's account, Dekar sees this as a threat."

"And you?"

"There have been terrible raids against Dekar's northern hunting camps. Our own farmers in the northern provinces have felt harder raids from the men in the North than in any season past. Combine these tidings with the tales from Verdant Hall and our own folk here in Damris, and I'm afraid that I, too, see danger abroad."

"But the Sorcerer, Father. What proof have we it's this . . . this legend who authors the raids? There are raids every autumn on our farmers. Often as not it is the Elvish king who orders them." Garth shrugged. "It's been that way for as long as we know. Dekar has had hunting camps violated before this and rightly put it to our credit."

"Aye, Son, what you say is true. But what you fail to take into account is the fact that our farms are not simply raided for their harvest and stock, but left ruined and bereft of the folk who worked them. Rumors of fell magic are abroad in the land. No, I agree with the Elvish king: A time has come for us to put our differences aside to defend our lands against something worse than each other's armies.

"Darun advises me that the Elvish king is willing for the treaty to be ratified at the earliest moment."

"So," Fenyan, who had been silent till now, drawled, "my brother takes a wife."

Alain put aside the sharp words that leaped to his lips. "You understand the feeling of the council, Fenyan. It is agreed, by them and by me, that this treaty is needed."

Fenyan made no answer. Garth, seeking to lighten the strain between his father and his brother, slapped Fenyan's shoulder. "Come, Fen, be the first to congratulate me." He turned to his father. "Did Darun say when the Elvish king wishes the wedding to take place?"

"Just as soon as preparations can be made."

"Then it's settled." Garth raised his cup and met the eyes of his father and brother. "Congratulate me, my lords," he said, making affectionate use of the address.

Fenyan snorted. "You're eager indeed to accept an Elvish wench, Brother."

"My wife," Garth corrected. The laughter left his eyes.

"That won't transform her into something human. It's glad I am that a wife already warms my bed, and sorry for you that a witchy elfling will occupy yours."

Garth's eyes glittered darkly, faintly dangerous. Though his brother had made no secret of his antipathy toward the treaty, he hadn't shown himself so openly hostile before this.

"You'd do well to practice your manners, Fen, before your new sister-in-law arrives."

"I will not name an Elvish witch sister!"

"Enough!"

Alain slammed his goblet down on the edge of the brazier with force enough to claim their attention. Subdued, Garth looked away, but Fenyan showed no regret. Alain drew himself to his full height and stepped toward his eldest son. "I'll hear no more, Fenyan. Your thoughts on the matter have been heard in council and in private. The thing is settled. You'll dishonor neither this house nor the treaty with talk like this again."

"Father, I—"

"I have spoken, Fenyan. No doubt my summons has taken you from some business of your own. You're now free to pursue it."

It was dismissal of the curtest kind. Fenyan did not speak further, nor did he look at his father or brother before he took his leave.

CHAPTER 2

The late afternoon sun cast a golden light on the garden, warming the underlying chill of the air. A soft breeze, filled with the dusty fragrance of herbs past their prime, greeted Nikia as she stepped out of the solar.

"The air smells so good, Lizbet!"

"Aye, *Halda*, it does. It's not that the air within is foul. It's not. Yet . . ." The Elvish waiting woman let her thought trail and shrugged.

"No, not foul. But damp. Aye, damp. It's all that stone! I have never seen so much carved stone before, Lizbet! A great labor must have gone into the making of this Mannish palace."

"Citadel, they call it."

"Citadel." Nikia sighed. It was a warlike word for the chosen residence of the Mannish kings. "I'm glad that you will remain here in this . . . Citadel with me, Lizbet. I feel so foreign here."

"It's because we are, *Halda*." Lizbet's was a practical mind, and she saw little benefit in soothing her mistress's fears by pretending that they did not exist. Better to face doubts than to ignore them. She faced them now, but her eyes, the light dawn-blue that clearly spoke of her northern ancestry, softened. "This place is little like our homeland, but still it's shaped in its own kind of beauty. Stone, they use, where our craftsmen use wood. And high they build, while our homes and halls lounge and stretch through the forests. Home, though, child, is what you make it."

Or, she thought, patting a stray wisp of her ebony hair back behind her canted ears, what you are allowed to make of it. This thought she did not speak aloud.

"Don't worry, *Halda*. We have been welcomed royally this day, and I think that your father is pleased."

"Aye, it can't be said of King Alain that he stints in his welcomes."

Alain, accompanied by Prince Fenyan, his council, and a train of lords and ladies whose sumptuous, glittering dress reminded Nikia of a sweep of lustrous birds, had ridden from the city to meet and escort Nikia's bridal party to Damris. And yet Prince Garth, the man who was to be her husband, hadn't been among them.

Nikia was curious about this at first, then frightened. Was he so reluctant to take an Elvish bride that he would not even come to meet her?

Phrasing her question carefully to cover her distress, Nikia inquired of the Mannish ambassador who rode close behind her. During the weeks that he had been at her father's court, Nikia had learned to like the tawny-haired Darun, Lord Calmis. His diplomatic skills were polished and perfect, yet she sensed that should he put them aside, still she would find a kindly man. His brown eyes told her that. On all the long ten days of the bridal journey from Verdant Hall, nestled in the forests, through the wide meadows rampant with autumn flowers, and around the river-linked small lakes known to both elves and men as "The Diamond Chain," Calmis had been both a companion and courtier. She wondered, though, as he answered, who spoke, the companion or Alain's ambassador.

"It's a tradition, *Halda*," Calmis assured her gently. "It's considered ill luck for a betrothed couple to meet before the wedding. Garth is within the Citadel."

"When may we meet?"

"Why, this evening, *Halda*, at the wedding feast."

A thread of panic chased through Nikia then. How would she know Garth? How would she greet him? What would he be like? The questions showed in her eyes, and Calmis smiled. Leaning across the neck of his horse and dropping his voice low, he said, "I admit that I have a prejudice, *Halda*. He's my lord, but I assure you that Garth is a likely young man. Look to his father, the king, and sweep, in your imagination, thirty years from his face and form. You'll see Garth."

Nikia glanced aside, watching the Mannish king through eyes veiled by silvery lashes. He was broadly built, thick-chested and wide-shouldered, though not so tall as his son, Prince Fenyan. His face was browned and squarely handsome, his eyes black and hard.

Might I sweep away that hardness of eye as well? she wondered. Or will my husband be as forbidding as his father?

Nikia said no more but rode in silence into the city of Damris. She tried not to think how strange it was to hear the clap of hooves on cobbles, and that clap echo from stone-built house to stone-built house, and those echoes chase themselves around the alleys and byways of the Mannish city. People crowded in the narrow streets and leaned from high windows. "The Rainbow-eyed," Lizbet had named these folk. Where Elvish eyes were northern blue or southern silver, these Mannish seemed to have found the colors for their own eyes— green, slate and noon-sky blue, storm gray, fawn and catkin brown, changeable hazel and nearly black—in a rainbow's ribbon. Acknowledging the greetings of the people lined along their route with simple grace and dignity, she strove to hide her mounting fears from those who called out to her.

And many did, welcoming her with glad cries and the flow-ered bounty of the meadows.

These were the women. If their men stood silent, watching the ride of recent enemies into their city, the women of Damris seemed willing enough to have her. Perhaps they saw in the

Elvish princess a woman like themselves. It might have been
that they said among themselves, "Poor child, to be made a
bride in a strange land! Be glad that her lot hasn't fallen on our
daughters!"

Nikia shivered now in the garden.

"You are chilled, *Halda*. I'll fetch your cloak. The servants
have doubtless retrieved our luggage from the baggage train by
now," Lizbet said.

"Will you be able to find your way back to our chambers?"

The waiting woman smiled, lifted her hand to Nikia's
cheek, and brushed aside a silvery strand of hair that had
escaped the golden net of her headdress. Lizbet had served
Princess Nikia since the death of Dekar's queen. Nikia had
been but three years of age then. "I'll ask the way."

Alone, but comforted by the gardens around her, Nikia
stood for a moment to take in their beauty. She recognized
many of the hedges and shrubs forming the carefully tended
borders. These, at least, were old friends in a new home.

The gardens filled the courtyard in a circular pattern,
hedged around by short evergreens. Within that border ran
two circular paths, the outer much larger than the inner. Walks
led from the outer planting inward, much like the spokes of a
wheel. Nothing flowered this late in the season, but enough of
the plantings still grew to show Nikia that this was an herb garden.

She strolled along the paths, identifying by their look and
smell rosemary, mint, basil, and fennel. The basil was far past
its full beauty of late summer, but when Nikia ran her fingers
lightly along the underside of a leaf, a sweetly pungent scent
drifted on the cool air.

The Elvish knew herbs for magical plants. Their healers used
chamomile to soothe nervous disorders and to banish weariness. Rosemary, taken in proper measure, would strengthen
the memory. Nikia knew it as elf leaf, aptly named for its many
magical uses. It was also said among the Elvish that where rosemary flourished a woman would reign.

Though she had seen the Mannish king only briefly for the
first time that day, Nikia had no doubt that Alain ruled with a

strong masculine hand in his stone Citadel. She wondered what he'd think of the Elvish ideas about the pretty little hedge growing in his garden.

He would think, she realized suddenly, that it was all non-sense of the most suspicious kind!

Nikia shivered again, wrapping her arms tightly around herself. They feared magic, these Mannish people. They mistrusted it, did not tolerate it around them.

The thought brought back the memory of her father's warning words on the night before the bridal journey: "Don't use your Elvish skills in your new home, Daughter. It's enough that you're the child of an old enemy. Give them no reason to complain against your magic."

Fires, then, must be lit in a difficult way, with wood and flints. Nikia supposed that servants performed that task here. No little blue globes of cold light could be called upon to illuminate a dark corridor; torches must be sought instead.

And yet, she thought, Alain does have a mage. "The king's mage," he is called. How does he fare among all this doubt and mistrust? His lot must be a hard one!

Sighing with sympathy for a man she had never met, Nikia continued her stroll around the garden. Her thoughts returned to herself only when she became aware of someone watching her. She thought, before she looked up, that it was Lizbet, reluctant to enter and disturb her reverie. It was not.

Standing just inside the far gate, a small dark man watched her closely.

"My lady," he said, his voice so soft that Nikia almost missed his words. "May I enter?"

"Yes, of course."

He took the most direct path through the garden to where Nikia stood. His robes were dark, the hood of his cloak thrown back so that Nikia could see his eyes, cat-green in his sallow face.

Stopping before her, the man stood silent for a long moment, his glance traveling the length of her. Nikia knew that his eyes, taking in her silver hair, her elegantly canted ears, and her long Elvish face, missed nothing.

"You are the Princess Nikia?" he asked.

She inclined her head. "I am."

"I missed meeting you this morning, my lady, but I was unfortunately delayed. I am Reynarth, the king's mage."

He of whom she had only just been thinking! Nikia acknowledged him with a smile. Perhaps here was a comrade in this place of folk who fear magic! "My lord," she said, proud to employ the courteous address that Darun had taught her was proper. *Halthe*, it meant in the Mannish idiom. "My lady," she knew, meant *Halda*.

The mage laughed sourly at that. "Oh, hardly, my lady. Only Reynarth."

Nikia blushed for her error. His amusement made her feel foreign and provincial. "You are one of Alain's counselors?"

"Yes." Reynarth continued to regard Nikia steadily with his hard eyes. Her discomfort grew.

Much of what Nikia had heard at her father's court came back then as quickly remembered impressions. Even the least and youngest of the Elvish could master the spells necessary to light a fire, call light, or charm a bird to hand. Magic, among Dekar's people, was a natural skill. But there was something different, the Elvish knew, about the magic of men. They worked with powers more primal than natural. Dekar's mages said that a Mannish magic-user was more sorcerer than mage, dabbling in whatever powers he might find, not caring whether they were dark or light. Small wonder, then, Nikia thought, that the Mannish distrust magic!

Reynarth seemed to sense something of her thoughts. He quickly arranged a smile on his lips, but it did not reach his eyes. He came closer, and Nikia resisted the impulse to step away.

"How pleasant," the mage said, "to meet the hope of two kingdoms here in the Queen's Garden."

His words almost echoed those her father had spoken when he had presented her to Alain before entering Damris. From Dekar's lips, they had been full of hope and promise. From the lips of this mage, they sounded like an epithet.

Nikia was spared the need to reply by a commotion at the far

side of the garden. She heard sounds of a scuffle, the excited
bark of a dog, and a frustrated curse. Suddenly the little wood-
en gate burst open, and a small gray hunting bitch leaped
through and into the garden. The bitch, her coat rough and
stiff with mud, darted this way and that, followed closely by a
young man in stained, dirty hunting leathers. As he chased
her, he called loudly in what Nikia at first thought was anger.
But then she heard the laughter in his voice. She could not
help but smile.

The bitch made her way toward Nikia, and the Elven acted
instinctively. She held out her hand and used the small spell all
Elvish employ when they wish to let a creature know that trust
may be given.

The gray bitch paused in her flight. Lowering her head, she
advanced toward Nikia slowly. She stopped some paces away
and stretched out her muzzle as far as she could. Sniffing
Nikia's fingertips, the bitch snorted, wagging her tail in
acceptance.

"You have a charming way with animals, my lady." Reynarth's voice was low, his words insinuating. Nikia glanced at
him sharply, suddenly frightened by his knowing smile. She
knew she shouldn't have used the spell. How quickly she'd
forgotten her father's warning!

"I—I always have," she said. But it was too late to hope that
Reynarth had not sensed the spell. His glittering green eyes
told her that he had.

"Perhaps," he said, as though she had not spoken, "you will
teach me that spell someday."

"You've caught her!"

Startled, Nikia gasped.

"Many thanks, my lady!" The young man came hurrying up
behind the bitch, laughing silently. He seemed to have been
rolling in livestock pens. The musty odor of mud and animals
clung to him.

"No, not I," she said, turning from the mage. "She came to
me willingly." Unhappy that the lie had sprung so easily to her
lips, Nikia lowered her eyes.

"Well, you have my thanks anyway." The newcomer went

down on his heels beside the gray bitch, purposefully running his hand across her shoulder and flanks and down her legs. Satisfied that she was sound, he let his hand linger gently on her side, stroking her ribs.

"Her name is Misty Morning. She's breeding. It will be her first litter, and one that I've been waiting for."

"She's lovely."

"Lovely enough," Reynarth drawled, "but rather stupid for all of that."

His words, which seemed to imply criticism of the young bitch, were innocent enough. Yet Nikia sensed that the criticism was not of the bitch alone.

The young man seemed to feel the same way. He gave Reynarth a long, measuring look. "Are you taking the evening air, Reynarth? I'd have thought you'd be preparing for the feast."

Reynarth bowed his head, a small inclination. "I was making the acquaintance of the lady, my Prince. Enchanting, she, and my sense of time seems to have been spirited away."

Nikia looked harder at the young man. She saw now that his resemblance to Alain was marked. She realized in that moment that she was in the presence of the man who was to be her husband!

"*Halthe Garth*," she said, striving to keep her voice steady.

Understanding lit his eyes. "You're the Princess Nikia?"

"I am, *Halthe*."

Garth reached down to fondle the gray bitch's ears. When he spoke again, his tone was cool. "You'll excuse us, Reynarth, I'm sure."

The mage recognized the dismissal. He inclined his head again, but not so deeply that Nikia missed the sly look of speculation in his eyes. He left them silently as he had come.

"My lady, you look discomforted."

"I? No . . . oh, well, tired perhaps. So many people. So many new faces. I— Oh!"

"What is it?"

"The custom, the tradition! It has been violated!"

Her distress was real, and Garth frowned. "What custom is that, my lady?"

"*Halthe* Calmis—Lord Calmis—explained it to me. We aren't to meet this soon before the wedding. Oh, my indiscretions mount and mount!"

Garth shrugged. "Truly, my lady, you haven't been here long enough to mount up indiscretions. As for this custom, it'll be our secret that we've met here. If you tell no one, neither will I. And, truth be told, I was curious for a look at you."

He was a direct youth, this Prince Garth!

"And you, Lady Nikia—weren't you curious?"

"Aye," she whispered shyly.

"So our curiosity is satisfied. For now. I trust that your other indiscretions are as small."

Not so small, she thought, but perhaps not so large. Something about Garth invited confidences. Nikia responded to his easy manner with the truth.

"I'll confess, *Halthe*—my lord, rather—that I called your Misty Morning with more than a whisper."

Though her words sent a prickle of fear racing up his spine, Garth felt sorry for the uncomfortable flush that still stained her cheeks. He reached out carefully and touched the sleeve of her gown. He would rather have taken her hand, but he sensed rightly that she was yet nervous and afraid.

"You employed magic? Well . . ." He did not examine his feelings then, for it seemed to him that hers were the more important. He reached down and tugged at the gray bitch's ears, causing her to wag her tail and lick at his fingers. "She seems unchanged to me, my lady."

They were silent again for a long moment. Nikia was about to speak when Lizbet called from across the garden. Hesitating at the solar door, she stood with a blue woolen cloak in her arms. Nikia beckoned her forward. Lizbet came hesitantly, bowing deeply to Garth when Nikia presented her.

"Please pardon me, *Halthe*," Lizbet said. "I've come with a cloak for my mistress."

Nikia took it with thanks. Its warm familiarity cheered her.

After an awkward moment of silence, Garth bowed to them both. "Excuse me, my ladies. I have to get Misty Morning back to the kennel, and I have some things that need tending before we meet again." He laughed ruefully and took a swipe at the mud-stained hunting leathers. "Not the least of which will be clean clothes." He left with no other word.

"Lizbet . . ." Nikia's voice softened as she watched Garth leave. "I think that I will like that young man."

Lizbet made no comment, but her eyes were bright with satisfaction. She had made her own judgment about Prince Garth, and he did not suffer for it.

CHAPTER 3

Stained with shadow, the tower chamber was cool in the autumn twilight. At the scent of human approach, the small creatures who lived there—the white rats, the snake, and the falcon—came awake. Chittering, the rats scrabbled against the wicker of their cage. The snake reared its spade-shaped head, darting a forked tongue and hissing. Only the falcon remained silent.

Reynarth smiled, a grim pulling of his lips. "Peace, little ones, peace," he whispered. The creatures fell silent.

Reynarth moved slowly across the dark chamber, touching, here and there, the objects that filled the room. He felt, in passing, the roundness of a globe, a small thing, not large enough to fill his two hands. His smile vanished.

The mage closed his eyes and called to mind the simple spell that would banish the darkness. He relaxed every muscle, then drew a soft breath. Finally he pressed the palms of his hands together and visualized his need.

"Light," he breathed.

Torches, dormant until now in their wall brackets, sprang to ruddy, crackling life. The hearth, filled with new kindling and silvery dried logs, leapt with light and heat. Warmth bled quickly into the room, and Reynarth smiled again. Even the smallest display of his power never failed to please him.

"Simple enough," he told the falcon, "even for one who was not born with the skill but must acquire it through study."

The falcon regarded him with a haughty eye.

"So, my friend, you sneer at feats that once impressed you? Do you sense all this Elvish magic and pity my poor human skill?"

Reynarth glanced at the falcon's perch. The silver linked chains that bound the hunting raptors of the Citadel did not hold this bird. He crossed the room and stroked the falcon's soft breast feathers. "Still, my magic holds you firmly enough, doesn't it?"

Satisfied, he returned to his worktable and picked up the globe. He moved a small stool to the center of the hearth and placed the little sphere on the stool. Sinking down gracefully, he settled on the cool stone, drawing a long, steadying breath. His eyes rested on the globe.

Having form, it appeared at first not to. It was round, one could tell from the feel of it, but to look at it, one saw only an unedged clearness, reflecting nothing now, yet capable of reflecting everything. It acted on the eyes of a beholder much as fine, polished silver: There was form and outline, but dimension was not easily perceived at first glance. It was a power stone. Conferring no power, no skill in things magic where skill did not already exist, it instead reflected and enhanced the energy of the one to whom it was attuned.

Reynarth leaned forward and touched the globe lightly with the fingers of one hand. "I wish to see," he whispered. Concentrating, he bent his mind carefully toward the thing that he sought.

Clarity faded to a gray, moving fog through which objects took dim shape. There was no sound, no sense of feeling—there were simply images, clearing slowly, resolving into pictures. Reynarth followed the images where they would take him; what he wished to see would soon be revealed.

As from another room, he heard a voice. "Now, *Halda*, you must not linger."

There was laughter, and then a sigh. Though his body remained in the tower chamber, his senses had gone to the bedchamber of the Elvish princess. Reynarth drew a long breath again. This time it did not serve to steady him as it had before.

"Don't worry, Lizbet. I'm finished."

A graceful arm rose from an oval bathing tub of gray-veined marble. Startling in its smooth whiteness, the arm reached for something that was out of Reynarth's sight.

Water sighed, running from a rising body. She was beautiful. Her white skin gleamed; her limbs were long and smoothly muscled. A silvery mass piled high on her head, her hair seemed to Reynarth like a crown. Desire ran, liquid fire, through him even as hatred turned his heart to ice.

Nikia turned, her image tiny in the globe, her presence immense in his mind. She bent, found the towel, and covered herself.

Suddenly the image vanished. Filled with fire and ice, angered by his body's reaction to her, Reynarth wanted to turn away. He could not; there was more to see.

The images ran again, too swiftly for him to tell one from another. A long, soft moaning came to his ears: the sea wind in passages of dungeons where he had never been. Laughter whispered, thin and evil, around a sharp, bitter wail. And she was there: Northern Enchantress, Sorcerer's Mistress. Yvanda . . .

If the image of the Princess of Elvish had filled his mind, this one filled even more: It filled his very soul. In memory, he had never been able to recall Yvanda's face with accuracy: It was black . . . no, white as the moon's light. Long and sharp? No, round and soft! Her hair flowed darkly down her shoulders, and yet it was bound, high on her head, a weighty crown of gold.

With a sickening sense of familiarity, Reynarth felt himself fill and empty, rise and fall. He groaned and became silent.

She was Yvanda.

So, the little princess has arrived. . . . As with her image, the voice of the Enchantress eluded description. Reynarth heard gentle softness, felt imperious demand.

"Aye, mistress, she is here."

A lovely little creature. I see her still in your mind's eye. Ah! I see something else as well. You desire this Elvish wench?

"No, mistress, not at all!" His protest was swift, but it was a lie. He could not have said to whom he lied—Yvanda or himself.

She laughed, and Reynarth shivered with cold. *Never seek to hide the truth from me, mage. It does you no good, gives you little credit. Have you so easily forgotten the deaths cast to the Elvish account?*

"No, no, I have not."

She sighed and Reynarth heard perfect sorrow. His heart ached within his breast, for her sorrow and for his own. He closed his eyes.

So? I think you have, mage. I think you have forgotten what these Elvish owe you.

"No," he whispered, knowing as he spoke that his protest would not be acknowledged.

Be there again, mage. Know again what these enemies owe you. . . .

*   *   *   *   *

. . . He stood in carnage. Around him lay the shattered and burned remnants of what had been, only days ago, a thriving village. It had been too close to the Elvish borders. He had known that it would one day feel the bloody hand of war, but even that knowledge could not have prepared him for what he saw now.

The small shops were burned ruins, the little wooden houses had been fired and lay now as so much ash and charred timber. The streets, not cobbled as were the streets of larger towns, but only soft and brown dirt, were fouled with the corpses of the villagers and their stock and fowl.

The place stank of death and rotting, was filled with the irrevocable silence of the dead. He'd been born here and had spent his childhood here, a happy time marked by the gently passing seasons of a farmer's year.

It was horrible to him, as he moved among the dead, that he could recognize even now the faces of people he had known and loved—the smith, the baker woman, the tavernkeeper. Ah! The old man who had first taught him that there was magic in the world! Only an insignificant village mageling, Cadron had possessed enough skill and knowledge to recognize the greater talent of the young boy Reynarth.

"Take what I can teach you, young one," the old mageling had said, "and then depart from here and learn more. You'll do well. There is a great talent in you."

Reynarth quickly went down on his heels beside the old man and turned his still form gently to face the setting sun. His face was stiffened, drawn with pain and the final realization of death.

"Cadron," he whispered, "Oh, Cadron, my old teacher . . ." But the old man was beyond hearing now.

There had been others to find, the folk who peopled his childhood, the folk who lived in his memories of a sunny time of peace and learning. And there had been Illeah. Sweet Illeah, the girl who would have been his wife someday.

"Only wait a few more years," her parents had pleaded. "Only a few more years until she is ready . . ." No woman of Alain's court had moved Reynarth's heart the way Illeah had. No high-born lady's loveliness touched him the way this girl's childlike beauty had. And now she was dead.

It had not been a clean or easy death. He saw that now as he held her shattered body in his arms. She had died for some soldier's sport.

Above the wreckage of his past, the vultures wheeled in long, lazy flight. They could wait, their insolent drifting said. They could wait. . . .

* * * * *

The coolness of his chamber in the Citadel gradually replaced the memory of Reynarth's pain. He shuddered but he did not weep. His tears had been long spent for this pain, though the grief had not gone. It lived and grew, fouling his heart and soul with memories of love despoiled.

Never forget it, mage.

"No," he sighed. "No, I haven't forgotten. I never will."

And never forget who did this to you. Never forget that it was the hand of the Elvish king that reached out and crushed what it was that you loved.

"No."

Tell me, then, what you have learned.

Reynarth brought himself back from the past with an effort, straightening his spine and lifting his eyes again to the globe. "Little enough. Only that this treaty will be sealed by the marriage of their two houses. The kings are meeting even now, dealing in the formalities. The wedding feast will take place tonight."

Tonight? They lose little time.

"They've grown fearful. They want to confirm this treaty as quickly as possible. Dekar has brought his daughter and the Ruby of Guyaire."

What is this ruby?

"One of the symbols of the Elvish right to rule, he says. It's to remain with his daughter, but it's no secret that Dekar met great opposition from his advisors. A great talisman, this ruby, and one that his advisors would have kept in Verdant Hall."

And yet he gives it to Alain?

"No. He gives it to his daughter, and he has made a great show in council of the difference."

Ah. He is wily, this Dekar.

"Careful. He wants this alliance as much as Alain does."

And Alain's people? How do they feel about this alliance?

Reynarth chose his words carefully. "Most of his council is willing for the treaty to be sealed. A few are doubtful, but only Prince Fenyan openly expresses that doubt."

Someone to consider, this Prince Fenyan. . . .

"Aye, mistress, he is. His loyalty to his father and his father's cause is beyond reproach. But there is his own cause to consider, his inevitable ascension to Alain's throne. He doesn't like an alliance with an old enemy."

*Watch him carefully. He may be a tool. You have done your
work well, mage. I am pleased. It will be your part to keep this
alliance off balance. If you do it well enough, you may claim
any reward you wish.*

Swiftly the memory of Nikia rising from her bath returned
to Reynarth's mind. Yvanda laughed.

Aye, even that. She would be a fitting reward, I suppose.
Yvanda's laughter cut through the mage again, painfully,
pleasurably. Then her image faded and was gone, replaced
almost at once by another.

A towel rubbed pale skin to quick pink. Nikia released her
silver hair to foam like water over round shoulders, hiding
from the mage's view the childishly small breasts, the graceful
curve of her hips.

Reynarth moaned, heard the sound, and turned away from
the globe. Witch! He could not have said on whom he laid the
name—Yvanda or the Elvish princess.

* * * *

Hands clenched to still their trembling, Nikia stood before
the polished silver mirror to view her gown. Misty green in col-
or, its light fabric shimmered with subtle, silvery stitching. It
flowed from her neck to the tip of her dove-gray slippers in a
soft, clinging line. A belt of silver, wrought in the shape of
simple flowers, each linked to the other by a tiny pale green
jewel, hugged her waist. Earrings of the same pattern decorated her ears. As befit an Elvish maiden going to her marriage
feast, her hair fell about her shoulders, undressed and
unadorned.

Stepping back from the mirror, Nikia touched a strand of
hair here and another there. Impulsively she shook her head.
Her hair spilled forward, hiding the slim, tapered ears that
marked her so clearly as a foreigner in this place.

At that moment, the soft murmur of her father's voice drifted in from the sitting room. Nikia smoothed her gown and
turned to welcome him.

"Daughter!" Dekar took her in his arms and kissed her forehead. He had a gallant compliment for Lizbet, who stood

behind him in the doorway. She accepted it, blushing, and then excused herself. It was plain that Dekar wished to have a moment alone with his daughter.

He held Nikia at arm's length, admiring her gown. Yet, though he smiled, the smile was touched with sadness. Carefully he brushed her hair back, letting the silver lengths flow down her back. He touched her earrings. "These are too lovely to hide, child." Nikia caught her lower lip between her teeth but remained silent.

"Your husband will be the most fortunate of men, Nikia. I pray that he understands that," the Elvish king went on.

She did not know what to say, and in truth, she did not trust herself at that moment to speak any but conventional words. Shaking her head, she took Dekar's hands in hers.

"Let us not speak of that now, Father. The marriage is made. Surely if I go to my marriage with a willing heart, my husband's must follow."

They were brave words, and she felt a certain confidence in them. As she spoke, a picture of the young man in the garden, smiling and jesting, rose in her memory. She had liked him then. She instinctively hoped that this liking would be enough for now.

Dekar lifted his daughter's hands to his lips. "You are a fine young woman, Nikia, and all that I might have hoped you would be. Your position is not an easy one, and I almost regret that I have placed you in it."

Did he regret it? Nikia did not know. She thought that he spoke his words in sincerity, and yet she knew that no plea would release her from her role as treaty warrant. Deliberately she put the thought away from her.

"No, Father. What am I but a pampered child if I don't understand my duty and go where it leads me? But come, we'll be overdue at the feast."

Dekar sighed. Her words were a release, an absolution. "We aren't overdue yet. These Mannish surround everything with such great ceremony. We have a few moments still."

He reached inside his dark brown robe and took from some hidden place a small pouch of golden silk. With deliberate care, he spilled the contents into his hand. Nikia caught her breath. Named for an Elvish prince whose history was now only dim legend, the Ruby of Guyaire lay like a frozen piece of crimson sunset in her father's palm.

Dekar slipped the necklace over her head. The chain was of purest silver, the tiny links forged so tightly together that they seemed one liquid line of moonlight. From this chain depended the ruby, large and beautifully formed in the shape of a teardrop. Its perfectly cut facets caught and threw back the firelight.

Nikia took the ruby in her palm, her hand trembling. The jewel sent pale red shadows spilling across her fingers. This was the legendary heirloom of her father's house. One of the three symbols of Dekar's right to rule, the ruby had been in her family for generations uncounted.

It had been said in council that the ruby should not be allowed to be sent from the House of Elvish. But Dekar had prevailed, giving as his reason that Nikia was the heir to the House of Elvish and as such had every right to the ruby.

It cost Dekar much to send the ruby from his keeping. No king or queen of Elvish had ever given it over to the care of another while he or she yet lived. Its departure was the measure of the old king's desire for the alliance that Nikia's marriage solemnized.

"Father," she whispered, "I never thought to wear this while you live."

"And I never thought to give my daughter in marriage to a Mannish prince. Strange times breed strange actions, my child. The jewel is as much a part of the treaty as your marriage to Prince Garth."

"Does Alain covet it so?"

Dekar shook his head slowly. "It was my first thought, and one that is still in the minds of some of my advisors. But I think not. The jewel will remain with you. But Alain understands its power as a symbol and recognizes that there is where its true value lies.

"By your marriage to his younger son, you will found a new house, Nikia. Your child, son or daughter, will rule Elvish. We will bind our two kingdoms through the generations, and not simply for a single lifetime.

"The rulers of the two kingdoms—your child and Prince Fenyan's—will be cousins, raised as kin. I know you understand the reason for this."

She did. Hereditary enemies are not drawn into alliance easily or gently. The reasons must be grave. From the things that Nikia had learned during the treaty negotiations, she knew just how grave the reasons were. There was an unease among the Elvish mages and among Alain's counselors. A formidable power grew stronger in the North. None named that power; few spoke of it aloud. But when kings set mages and counselors about them, they are wise to heed their warning words.

Nikia thought suddenly of Reynarth and wondered what part he had played in the treaty negotiations. She did not imagine that he viewed it with favor. And yet he was the king's mage, the only mage on Alain's council. He must have had some part in those warnings.

She adjusted the ruby so that it lay, heavy and beautiful, on her breast. "I understand, Father."

Dekar was pleased. He leaned down to kiss her forehead again. "Tonight is the first night of the harvest season. Though we aren't among our own folk to celebrate and give thanks this night, I will give thanks to the gods for the fine daughter they have given me."

Nikia did not know for what she would thank the gods. Soon she would be alone, among strangers who were only recently enemies. Nikia clenched her fists again to hide the shaking of her hands. The next time she returned to this chamber, it would be with her husband.

Though it was not appropriate during harvesttide, she would, instead of offering thanks, seek the boon of their grace.

CHAPTER 4

Nikia was wed to the Mannish prince almost before she realized it. In a great hall filled nearly to overflowing with Mannish lords and ladies, Elvish *Halthin* and *Haldain*, and servants of every description, she took her marriage vows.

Standing before his daughter and beside the Mannish king, Dekar spoke the solemn words of ritual:

"Nikia, Princess of Elvish, Daughter of Dekar and Malteir, heir to the throne of the Elvish, Keeper of the Ruby of Guyaire and the hearts of her people: Will you take now, before this company, the wedding vows?"

Nikia met her father's eyes. "I will."

"Vow you to keep the hearth and home of this man?"

Her answer trembled upon her lips; her voice was a pale, whispering shadow. "I vow this now."

"And, Garth, Prince of Mannish, Son of Alain and Laina"—Alain's voice was deep, steady, and quiet—"second heir to the throne of Mannish lands, Vice-General of the King's armies, Defender of the King's people: Will you take now, before this company, the wedding vows?"

"I will."

"Vow you to accept to your hearth, lands, and home this woman?"

"I vow this." There was nothing of the tousled and muddy young man of the afternoon in the prince now standing beside Nikia. Attired in a doublet of burgundy velvet over gray hose, he seemed taller than she had at first thought him. His boots were soft and low, and he wore at his side a short ceremonial sword. Upon his brow, nearly lost among his shaggy brown curls, he wore a slim circlet of gold.

Nikia shivered. This man was her husband!

The two kings, each having administered the vows to his own child, joined together then, speaking in somber voices as one:

"By the exchange of tokens will we, the company gathered to witness these vows, and you, the two who agree to join in marriage, recognize that this union is made, and once made, cannot be undone."

Garth took Nikia's left hand, bringing it first to his heart, letting her palm rest there upon his breast, and then to his lips.

"My lady," he murmured, "accept my ring. Having no beginning, having no end, let it symbolize our union."

It was a simple ring, almost a duplicate of the coronet that he wore. Garth slipped it, warm from his hand, onto her finger.

I am bound! As best as she could, Nikia put down the sudden rush of fear and loneliness that swept over her.

"*Halthe.*" Though her voice was as low as his had been, it was not as steady. She had no ring for him, for rings were not part of an Elvish wedding. She had, instead, the wedding cup of her family. Carefully Nikia spoke the words that would have been traditional had she married an Elvish prince, words that Elvish women had known from times forgotten.

"I give you now the cup, in earnest of my acceptance of my husband and his family, and of his hearth and home. The simple decorations—runes bearing the names Gebo, Uruz, Inguz, Wunjo, and Berkhana—signify my faith that our union will be filled with those things that each rune represents: Partnership, Strength, Fertility, Joy, and Growth. *Halthe*, Husband, accept my cup."

I am bound! she thought again, drawing a ragged breath. I am bound to a man I have never seen before this day. I am bound by his laws and our own; by his vows and mine. Oh, Father! Why have you sent me away?

She chided herself at once for those thoughts and turned to her husband, for such this stranger was now, as he lifted her face for his kiss.

"Little wife." He cupped her chin in his hand and placed upon her lips a small, chaste kiss. "Am I such a troll that you must look so frightened?" There was laughter in his voice, but it was covering something else.

"Forgive me," Nikia whispered, not able to see what that laughter was hiding.

"No. There's nothing to forgive."

She met his eyes, then smiled with relief. She was able to see, then, what the laughter hid. It was, she realized with surprise, a fear not unlike her own. Nikia felt her heart warm toward him. Slipping her hand into his, she let him lead her forth to open the feasting.

* * * * *

In the darkness of his chamber, Reynarth watched the courtyard from his window. Far below, the torches of servants running to and fro, guiding the few early departing guests, resembled the dimly flickering lights of fireflies. No sound came up to him at this height. The lights seemed distant and unreal.

He turned from the window and closed the shutters. It was in darkness that Reynarth was most comfortable.

He found the globe by instinct and touch, took it up carefully, and brought it to his bed. Breathing deeply, he set in his mind who it was he desired to see. As ever, sound preceded image. The voice he heard was inquiring and familiar.

"Nikia?"

"I am here."

Reynarth let his breath out softly, almost involuntarily. He had come to his chamber and taken up the globe with the intention of viewing this scene. Why then this sudden, heavy ache?

Witch, he thought. Witch! Have you cast some evil Elvish spell of enchantment? And well she might have, he realized. She had sparkled at the feast, all eldritch glow and silver, alive with the attention of all those present. The music of Alain's bards had paled beside the sweet song of her laughter. No flower graced the Great Hall that was more lovely than the blush of her cheek.

How could an enemy be so beautiful?

"Witch," he said aloud, his voice low and deadly. "Cast what spell you will, you will always be an enemy!"

As Reynarth watched, Garth crossed the bedchamber to the window seat where Nikia stood, quietly looking out into the night. Gently his arms slipped around her waist, and she did not start but only leaned back against him. They were silent for many long moments, unmoving, as though this still embrace would last the night.

But it did not. It was replaced by others more ardent, and in quick succession.

Reynarth watched as Nikia gained, at the hands of a patient and kind young husband, the knowledge of the ways between men and women. When it was over and they lay still, breathing softly in the dimmed glow of the hearth light, Reynarth turned away from the globe. He raised his hand absently to wipe his lips. His fingers came away stained with blood, and he thought that pain might be ignored but never denied.

CHAPTER 5

The weather turned foul for a fortnight after the wedding feast. The deep stone windows of the Citadel were shuttered against the wind and rain. Folk went about in their warmest clothes by day and did not leave friendly hearths by evening.

During this time Nikia discovered a friend in Fenyan's young wife. The youngest daughter of Lord Karo of the northern province of Raeth, Gweneth had been five years chatelaine of the Citadel. She was a lovely woman, whose black hair and gray eyes excited the envy of many women of the Citadel, and the admiration of all the men. In her sixth month of a long-desired pregnancy, Gweneth welcomed a woman of her age to the family group. The princess acted toward Nikia in all ways as one reunited with a lost sister. Nikia found that the comfortable familiarity acted as a buffer against the stares and murmurings of the servants, the whispering of the other ladies of the Citadel.

As the Citadel's chatelaine, Gweneth knew the great stone palace intimately. She took quiet pleasure in guiding Nikia from the huge structure's top to its bottom, showing her the vast rooms and corridors, teaching her how to find her way about the place.

The Great Hall, which had hosted Nikia's wedding feast, was the Citadel's central room and its largest. From the palace's first floor, it rose in sweeping, windowless stone to the heights of the Citadel. The galleries and corridors of the succeeding floors were reached by one of two broad-stepped stairways. Guest chambers, residential suites, and reception halls all fronted the stone-floored corridors circling the well that was the Great Hall.

In every room and hall, Nikia was struck by both the beauty and the stone-hard coldness of her new home, barely relieved by rich tapestries and delicately embroidered silk wall hangings. In nothing but the furnishings did she find the warm beauty of crafted wood. As she followed Gweneth from one room to another, it was not the dark and unfamiliar stone that sent pangs of homesickness through her, but the sudden glinting of a flame's reflection in the highly polished oak of a chair's arm or the scent of wood, smoky and warmly gray, evocative of her forest home.

Under Gweneth's cheerful instruction, Nikia discovered the pattern of the place and was soon able to make her way about with little of her earlier difficulty. It was Gweneth, too, who introduced Nikia to Riche. It seemed that Nikia, as a lady of this royal household, required a page to run her errands through the Citadel.

"He's a fine lad, Sister. You'll be pleased with his service. Though he's but ten years of age, he performs his duties and tasks well and with a willing heart." Here Gweneth's light eyes sparkled with mischief. "Riche has taken a fancy to serving you."

And so it was that the lad, dark-haired and dark-eyed, accompanied the two of them on their tours of the Citadel. Nikia liked him at once, for Riche had the ability to be near at hand and yet not intrusive. And though his fascination for the new wife of his prince was evident, Nikia was pleased by it. She hoped she'd made another friend in this cold stone palace.

On the third day after her marriage, a day filled with leaden clouds and fitful bursts of heavy autumn showers, Nikia, Gweneth, and Riche ended the morning's tour of the first floor of the Citadel in the large solar which led into the garden Nikia had found so congenial on her arrival at Damris.

The Queen's Garden, Gweneth told her, was the oldest on the vast grounds of the Citadel. It was named for Ylin, the first Queen of the Mannish.

"There's not much known about Ylin in these latter days," Gweneth said, peering out at the forlorn, rainswept garden, "but there is a song or two in which she plays some part. Your bards will be pleased to make these known to you."

"My bards?" Nikia asked.

Seeing her puzzled look, Gweneth laughed. "No one's told you?"

Nikia raised her eyebrows. "Told me about what?"

"I'd have thought that Garth, at least, would have told you about your duties as Lady of the Bards."

"It's a lovely title, but, no, he's said nothing."

Gweneth shook her head. "Garth has little care for the bards unless they are entertaining him with a bawdy tale or tavern romp. I'll tell you, then. It is a tradition of the Citadel that the queen will hold the title of Lady of the Bards until such time as her son weds. Then his wife assumes the title. When the next son weds, the title and duties fall to his wife. That is you now, Nikia."

"And what are the duties? Have I been neglecting them without knowing it?"

"Not at all. The duties are not difficult or many. You're simply their patroness among the royal family. When the position was mine, I would visit them daily, hear their new songs, and escape quickly. My own voice is a mere croaking compared with theirs. I've heard you sing of an evening, Nikia. You'll do fine."

Gweneth leaned closer to the glass-paned doors leading to the garden and murmured something that sounded at once surprised and annoyed.

Nikia followed her gaze. Two men walked the large outer

path of the garden, cloaked and hooded against the rain. She thought that one of them was Reynarth. There was something familiar about the graceful, catlike stride. Nikia shivered.

Gweneth urged her to come away from the door.

"Nikia, send Riche for a mantle if you're chilled."

Though the page moved at once, Nikia shook her head. "No, I'm fine. Stay with us, Riche." She turned to Gweneth. "Who was that with Reynarth?"

"Reynarth?" Gweneth's pretty gray eyes did not meet Nikia's. "I don't know that it was the mage. As to the other . . . ." She shrugged. "He is my husband. I can't imagine what he is about walking in this rain." She spoke lightly and laughed a little as though to show Nikia that she took no great account of Fenyan's foolishness.

Nikia never would have applied the word "foolish" to Prince Fenyan. The words "crafty" and "cautious" seemed appropriate. He was forever watchful, always gauging what was being said or done, and reckoning it somehow against his own notions. He never failed in the courtly politeness that marked the manner of his family. His words were always correct, and he was ever attentive. And yet Nikia could not escape her picture of craftiness.

Like a fox, she had once thought, then chided herself for unkindness.

Nikia had seen, only that morning, the beautifully framed portrait of a young woman dressed in royal robes and jewels. This, Gweneth had said, was the late Queen Laina, who had died many years before when the princes were but children. She had been beloved of the king. Alain mourned her still.

And well Nikia could imagine that Alain had loved his wife. The portrait showed a slim, tall creature, whose hair was the same reddish color as Fenyan's and whose eyes were a slaty blue. Her face was rounded and lovely; her complexion, as represented by the artist, was cream touched with rose.

But there was no hint of the foxlike craftiness of her son in the portrait. Nikia wondered what had happened to the queen's eldest son to form his character thus.

Toward Gweneth he was carelessly kind, as one would be to a

pet of whom one was fond. His compliments to her when they met in public were correct, but seemed, at least to Nikia, to lack any true feeling. He responded to his wife's smiles with smiles of his own, but reserved his initiative for the ladies of the court. Nikia wondered how Gweneth felt about this.

But she could only wonder. Gweneth accepted her husband's lifeless compliments gracefully, and she studiously ignored his dealings with other women.

*   *   *   *   *

On the last night before Dekar returned to Verdant Hall, Garth joined Nikia in their chambers as she dressed for dinner. They had been apart the whole day, as they had been on most days since the wedding. The councils that her father and Alain convened claimed most of Garth's time.

Nikia learned a little of what happened during the councils at evening dinner, but only those things fit for the ears of those not privy to the council. At times, late at night, because she insisted, Garth would speak of council matters, and here Nikia gained a stronger knowledge.

Although the alliance between the two kingdoms was cemented by the marriage, there were specifics to be worked out. Among these was the assignment of border patrols in the northlands. There brutal raids savaged both their lands. Reports of farms burned and laid to waste grew ever more frequent.

As a dark cloud on the horizon, reports had come to Dekar only days ago that several of the hunting parties usually sent out to the northern mountains this time of year to secure food for the winter had not returned. Searchers found no word, no sign of the hunters.

But today something more had happened. In the days since their marriage, Garth had clearly set himself to be an amusing and congenial companion to the lovely young wife his father had chosen for him. If he found Nikia's beauty foreign and strange, he also found her willingness something to be encouraged. Amusing and befriending the Elvish princess was not an onerous task if it yielded a companionable and compliant wife who enjoyed his company by day and by night.

But now he was silent, pacing the length of the room with white-knuckled fists, scowling at each wall of the little chamber that forced a turn in his prowling. Nikia judged it best to keep her peace.

Garth snarled impatiently. "How can you stand these chambers, Nikia? There are storerooms in the kitchens larger than these!"

"They aren't small for me, Husband, but small, I imagine, for you, who must stride the length of them like some creature in a cage." She was careful to keep her voice light, but in truth she did not know how else to answer.

Garth stopped his prowling and passed his hand through his rumpled hair. It was a habit Nikia already recognized, and one in which he must have been indulging all day from the look of him.

"Tell me, Garth," Nikia said quietly. "What's wrong?" She settled herself against the headboard of the bed and swept aside the colored hair ribbons she had been sorting. "Come, sit with me."

He did and, resting his chin on her head, rubbed his cheek against her hair. "Elvish lady," he said at last, "I'll be leaving you for a time."

Nikia sat up, breaking his embrace.

"Ah! Little wife, will you miss me?"

She had the grace to blush, for his look was a comical mixture of leering and laughter. "Of course."

Garth offered a crooked smile. He settled her back firmly against the headboard and resumed his embrace. "There's been another messenger to the council."

"From my father's hall?" Nikia thought of the lost hunting parties and shivered. The summer's rumors of soul-reft walking dead moved like ghosts in her heart.

Garth rubbed his hand along her arm. "No. This time from our northern borders. The news is bad. For some months, we've had patrols on our borders. These patrols have been, so far, fairly successful in keeping the raids on our farmers to a minimum.

"Not so anymore. Word came this morning of three more

raids. The messenger was the only survivor of a patrol that was overpowered by northern raiders. He saw Mannish swords and shields being used by the raiders. And now we're two patrols short.

"I . . . I am going to lead a force to the border."

"You! Why, Garth?"

Garth raised an eyebrow. "They tell me that I am quite a credible soldier and commander."

"I'm sorry," she whispered, confused by her reaction. "I'm sure you are. How long will you be gone? Do you go to fight?"

"Not to fight . . . only to gain a firsthand knowledge of the situation to bring back to my father and the council. There have been too many rumors, and those too fantastic to allow us to lay any reasonable plan. I expect that I'll be back within a week. Perhaps ten days at the most."

"New rumors?"

"Aye, of wild things . . . fantastic things. They don't bear repeating. I'm going to do my best to get at the truth of them."

But Nikia insisted. "What are the rumors?"

Garth scowled impatiently. "Nikia, why frighten yourself with nonsense?"

"Can they be nonsense when you won't tell me?"

Garth eyed her sharply, put off balance by her interest in matters most ladies of the court would consider beyond their spheres. Were Elvish ladies trained to matters military? Did they learn statecraft at the knees of their fathers? Or was she, her silver eyes bright now with her need to know the latest news, as unusual in her homeland as she was here? He considered evasion, but then discarded it. Her fate had been joined to his by these rumors and the fear they engendered in two kings. He owed her at least honesty.

"At first we were hearing simply of raids. But there have always been raids on the northern borders."

Nikia nodded, thinking again of the horrible tales that had haunted her father's court through the summer.

"Cattle have been stolen before from the farms, crops damaged. But it's different now. Now the reports tell of wholesale slaughter—farms burned, whole families killed or vanished. Your father has heard the same. On the farms, wells are fouled so badly that they won't be pure for years. And the fields . . . I don't know what's happened to the fields. They're ruined somehow and will not grow crops for generations to come."

Garth's eyes clouded with grief when he spoke of the murdered folk and wasted lands. Nikia covered his hand with hers.

War had been a part of her life since she could remember. Her father's chief occupation for all the years she had been alive had been planning campaign after campaign against Alain and his armies. Battles raged; warriors died or returned to be covered in glory. It was the way of a war fought out of habit, one that continued, in its unhurried way, for generations. But never did they seek to inflict the kind of damage that would take lifetimes to repair.

"Garth, this is war on generations yet unborn!"

Garth laughed grimly. "I suppose so. But, Nikia, only a year ago our people were enemies."

"I know that. I'm not justifying one type of war against another. I don't think any war can be good."

"You are a woman. And so it is with women."

Nikia drew back. With a swift gesture, she flung her starlight hair over her shoulder. She was, Garth thought, his eyes on the tapered cant of her ears, very suddenly Elvish royalty and not at all a lady cast adrift in a foreign court. When she spoke, her voice was as cool as moonlight.

"I know it's not customary among the Mannish folk, but some of *our* greatest rulers were queens. Check your own history, Prince Garth, and see if those women did not inflict some little damage on the armies of Mannish!"

One of the first lessons Garth had learned as a child was that amusement can often be the best answer to anger. The tactic had nearly always worked against Fenyan's adolescent rages, and it worked well even now against the cold, tight-lipped fury that frustration could produce in the elder prince. With the instinct of one reaching for a tried and proven tool, Garth grinned. He took Nikia's hands and rubbed her fingers almost absently until her hands unclenched.

"Do you propose to imitate history here, Elvish lady? Come, no angry words now."

"I'm not angry."

"Perhaps a little insulted?"

Nikia smiled. "No. Not even a little. Let it go. I won't interrupt you again."

"I imagine not. There's nothing else to tell."

"I have heard little that seems more than ugly, Garth. What are these new rumors?"

"Foolish things. The rider who came in this morning spoke of the raiders he encountered as though he had fortified himself too liberally with good wine along the way. He spoke of demons . . . large and ugly creatures, neither Mannish nor Elvish."

Nikia shuddered. "Perhaps fear colors his description."

Nikia felt Garth was holding something back. She read a secret in his eyes, but all her questions would not release it now. "Demons," he had said. "Large and ugly creatures." And the mages in Dekar's court had been saying for many months now that some unnamed power was growing in the north. They attributed sorcery to that awful power—a brand of magic so foul and twisted that it was an evil even to think on it.

She voiced these thoughts to Garth, and he was silent for a long moment.

"Legends speak of the small folk called dwarves who delved in your northern mountains for jewels to fashion rich treasures. Should I stop and see if I can find their hidden treasure houses?"

"You mock me," she said, her anger rising again. Nikia slipped quickly off the bed and crossed the room to the window overlooking the Queen's Gardens. Light spilled into the night from the solar. Someone walked the round paths, but Nikia could not see from this distance who it was. She turned to face Garth.

"What does the king's mage say to all of this?"

"Reynarth? What he usually says: 'We can't base our preparations on rumors, but neither can we waste time chasing every tale, magnified by fear, to its root.' Mage talk."

Nikia returned her attention to the window. The figure below had stopped pacing and stood still in the center of the garden. She had the clear impression that the person in the garden was looking up at her.

Nikia turned away again. "And yet you are going."

"I am. I agree heartily with the first part of Reynarth's advice, and my father, and yours, both feel that it would be no waste of time to put down rumors of this sort. Once something like this spreads, Nikia, it can do more damage than if it were the truth."

She agreed. The course seemed a prudent one. Nikia returned to the bed and sat on the edge. "My father leaves tomorrow."

"I know." Garth reached for her again, and she slipped comfortably back into his arms. The imperious Elvish princess was gone. "And I have an idea that you should occupy your time by finding us a larger chamber than this."

"Indeed? Something to accommodate your pacing needs?"

"Yes. And your time will be taken up with your other duties. Dail will be returning to the court within the week. He'll be anxious to meet his new lady."

Dail, she knew from Gweneth, was the chief among the bards. He had been gone from the Citadel for several months, and when Nikia had expressed the opinion that his wandering seemed to her unusual, Gweneth had only laughed and said that she would not think so once she had met Dail.

She and Garth sat for a long time in silence, each lost in private thoughts. Nikia did not know what Garth's might have been, but her own were colored with confusion and fear.

CHAPTER 6

Although bustling with activity, the Citadel seemed empty to Nikia. Her father and her husband had left Damris in the early morning, planning to ride together until their ways separated.

Nikia had made a formal, cool farewell to her husband in the morning. She was yet a child, who thought herself a woman. And like a child, she did not wish to weep before him when she did not know why it was she wept.

My father and my husband, she thought when she accepted Garth's small farewell kiss on the steps of the Citadel, are leaving me alone in this huge pile of stones. The one anchors me here, while the other is my tie to home and the forest. Isn't that reason enough for tears?

No sparrow cast adrift in winter gales could have felt more desolate.

Lizbet did her best to cheer her mistress, but since she viewed her king's leaving as the severing of her own connections with the Elvish folk, she provided small comfort.

By afternoon the rain that had plagued the city for a fortnight ended. The sun won through high clouds fleeing before a brisk autumn wind. Nikia, weary of weeping, left Lizbet to her own tears and rang for Riche.

"Please find the Princess Gweneth, lad, and if she's not occupied, tell her that I'd welcome her company."

Riche must have run with the message or else met Gweneth in the corridor. At any rate, no sooner had Nikia bathed her face in cold water and felt the better for it than Gweneth appeared in the sitting room.

Nikia told her of Garth's suggestion that she find larger chambers for them. "I hope our moving won't inconvenience anyone."

Gweneth gave her a questioning look and then smiled. "How can it? This is your home as much as anyone's. I thought that you'd want larger rooms long before this."

It had not occurred to Nikia that she might move, simply because it had not occurred to her that she would wish to. The little suite that had been given her on her arrival had become the nearest thing to a home that she had in the Citadel.

She threw a warm mantle over her shoulders, for it was still chilly even if the sun did try to shine. Suddenly she was eager to find her new chambers, to choose a new home within this strange and cold Citadel.

When Gweneth mentioned a suite of chambers near her own apartments, Nikia assumed that she referred to the chambers she shared with Fenyan. She was mistaken.

The two of them went first to Gweneth's chamber, for she, too, wished a mantle. There Nikia waited for her in a small sitting room that served as a kind of antechamber to her bedchamber. When she looked about her, Nikia could not mistake the touch of a woman's hand in the decorations. Daintily embroidered pillows were arranged on the delicate little chairs that were placed about the sitting room. There was in all no sign that a man lived here.

The limited view she had of the bedchamber from where she stood showed the same feminine touches within. Her conclusions half-formed, Nikia decided not to air them before

Gweneth with questions. And yet, when Gweneth returned, she must have seen Nikia's thoughts in her expression, for when she rejoined the Elven, it was with a sad little laugh that was meant to sound careless.

"Yes," she said, placing a blue wool mantle around her shoulders. "I meant 'my chambers' when I said it. Fenyan and I do not share the same abode."

Only ten days ago, Nikia might have innocently asked if it were not the custom among the Mannish for a husband and wife to share chambers, but she knew better now.

Gweneth fumbled awkwardly with the clasp of her mantle, a large silver pin shaped like a bird and studded with blue jewels. Nikia quietly fastened it for her.

"There," she said, stepping back as though to view the effect.

Gweneth raised her head then, and Nikia saw her swallow as though to firm the trembling of her lips. Her eyes were bright with unshed tears, but she met Nikia's eyes with a smile. "Thank you, Sister."

"I can't think how we are expected to fasten the things when the clasps are placed directly under our chins where our eyes will not go," Nikia said.

"No," Gweneth replied softly. "I meant to thank you for not asking the usual question."

Nikia looked away, not wishing to encourage any confidence Gweneth would not be comfortable offering.

Gweneth shook her head, and her long, dark hair fell across her face, hiding what Nikia was sure were tears on her cheeks. "I can't complain of his treatment of me. And he does have cause to complain of me."

"Of you? How could he complain of you?"

"I am his wife," she said, and now Nikia could barely hear her voice, so low with pain was it. "But I can't seem to become the mother of his child."

On the last word, her voice faltered, despite her attempt to keep it firm. Nikia felt the sharp stab of her pain. It was the pain of a wife who is denied her husband's love and comfort and blamed for not producing the very thing which might bring her the love she so badly wanted.

It had been common knowledge throughout both kingdoms that in the five years of their marriage Fenyan and Gweneth had failed to produce the heir Alain needed to assure the continuation of his line. There were two sons, of course, but Garth's first child was prohibited, by the marriage treaty, from entering the line of Mannish succession. And though any child which followed was eligible for the succession, there was a disturbing gap. Gweneth's three pregnancies had all resulted in miscarriages after the fourth month. She was great with child now, though, with this pregnancy well into its sixth month. There was hope.

An ache of sympathy rose up in Nikia, closing her throat with the grip of tears so painful that she could feel it in her very fingertips. She went to Gweneth instinctively and put her arms about her. Gweneth stood tense within Nikia's embrace, as though she still fought to suppress her grief.

Poor woman! Nikia thought. Poor, poor woman, who spends her days in grief and her nights in blame! Nikia thought of Fenyan, of his easy flatteries and constant flirtations.

She was not so foolish as to think that the marriage of Fenyan and Gweneth had been a love match. Folk of our station seldom marry for love, she realized, and the best that can be hoped for is that an affection will grow between husband and wife. But she was angry nonetheless. She thought of Garth. His easygoing, merry ways had charmed her from the moment she had first met him in the Queen's Garden. She wondered if he would grow cold and grim if she, too, was unable to give him the child it was her duty to produce?

They did not find Nikia's new chambers that day.

* * * * *

Nikia's plans to find and furnish a new suite were laid aside for a few days, and during that time she saw little of Gweneth. It might have been that the long-suppressed emotions so suddenly let loose on the day of Garth's leaving had left Gweneth embarrassed. Nikia could not be sure. She was careful not to intrude and spent her time with Lizbet, sitting in her rooms listening to her play her little harp, or walking in the gardens. Nikia soon grew restless and bored. This became apparent even to Alain, for he told her at the evening table one night that Dail would be returning on the morrow and that the chief bard was said to be looking forward to meeting his new lady. The king said this with the air of a man holding out a pretty toy to a child he hoped to charm away from petulant boredom.

Does he think me a child? Nikia wondered as she slipped beneath her covers that night. Does he see me as a pretty little creature who must be amused and kept happy?

She suspected that perhaps he did. She did not see the king often, except at the evening table, and then he spoke to her as though she were his little daughter, a girl not yet out of the nursery. When Nikia contrasted this with his manner toward Gweneth, she knew her conclusion to be true.

She thought, at first, as she lay alone in the bed that seemed oddly too large this night, that it was because he did not know her well, and so fell back on a gentle, avuncular style of dealing with his son's wife. But closer reflection being the more honest, she realized that this assumption of roles was in part her doing.

She *was* bored. Her duties were few, consisting of meeting with her bards in the morning, a courtly affair during which she was treated as some kind of foreign deity. They behaved as though they were worshipers who were too new to a strange shrine to be comfortable in its presence. Nikia soon grew too uncomfortable among them to enjoy these daily meetings.

Aside from this, she did little. The position of chatelaine of the Citadel was Gweneth's, and she seemed to enjoy it greatly. She it was who saw to the running of the Citadel, from the planning of the meals to the assignment of duties to the lowliest page. Nikia learned to envy her friend the work that she so enjoyed.

But Gweneth needs it more than I, Nikia thought as sleep came creeping slowly around her, for it is her comfort to be useful when she finds only blame in her marriage.

And yet Nikia knew she would have to find some useful

employment. She wanted to erase the picture of a petulant child that she had created in the king's mind.

Nikia gave herself no more time for reflection. Perhaps because she was tired, perhaps because she did not want to wonder why it was, she curled on one side of the bed as though she had already formed, in these few short weeks, the habit of nesting there beneath Garth's arm.

* * * * *

Dail proved to be the key. He was a slim man, dark and wiry. His blue eyes contrasted oddly with his black hair. Nikia knew that the Mannish of the northern mountain regions, much as the hunting Elvish folk, were seen more frequently with this coloring than any other. His skin was fair, almost white.

When Nikia first saw him, he was surrounded by his bards, the same solemn souls who daily placed her on that uncomfortable pedestal to stare at her and wonder what was to be done with her. She had never thought to see them so animated and joyful. They hemmed around him closely, laughing, questioning, and Nikia knew that they saw him in the light of a teacher, or they gave him the teacher's honorific of 'master,' but this did not detract from their affection for him. Nikia, standing quietly in the doorway of the Great Hall, envied him sharply.

He joked with them as he tousled the hair of one of the younger students. He called each by name (while Nikia had not, in more than two weeks, been able to remember but a few of their names) and promised all of them that their lazy days were over.

Yet, if she envied him, Nikia felt no enmity. His charm was natural and easy; his voice, laughing above the chatter of his fellows, was merry. It was the bards she envied more than Dail. She felt at once that she would like to be a part of that group gathered to welcome a friend.

Nikia did not like to intrude, and so she backed as quietly out of the doorway as she could. She was not silent enough, however, for the group of bards and bardings grew suddenly still. All eyes turned at once to her. One of the youngsters dropped to his knee in his best courtly manner, while another swept a low bow. The others contented themselves with remaining silent and watching.

Dail did none of those things. With the look of a man who delights in a beauty suddenly found but unlooked for, he crossed the hall to her, catching a better grip on the little harp case across his shoulder as he came.

"Madam . . ." Nikia thought his voice sounded like music. "For I take it that you are the Princess Nikia, Lady of the Bards?"

Nikia nodded, feeling like a child caught listening where she should not be.

Dail bowed and took the hand she extended to him. "Madam, I've looked forward to meeting you for some time."

She murmured some welcome and thought that he was nothing like his stiff, uncomfortable fellows. He seemed bent on conversation, and his eyes still held that odd light of discovery. "In fact, I bear a message for you, madam, from your husband."

Dail reached into the leather pouch that he wore at his belt and took out a small folded parchment. It was sealed, and the superscription bore her name in a careful hand. Nikia was caught between the wish to open it at once, to read what message Garth had sent, and the wish to maintain some dignity before the bards. Dail cocked a thumb at his bards.

"I'd like to speak with you, madam, when you find it convenient. But I want to get my lazy fellows working first. There are new songs to learn. Can I join you here in an hour?"

Nikia nodded absently. She was not thinking of what he had said, only of what might be in the message from Garth.

"Good. I thank you."

"Dail, when did you meet with Garth?"

"Three days ago. He was well and had just left your father."

"And my father? Did Garth have any word of him?"

The bard shook his head. "No, madam, but that can only mean my lord had left the king in good health."

"Yes, of course. I will meet you here in an hour, then."

Nikia watched the bards return to their places, then fairly flew to her chambers.

* * * * *

Fenyan did not dwell on the perfection of the day. He noted it the moment he stepped into the Queen's Garden, cast a glance at the clarity of the sky, observed the mildness of the breeze, and even smiled at the pleasant mixture of scents with which the herbs filled the air. But he had neither inclination nor time to dwell on these things.

That morning the council had received a message from Garth. Foul weather was delaying his journey to the northern borders. He had hoped to return to Damris within ten days' time. This would not be possible now. The message had left the council restive and his father impatient. Doubtless, Fenyan thought wryly, this will not please the Elvish princess at all.

He permitted a brief digression of thought. The Elven had behaved, so far, like an abandoned child. Her inability to find occupation or amusement was, to Fenyan, annoying. She spent much time with her waiting woman, doubtless exacerbating her self-proclaimed loneliness in the privacy of her own chamber. Some of her time, it was true, was spent with Gweneth, exclaiming about how much she missed her new husband.

Fenyan snorted. His brother and his foreign bride had spent as much of their time together as they could after their wedding. Doubtless we will soon hear that Nikia is carrying a child.

His smile faded. Aye, a child—the warrantor of the treaty, a child more eagerly awaited than my own. Anger rose quickly then. A child, he thought, clenching his fists, whose coming will eclipse the birth of my own heir and the heir to Alain's throne. Thanks to an Elvish witch . . .

Fenyan stopped this line of thinking and controlled his anger with an effort. His last thought brought him to the primary matter of his consideration. Gweneth, too, had kept much to her chambers of late. His first reaction had been concern. Was she ill? Did this presage another disastrous miscarriage?

Fear tumbled through him at the thought. He prayed to various gods that this not be so, but Fenyan was a practical man. While he petitioned the Mannish deities, in whom he had little faith, he had also petitioned a finite source: Reynarth. The mage had promised to visit Princess Gweneth and advise Fenyan of her condition. It was this report that Fenyan now awaited. He did not wait long.

"My lord?"

Fenyan looked around to see the mage entering the gardens from the outer gate. "Reynarth, have you seen her?"

"Aye, my lord." Reynarth closed the gate behind him and did not speak until he had come to stand beside the prince. "I have seen your lady wife."

"Is she well?"

"She's easily wearied, my lord. But I found her well enough otherwise."

"And?"

Reynarth raised his eyes to meet Fenyan's. He smiled. "I find no need to fear."

"I always fear in these matters," Fenyan snapped.

"I think for now you need not. I gave her a brew of plantain and amaranth, for rest and strength." The mage smiled now. "Come, my lord. She has never carried so long as this."

Fenyan took a quick breath, decided to accept the mage's word, and changed the subject. "Dail has returned."

"So I've heard. And with a message from Prince Garth, I'm told."

"Yes. You missed little but dithering at council. Lords Liam and Celedon call for swift mobilization of our armies. Darun and my father are for waiting for Garth's return."

"They may be right, my lord." Reynarth's tone was again careful.

"Indeed? And how would you have said?"

"I? I would have agreed with the Lords Celedon and Liam— but, no." Reynarth stopped abruptly, as a man does who has a second and better thought. "No," he resumed, "I am sure your father and Lord Calmis are correct. There is, after all, the Elvish alliance to consider. The king can't plan any campaign without consulting Dekar. And it was the Elvish king who desired word from the North before committing his forces."

Reynarth drew a long breath and let it out slowly. "There is a treaty to consider now, my lord. Alain is doing everything he can."

"Aye. He waits while the season advances. Soon it will be winter, and then no campaign can be launched."

"Well, yes, but as I said, there is a treaty now."

"Damn the treaty!"

Reynarth feigned shock. "My lord!"

But Fenyan was gone, leaving the garden with balled fists, angry with the impotence the treaty had thrust on his father.

Reynarth watched him carefully, then smiled briefly. Fenyan was not the only one waiting for a report from him. Yvanda waited, too, and she was not one the mage liked to make impatient.

* * * * *

It was not meet that a princess of the house should await the attendance of her chief bard. However, Nikia was in the Great Hall some short time before Dail arrived. Garth's message was brief and seemed swiftly written. It assured her of his well-being and said that he would return as quickly as his mission would permit. Much as she welcomed the news, Nikia found herself anxious to speak with Dail, to ask him in greater detail how he had found her husband.

The hall bore little resemblance to the feasting place it had been on her wedding night. It was little used by Alain and the court except on state occasions, and now it seemed far larger than it had a fortnight ago. It stood empty now but for a long table in the center of the hall. The braziers and torches had been lighted. In the hearth, a fire blazed. These things were attended to each morning, by the servants, for Nikia's meeting with her bards. But after her meeting, the hall went unused, the fire was allowed to die away, and the torches burned out.

Standing before the hearth, taking warmth from the crackling flames, Nikia felt small in the vast and vaulted room, like a little doll in a child's toy castle. Around her and above her, shadows danced on the stone walls. Sounds magnified and carried far in the vastness. It was why the hall was chosen for the bards' work. Now her own sigh carried around the hall.

"Lady?" Nikia turned to see Dail standing in the doorway. She had the instant impression that he'd been standing there some moments before he announced himself. *He watches me,* she thought, *and wonders what kind of lady his bards have now.*

"Please join me, master."

Dail still carried his harp, a small thing, little bigger than the lady's harp that Lizbet played. Nikia watched the bard as he walked the great length of the hall. The light of pleasant discovery that had danced in his blue eyes only an hour ago was tamed now, softened.

"Thank you for waiting for me, my lady. I underestimated the time it would take to get those fellows settled to work."

Wine had been placed on the broad table. Nikia poured two goblets full and offered Dail one. Dail waited for her to sip first, as was proper, and then drank heartily of the wine.

"Elvish wine," he said, looking at her over the rim of the goblet.

"From my father's own vineyards." Looking about her, Nikia saw that the only place where they might sit was at the long table. It seemed foolish to do so, they being only two, so she dropped to a comfortable seat on the first step of the carpeted dais.

Dail cocked an eyebrow at her assumption of so humble a seat, but he made no comment and seated himself two steps below her.

"Tell me, Master Dail, how did your people keep supplied with Elvish wine during the war?"

"Not easily."

"Well, it is to be hoped that the situation will be remedied now."

They were silent for a long moment, Nikia because she did not know what to say, and Dail for reasons of his own. Still silent, the bard set his emptied goblet on the step and finally removed his harp case from his shoulder. The instrument he removed from the soft old leather was of breathtaking beauty. The wood frame was polished to a soft glow. Its strings whispered music of their own making when Dail moved the harp.

"The harp is called Dashlaftholeh."

Nikia recognized the ancient Elvish word at once: "Songbringer," in Mannish speech. She had thought when she first viewed the little harp that it must have been of Elvish make, and its name confirmed this.

"Where did you come upon an Elvish harp?"

"Oh, it is an ancient thing."

"I know. The craftmaster who created that harp has taken his place in legend. How did you come upon it?"

"It was given to me long ago by my own master. How he came to have it I don't know. It is a beauty, isn't it? I've been well served by my Dashlaftholeh."

"Will you sing for me?"

Dail nodded and lifted the harp lovingly, running his hands and string-calloused fingers along the ancient frame. The song he sang was an old one, far older than the harp itself.

> "In fallen cities, fair and golden,
>   In ancient times misplaced,
>   There hangs a banner
>   Tattered and faded.
>   In fallen cities.

> "In ancient ballads, sweet and bitter,
>   In loving song portrayed,
>   There lives a race
>   So fair and wise.
>   In ancient ballads."

Dail stopped his song after two verses. The sad old melody lingered for a breathless moment after he had fallen silent. Nikia had known those verses all her life.

"You must have traveled among the elves at some time."

Dail shook his head. "At the risk of hide and harp? No. My own master taught me the song. It suits this harp well."

"We sing it in the evening at my father's hall. It's the last thing we hear before we retire for the night. I've missed it."

"Then I'm glad I was able to sing it for you." Dail's eyes

lighted then with a sudden thought. "Do you know the other verses?"

"Only a few."

"Would you teach them to me?"

Nikia smiled at his sudden eagerness. "I don't know all the verses. The complete song is lost to us."

Dail placed Dashlaftholeh in Nikia's hands, and she set the harp gently on her knee. When she touched them, the strings sighed. The instrument was perfectly tuned, as she might have expected. Her fingers found the melody at once.

> "Upon a sea cliff, rock and carven,
>   Once was a kingdom,
>   Ah, bold and valiant.
>   And none could conquer those,
>   Fair and wise,
>   But one, and he was nameless.

> "Who sent them fleeing, terrified,
>   In ancient times misplaced,
>   To leave their banner
>   Blue and silver, Green and golden,
>   Far from the cities?"

"I'm sorry, but that's all I know."

"For this much I thank you. You have a lovely voice, my lady. You'll make a good Lady of the Bards."

"I don't think so. Your bards seem to regard me as some sort of idol to be stared at and sung to. Not to be spoken to, however."

Dail's smile was mischievous. "I know. I've heard much the same from them. It's because you are strange to them, lady, and they don't know how to approach you. You are different."

Nikia caught her lower lip between her teeth. She reached up to tuck her hair away from her face. As she did, her fingers brushed the elegant cant of her ears. She saw herself, suddenly, with the eyes of those around her. How foreign in appearance she must seem to them! Silvery eyes, slanting upward in a face that was not so pleasingly rounded as the Mannish women's, but rather longer, with a more pointed and narrow chin. And her ears, tapering to a slim point at the top—a sure mark of beauty among the Elvish, but certainly a mark of the alien among her new people.

Dail spoke as though he had read her thought. "Different, my lady, but certainly beautiful."

"My own kind might say so, yes."

"Among any kind. I don't doubt that you've simply left our bards at a loss for words."

"A pretty compliment! I thank you. And yet, somehow, I don't think you quite describe the bards' problem. No matter. We will get on later if not sooner." She glanced at him and was suddenly, sharply, reminded of Garth. She told him this, and he shrugged.

"With good reason, I imagine, lady. I'm cousin to the princes."

"A cousin!" Nikia was genuinely surprised, for she had heard nothing of this before and wondered now why she had not.

"Well, a cousin of sorts. Their mother and mine were sisters. But the queen was wed to Alain, and Tahrah, my own mother, was wed to no man. So you can see that the kinship is only privately claimed."

She nodded her understanding, yet she could not but feel more comfortable in his presence for the kinship. He was older than Garth by perhaps ten years, and there were the beginnings of streaks of gray around his temples. Nikia thought that this might be what her husband would look like ten years hence.

They sat for a long moment in silence, but this time it was not an uncomfortable interlude. Dail watched her, and she carefully watched the hall. The shadow-stained walls seemed less cold to her now, and the hall itself less imposing. Nikia supposed it was always so when one is comfortable, and she wondered if she might number Dail, with Riche, Gweneth, and the Lord Calmis, among the friends she had made in Alain's court.

"You smile, my lady. Why?"

"I hardly know myself. Perhaps it's that I've had word of Garth today."

"Then I'm glad I brought it."

She regarded him closely and saw only sincerity in his expression. "That's kind of you to say. How was he, really?"

"As I told you, lady, he's fine. And looking forward to completing his mission for the king and returning here."

Nikia's happy thoughts scattered at once. The room seemed dim again.

"I'm afraid for him," she whispered.

Dail didn't answer but watched her in some surprise. Such devotion so soon? he wondered. Well, likely not. But she's young and far from home. If Garth has been kind, and he would be, wouldn't she easily attach her affections to him?

Nikia shivered. In the silence falling again around them, she heard the crackling of the fires and the whispered breathing of the torches in their cressets. It seemed to her then that the soft sounds were slowly translated to words. Frowning, Nikia leaned a little forward. If they were words, they were in a language she did not know.

"Lady?"

"Hush! A moment," she whispered. What are these words? They were words, she was sure. Might it be some trick of acoustics that brought her a servant's conversation from the corridor? Nikia did not think so. She heard two voices—one a man's, and the other one she could not place. Was it a woman's? She thought so at first, but then its timbre seemed to deepen. A sudden chill spidered along her back and arms. Nikia drew a deep breath and closed her eyes.

What language is that? She took no heed of Dail's hand on her arm. Her head was light, her breathing difficult, but she paid even less heed to this.

Dail grasped her arm harder, let Dashlaftholeh fall with a sudden jarring cry of its strings, and steadied her. All color had drained from her face. Her eyes, when she opened them, were glassed over, their silvery pupils wide and searching.

"Lady!" Nikia heard him then. Returning to herself, she

shivered and gasped. The walls of the Great Hall seemed to have closed in on her; she could not find enough air to breathe.

"What's wrong?" His eyes were hard, searching her face.

Nikia shook her head slowly, forcing herself to breathe evenly. "I—I don't know. I heard . . ." But she let her words trail away. What *had* she heard? She did not know. Words? A conversation? No, it could not have been.

"What did you hear?" Dail asked, concerned.

"I—nothing."

"Are you ill?"

Nikia shook her head. The lightheadedness had vanished now, and she found herself steadier. She smiled and rose slowly. "I'm well, thank you, Master Dail. I didn't mean to frighten you."

Her reply was distracted, absent. Dail eyed her carefully. The color had returned to her cheeks, and her eyes no longer seemed to search for something he could not see.

"Lady, if you are sure—"

"Dail, please excuse me. I want to go to my chambers to rest awhile."

"I'd be glad to fetch your waiting woman or a page, if you wish it."

"There's no need. Thank you for your concern, and for the song that I've missed."

Dail bent to pick up Dashlaftholeh but did not, as he once would have, immediately inspect the harp for damage. Instead, he watched the princess leave the hall, wondering what had caused her ill turn.

After a time, he turned his attention to the harp. When he had satisfied himself that Dashlaftholeh had taken no harm from its fall, Dail returned to his seat on the step of the dais.

The new Lady of the Bards was much on his mind.

CHAPTER 7

It was a comfortable group who gathered in Alain's reception chamber for the evening meal. Convinced that she had simply been overtired, that she missed her father and husband, Nikia determined that the voices she thought she'd heard in the afternoon were no voices at all. There had been no words to hear, she decided, only the whispering of the fire in the hearth, the torches on the walls. The Great Hall was a cavernous place, tossing back echoes as a child would toss a ball. With only a little effort, Nikia soon fell in with the mood of her companions.

Dail was a welcome member of the party. During the meal, he amused them with tales of his wanderings, and afterward, he kept each spellbound with his songs. Alain had always had a bard attend after the meal, and at those times the music and songs served as a pleasant background to the conversation. When Dail sang, it was different. No one spoke or even seemed to move during his performance. No one wished to miss even a single note or word, so beautiful was his voice, so beguiling was the music he coaxed from Dashlaftholeh.

Nikia made herself comfortable near the hearth, with Lizbet beside her. Lizbet's hands were never idle, and even now she worked on a simple bit of embroidery. The Lord Calmis sat on a low stool that was placed so that he appeared to be in attendance upon Nikia.

Nikia could see that this little deception did not fool her waiting woman. Lizbet's eyes would stray from her work from time to time to rest on the man at her feet. At such times, her handsome face would color slightly. Nikia approved of the bloom on her cheek.

Even Gweneth smiled. Fenyan, in the absence of other ladies to flatter, turned his full attention to his wife. A rose gone too long without the sun, Gweneth bloomed under that attention.

Nikia thought that the pleasant mood was all due to Dail. His songs that evening were all amusing ones, and Dashlaftholeh's voice was so tripping and glad that she was not surprised to find that her feet were restless and longing to dance to the melodies.

When Dail paused to ease a throat gone dry with singing, the king rose to join Nikia. They were not especially formal during these evening gatherings, and no one, except Lizbet, felt obliged to rise at the king's approach. Nikia quickly slipped her feet to the floor, however, and gestured her husband's father to join her on the low settle.

"It does me good to see the laughter return to your eyes."

She smiled at that and had the good grace to blush a little at this royal attention. "Thank you, sire. How could one help but be merry when Dashlaftholeh and his master touch our hearts so gaily?"

"Aye, he has a way with him, our Dail, and few can hear and not wish to sing or dance. It would have been my great pleasure to have him attend us at your wedding feast, but at that time he was far away. The wedding was on us all so swiftly that we had little time to call him back from his song gathering. Still, I wish that I had been able to show off my finest bard to your father."

"He would have appreciated the music. But you said Dail was song gathering? Your chief bard?"

"Oh, aye. There will always be something of the wandering bard in Dail. He can't resist the song of the road. He'll tell you that a chief bard won't ask of his bards and bardlings what he won't do himself. But the truth is, he simply loves the road songs."

Alain settled himself more comfortably on the couch and asked Lord Calmis if he should not refill the Lady Lizbet's goblet. Calmis took the meaning of Alain's request at once, and Lizbet accompanied him to the sideboard set out with wines and fruits for enjoyment after the meal.

When they were alone, Alain said quietly, "I've had a message from my son."

"As have I, sire. He tells me he's well, but that his return will be delayed."

"Yes. The weather has turned foul in the North. Daughter . . ." Here Alain paused, as though gathering his thoughts. When he continued, his expression was sober. "Did Garth tell you about the errand he's undertaken for me?"

"Yes, sire."

"There's a task that I want you to undertake. It might assist both your father and me."

Nikia's interest was piqued.

"Time weighs heavily on you, Nikia. I understand that you are used to a more active life than has been yours here at the Citadel."

"It's true, sire. But Gweneth has been kind, and she has been spending much time with me, helping me to become accustomed to my new home."

The king's eyes left her then and went at once to Gweneth. She was seated on large pillows placed for her comfort in one of the two window seats across the room. Fenyan was refilling her wine goblet, and her eyes were bright with happiness, her face flushed and glowing.

Nikia wondered if Alain blamed Gweneth for his lack of a grandson. It would be an easy thing to do. She wondered, too, if there were any youngsters in the servants' quarters or among the lesser nobility who bore the fox-red stamp of Fenyan's fathering.

The king's eyes were thoughtful, considering. He renders no judgment yet, Nikia realized with a small sigh.

"Now to your task, Nikia. Dail tells me that he's heard much the same rumors as we have here. He relates, in various versions, the same tales of demon-warriors and foul magicks in the North."

Nikia pulled her light cloak closer around her shoulders against a sudden chill. She was reminded of the thing found in the reeds at the riverside near Verdant Hall earlier in the season. And hadn't there been a tale of something dark and wicked outside a tavern in Damris? She knew little of the details, but she had heard enough to know that it was something frightfully unnatural. She remembered the whispering voices in the Great Hall. Those were nothing but echoes, she told herself sternly.

"I imagine that nothing travels faster or farther than rumors, sire, not even bad news."

"Dail agrees. He suggests that we are seeing the outcome of a subtle ploy of our enemy to the north."

"You think, then, that these demon-warriors don't actually exist?"

He only shook his head. "It is what I hope Garth can tell us. And if the rumors are not true, then it hardly matters anyway. For if they let fear pave the way, the greater measure of their job will be done for them.

"What Dail suggests is that we counter the enemy's rumors with a weapon in kind. I'm not suggesting that we sow the same kind of rumors as he does, but that we work to root out the fear with a reaffirmation of our own strengths."

Nikia was puzzled but said nothing. She waited for Alain to continue.

"I don't expect that you have any knowledge of our legends and tales of valor, but I'm sure that you have access to the same kinds of legends and stories of your own folk. What I've asked Dail to do is to transform those tales—the legends of your folk and the Mannish folk—into songs. These songs will be sent out among the people through the bards, and it is hoped that they will give the folk a rallying point."

"Songs, sire?"

Her expression reflected her bewilderment, and Alain laughed. "Songs, Daughter. Don't think that this is how we intend to defend our lands, your father and I, but it's no small gain to replace an ugly rumor with a brave song."

"And you wish me to work with Dail to assist him with the Elvish legends?"

"Exactly. Can you do it?"

"With pleasure. I hope that we can accomplish what you wish."

"I know you will. Tomorrow, send to your father and ask that he have his scribes prepare whatever material you need to begin your task."

It was Nikia's turn to laugh then, and she answered the king's puzzled look at once. "That won't be necessary, sire. The Elvish have no written record of their legends of valor. Ours is a spoken tradition, and each elfling is taught the ballads and tales from the cradle. A child of Dekar should be embarrassed before all if she can't call up any song or tale of the Elvish at will."

They might have spoken further, but at that moment, Dail placed his hand on the harp, and the room fell instantly silent again. Alain rose to leave, and Nikia was soon rejoined by Calmis and Lizbet. She did not know what had gone on between them while they were away, but she thought that Lizbet's eyes had never sparkled quite so brightly before now.

That night, Nikia was happy. She had a task to perform, and Dail's songs banished her whispering fears.

* * * * *

Dail stopped beneath the arch leading into the Great Hall. Nikia, it seemed, had convened his bards already. Some purpose had brought her here early, and that purpose now stiffened her chin and squared her shoulders. His bards, he thought, were about to fall before such purpose—or at least their mule-minded stubbornness would.

They ranged, sitting or standing, before the Elvish princess as though they were warriors defending a walled city against attack. Their problem was not, Dail thought, a matter of their being accustomed to Gweneth's patronage these five years past. It was a matter of their being unsure how to approach this new lady, this lovely daughter of the Elvish king. She was a silver-petaled starflower, transplanted suddenly into a garden of tamed herbs. The herbs even now did not know what to do about the starflower. The starflower was about to address the matter.

"I give you good day, my friends," she said, her voice light and nearly as bright as her smile.

Though he had at first intended to join Nikia and the bards, Dail kept to his shadowed corner. If Nikia was going to work as closely with his bards as her acceptance of Alain's charge demanded, she must win them to her with no assistance from him.

Donkey-minded, they murmured their best wishes for her health and well-being. Banz, Dail's capable second, rose from his place and bowed neatly.

"Welcome, Princess. How may we be of service to you?" the bard asked politely.

She laughed, at first to lighten her words, for she wished to offer no offense, and then to see the comical look of puzzlement on his face. "Banz, you make me dizzy with all this bowing!"

"My—my lady, I do not know what you mean." Banz was clearly out of his depth and did not know how to answer her unlikely remark.

In the shadows, Dail grinned and hoped he was invisible.

"The bowing, sir," Nikia resumed. "It makes me dizzy to see it. I don't require more than simple courtesy from you in these meetings. I'd much rather have your attention and cooperation."

She smiled again, and Banz seemed to want to bow again. He caught himself in time and simply inclined his head.

There, Dail thought. Now you have it, Banz!

"Thank you, Banz. . . . My friends, I understand that you

have been accustomed to having the Princess Gweneth as your lady and that I'm unusual to you."

Dail leaned against the stone of the arch, approving her directness and her direction. She has the heart of a battle commander, he mused, who doesn't wait but presses the advantage.

"We are new to each other, and you are the largest group of Mannish folk I've ever had to deal with. Until now, it has been easy, if not comfortable, to let you treat me as though I were some strange creature of whom you were not quite sure." She paused for a breath, to see if any conquests had been made. None, it seemed, had. She was not daunted.

"It would be easy for us all if we had time—days or weeks— to get to know each other. We don't. I've accepted, in your names and my own, a charge from the king. There is a task before us, one for which we have not been afforded much time. In order to perform this task, I will need the cooperation, the humor, and the understanding of all of you. I will give you those things when they are needed from me."

Banz stood. This time he did not even attempt to bow, but only inclined his head. "Lady, it was not our intent to treat you without consideration, but as you've said, we are new to each other. You are our Lady of the Bards. We will give you whatever you need."

Dail knew that his second smiled, he heard it in his voice. Banz, caught and held by her beauty, her open and courteous way, was Nikia's man now. None fell more completely into love than Banz.

Tall and slim as a birch in the forest, with eyes the color of stars, hair like a spill of moonlight, Nikia would surely send Banz soaring, composing songs for her that he could only hope approached the worship she was due.

Dail stepped away from the arch and into the hall.

As Nikia had explained to the bards, there was a task that needed doing and not much time afforded for it. Certainly there was no time to waste launching flights of fantasy to the glory of an Elvish starflower, a girl wed to both a prince and a kingdom.

Dail greeted his bards and their new lady briskly and set all to work, almost before they could return his greeting.

* * * * *

Thick gray fog clung to the foundations of Souless. It never lifted but instead drifted, slowly and treacherously, as though it were alive. It cleared in some places, almost, and thickened in others with an impetus that had nothing to do with the vagaries of air current. The fog bent to the will of one who had determined its random floatings in a time that lived now only in legend. Men and Elvish said that the fog was the outpouring of the evil magic concocted within the fortress.

It was not; the fog was a tool, called up and controlled by the feared magic—a part of it, not a result of it.

The fog was one of the Sorcerer's smallest skills, one that required the least portion of his capabilities, and one to which he had long ago ceased to pay attention, knowing that it was fulfilling the task he had created it for: disguise, fear, and distraction.

It did not hide the sounds drifting helplessly, horribly from the dungeons of Souless.

The place had been called, long ago, by another name. Solace, named for its function. It had been, then, a place of peace and beauty. It had been a place of healing and hope, presided over by one who was not a god but who was a child of both god-spirit and earth-spirit. Yvanda was the god Lif's daughter, and her mother was the world itself. She was the only one of her kind.

Solace had stood against the First Dominion of the Sorcerer and survived. When the Second People fled from the East, driven out by the Sorcerer's evil, she provided, to those few who had made their way to Solace, healing and comfort. They pledged their gratitude then, so fervently that she knew they would have conferred upon her the godhood that had never been hers.

"No," she had said, "I am no goddess. I have long life, but not beyond the eternity you yourselves possess: my spirit. Take your worship and give it where it belongs—to the true gods.

They are the same here as the ones you worshiped across the sea. My place is here, at Solace. My reason to be is here."

But they protested, falling down on their knees to her, holding up their hands to her.

Still she resisted. "I am neither god nor human. There is, in my path through life, no way to turn aside. My name is Yvanda, and my place is here. My purpose is other than godhood. The small concerns of your folk, of those you will find already living in these lands, are not mine."

But they did not comprehend, and she knew of no other way to make them understand. She was a being who existed for a single purpose. She had not, as they did, the right to choose her way in life. Her heart, her spirit, her very form, were created for the single purpose of offering solace. A godly experiment, she thought as she watched them ride away. A creature made to serve only one duty, a creature made to walk only one path.

She knew that these folk considered themselves the children of the gods. It was not so. They were the children of the world, sprung from its animal loins. Their spirits, their capacity to see and create beauty, to know and venerate the works of the gods, were gifts bestowed upon them by the deities, not a birthright.

Alone again in her palace, she thought, I am the only child of the gods. I am something they tried once and, in their wisdom, never tried again. I am healer, comforter, the thing that fills the void when all else is gone.

She was, in the eyes of one who walked the world, the folly of the gods.

There had been a terrible war. The refugees rallied in their new home and made for themselves magic which stood for a time against the Sorcerer. When this magic failed, they found among the First People a thing to defend them against their great enemy.

But their concerns were not Yvanda's. The gods' child waited in her palace and gave to those who fled there the comfort they needed, mending broken spirits and filling emptied hearts. She could not have done otherwise. To give solace was to receive life.

When the wars were over, after the newcomers had beaten back their enemies, there was one more who sought her comfort. He was the Sorcerer himself.

She prayed and she pleaded. She went to the highest place, and she cried out to those who had created her. They did not offer her anything save to reiterate her duty.

"He is foul!" she cried. "He is filled with evil. Nay, he *is* Evil!" But her weeping could not change them. They were gods, and they saw a different pattern than she.

"He will rise again! He will take from me the succor he needs, and Evil will rise again!"

Evil, they told her, had never fallen.

"He will make filthy all that I am. He will pervert my every reason for being!"

But now her gods did not answer. They knew her reason for being, and it was not what she had thought it.

"Do not abandon me!" she screamed. They remained silent. "Do not abandon me," she whispered. But the Sorcerer's foot was already on her shore, and she was compelled to offer him solace. And the life that she took back was twisted and bitter, for it was Evil's life. Abandoned, she grew to hate. And in hating, she abandoned her spirit.

She became, in time, not a well of solace but a creature who was soulless. The gods forsook their only child, for it was she, they knew, who might prove the Sorcerer's weakest link in the war that only seemed to have been won. How they counted the sacrifice of their child, only they knew.

But she was not, in the end, forsaken. Lif, who was said to be her father, moved in secret and granted the only boon to his daughter that he could. That memories of her former gentle life would not haunt her, torment her, Lif banished them as though they had never been. It was a deity's reckoning, Lif's— the reckoning of one who had no past, no future, only continuing. The reckoning of a god who could not imagine that dreams from a better past could comfort one against whom that past was sealed.

*   *   *   *   *

The Sorcerer took up the wine goblet from the polished stone table at his side, saw that it was empty, and gestured absently to the servant who hovered in the shadows behind the throne. He glanced at the woman seated on the top step of the dais.

He did not speak but watched her as she sat, her fine head tilted just slightly, a small distracted half-smile curving her full lips. A glitter both deadly and exciting sparked in her pale gray eyes. One long-fingered hand moved in a graceful gesture as she reached up to tuck a strand of black hair back into the artfully simple arrangement that seemed to flow, as a dark river, down her thin shoulders, across her small back, and finally to lie in waving blue-black foam across her knees.

He smiled now, a smile that showed white teeth longer than most men's. Though one-handed, he was darkly handsome, with the beauty of a deadly thundercloud lit from behind. His hair, thick and long, framed a face that might have been sculpted from dark stone, all high cheekbones and thin, wide mouth. His eyes, first one color, then another, were cold, hard, reptilian. Those changeable eyes rested on Yvanda now, and he remembered the best thing about her: She was his. She was his as surely as this fortress, Souless, was his, taken violently and made irrevocably his possession because she could not have chosen.

Her wants or needs would not have made a difference to him, but they did add a dimension to the possession which he would not willingly choose to disturb. She was a witch, and as such, she had values aside from the intrinsic value of the fact that she was his woman.

He spoke, then, absently stroking his scarred, useless left arm with his right hand. "What do you hear, woman, from the South?"

Yvanda turned only enough to see him through brooding gray eyes. "I am afraid that I hear little of value, my lord."

She turned fully now, facing him, and brought one knee up, resting her chin on it, not taking her eyes from his. "The little Elvish princess has established herself in her new home. She and the Mannish prince have managed to consummate their marriage."

Yvanda paused again, remembering the pain and the excitement she had gleaned from Reynarth's memories. She preferred activity to voyeurism, but voyeurism coupled with the reactions of another was, after all, activity of a kind. "He is bound to me, that mage. He will tell us what we need to know, when we need to know it."

"You are certain?"

"Oh, aye, I am certain. His bonds are doubly tight, my lord. He is bound to me by pain, and to the little princess by hatred and lust." She laughed aloud. "No man can escape those bonds!

"And what has he told me? Little enough. The prince has been sent north to validate rumors of demonic warriors. No move will be made by the alliance before his return. I think, my lord, that he should be allowed to return."

"Indeed?"

"Let him come back with the truth. They will have the whole winter, then, to contemplate the demonic armies that will sweep down on them in the spring."

There had been something else in the mage's last report. It was not a verbalization, just a thought image she had caught unawares from him. She had seen, in his thoughts, the picture of the little princess with her bards. She had heard, as from a great distance, the princess's voice, telling the ancient ballads of the Elvish. A counter move, Yvanda realized, but not one worth discussing with her lord just now. Let them trot out their old tales, let them comfort themselves before their winter hearths with the doings of heroes long dead. It would do them no good.

"What else, woman?"

Yvanda felt the Sorcerer's eyes close on her. There was no need to mention the song-crafting. To cover her hesitation, she rose, stretched slowly, and turned in such a way that the thin material of her robe was rendered nearly useless as covering in the light of the fire behind her.

It was time to distract him, time to assure herself a few moments to consider the political events that were taking place in the South. Yvanda had the useful ability to separate her mind's functions from those of her body. This she did now as she leaned forward, resting each hand on her lord's shoulders. She took care that she did not flinch from his withered left shoulder.

"My lord," she murmured, "you may be sure that I have told you everything that I have learned from the mage."

The Sorcerer's eyes, black as agate now, grew sharper, brighter, his breathing more quick. The deliberateness of the seduction, not as subtle as she might have wished to think it, did not escape him. She was thinking, evaluating something, and he knew she might possess a piece of information that he did not.

What good, he wondered, would this piece of information be by itself—a cold, unadorned fact? Had she connected it with something else yet? It would be worth his time to wait until she had, to wait until it meant something to her, and so to him.

There was nothing he could not take from her if he truly wanted it. Let her play her little games, he thought. It does not matter. And if her intrigues keep her contented, let them. I am her purpose now. Without me, there is no life. Alone, she is the abandoned plaything of her wretched gods, without even the memory of their grace to sustain her.

He would watch her carefully, but he would balance his watching against his need for her powers. . . .

Smiling, and with no gleaning of his thoughts, Yvanda wound her arms around the Sorcerer's neck. It was working. Witch's sense told her a moment before his body did that he had accepted the seduction. She was not unaware that it was for reasons of his own rather than his body's desire. Still, as his weight bore her down before the fire, she knew that she would now have time to think. And in thinking, two pictures were called into the part of her mind that did not admit the Sorcerer: the mage Reynarth and the little princess Nikia of the Elvish. It was the latter on which her mind fastened.

There was something about the little princess, a power near her which could not lightly be dismissed. The Elvish had grown weak and careless in their magic. Still, the potential to use it as it had been used in the past was still there. And as she knew that the power was there, so did she know that the little Elven was unaware of its presence. It was a raw power, a huge and untapped strength. *The strength of your ancient fathers?* Yvanda asked the image in her mind. *I doubt you have the will to wield that, little Nikia.*

Yvanda cried aloud in triumph, and if her master believed it was from pleasure, she thought, why, let him think so.

CHAPTER 8

As was her custom, Nikia returned to her chamber in the early afternoon to take a light meal. Riche had laid out fruits, cold meat, and a light wine on a sideboard in the sitting room. Nikia found him resting on his heels, repairing the fire.

Fresh from her first successful morning with her bards, fired by her new task and purpose, she greeted him with a dazzling smile. She looked about her, expecting to see Lizbet, but found her missing. "Where is the Lady Lizbet?"

"My Lady Lizbet has gone riding."

"Riding?" Nikia could not keep the surprise from her voice. Lizbet had kept close to their chambers since their arrival at the Citadel. Nikia could no more conceive of her going riding of an afternoon than she could imagine her deciding that it would be pleasant to take a swim in the river. Lizbet, a good horse-woman, had always enjoyed a ride out on a fine afternoon when they were at Verdant Hall, but she had been a solitary and somewhat lonely figure since coming here. Nikia was surprised indeed, but not displeased.

"With whom has she gone riding, Riche?"

Mischief gleamed in the lad's eyes. He could no more control their sly sparkle than he could dampen his irrepressible high spirits. "The Lord Calmis. But the lady asked me to tell you that she will attend you this afternoon."

Nikia tousled the little page's dark hair and dismissed him. Then she turned to the sideboard, surprised that her appetite, usually small, was hearty this afternoon. She set to the fruits and meat, enjoying the meal and the sense of satisfaction over her morning's work.

* * * * *

Gweneth joined Nikia in her chambers shortly after she had finished her meal. It was in Nikia's mind that they had never located new chambers for her and Garth, and she asked Gweneth if she would assist her with the search again.

Gweneth agreed at once. "We can start right now."

There were many suites throughout the Citadel from which to choose, but Nikia liked the idea of being near her friend and so found the second set of chambers she was shown much to her liking.

The suite was larger than the little one she presently occupied. There were three bedchambers, instead of two, and a central room, which might better be called a reception room than a sitting room. The suite occupied the side of the corridor opposite Gweneth's.

"It's lovely," she said after she and Gweneth completed their tour of the suite. They were back in the reception area, a room wider than it was long. Doors led from the side walls to bedchambers. There was a single chamber on the north side of the suite; it would be a fine place for Lizbet. A second, smaller chamber led from the south wall, and from that to another, much larger room. This room she would share with Garth.

Nikia smiled. The rooms had plenty of space for Garth to pace should he find himself so inclined.

She envisioned warm tapestries hanging on the cold stone walls. In each of the bedchambers, as well as the reception area, the window embrasures settled deep within the Citadel's stone walls. These cold stone seats she would cover with pillows. In the spring, when the sun was warm on the Citadel walls, she would have fragrant herbs and flowering plants placed in planting tubs so that she would be surrounded by greenery, small reminders of the forest home she missed.

"I feel truly at home here, Gweneth. These chambers are perfect."

"I thought you'd find them to your liking. And now there's something else I want to show you. I've heard about the task that Alain has set for you and your bards. There's something in the store rooms of the kitchens that might be a help to you and Master Dail."

Nikia could not think what would be hidden away in those musty store rooms, which she had seen only once, that might be a help in her songmaking. She asked Gweneth what she had found, but her friend only shook her head, the light of mischief in her gray eyes.

"You may tease for an answer all you wish, Nikia, but it will only delay the finding. Come with me."

It was plain to Nikia that her friend was pleased with herself, and her find. She questioned Gweneth teasingly, hoping to get some clue of what she felt was so interesting. Gweneth gave her none, but only led her down through the Citadel to the kitchens.

The kitchens occupied the ground floor of the Citadel. Because the palace was built on the hill crowning Damris, the kitchens were reached by traveling down a flight of stairs from the first floor of the entry level of the Citadel. These cavernous rooms had stone walls with high vaulted ceilings blackened by countless years of cooking smoke. Nikia found the bustle of activity and the good, rich smells of cooking and baking welcome and pleasant.

They were greeted with great surprise and a flurry of bobbing and knee-bending. A large woman, whom Gweneth addressed as "Mistress Cook" and who clearly reigned in this good-smelling domain, welcomed them.

When they passed through the preparation room, filled with long tables over which many assistant cooks worked to prepare the evening meals, Nikia spotted Riche. Caught with his fingers in a fine, sweet-smelling batter, Riche was about to come to quick grief. Before the assistant cook who had caught him at his theft could make good her threat to have him tossed from the kitchens, Nikia claimed his service.

"You've saved me, lady," Riche said, taking his fingers from his mouth. "How may I serve you?"

"As a guide," Nikia said. "Through the store rooms." She smiled. "I've no doubt you know your way about."

His eyes narrowed a bit, then he nodded. He bowed to Gweneth, for he was not so free with others as Nikia encouraged him to be with her, and took up a branch of candles.

The store rooms led from the preparation room back into the under areas of the Citadel. Guided by Riche's light, Nikia and Gweneth picked their way through the herb rooms, cool, windowless places built deep so that no light would disturb the flavors and colors of the herbs and spices stored there.

Nikia liked the smell of these rooms and lingered behind for a moment to enjoy the scents of the large green bunches of partially dried plants. The herbs were not the harvest of the Queen's Garden. That place was only for pleasure and decoration. These came from the vast gardens spread along the outer grounds near the kitchens.

At Gweneth's urging to hurry, Nikia left the herb rooms and followed her friend into a root cellar, packed with barrels of drying fruits and pickled vegetables. Nikia marveled at the produce being preserved for the winter. Here were long shelves of preserved fruits and little stone pots of the sweet jams and conserves which were so new and delightful to her. More than once Garth had found occasion to laugh at his wife, caught with her fingers in an irresistible jam pot.

Gweneth called again at the door leading to still another room. "This is the place," she said mysteriously.

Nikia followed her friend through the door and stood for a moment, catching her breath in the close, heavy air. This last room was a large place, perhaps as large as all the other rooms combined. Cobwebs drifted like fine, gray lace from the ceiling and walls. The ceiling here was lower, and the room was filled with boxes and barrels packed with kitchenware that had not seen use in many years.

It was difficult for Nikia to make out more detail, for the branch of candles, which Riche held as high as his arm would permit, sent shadows lurching all over the walls and ceiling, pooling on the floor. Nothing was fully illuminated; all was only half seen.

Before she realized it, Nikia's hand moved to form a cup. She closed her eyes, breathing lightly, instinctively calling up the spell that would fill her cupped hand with a cool, blue fire. The witch-light was half-formed, its blue shadow already touching her palm, when she caught herself and let her hand drop.

No! Not here, she thought. But instinct was so hard to tame! Satisfied that neither of her companions had seen her indiscretion, Nikia sighed.

Gweneth took the candles from Riche and held them higher, to afford them better light. Barrels and trunks sprang out from the dark; Nikia heard the skittering in the corners that bespoke of the startled residents of this place. She shivered and looked away from the yellow eyes glaring at her from the lid of a barrel in the farthest corner.

"You needn't fear, my lady," Riche said, coming to stand beside her. "The rats resent the intrusion, but they fear us, too."

Nikia did not mind the little mice of the field, but the thought of their larger cousins, lurkers in dark, damp places, set her to shivering. Dekar's *lifras*, the keepers of his hall, daily renewed their banishing spells to keep Verdant Hall free of the insidious river rats. It seemed that the Mannish Citadel could do well with a *lifra's* spell. But no *lifra* lived here, and should he, no spell would he be able to cast for the sake of the Mannish, who would likely fear even that simple boon.

No, she mused, these folk would easier live with a rat than banish him by magic. It would be a long time, she decided, before she understood her husband's people.

Gweneth bent over two trunks, one larger than the other, and endeavored to pull the smaller one out to the center of the room. Riche hopped off the barrel near his mistress where he had perched and lent his back to the effort.

"Thank you, lad." Then she turned to Nikia. "I had these placed down here several years ago for lack of a better place to put them."

The small trunk was unadorned, and Nikia saw at once that it was very old. "Have you come to show me cooking treasures, Gweneth?"

"Oh, you'll appreciate what we find, I think." The lid was rusted, and when the top was finally raised, the hinges cried their protest with ancient voices. Nikia drew closer to the light. The trunk was packed full of small books whose leather covers and bindings were ugly with damp and age. The musty, dark smell of mildew drifted into the close air. "What are these?" she asked.

Gweneth took one of the books from the top of the trunk and held it out. The little book was filled with the close writing of many different hands. Some passages were only long scrawls, while others were neat and legible. She could not read any of what she saw. The light was too poor for that. Puzzled, Nikia glanced at Gweneth.

Gweneth pushed her dark hair back from her face with the heel of her hand. "Travel logs, they are called. It was the custom, a long time ago, that the travel shelters across our land be furnished with books such as these for the folk to use. In them, you will find many things—the brief musings of a traveler before he takes his night's rest, bits of tales and songs, pieces of local gossip from years past."

These were treasures indeed! Nikia held the little book closer to the light but was still not able to read much. She longed to cast the spell for witch-fire but managed to curb her impatience.

"Gweneth, this is a treasure trove! Tell me more about these books, this custom. Are they still used?"

"I'll tell you, and gladly. But come, we needn't linger here in the dark to talk. We will have these trunks brought to your chambers. There we can talk."

Nikia could not wait for the trunks to be moved, however.

She filled her hands with as many books as she could hold. Her imagination sparked, she was certain she would find many things useful to her new task.

* * * * *

Nikia was amazed by what innocuous thoughts so many travelers could have. The books held many accounts of the weather—the constant lament, in many hands, of the journey—and often comments that seemed to make no sense to her at all, but which must have meant something to the writer for him to have taken the time to note them.

Nikia set aside the third of the little books that she had brought to her sitting room and leaned down from her chair to poke at the fire. "I'll have a lot of reading to do if I'm to win-now anything from these logs." Nikia had been too eager to plunge into their trove to listen much to Gweneth's explanations, but now, three books behind her, she was ready.

Gweneth settled herself more comfortably and took up the little silver goblet of wine she had poured but not touched. "It's a simple tale. Many years ago, long before the reign of King Alain, or even his sire or grandsire, the custom fell out of use, but when it flourished, folk observed it faithfully.

"Once there were travel shelters placed at regular intervals all across our kingdom. They were not elaborate affairs. We can still see the ruins of some in the northern mountains, where customs die more slowly than here in the South. It was the duty of the bards to collect and replace the logs at each new quarter of the year. It took about that long for a log to be filled.

"The folk who traveled and used the shelters were encour-aged to make use of the books, as I said before, filling them with their thoughts and songs and tales. What the bards mostly garnered was local gossip and the praise of fine weather, or the cursing of foul. Just as often, they were rewarded with a new tale or a song so old it was long forgotten."

Nikia was fascinated all over again. "Why did the custom stop?"

"The kingdom became involved again in a war."

"I wonder how much use my old Elvish grandsires would

have made of these complaints about the weather."

Gweneth shrugged. "Some things might have found their way into the logs that never should have."

Nikia thought it a pity that so lovely a tradition had become a casualty of the age-old war only lately ended. Picking up a book again, she determined that she would approach Dail with the idea of renewing the custom. She smiled and settled comfortably to reading again. For the first time since coming to Damris, she began to feel as though, someday, this place might seem like home.

* * * * *

"The Princess Nikia is breeding."

Fenyan dropped the empty wine goblet and listened to the hollow ring it made when it hit the stone floor. It was better, somehow, to listen to that little hollowness of sound than to consider the news that Reynarth had just given him.

"My lord?" The mage's words were quietly spoken, his tone solicitous.

"Yes . . ." Fenyan reached for the goblet, snatched it up, and placed it carefully on the table. "Yes, I heard you."

"Isn't that good news?"

"Of course." His reply was automatic, words spoken out of reflex. It was not good news: It was bad news. But what was even more disturbing to him was that he did not quite know why he viewed the news of Nikia's pregnancy as bad. Garth would be happy. More importantly, so would Alain.

And, he realized, the council would be pleased. There would be firm and irrevocable validation of the treaty. The Elvish princess was pregnant.

"How do you know this?" Fenyan asked in a flat tone.

"Oh, it's easy to see for one who knows how to look."

"Has she been to you?"

The mage smiled sadly. "No, my lord. I would be the last person she'd come to. I think the princess dislikes me, though I don't know why. Perhaps she has little faith in my Mannish magical skills. I doubt that she will seek my aid and advice as your lady wife does. But, still, it is true. She is breeding."

"Has she told anyone?"

"I don't think she knows it yet herself."

Fenyan grunted acknowledgment. So quickly! So easily! And he began to picture a future in which the children of his brother, so easily conceived and brought to life, filled the court. The converse of that picture sent another ripple of anger and fear through him. He saw a future in which there was not a single child of his own to take its place in the line of succession. But that thought he quickly cast aside. Gweneth was entering her seventh month and showed every sign of being able to carry this pregnancy to term.

"Damn!" he muttered, "Damn the woman! She'll no doubt breed like a rabbit. In a matter of years, there'll be part-elflings all over the place."

Reynarth rose from his seat by the window and filled the goblet Fenyan had placed on the little table. "You must congratulate her, my lord, when she makes the grand announcement. It's what your father, and hers, planned when the treaty was arranged. Don't think of elflings, but of a treaty coming to fruition. That can only be a good thing."

Of course it must be a good thing. Fenyan knew that the mage was right. Still, he felt at odds with his reactions, and he felt threatened as well.

Fenyan rose, ignoring the wine Reynarth placed before him. "There are matters I would like to attend to before I join my father at dinner."

The mage rose from the seat he had resumed. He bowed once and smiled again. "Of course, my lord."

Fenyan cursed again, silently, as he watched the mage leave. *A pack of elfling brats to overwhelm the poor little son that I have tried so hard to sire!*

* * * * *

In the corridor outside Fenyan's chambers, Reynarth smiled. He had been able to predict the prince's reaction nearly to the words he would choose to lament the news.

Fenyan was much the easier of the two princes to read. It was partly due to the young man's personality, partly to the demands that being the king's heir made on him. In another pair of brothers, it would have been Garth who skulked jealous and afraid. But there was sun in the younger prince's soul. Sun had seldom touched Fenyan since the death of their mother. Never, since the death of Laina, had Fenyan been certain of anything, of anyone.

Something about Fenyan's reaction struck the mage as useful. He could not think of a place to use it yet, but he had no doubt that a place, and a time, would present itself soon. His smile fading, he left the corridor and headed for his own chambers.

In the darkness of the tower, in the laden darkness of his heart, Reynarth took up the small, colorless globe. A branching thing, a thing unsatisfied with caging, his spirit flowed outward, channeled by the globe. It sought and found Nikia.

He had watched her often before Garth's leaving. The two of them had moved as in a dance. Small figures in the globe, they met and spoke, came together and loved, and fell at last apart.

I should have withered the seed in his loins! Wretched Elvish witch! he cursed silently.

Reynarth stirred, reacting to the heat that warmed his blood. He watched her now, unmoving in sleep but for the gentle rise and fall of her breast. Her hair, a silver tumble loosened for the night, washed over her, hid from his view her softly rounded shoulders and arms. Her bedcover had fallen away. He drew a long, ragged breath. There was no change in her appearance. Nothing yet presaged the swell of belly and hip as her body accommodated the growth of the child only he knew was there.

She would not become ugly in pregnancy. She would, he knew, become still more beautiful. I should kill the child in her womb even now! But he must not. He tried to put down his anger and his lust.

Aye, even that! She is so lovely where she lies, unknowing, sleeping at peace, as though awaiting a lover with perfect trust. A lover . . . Blood burned through the mage's veins. A lover who would come swiftly, slip beneath the bedclothes, and stroke that silken skin. A lover . . . His body ached, but he felt it only as from a distance now. A lover who would dip his hands into that silver river of hair, one who would possess every part of her foreign Elvish body. . . .

"Ah, witch!" he cried aloud. "Witch! You can't do this to me from so far!" He jerked to his feet and reeled away from the dizzying pull of the globe. Knees trembling, heart racing, he staggered until he dashed a knee against the foot of his bed.

"Witch!" he growled once more, his voice an animal sound. "See if that child grows within your womb for long!"

CHAPTER 9

The fields wore black scars, as though some fiery-hoofed beast had run amuck in them. Though fire, Garth noted, could never have done this damage. In fields as full as these had been with the stubble of recently harvested crops, fire would have run its course straight to the mountains. He squinted into the sun and the hard blue sky. No smoke plumes stained the black ridge of the foothills or the green, climbing heights of the Kevarths. Indeed, it seemed as though the waste and destruction ended at the precise edges of this luckless farmer's land. His fields lay like fragile black lace, lines of spoiled crops intersecting slim, golden lines of wheat or oat chaff. Ruin had been capricious in these fields.

It had not been capricious in the barnyard, or in the cottage.

Though Garth and his men had searched from the empty cottage to the ruined barn, stepping gingerly around the bloated bodies of milk cows and plow horses, they found no man, woman, or child. None living; none dead. And yet, about the cottage hung something strange and more chilling than the mourning winds of late autumn. To Garth, the place seemed like the shell of a turtle ripped, bleeding, from his little dark fort.

But there is no blood in the place, Garth thought, turning away from the fields. Or none that he could see. He ducked out of the sun and into the cottage again, and again he winced as though stepping into a place where horrible murder had been perpetrated only moments ago. The chill spidering up his neck, the roll of nausea in his belly, argued that the walls of the place were spattered with blood, the floor ankle-deep in it.

But the floor was only hard-packed dirt, recently broomed; the walls daub and wattle, chinked and needing repacking. Places stood set at the small table before the hearth as though for a meal. In the hearth, a kettle perched on a wrought-iron tripod, its contents burned but yet identifiable as someone's morning pottage.

A cold wind from the northeastern arm of the A'Damran blew in fitful gusts, reaching with icy fingers through the chinks in the cottage walls. Garth listened to it for a long moment. It was not that the wind could carry any message he might hear or heed; it was simply that he was loath to look again at the last thing in the cottage to testify that a family had indeed lived here.

Outside in the bright sunlight and winter-chased cold, one of his men cursed loudly, a ragged sound. Kesin, who would captain this border patrol after Garth returned to Damris, raised an abrupt question. Garth listened for the reply of the one who cursed, did not hear it, and shook his head. Dead chickens, mutilated goats, he thought wearily.

And vanished infants. The thought came even as his eyes were drawn toward the shadowed corner near the hearth. The cradle, made of rough wood, did not lay empty. A small doll, crafted of corn husks, lay on blankets meant to cover a babe. Garth touched the dry leaves of the manikin's body. The toy had been made only recently; he could still feel the resilience of husks from this year's crop.

Even as he realized this, Kesin's hoarse cry of dread rent the eerie silence. Garth ran from the cottage. He saw, on the dark ridge of the Kevarths' foothills, a progression of creatures spawned in nightmares.

Kesin shuddered suddenly and turned his eyes away. "What *are* they?"

"I don't know," Garth said, shading his eyes against the sun. An echo of Kesin's shudder jerked through him.

There were a dozen of them, whatever they were, and mounted. Like ghosts on the march, they drifted along the ridge, silent and gray against the vivid green of the Kevarths' pine-forested slopes. Things that were neither men nor elves, whose arms were too long, whose legs were too many. Things with misshapen, slanted heads, wearing the armor and carrying the shields and weapons of Alain's soldiers.

As though it sensed Garth's eyes on it, one of the creatures dropped out of the line, turned its mount, and looked down into the valley. Sun glinted along the creature's skin as though its hide were armor. Like a stench, a sense of *wrongness* flowed down the slope. Then the thing raised its long, slanted head and howled. Garth knew the sound for laughter.

"To horse!" Garth shouted, and Kesin picked up the cry. But though they rode furiously, though it was no great distance between the blasted fields and the haunted ridge, they closed with no enemy, ghost or human. Cold sunlight danced along naked sword blades, gleamed on the tips of barbed arrows, and mocked the impotent fury of warriors whose quarry had vanished. The ridge was empty, deserted as though not even the smallest stoat had ever hunted a vole there.

Shivering in the cold sun, Garth remembered the empty cottage, the empty cradle. Unaccountably, he thought of Damris, of the Citadel and Nikia. Rumors, he had told her so many days ago, we go to find the truth in the rumors.

To the song of unblooded blades sliding home into their sheaths, of curses muttered and prayers set loose to fly to the gods, he thought that there were no rumors. There was only the desolate truth pictured in an empty cradle, framed in a deserted cottage.

It will soon be winter for us, he thought sniffing the air. He looked over his shoulder at the ruined farm, lying like a black-

ened and festering wound on the land. For those vanished people, winter had already come.

* * * * *

Garth returned to Damris with the first snowfall. He went to
Nikia in the afternoon and found her sitting before her warm
hearth alone, reading as she had been since she found the travel logs. He was full of the breath of winter, his brown hair wet
with clinging snow, his face burnished red by the cold winds.

Garth caught her up, hugging her to him, and she, heedless
of the ruin his wet cloak made of her gown, delighted in the
warmth of him and in the happy tripping of her heart. She had
missed him and not realized it so fully while he was gone as she
did now that he was back. She had a gift to welcome him home
with, a gift of news, a promise of joy.

And when she gave the news to him, he laughed, swung her
about, and then, bethinking himself, set her gently on her
chair by the fire and went down on his knee beside her. He was
to be a father, and he could find no words to frame his joy.

Garth rested his forehead against his wife's knee, as though
her living warmth were a talisman against the memory of the
child-reft cradle, the abandoned doll in Harvest Run. "When,
love?"

"I . . . I don't know." Her laughing stopped then, and she
grew more serious. "There's something we must consider. My
own folk bring a child to term in something less than seven
months. I know that the Mannish women bear in a term of
nine months. I can't honestly say when the child will be born."

"Have you been to the physicians?"

"Aye, certainly. They caution and shake their heads. I think
they can offer no answer either."

Garth's eyes grew dark with concern. He sat on the floor at
her feet. "Do they think that all will go well with you?"

Nikia nodded at once. "I'm sure it will. We're not so different a folk that I can't bear your child, Garth. It is only that we
can't say when the babe will come. I think that the longer term
will hold. Midsummer will see our child born."

As he rested his head on her knee, Nikia thought how much

she had missed him. She had been hugging her secret to herself for nearly a week. No one was privy to it but the physicians and, of course, Alain. The physicians had run to him like old women with rich gossip the moment she had left them.

Garth looked up, as though reading her thoughts. "My father knows?"

Nikia nodded.

Garth grinned and said, "He didn't say so, but he hurried me from his presence nearly the moment I arrived, telling me that I'd better attend the wife I'd neglected." He shook his head fondly over the memory. "I understand now why he was laughing. Have you spoken with him?"

"Yes, I have. He's pleased, and his manner is so solicitous that I fear that I must break like fine porcelain if I so much as lift a finger for myself."

Garth laughed. "Who else knows?"

"No one. I didn't wish to have you greeted in the courtyard by the stablemen with news I would tell you myself."

"Secretive wench. . . ." He hugged her knees, then rose suddenly to his feet. "There will be a feast tonight. What a fine cause for celebration!"

There was no containing his joy, and he paced about her little sitting room.

"You'll be glad to know, husband, that I have found you a larger place for your pacings."

"A new suite? Excellent! You've made wise use of your time, Elvish lady."

Nikia did not acknowledge the double meaning of his remark but only inclined her head. "Thank you, Husband." The sparkle in her eyes belied her prim tone.

They were silent for a moment, Garth pacing off the room as though it could not contain his energy, and Nikia sitting in her place by the hearth. She was well content with herself. Messages had been sent to her father that morning. She only wished that she could be with Dekar when he heard the news. He would be pleased, she knew, and proud to know that his daughter was well on her way to fulfilling his hopes.

Garth stopped in his ramblings and looked about the little

sitting room. "Where is the Lady Lizbet? Have you lost your faithful shadow, love?"

"It seems I have. And to the Lord Calmis. Lizbet finds his company more stimulating than mine."

"No matter now. I'm home, and we will leave the Lady Lizbet to Darun and wish them the joy of each other." He grinned again and ran his fingers through his shaggy hair. "It's good to be home, love."

The grin faded too fast. Nikia hesitated before she asked her question. "What did you find in the North?"

His eyes were suddenly grim. "I did not find rumor."

"I don't understand," she said, but she was afraid that she did understand. "Garth? The tales are true?"

"Demonic warriors? I don't know. I don't know only because I don't know what I would name a demon. But, yes, there are warriors that are huge and misshapen and grim. They seem to be invulnerable in battle, and terribly strong."

Nikia's voice trembled. "Did you encounter these warriors?"

"No, but not for lack of trying. I saw them from a distance, Nikia. And I heard the reports of trusted captains who did engage them in battle.

"But enough of this now. We have something happy to celebrate tonight, and celebrate we will. And we will hope that our good fortune is a sign that the alliance was well taken, and that we will, in the end, triumph."

But Garth's voice was flat, emotionless. Nikia shivered. She rose, gathered the scattered log books, and kissed him gently. "We will feast tonight, and we will celebrate, for I know that it is as you say: Our good fortune will be the good fortune of both kingdoms."

* * * * *

"Dail!"

"Welcome back, my lord."

Garth took the bard warmly by the arm, clasped his hand, and smiled. "You look better now than when I last saw you."

Dail grinned wryly, recalling the cold, rainswept campsite

they had shared on the night before he had started back to Damris. "I can say the same for you."

Garth glanced around the council chamber. It was, but for the chief bard, empty. There were goblets set at each of the eight places, and little stone flagons of wine stood at intervals along the length of the table. Behind the head of the table, an arm's length from his father's place, hung a large map of the Elvish and Mannish kingdoms.

"It looks to be a long session, Dail."

"Undoubtedly. The council has been awaiting your return and your report."

"Well, they'll have it, for all that they won't like it."

"Trouble?"

"Trouble. Why have they brought you here today?"

"A bard's report, my lord." And he told Garth briefly of the task that Alain had set for his bards.

"Song-making, eh? Well, it's an interesting tactic. How do you progress?"

"Your lady wife has been of great assistance. She has the ability to select the right legend. And if she is not yet a craftswoman, she shows talent."

Garth smiled at that. "Aye, she has shown quite a talent for crafting."

Dail did not miss the certain pride in his tone. "An interesting statement from one who has not heard her songs."

Garth laughed. "I am to be a father by midsummer."

"Congratulations, my lord." Dail's words were simple, the thought sincere, but in his heart another voice spoke. It spoke in confused whispers, and it spoke softly. Dail could not understand it at first, and he wondered at it. It was the voice of disappointment.

"I'll miss her work," he said quickly. For surely, he thought, that is the source of the disappointment.

"Oh, I doubt that you'll lose her for some time yet, Dail. If she loves her work, as it seems she does, she won't be soon parted from it."

Within moments, the council chamber began to fill, and shortly after that the council was called to session. Dail took his seat at the farthest end of the table. He fought to still the confused whispers in his heart. It was not a difficult task, for the news Garth brought back was of trouble, and soon he had thought for little else.

"The borders," Garth said grimly, sweeping his hand across the northern arc of the map, "effectively no longer exist. The raids have increased in frequency and brutality. There are no longer bodies to be found on the stricken farmsteads. I don't know what this means, my lords. I only know that what we found were dead cattle and ruined fields, but no bodies. People speak of horrible things. They tell tales of hordes of demonic warriors sweeping in from the northern shores. They tell of vile magicks that leave their fields blasted and ruined, and of creatures they call 'Darklings.' "

Darklings. The word had a poetic, but ominous, ring to it. Dail shivered. He well knew the fanciful turn of speech of his own northern folk. Here was a word that must be defused.

"My lord," he said.

"Aye, Cousin?"

"Have you any description of these Darklings?"

"I have. 'Lifeless things,' I was told. 'Things that can't be killed, for you can't kill the dead.' That's the description I have."

A murmur swept the chamber. It was Celedon who spoke first. "Surely, my lord, that can't be! Come, now, you can't believe that the dead walk!" He glanced about him, a smile of denigration ready on his lips.

"Aye," Liam agreed. "Aye, my lord. The dead don't walk, else they would not be dead."

Garth glanced at his father, but Alain remained silent. Did he believe the report? Garth could not tell. He watched the councilors carefully. Liam's and Celedon's expressions held not merely doubt but disbelief. Fenyan's expression was grim, and in Dail's eyes he read a look of warning. He glanced at Calmis, but the ambassador's expression was unreadable.

Good tactic, Darun, he thought. Reserve your thoughts for yourself at the moment.

Reynarth had turned away, his eyes fixed on some point

across the room. Garth resisted the impulse to see where the mage was looking. He could not be distracted now.

"My lords," he said, his voice quiet and calling them back to order, "I have seen what the folk describe."

Celedon laughed. "You tempt me to doubt your credibility, my lord."

Garth's eyes narrowed. Here, he realized was intractability. "I have seen the empty farms. I have seen the deserted villages. I have been inside the cottages, emptied as though the people had fled and not had time to take even one piece of clothing, even one stick of furniture. I've seen this with my own eyes, Celedon.

"Father," he said, turning the topic away from their disbelief. "I've seen those things, and I've seen the enemy's warriors. They are strange, ill-formed things and incredibly strong, if my captains are to be believed."

Alain rose to his feet. He looked suddenly older, Garth thought, as though the tale he'd heard had aged him considerably. Not the tale, Garth realized then. The toll is caused by his believing it.

When the king spoke, his voice was firm. "We must prepare for one last winter campaign. We have, for the most part, the warriors we will need. But what we must do now is to apprise our ally of the situation and coordinate our campaign with his."

"Your Grace?"

Alain glanced around. It was Reynarth's first word since Garth had begun his report. "Have you a suggestion, Reynarth?"

The mage rose from his seat. He bowed respectfully. "Aye, Your Grace, I have. It's this: I suggest that we make whatever move we must without delay."

"It's what I intend, Reynarth."

"Aye, I understand that, Your Grace. But coordination with the Elvish king will take time. Can we afford the delay? Have we the time before winter grips the North?"

"We will make time, Reynarth. We'll send messengers now, as quickly as we can."

Reynarth nodded. "Aye, Your Grace. And I will use my weather skills to assist where I may. But please, Your Grace, we all know what a northern winter can be like. Don't delay a moment longer than you must."

"I intend," Alain said firmly, "to delay not at all."

Reynarth resumed his seat and did not speak again throughout the rest of the session. He needed time to think. He took that time, now, while taking in, as well, as much information about the coming campaign as he needed.

* * * * *

The fire in the hearth was only a dim orange glow of coals, giving off little heat. Heavy winter silence filled the bedchamber. For the first time in many nights, Garth was again in Nikia's bed, and she was content to curl up against his warm back and lie in the silent darkness to think.

The feast had been all that she had expected. There was great joy when Alain announced that she was with child. The folk, from the servants to the noble guests at the tables, were delighted.

Nikia smiled into the darkness. It seemed that it was a simple thing, after all, to please these folk. Garth's skin was warm against her back, and she sighed with happiness to hear his even breathing beside her, to know that he was safely returned.

Wine had flowed like water that night. The bards had sung and played their very best tunes. Each song they presented was a jewel. At one point, and now Nikia blushed in the darkness to think of it, Dail delighted the assembled folk with a quick and laughing series of nursery songs. She could still hear them. The guests quickly caught the tunes and remembered the words, and the songs were sung by all. They laughed when Dail was done, and several women advised Nikia that she had best learn the little songs before the summer.

She assured them that she would do her best and, perhaps because the wine had flowed too freely into her cup, regaled the company with the first Elvish children's song that she could remember.

"These the colors of the fall," she had sung.

> "These the colors of the fall;
>   Fire guards them all:
>   Red as blood
>   Spilt in war,
>   Green as summer growing.
>   Blue as the sky
>   Above us all.
>   White as water flowing."

Nikia smiled again. Aye, the wine had flowed freely.

But not everyone had laughed. She shivered in the dark and huddled closer against her husband. There had been one who did not laugh, one who watched her instead with suddenly arrested attention. Here, in the close darkness of her bedchamber, she could still feel Reynarth's eyes on her.

Slowly she sat up, drawing the bedclothes about her, shivering in the chilled air, trying to recall the evening. It seemed, from that point and through the rest of the evening, that she had completely captured the mage's interest.

Nikia stared into the darkness now, her eyes drawn first to the fire, and then to the little crystal case which held the Ruby of Guyaire. The case had been a gift from Garth, presented to her during the course of the evening. "To hold your treasure," he had said gently, his eyes alight, "as you hold mine."

The crystal case sat on the dressing table where Lizbet had placed it only an hour ago. Inside, the Ruby of Guyaire glowed redly, a jeweled heart in the crystal case.

Reynarth's green eyes had hardly left her the whole night after she had sung her little song, she realized once more.

> "These the colors of the fall;
>   Fire guards them all:
>   Red as blood
>   Spilt in war,
>   Green as summer growing.
>   Blue as the sky
>   Above us all.
>   White as water flowing."

The words repeated themselves over and over in her mind, until she was nearly convinced she actually heard them spoken in a dry, whispering voice.

She shivered again, but not with the cold. Nikia closed her eyes, bowed her head, and tried to banish the haunting words. At first she denied, within herself, that this was a voice she had heard before. That voice had spoken words foreign to her, in a language she could not even guess at. This voice spoke the silly familiar words of a nursery song that she had known all her life.

"*These the colors of the fall. . . .*" Garth stirred beside her. She had whispered the words aloud, and he, as though they penetrated his very sleep, stirred, turned on his back, and smiled.

Nikia slipped from the bed. A restlessness was upon her, banishing the comfortable contentment that she had felt only moments ago. She crossed the room, stepping from rug to rug to avoid the cold flags of the floor.

I must put this away, she thought, picking up the little crystal case. The ruby glowed, almost pulsing, transforming the crystal to rose. The fire in the hearth leapt and then died.

Nikia placed the case on the mantle and arranged some logs on the embers. They would not catch. Kindling first! When am I going to learn this! But there was no kindling to be found, and she was so cold! With a gesture and a thought that she had not had occasion to use this month past, Nikia leaned toward the fire and commanded it.

Light sprang up. Across the room, Garth turned again in the bed. He threw an arm across his eyes and murmured something that Nikia could not hear.

Nikia stared at the fire. She tried always to remember her father's advice. Instinct, as she had thought in the kitchen store room, was indeed a hard thing to tame. She had called Garth's little bitch on that first day, then almost cast the spell for witch-fire only a few days ago, but until now she had never commanded the fire.

Had Dekar never warned her against using her little spells, Nikia would have known from the very first that they would not be welcome among the Mannish. She had no wish to inspire the awe and fear that Reynarth did. The servants who passed him in the corridors and those who waited at table invariably made some little hand sign when they were out of his view. It was, she knew, the sign against evil. Nikia did not want anyone to use that gesture against her.

It was enough, she thought now, that they still gave her covert glances when they thought they were unobserved. It was enough that they seemed, at times, to watch her as though she might do something untoward. She remembered again that day in the store room. What would Riche and Gweneth have done had she simply called up the little blue light instead of suffering the poor illumination of the candles? She did not like to think what her friends' reactions would have been.

But not tonight, she thought, not tonight. . . . Tonight I have managed to please. How quickly those smiles would have vanished had they been able to see her now!

Nikia put aside that thought. After all, no one *had* seen. She reached for the crystal case, then sank down on the thick rug nearest the hearth. She was confused, and that dry voice whispered still in her mind: *These the colors of the fall . . . of the fall . . . these the colors of the fall . . . red as blood . . . spilt in war.*

She closed her eyes against the sound, but that only made it clearer in her mind: *Red as blood spilt in war . . . these the colors of the fall . . .*

The voice laughed, and she feared it. She leaned forward, her arms across her belly as though to protect the life within. *Green as summer growing . . . blue as the sky . . . these the colors of the fall . . . red as blood spilt in war . . . red as blood . . . red.*

Trembling took her. She was afraid on a level far deeper than she had ever been before. *These the colors of the fall. . . .*

Would that voice repeat those words forever? Nikia pressed her hands to the sides of her head. The ruby's case fell to her lap and lay there, a blood-red eye staring at her. *These the colors of the fall . . . red as blood . . .*

"Stop!" she cried suddenly, hardly recognizing her own voice, so shrill and full of terror was it. "Stop!"

"Nikia!" She jerked her head around and saw Garth, standing at the bedside. His face was hidden in the shadows, but she could see, even through her fear, the tension of his body. He crossed the room quickly, raised her gently to her feet, and held her for a long moment. "What are you doing out of bed?"

"I—I was cold. I came to make up the fire."

Her words drew his eyes to the hearth, and then she saw him look downward. He let her stand alone for a moment, and the chill of fear returned. He bent to pick up the little case and placed it on the mantle. Then his arms were around her again, and the whispering voice faded.

"Nikia, what is it?"

She shook her head against his shoulder. "I don't know, Garth. Truly, I don't know."

He guided her to the bed, removed the robe, and tucked the bedclothes around her. Then he slid in beside her, and Nikia lay against him, her head on his shoulder.

"Your heart is beating like a rabbit's in the chase, love." Garth bent down to place a light kiss on her cheek. "Tell me what's wrong."

What could she tell him? Could she tell him that she had commanded the fire? Could she tell him about the whispering voice in her mind? Nikia looked into his honest eyes, brown eyes the color of a deer's coat in summer, and saw concern and puzzlement there.

"A voice," she whispered against his shoulder. "I heard a voice. A whispering voice. It repeated the words of that silly little children's song. *These the colors of the fall. . . .* " She shuddered and could not continue.

Garth laughed gently. "Well, love, I can give you three answers to your 'voice.' "

There was something comfortable about his laughter, and Nikia wanted to believe in his answers before she even heard them.

"Wine, nightmare, or your new condition." He laid a gentle hand on her belly. "And were I to choose, Elvish lady, I would lay it at the door of the first and the third."

It might be true. It might be that the wine she had drunk had served her an ill turn. "Do you really think so?"

Yawning, Garth nodded. "Yes, I do think so. Come and sleep now. In the morning you will forget this. But if you do not, you might seek out Gweneth, who has had some experience of the fears and vapors of pregnancy. She'll set your mind to rest."

Nikia kissed him. If she doubted his explanation, she did not say so. She slid down farther beneath the coverings and eventually she slept.

But she did not sleep well. Instead, her dreams were filled with restlessness and whispering.

CHAPTER 10

Snowstorms gripped Damris with icy hands. The A'Damran was a black, ice-laced ribbon winding through the white-mantled fields beyond the city. The winter's silence filled even the bustling halls and corridors of the Citadel. It was, for Nikia, the beginning of a winter of the spirit.

She moved among the folk of the Citadel as a strange woman-child who walks in haunted places, a fearful ghost. Haunting, she was in turn haunted. Waking and sleeping, she was filled with foreboding and the whispering voice that came unheralded and made of her sleep a shambles, of her waking hours a nightmare. And the long ache of homesickness dogged her more closely than her own shadow.

She had spoken with Gweneth, at Garth's suggestion, and received her friend's reassurance that the early months of pregnancy are often filled with strange feelings and uncomfortable nights.

"For my own part," Gweneth had said, taking Nikia's hand in her own, "I knew at once that I was pregnant again when I began to smell, here, there, and everywhere, the scent of mountain roses."

Nikia had smiled, shaking her head. "A pleasant enough warning."

"Aye, and one my own mother claimed to have experienced after my conception, only she smelled, constantly, she said, bread baking." Gweneth laughed. "Pleasant enough, too, though she often said that she grew heartily sick of the smell after a while. No, Nikia, this will pass. No one knows what fancies a woman's mind will bring when she is breeding. But you'll come through this winter to a fine summer and bear, I hope, a son for Garth."

Though Nikia tried to hide her doubts, she was unsuccessful, for she saw them mirrored in Gweneth's own concern.

"Nikia, you have been to the physicians?"

"Of course."

"And they assure you that you will be well?"

"Yes."

"Have you considered applying to Reynarth?"

Nikia shivered, though she could not have explained why. She shook her head.

"I know he is a forbidding one," Gweneth said, "but I've often found his brews of herbs and wine soothing and restful." She smoothed her hands over her belly as though caressing the babe within. Nikia marveled at her calm assurance after so many losses.

"I think you may be right when you say that I'm only experiencing some silly fancy born of my condition. You are right, rest and quiet are all I need."

Yet though she made every effort to rest and took her duties only lightly, Nikia did not thrive.

Instead, she grew pale and thin, and she moved and spoke with a nervousness unlike her usual manner. Gweneth had successfully entered her eighth month of pregnancy, and for a time Nikia had been able to put aside her fears to join her friend in preparations for the long-hoped-for arrival of Fenyan's heir. But only for a time. While Gweneth bloomed under the influence of her condition and joy, Nikia looked as though she sickened daily. She was constantly weary; her restive seeking for occupation faded. To some, it seemed as though the child she carried sapped her strength and vitality.

Nikia did not think so. The tiny life growing within was the one thing on which she based her ability to survive her torment. If she was strong, if she was able to endure her nightly fears and daily terrors, it was for the sake of her unborn child. She would linger for hours before the fire in her sitting room, warming herself, dreaming of forests alight with winter starlight, and of her child.

She knew that her little group of friends watched her with concern, but there was little that she could do to reassure them. All her strength was for reassuring herself.

"It's simply your pregnancy," Lizbet assured her gently. "That's all. It is so with many women, my child. You must rest, and not overdo, and you will be fine."

Nikia wondered how much Lizbet believed this comfortable explanation. The waiting woman's eyes were often sharp with concern, her face drawn and shadowed by doubt. In their dawn-blue depths, Nikia read her own desire to be once again beneath the snow-burdened eaves of the forest.

Garth, too, had seized on this reason for his wife's listlessness and pallor. "Winter, Nikia, is a difficult time at best for an active woman. There's little enough to do but keep warm, and now you must use your strength for not only yourself but another. Come spring, you'll see. The first warm touch of the sun and you'll bloom and strengthen."

It was but another version of the refrain that Lizbet and Gweneth played, and like them, Nikia did not think that Garth believed it. Physicians attended her daily, pressing strength-giving brews on her. She took them dutifully, but she did not benefit from them.

Nikia worked with her bards as often as she could, although not as often as she would have liked. When she could not join them, she spent her time in her chambers, reading and rereading the little treasure of travel logs she and Gweneth had found.

That time, she knew, was not wasted, for the logs had yield-

ed many old songs that would be appropriate for Dail's use.
And when she could not meet with her bards, Dail joined her
in the afternoon to keep her company, to teach a new song, and
to help with the reading.

Of Alain, Nikia saw little during that time. The last campaign before winter had been a failure. Caught in the foothills
of the mountains, the combined armies of Alain and Dekar
had been forced to turn back. None could cross the mountains
in the fierce storms that descended from leaden skies. Now
Alain and his sons were ceaselessly occupied with preparing a
strong defense of the borders for the spring. This year, they
would not be taken unprepared.

Messages went back and forth between Alain and the Elvish
king. It was not unusual to see a group of Elvish *halthin* and
captains in the Citadel now, and Nikia wondered uneasily
what reports of her they were taking back to Dekar.

She could not avoid these visitors, nor did she wish to, for
many of the *halthin* and captains who were working with Alain
were men she had known since childhood and friends, in their
way. At those times, Nikia felt better, and she endeavored to
put a good face on her illness and appear the charming Princess
Nikia that they remembered.

She judged her efforts successful. The messages they bore
from her father were all of hope and happiness. None indicated that Dekar was aware that his daughter did not flourish.
For this, Nikia was grateful. She began to hold a half-belief in
what those around her said—that she would do better in the
spring, that she was only encountering a normal difficulty of
pregnancy. She liked to hope, and she often felt better when
she did.

But not for long. A day would pass, or perhaps two, and the
dry whispers would be silent. Sometimes even a week would go
by, long enough for her to think that perhaps it had been only
the fanciful imaginings of pregnancy. It would not last. Walking along an empty corridor, standing silently by a window
watching the snow fall, or even in a sleep that was sound for
perhaps the first time in a week, she would stop or wake to
hear, faint and far away, the words of the child's song she had

come to hate, or the sound of the alien language that was more than loathesome to her. And the haunting would begin all over again.

Nikia grew to fear the interludes of peace almost as much as the times of fear.

* * * * *

For one who watches the little Lady of the Bards so ceaselessly, your taste in music is remarkably simple and limited. Yvanda's voice was filled with amusement, and with impatience. It was soft, yet it was hard. There was a demand for an answer, and a solution all at once.

"It's a child's song. It stays with me for some reason."

And how does the Lady of the Bards?

"She weakens daily, as I predicted."

You are taking care, I hope, to make it look as we planned.

"Of course. She hears voices, whisperings in the night. They wear on her, and she doesn't know where they come from."

Voices? Your voice?

"Aye, lady, mine, but I have taken care that she won't recognize it. Little nonsense words are all that she hears."

Ah, the song again. Tell it to me, mage.

Reynarth ground his teeth in frustration. It was, as she said, with him always. It stayed in some little corner of his mind, only to reappear and peep out from time to time. He repeated the words as she demanded, and he endured the laughter he expected.

"The song has nothing to do with our business, lady."

Indeed, except that it is useful enough against the Elvish princess. Well. I compliment you on your weather skills, mage. You made a fine job of blocking the last campaign.

"Thank you, lady." Something moved between them, something ebbed and flowed, rose and fell. It was understanding.

There will be no more border raids this season, mage. There are preparations to be made.

"Aye, lady, I understand."

And there are things at Damris that will need your own

attention as well.

"Aye." Reynarth settled his position more comfortably. He smiled.

You are amused?

The smile died. "No, lady."

Ah. Perhaps you anticipate the pleasure of your work. It will be up to you, mage, not to damage the thing that you desire as your reward. I care not whether she lives or dies. I care only that my ends are accomplished. There must be no heirs to the thrones of the two kingdoms.

Reynarth nodded.

Answer me, mage.

"There will be none, lady."

See that it is so. And she was gone.

Reynarth was abruptly emptied of her presence, her thought, her being. Exhausted, he fell back against the head of his bed. Breathing slowly to calm himself, he raised trembling hands and covered his eyes. In the darkness, he knew that he must choose his path with care now.

These the colors of the fall. . . . Damn the song!

Reynarth got to his feet, picked up the little globe, and replaced it on his worktable. Why was the song persisting? What was there about it that caused it to continue and continue in his mind?

Foolish children's song, he thought. It haunts me as much as it haunts the Elvish witch. They fashion these things so the tune will repeat endlessly in a child's mind, aiding an immature memory. And what, he wondered bitterly, is so important about the colors of the autumn that they must be drummed endlessly into a child's head? Something must have been, at some time. . . .

Shrugging aside the concerns of the ancient song-maker who thought it so important that a child learn to recognize autumn colors, Reynarth returned his attention to his worktable. He touched an object here, checked the scent and texture of a bundle of herbs there. He did all the things that he normally did when resisting the impulse that had become such a part of his life.

In the end, it did not matter. In the end, he reached again for the globe. He took it between his two hands and dragged up a stool with his foot, drawing a long breath and clearing his mind.

He called silently for that which he wished to see. The globe clouded and cleared. She would be working with her bards at the song-making. It was where she always was at this hour of the morning when she was feeling well enough. She should be feeling well enough this morning, for he had not 'haunted' her too badly of late.

The globe showed him the hall, filled with the sounds of the song-making, the fitful starts and interruptions of bards crafting. It was to Reynarth, however, empty. Nikia was not there. He scanned the room quickly. No, she was not there. Neither, he realized, was the chief bard.

The mage listened for a moment to the song they were trying to sing. It was a light melody, etched out in quick, tripping chords. The words were simple, the phrases short.

"... *his saddle is leather, his bridle is gold, the jewels are the shades of the fall.*"

Another simple rhyme encased in a naggingly persistent melody. Reynarth cleared the globe with a short, growled thought. He was frustrated, he was angered, and he was disgusted with the foolish songs that seemed to be infiltrating the court these days.

Let them sing, he thought bitterly. It will do them little good.

And then he laughed to think that these cradle songs would never be sung to a child of Alain's house, either rightly born or born of an Elvish witch.

CHAPTER 11

When he allowed himself to think about it, Dail knew he was in trouble. He tried, often and hard, to ward off the trouble with thoughts of Kysla, she of the petal-soft skin who welcomed his visits to her home in the Street of Taverns; of the Lady Evline, Celedon's lovely copper-haired daughter; of Lainde, who served him at table and whose flashing, sapphire eyes held such promises as to make a man's knees weak.

Yet wild Kysla, sweet Evline, and mischievous Lainde were no talismans to protect him now. What were fair skin, copper hair, and sapphire eyes when compared with the eldritch beauty of Elvish's transplanted starflower, Dekar's daughter, Garth's wife?

Oh, aye, he thought, taking up a traveler's log and dropping to a seat on the floor before Nikia's hearth. Trouble has found me. And if I hear one more of Banz's wretched paens to her beauty, I will twist his neck!

Nikia sat opposite him, her moonlight hair pulled back from her face and twisted high on her neck. Dust from the musty log she studied smudged her time-faded rose gown, her fingers, and the tip of her chin.

Before he thought, before he could stop the hand that seemed to move without his will, Dail reached up and wiped the dust from her chin with his thumb.

She looked up and smiled with the light of all the stars. "The dust of ages, looking for a new home."

Dail tried for a light reply and found that words had deserted him. And why should his words, his tools, his materials of crafting, have stayed behind when his sense had flown? He shrugged and returned to the book on his knee. He told himself that he was a benighted wretch and no better than an adolescent boy whose good sense flees before the first beautiful face he sees. His thirty-five years should have left him wiser than this!

He wished heartily that Garth were here in Damris and not at Verdant Hall. It was far easier to retain his wits when Nikia's husband was nearby. But Garth had ridden out nearly a week before with a returning party of Dekar's *halthin*, accompanied by Darun Lord Calmis and the king's mage. The prince and the two council members were to present the ideas that had been worked out among his deputation and Alain's council for the spring defenses in the North.

Aye, Garth is gone, and Darun with him, and these two Elvish ladies have no one for company but a heartsick bard who has managed to lose every bit of the good sense the gods once granted him.

As though she spoke to his thoughts, Nikia glanced up at Lizbet, silent and still in the window embrasure, and said, "Lizbet, I believe you are quite . . . pining for something."

Lizbet looked around, saw Nikia's smile, and answered with one of her own. There was a look of hesitant hope in her eyes, for it had been many days since Nikia had spoken so lightly.

"Not I, *Halda*." Rosy color tinged the waiting woman's cheeks, and she turned her face away to hide her smile.

Dail spoke up then. "I think all your best efforts could not supply this particular lack, my lady." But Darun's efforts, he thought, can and will. And in that, the bard counted Calmis fortunate. The ambassador's fortune lay not so much in the fact that his lady was lovely, though she was, with her raven hair, dawn-blue eyes, and upswept brows speaking of Elvish mystery. In Dail's opinion, Calmis's fortune lay in the fact that his lady loved him.

Lizbet shook her head. "What do you know of it, Master Bard?" she challenged. The sparkle in her eyes was laughter.

"I would betray no secrets, Lady Lizbet."

"Secrets! I have not one secret!"

"Oh, one, I'm sure."

Lizbet returned her attention to her embroidery and Nikia laughed. That laughter rang in Dail's soul like the song of birds greeting spring. "Why, Lizbet," she said, "I do not believe that you have ever held a secret from me."

"No. I never have."

"Until now?"

"Not even now, Lady Nikia."

Dail said, "The blush betrays you, Lizbet."

Lizbet gasped and colored deeper. "You are a scandalmonger, Master Dail. I cannot sit here and listen to this silly chatter." She bobbed a neat curtsy to Nikia and nodded to Dail. "I am sure that you will excuse me for you will wish to get on with your gossip." Lizbet left in a flurry of skirts and dignity.

"It does me good to see that," Nikia said, picking up her book again. "I like Darun. It would be a good match." She smiled and looked up. "Dail, do you think that Darun is serious about her?"

"I can't speak for him. But I will say that I have never seen his attentions linger quite so long on one lady."

"You make him sound quite a rake."

Dail grew serious then. "I don't mean to. But still, it is true that Darun has remained unattached for a long time. And he's always acknowledged the advantages of that condition."

Nikia was satisfied with that. "And what of you, Dail? You look to be making a long career of your own unattachment."

"Well, I suppose I haven't been as fortunate as Darun."

There was a note of sadness in his voice, one that Nikia was sure he was not aware of. Did it hint, she wondered, at a past love? Did it speak, however softly, of some unfulfilled love?

"Lizbet is right," she said briskly. She returned her attention to her book. She had no wish to cause him hurt by bringing up what must be a sad memory. "We do gossip. And to no end."

They fell silent again, reading. Nikia had made her way, with Dail's help, and at times Gweneth's, through half the first trunk of books. All were quite similar, and for a while her attention wandered from her readings again. She took in the words, storing them someplace within, and let her thoughts roam. But she was brought back suddenly by the small cramped writing on the page she was reading.

She reread the passage. The writing wandered in a desultory fashion, uphill and down, on the page.

The night is cold, he had written, *and I long for home. I long for Varna, and I grudge each night that I spend away.*

> Summer green and autumn fire,
> Sky so blue above,
> Heartsblood red and water white,
> A sweet song for my love.

Nikia read the passage again. What a pretty rhyme, she thought. "Dail, do you know this rhyme?" She repeated it for him and he nodded.

"Every lover knows that one, lady. It's as old as reckoning." He put a skipping tune to the work, and Nikia wondered if he was thinking of his stony-hearted lady while he sang.

"It reminds me of something, Dail."

". . . *These the colors of the fall*. . . ."

Nikia shivered. Despite the comfortable fire in the hearth, a sudden chill crawled along her arms.

"Red," Dail said, ticking off the colors on his fingers, "blue, white, green, and orange. Interesting that in both the Elvish rhyme and the Mannish one, the things used to illustrate the colors are so similar. This song comes out of the northern lands. Do you know the origin of your Elvish nursery song?"

Nikia shook her head. "The song's very old, but I might be able to find out."

"It would be interesting to learn, lady."

Nikia sat silent for another moment, thinking about the similarity in the songs. As Dail had pointed out, the illustrations were almost exactly the same. And in thinking, another little rhyme came to her mind. "What of this one?

> "Oh, lady, sweet lady,
> How goes your fair pony,
> Your pony of sweet dapple gray?
> Oh, lady, sweet lady,
> His paces are handsome,
> He races to you when you call.
> I've saddled and bridled
> And dressed him in jewels
> To glitter upon your way.
> His saddle is leather,
> His bridle is gold,
> The jewels are the shades of the fall."

"The shades of the fall," Dail repeated. "That's a pattern I've found regularly among the Elvish songs you've taught us. Is there some special significance to the autumn season among your folk?"

"Oh, indeed there is. It's the harvesttide, the time when the hunter folk come into their own and the great hunting is done. After that, there is a harvest feasting, when all folk gather with their families to celebrate the fruitful season and give thanks to our gods for providing bountifully once again for their people."

Nikia sighed, remembering past celebrations, with Verdant Hall lighted with the soft glow of hundreds of blue hand-fires like stars. She was suddenly and sharply reminded that she had not been at her father's hall for this year's feasting. She had been, then, celebrating her wedding to Garth.

"Now, there's a pleasant custom," Dail said gently. "Here we just tally up the harvest and thank the gods for farmers." He was thoughtful for a moment, rubbing his knuckles along his jaw. "The colors of the fall: red for the trees, green for summer fading, blue for the sky, and white for the water. Orange seems to always represent fire. All colors we see in great splendor in autumn."

"*The jewels are the shade of the fall. . . .*" Nikia mused. "Perhaps it means that the lady's pony wore colored jewels on his bridle. He must have been a well-dressed little beast!"

Dail nodded absently. He rose slowly, his thoughts turned deeply inward, and placed the little book he had been examining back into its chest.

Nikia's interest was piqued. "What is it?"

The bard only shook his head. "A moment, if you will. I'll be right back."

Nikia was alone with her reading for only a short time before Dail returned. He was not alone this time, for he had called up Riche from somewhere, and between the two of them, they were bundling a thickly rolled tapestry.

"There, Riche," he directed, indicating the floor before the hearth. The tapestry fell with a thud, and Dail and Riche straightened.

"Dail, what—?"

Blue eyes bright, a smile dancing around the corners of his mouth, the bard toed the tapestry, unrolling it. Dust drifted into the air. Riche sneezed, and Dail stepped back, gesturing Nikia forward.

"The well-dressed pony, lady."

Nikia dropped to her knees and ran her hands over the yarns which made up the scene. Though her fingers came away dusty, the colors were still bright. The picture, highly stylized, was of a woman standing near the head of a horse. Unlike many tapestries, this did not depict a large scene with throngs of people and activities. The only subjects of the work were the lady and the horse.

She was a beautiful woman, and the artists had taken great care with the materials used to depict the raven lengths of her hair, her blue-silver eyes, and the colorful extravagance of her gown. It was the horse, however, that caught Nikia's attention.

This horse was not a pony, and it was bay-colored, not dapple gray, but the beast was caparisoned in a jewel-studded halter. Nikia looked quickly around for Dail. He was standing behind her, peering over her shoulder. He had seen.

> His saddle is leather,
> His bridle is gold,
> The jewels are the shades of the fall.

And they were! Five jewels adorned a golden halter. "Topaz," she said quietly, "emerald, sapphire, diamond, and ruby. The colors of the songs! Dail, what can this mean?"

"I don't know, lady. Perhaps nothing."

"How old this tapestry must be! It's done in a style I haven't seen about the Citadel."

"Aye, it's old. I don't know its exact age, but I warrant the Princess Gweneth could tell you. There isn't much she doesn't know about the Citadel or its contents."

Nikia agreed. "Riche, would you ask the princess if she is free to join us here?"

But there was no need for Riche to go, for there came a light tapping at the door of the sitting room, and Gweneth stood there, her face alight with curiosity. "I heard the bustle, Sister." Her eyes fell on the tapestry stretched out on the floor. She smiled. "Another hanging for your walls, Nikia?"

"No. Hardly that. Come and look."

"Why, I had this placed in storage several years ago," Gweneth exclaimed. "How did you come by the old thing?"

Dail answered, shrugging. "Riche and I found it just where you'd left it."

"Indeed! Well, you're welcome to it, although I can't imagine why such a musty old tapestry would interest you. Still, it is a charming thing, as old-fashioned as its execution is." Gweneth held out her hand for Dail's assistance and dropped slowly to her knees. "See? We have not used that one-dimensional depiction for many years now. It's gone out of style, in favor of a more lifelike rendering. Ah, what a lovely halter the horse wears!"

"Yes," Dail said thoughtfully. "Just what we thought."

Gweneth caught something in his tone. She glanced from

the bard to Nikia, then back to him again. "The halter is interesting to you, Master Dail? How?"

Dail shrugged. "I don't know just yet, lady. But perhaps—What can you tell us of the tapestry?"

Gweneth studied the wall hanging. She turned over one edge, and her eyes lighted with sudden eagerness. But when she looked up again, she only shook her head.

"I'm afraid I can tell you little. It was hanging in the Great Hall when I first arrived here. It didn't seem to be a favorite with anyone, and the Four Histories tapestry had just been completed, so it was replaced with that one.

"It is old, as I said, but how old I don't know. I would guess—" she frowned—"perhaps several centuries old."

Nikia gasped. "So ancient!"

"Yes, quite ancient, Sister. We have a tendency to cling to the trappings of the past. Or did, at least."

Dail chuckled at that. "Ah, yes. But when Gweneth came to us, she took her chatelaine's duties seriously. There was a mighty housecleaning, then, I can assure you!"

Gweneth flushed. "I think now that I may have taken my duties too seriously."

Nikia peered at the tapestry again. "Who is the lady in the picture, Gweneth? Do you know?"

"Why, Master Dail should know that." Mischief was full blown in Gweneth's gray eyes now.

But Dail shook his head. "I remember the tapestry hanging in the hall, but I don't think I ever heard who it represents."

"Queen Ylin."

"Ylin!" The information obviously surprised Dail. Nikia glanced from one to the other, having no idea who this Queen Ylin might be, except that she had something to do with the Queen's Garden.

"That can't be Ylin," Dail said firmly.

"I assure you that it is."

"Isn't she the lady who erected the Queen's Garden?" Nikia asked.

"Well, she designed it," Dail said, "but it is well known that no portrait of Queen Ylin exists."

Gweneth would not be swayed. "This is Ylin."

"And what of the song?" There was both interest and challenge in Dail's tone now.

Gweneth appeared puzzled by that. "What song is that, Master Dail?"

Dail's voice was low as he sang, and puzzled, as though he would question the words he had known so long:

> "Faceless mother, unseen but loved:
> Ylin fair and bold:
> Hearts will sing in lonely song
> What eyes cannot behold."

He finished the song, brief as it was, on a note that clearly indicated his bemusement. "That song, my lady. The one that has always told us that no portrait of the queen exists. 'Faceless mother, unseen but loved.' It has always been taken to mean that no man alive now knows the face of Queen Ylin."

"Well, one man and two women do now." Gweneth could not be moved. She sat back on her heels, and her expression was as firmly determined as Nikia had ever seen it. "Look." She reached out to the tapestry and flipped up the corner she had turned over when she first sat down.

Dail went down beside her. Nikia moved closer to see. The letters were etched in the dark yarn that had been used to color the lady's hair, and they plainly read *Ylin*.

"I can't believe it!" Dail exclaimed.

Gweneth laughed. "Believe it, Dail. And if you require further proof, you must remember that no single artist signs a tapestry of this kind, for they are the efforts of many who produce such works. And so this must be Queen Ylin. I didn't know until a moment ago. The last time I saw this, it was hanging in the Great Hall. Then I had a servant take it down and had no time to examine it."

"But, a moment," Nikia said. "I don't understand. How can you imagine that this portrait of so legendary a queen has hung in your hall for centuries and no none knew who it was?"

Gweneth shrugged. "It's very old. I am sure that it has

appeared, vanished, and reappeared in the hall many times over the years. It's easy enough, I imagine, for something like this to have lost its history."

"But a revered queen! This must be a very valuable discovery, then."

Dail and Gweneth agreed at once that it was.

"But still," Gweneth said, "I don't understand your interest in her if you didn't know that she was Ylin."

"It wasn't the queen we were interested in," Nikia admitted. "It was her horse."

"Her horse?"

"The bridle," Dail clarified. "And the jewels on it."

"What of them?"

"I was reminded of this tapestry when we were going over something we found in the logs, but it seems that the discovery of a portrait of Queen Ylin eclipses our coincidence. Still, it is interesting."

They were silent for a long moment, looking at the tapestry and thinking their own thoughts. Gweneth's were simple enough to determine. Nikia could tell by her expression and the way she ran her hands over the tapestry that she was already planning to have it refurbished and rehung in the hall.

Gweneth lifted a hand to Dail, and he assisted her to her feet. "How strange to find a treasure that has been lying in plain sight of all for so many years! But still, that is often the way of treasures, is it not?"

Gweneth was pleased, and Nikia was pleased for her. But she could see that Dail was still puzzled. She knew he wasn't thinking about Ylin. All of his attention was still for the jeweled halter.

CHAPTER 12

If Dail and Nikia responded to the finding of the Ylin tapestry with interest and fascination, Gweneth's reaction was quite different. She bundled it away with her the same afternoon of its finding, already laying her plans to restore it and to find a proper and honorable place to display it. She asked Nikia and Dail to remain silent about the find, and they agreed, for Gweneth did not wish to present the tapestry to Alain until it had been fully restored.

"Had I only taken the time to look more closely at it . . ." she fretted.

Although both Nikia and the bard assured her that it was not her fault—had not the thing hung for years uncounted in the Great Hall with never a word being said about it other than that it was an outdated, old-fashioned thing?—still, Gweneth was embarrassed.

But they agreed to keep her little secret, and so the Ylin tapestry soon took a place in the back of their minds.

Nikia did not know if the easygoing Dail would be able to

put all thought of the tapestry aside, though he did not speak
of it again, not even to mention the similar patterns in the
Elvish song and the Mannish rhyme, or the bejeweled halter.
Nikia decided that he regarded them all simply as coinci-
dences. After all, she reasoned, there are only so many colors to
sing about.

And so the afternoon's discovery slipped away, soon to be
forgotten among greater things that were passing.

Garth soon returned with messages from Dekar to his
daughter, filled with his loving concern and his impatience to
be presented with his first grandchild. These messages heart-
ened Nikia. Too, it had been many days since she heard the
dry, ghostly whispering. She dared to hope that it would not
return. She took her food with greater appetite, and her interest in those around her grew, sparked by the sudden feeling
that the matters of the court were passing her by and leaving
her behind.

In the days following the discovery of the Ylin tapestry, the
sun, like thin gold, lay gently on the land. The constant dripping of melted snow from the many roofs of the Citadel
seemed like music to Nikia. She looked forward to the spring
rains. If they were yet several long weeks away, she nevertheless
took hope in this sudden thaw.

Her father enthusiastically accepted the plans Garth had
presented to him for the increased defense of the northern borders. Messages were sent throughout the two kingdoms, calling in the levies of warriors to be used for that defense. Dekar
had promised the troops which had been requested, and more
if he could raise them.

In the taverns of Damris, the bright, bold military songs,
composed by Nikia and her bards, filled the nights with rowdy
cheer. They told again, for a new generation, the fabulous tales
of the ancient heroes who had never known defeat, who took
victory as their just due.

"And not only that," Dail told her, a gleam of satisfaction in
his eyes. "One of my bardings overheard a young serving woman in the kitchens humming the tune to 'Brindan's Quest.'"

This delighted Nikia. "Brindan's Quest" was the first song

her bards had crafted from the Elvish legends she'd taught them. It had been a difficult task to find suitable tales and songs, when so many of the recent ones celebrated Elvish victories over their Mannish foes.

Nikia had been obliged to go farther back in time to find tales and songs that would not recall memories of the recent wars. It appeared, now, that her search had been a success. Dail agreed.

"Aye, lady. Let a serving woman in the kitchens start to sing, and soon her lover from the town will pick up the song, and then his companions in the taverns. And so it will spread. Songs don't travel on foot but on wings."

And so, during those days of sunny interlude during a cold and bitter winter, Nikia renewed her hope for her own returning strength and for her people, both Elvish and Mannish.

But winter did return. It came quickly, on the tail of the night's cloak. The evening, so clear and star-filled, gave way to a dawn dirty and gray with clouds. The air, only the day before warmed by the thin winter sun, grew bitter and damp. No moon silvered the cold that night. A mourning wind groaned about the eaves of the Citadel, and from the kennels, late into the night, Nikia heard the howling of the hounds.

Early the next morning, Garth was told that his hunting bitch, Misty Morning, she who had romped in the Queen's Garden the day Nikia arrived at the Citadel, had died trying to give birth to her first litter. Not one of the five pups lived, for each was a still birth.

That night, the dark whispering returned to Nikia. Unable to sleep, she tried to keep still and not disturb Garth with her restlessness. She didn't want to have to answer his questions should he find her wakeful and sickening again. Lonely, silent vigil seemed easier. In the small hours of the morning, as the dawn crept with bitter gray light across the eastern sky, Nikia heard Lizbet's soft footfalls, her hesitant breath.

"*Halda?*" Lizbet's eyes were dark in the light of the single candle she carried. Shadows scrabbled uncertainly across the walls and ceilings. "*Halda*, the Princess Gweneth— Oh, Halda, please come quickly!"

* * * * *

In Gweneth's bedchamber, torches flared on wall brackets and the hearth was ablaze with a fire whose light glared across the bed. Branches of candles sent light into corners where the torches and hearth fire did not reach.

Nikia, shivering from her walk across the cold stone corridor, felt the heat reach out to envelop her in its suffocating arms. "Gweneth?" she whispered. She spoke to no one, and no one turned to acknowledge her presence. The bed, a tousled ruin of bedclothes, a twisted reflection of Gweneth's pain, was surrounded by men. Nikia recognized the three physicians at once. Fenyan stood near the head of the bed, his face white, his eyes glittering like blue jewels. His left hand covered one of Gweneth's.

At the foot of the bed, removed from the physicians, stood Reynarth. He, too, must have been summoned from his bed, Nikia realized, for he was clothed in a fur-lined bedrobe, the hood of which was thrown back from his face to lie on his shoulders.

Gweneth cried aloud, her voice hoarse, her breathing labored. Her cry carried the sound of despair.

Garth, shadow-silent, touched Nikia's shoulder. "By the gods, Nikia, what is happening? I heard you leave."

"Oh, Garth, I don't know! Her child isn't due for a month yet!"

"Love, I'd better go for my father."

Nikia nodded and heard him leave, but she stood, too frightened to take another step into the room. She watched, her heart racing and jerking with fear, as Gweneth convulsed with pain. She gasped as her friend's voice lifted and shattered in another despairing cry.

Gweneth twisted her head weakly and turned her sweat-damp face toward Nikia. She gasped and drew in enough breath to speak but could not, for another tearing pain wracked her body.

Nikia ran to the bed and took Gweneth's hand in her own. "You must not speak, Gweneth. Save your strength."

Gweneth screamed. The sound tore through the room,

sending a chill of fear skittering down Nikia's back. Fenyan turned away. Quickly Nikia covered the abandoned hand with her own. She tried not to feel the bone-wrenching pain of her friend's grip, concentrating only on providing the support Gweneth craved.

"Hush, Gweneth, hush. It will be over soon. It will be over soon, and you'll forget it all when you hold your babe in your arms."

Her words were babbled. She didn't know what she said. But she had heard women swear that the pain of childbirth receded quickly before the joy of motherhood. She did not believe that this was true. How could she, when she saw Gweneth's twisted agony? But still she avowed it, over and over. It must be, she thought wildly, it must be! Else why would women subject themselves to this torture again and again?

"Nikia! Oh, Sister—" Gweneth moaned. Her voice was a rasping now, thin with pain. "Oh, Nikia, my babe will not—will not come."

"He will, Gweneth. He will." Nikia glanced wildly about, seeking the confirmation of the physicians.

They stepped back from the bed, shaking their heads. Each sought the others' eyes and folded his lips in grim conclusion. Radag, the eldest of the three, motioned her to join them. Slowly Nikia rose, ran a comforting hand across her friend's forehead, and left the bedside.

"See, lady," Radag said softly, nodding toward the bed. "The child has come, but only so far. He'll not be moving any time soon. Perhaps not soon enough."

Nikia shuddered. The child had crowned; she could see the top of his head, the damp sheen of matted red hair and the gleam of darkly unhealthy skin. A sob caught in her throat, and she turned away from Gweneth's weakened efforts to bring her babe to light.

"The princess hasn't the strength to help the child. And if we take the child, we can't be certain that the princess will live. Aye, even so we can't be certain that the child would live."

Fenyan cried low. Nikia looked up sharply. His breathing

was harsh, his eyes large with fear.

"Fenyan," she murmured, gesturing him away from the bedside. She would not have this conversation over Gweneth's childbed. "There will be a way to save them both."

"The child is the one who must be saved!"

Nikia's mouth went dry. She knew in that moment that should there be a choice between the life of his child and that of his wife, Fenyan would choose the child. Aye, and why shouldn't he? A child is conceived for dynastic reasons, reasons that she should understand well enough.

"Brother . . ." Nikia took care that her voice was soft, pleading, and gave him the title she had seldom used before this. "Please, I know of a strength-giving brew that will help. Please, Fenyan."

"The mage has given her potions already."

"He cannot have given her this one. It's one my own people use."

"No."

"Fenyan." Nikia swallowed hard, reached out, and took Fenyan's hands. "My lord, I beg you. It can save them both, I think. I beg you!"

"The child." He shook his head, then winced as Gweneth's cries filled the chamber. "It's the child who must be saved."

His hands still in her own, Nikia dropped slowly to her knees. She lifted her face to him, careless of the tears tracing down her cheeks. "Let me try. I beg you, in the name of your wife who has loved you."

Fenyan turned his eyes toward Reynarth. The mage hesitated for a long moment. He watched the woman on the bed, and then his eyes went to the woman at Fenyan's feet. Slowly he smiled.

"My lord, if the Elvish princess has a remedy we haven't tried—"

"Please let me try!"

Reynarth continued as though he had not been interrupted: "—then I can't stand in her way. Strength is what your lady wife needs."

"My lord . . ." It was Radag. Caution and concern burdened his voice. "I won't guarantee that this will work."

Fenyan glanced from the physician to the mage. His gaze traveled then to the bed where his wife lay, moaning and seeking only breath now and not strength. Placing his hands on Nikia's arms, he lifted her to her feet.

"I ask no one to make guarantee for me, my lord," Nikia said as she rose. "I only ask that I be brought what I need."

Fenyan nodded slowly.

"Thank you." Nikia went back to the bed and gently stroked back Gweneth's tangled, damp hair.

"Sister," she whispered, "I will try to give you strength. Your child will come, if you only have the strength to help him."

There was no way for Gweneth to answer, for there was no strength left to use for speech, but she heard Nikia's words and she took as long a breath as she could. She would try a little longer. She would not give up now.

The physicians sent for the things that Nikia needed. They found the ripple grass, the elf leaf, and the lady's mantle, and mixed them, according to Nikia's direction, with strong red wine. As they worked, Nikia, silent and unheeded, summoned the bright eldritch lines of magic coursing through the veins of even the most humble of Dekar's folk. She wove them at her witchy loom, twining them, courage and strength, and created the healing spell that would bind her magic and the natural powers of the herbs together.

Trembling with fear and from a dance on magic heights she had not visited in many months, Nikia managed, with the aid of a cloth dipped in the mixture, to get Gweneth to swallow the potent drink. Strength, of a kind, resulted. For another hour, perhaps for two, Nikia could not tell. Gweneth used all her strength to help her child into the world.

The child was finally born, not wailing and struggling as most babes, but silent and still. The infant's skin was blue-tinged and puffy.

Radag drew away from the bed, swaddling the blood-stained infant in clean linen. "Bring me water," he said urgently to one of his fellows. "Make it cool and clean."

It was Nikia who went for the water, tested its coolness, and sprinkled on its surface the remainder of the herbs that had not been used for Gweneth.

"What are those, lady?" Radag asked, his voice sharp, suspicious. He held the child slightly away from the basin.

"Only the same herbs we used for the princess. They won't harm the child."

"Aye, but—"

"Sir, help me to bathe him."

Motionless, still, the child's limbs touched the fragrant water. His face, blue and swollen, contracted once, grimaced, and then his tiny head jerked as breath was expelled from his lungs.

"He breathes!" Radag whispered. "Thank the gods, the little prince breathes!"

"Aye," Nikia murmured, her voice shaking as badly as her hands. She immersed the child in the cool, herb-touched waters, cleaning his limbs, his body, and last his face. "Well and on his own now."

"The herbs?"

Nikia shook her head, glanced up, and smiled at the physician. "More the water."

"Magic?" The physician's voice was breathless, awed, and tinged with both fear and respect.

Nikia shook her head once more. "No, sir, not the herbs. The water stimulates him, shocks him a little, and he breathes to wail his protest at being brought out into the cold. Take the child, Radag, and wrap him warmly. He'll want watching for a time."

Radag lifted the infant prince from the basin and covered him again with a clean wrap. The awe was gone from his eyes now, and he became once again distant and cool. "I know that well enough, lady."

But Nikia did not hear. She'd gone to the bedside of her friend, taking up Gweneth's hands in her own. She glanced once around the room for Fenyan. His wife's birthing labor forgotten, he stood with Radag, assuring himself of his son's health, his eyes bright with joy, his face alight with his satisfaction.

"Gweneth . . . Sister." The exhausted woman moved her head slightly, weakly, and managed a small smile.

"Gweneth, you have a fine son."

"Is he well?"

"Only tired from his hard entry into the world." Nikia stroked Gweneth's wet hair. Then she reached behind her for a towel and dipped it into a basin of cool water. Gently, carefully, she bathed Gweneth's face. "There," she whispered. "Doesn't that feel better?"

"Aye. My son . . . a son? Sister, I have . . . given Fenyan the heir he desired. . . ."

"And well pleased he is. Be proud, Gweneth. Be proud of yourself and your son."

Gweneth's eyes were dulled now, but the smile gracing her lips was enough to speak of her joy. Nikia bit her lip, bowed her head, and knew that her friend was dying.

She must hold the child now if she is ever to know the joy of him. Aye, and should not Fenyan be here, at this bedside, to comfort the wife who is giving her life that his son may live?

"My son!" Nikia could hear his voice behind her, across the room, crowing with his pride and pleasure. "Look, Father. Look at the grandson I have given you."

She heard Alain's compliment, and then the compliments of others. Anger rose in her then, and fear, and something unnamed that might have been loathing. Nikia rose, pressed Gweneth's hand gently, and turned away from the bed.

"My lord," she said, not caring that she did not keep the edge of anger from her voice.

Fenyan glanced around, the child in his arms, his face alight with pride and celebration. "The child does well, Sister, thanks to your help."

"You thank the wrong woman." Fenyan frowned, not understanding. "Wretched man!" she hissed. She crossed the chamber swiftly, snatched the child from his arms, and, ignoring the startled gasps of Alain and Garth, bore the infant back to the bedside of his mother.

"Here is your son, Gweneth," she said, making her voice gentle again in spite of her anger. "Here is your child."

The room grew silent about them. The murmured questions of the startled men fell away. The sob of joy was all the breath that Gweneth could manage.

"Here is your son, Sister." Nikia went down on her knees and placed the child in the crook of his mother's arm. Weakly Gweneth moved her hand to touch the red down that was his hair.

Her eyes went to Nikia's. "You saved . . . my son."

"No, no, Gweneth. It was you who found the strength to give him life."

"Your magic . . . it was your magic. . . ." Gweneth smiled, her eyes bright for the last time. "I can smell . . . the herbs on him . . . so light and clean. Your magic . . . saved him."

"No. Hush now. It wasn't my magic that saved him, Gweneth, but your own."

Weakly Gweneth smiled and shook her head. "Not mine . . . I have . . . no magic."

"Aye," Nikia said through the clench of tears in her throat. She watched the light fade from her friend's eyes, watched as the last bit of feeble strength left her.

She is dying. Oh, Gweneth! Gently Nikia lifted the child closer to his mother. "Gweneth, kiss your child. He'll need to sleep soon, and the nurse is here."

Gweneth moved slowly, touching her lips to her son's head. "Your . . . magic," she whispered.

"No." Nikia bent to kiss her failing friend. "It was yours, Gweneth, that gave the child life. It was the magic of love."

Gweneth sighed. When she closed her eyes, Nikia knew that she would never again open them. The light was gone, the spirit flown. The child lying on the still breast of the Princess Gweneth would never know a mother's touch beyond that last, soft kiss.

Nikia looked up, and through the veil of her tears, she saw Garth standing above her.

"Come, love. Come away now." He lifted her carefully to her feet.

"The babe. . . ." She glanced back to the bed, but the child was not there. Already he was in Fenyan's arms again. If there was sadness for the death of his wife in his expression, it was masked by the joy of holding his son.

"Garth, she is dead."

"I know, love. I know."

"She died for the child. But . . . she knew him, if only for a moment."

"Aye, love, she did. And for that she must bless you."

Nikia let her eyes wander over the chamber. She and Garth were the only ones near the bedside now. The physicians, the mage, and Fenyan stood near the little prince, who lay now in his grandfather's arms. Nikia's breath caught in a sob. Even as it did, she met the green eyes of the mage. His regard was long and thoughtful.

"I am sorry, lady," he said unctuously.

"Yes," Nikia whispered. "So am I." But none of the others looked away from the child, and even before she had spoken her reply, Reynarth's attention was again on Alain and the infant.

Don't they care? Don't they care that a woman has died here this day? Can they only care about the infant, the heir? Nikia leaned wearily against her husband's shoulder. "Garth, please take me home."

* * * * *

When she crept into her bed, aching with grief, Nikia curled herself up into a small, trembling ball. "Garth, Gweneth is dead!"

"Aye," Garth said, stroking her hair. "Aye, but she has bravely given Fenyan the heir he needed."

Nikia was silent for a long moment. When she spoke, her voice was wracked with tears and sobbing. "I mourn her now, Husband, and I will mourn her forever, she who was a sister to me."

"I know, love." He took her gently into his arms and held her as a man would hold a weeping child. He was silent for a long time before he spoke again. "Love, *was* it magic that saved the child?"

Nikia looked up from her weeping and wiped the heels of

her hands across her eyes. "Aye, Garth, it was magic. It was love's magic—Gweneth's magic."

Garth held her tighter and spoke no more.

* * * * *

The Citadel was dark. Lights burned only where necessary. Despite the cold, no fires but the fires of the kitchen and the newly occupied nursery were lighted. The folk of the Citadel, servant and noble alike, went about silently, dressed in muted, simple mourning. What gray light the wretched winter day had provided fled now with the sun's setting. Winter's wind mourned about the eaves of the great stone castle, chorusing the sorrow of those within.

Servants grieved, and their grief was as genuine as though a beloved family member had made the final passage that is death. They went about their duties with swollen faces, some, or with hardened faces, those who did not weep easily.

In the darkness of the Queen's Garden, alone, the Princess Nikia made her way to the very center of the circle of winter-dead plantings. She was cloaked against the wind, but no mantle could warm the icy depths of emptiness which filled her heart. There were no tears on her cheeks, for those had been shed already. There was only emptiness, echoing with ghostly memory.

"My sister," she said to the cold and the night. "My sister is dead." There were gods, she knew, who must be told. There were gods, she hoped, who would watch for the spirit of Gweneth, daughter of Karo, wife of Fenyan, Princess of Mannish. These gods would reach out to that gentle heart and take it home.

Nikia went on her knees there in the center of the garden. She didn't feel the cold ground or the seeping dampness. She did not know which of the gods the Mannish worshiped. It would not, according to every standard she had been raised by, have been polite to inquire. She did not see that her husband's people worshiped any gods at all, although their speech was often touched by reference to some deities.

Her own gods were personal to her. An elf chose, throughout his life, the gods that were special to him. These gods he honored by the way he lived. The Elvish believed that a god needed no ceremony to make him a reality.

"Recognize me or no," the god Hori was said to have declared, "I care not. I am no more real or less for your worship. Know that I am here; come to me when you need me. But make me no bargains, for I need not your little worships and adorations in order to exist."

He was the god of mothers and children. He it was who saw the women safely through childbearing; he it was who watched over the little ones in their cradles.

"Honored One, beloved Hori, watch now for a spirit that has been ever kind and loving in this life. Watch for her, help her on her way to you, and receive her who was my sister, not in blood but in heart.

"Honored One, beloved Hori"—Nikia raised her hands now, and her eyes, to the starless sky—"receive her in your love for those who bear the children of this world. Comfort her, who is parted from the child she so desired.

"Honored One, beloved Hori," she whispered, "watch over her child, and love him."

The wind's harsh breath stilled to a soft sigh, as though the god Hori had heard her prayer. She lifted her head again and turned her face to the clouded night.

"Receive her, Honored One. Receive her as you have received my prayer."

The wind fell silent. The restless murmuring among the skeletal plants ceased. Nikia rose to her feet, pulled her cloak about her more tightly, and returned to the grim, mourning darkness of the Citadel.

* * * * *

"What was she doing?" Fenyan's voice was a harsh whisper, low and grating, as though he feared to be overheard. "Why was she kneeling out there, alone, in the garden?"

Reynarth shrugged, turned away from the window, and leaned down casually to place another log on the hearth. He didn't keep mourning darkness in his stony chamber, but light and warmth. Torches glittered on the walls, lighted candles flared about the room. The hearth's fire crackled merrily.

"Can I pour you more wine, my lord?" He glanced up at Fenyan, who leaned against the stone casement. The prince's face was flushed and a little swollen—not with weeping, the mage knew, but with the puffiness of too much wine. The prince had been celebrating. Quietly, Reynarth thought, but celebrating.

Fenyan's clothing was simple—a dark tunic, black hose, and low, soft boots the color of charcoal. A pin of blackstar ebon-crystal held his short cloak closed at the throat. His valet had found him clothing appropriate for one who has lost a wife.

But the light in his eyes belied the darkness of his garb. Fenyan had his son now, and there was no room in him for more than the outward trappings of mourning.

Reynarth, however, had no cause to celebrate. Gweneth was not supposed to be dead. She was supposed to recover from yet another miscarriage, eventually from the death of the child, and continue to miscarry the pregnancies that her husband, in his quest for an heir, would engender.

But the child had lived. And the princess had died.

Reynarth still didn't understand what had happened to his spell. The bitch in the stables, spirit-tied to the princess through dark, hard spells to become Gweneth's magic Other, should not have died either. Only the litter, the child's spirit-shadow, should have died. Reynarth clenched his fists. That, at least, had happened as it should have.

There had been some danger, he knew. There had been some room for error. But even with the death of the bitch, still he had thought that the princess would live. And when it became apparent that she would not, he had hoped that the healing spell the Elvish witch had used would save Gweneth's life. It had not.

"Yes, Reynarth, more wine." Reynarth refilled both goblets and rejoined Fenyan at the window.

"Is she gone?" Fenyan asked.

The mage nodded. "Aye, gone." He put the goblet to his lips, tasted the sweetness of the wine, and set it down again.

"Praying to her Elvish gods, no doubt. She claimed to have been fond of the princess."

"Yet for all that, she did not help."

"I'm sure she did her best, my lord."

Fenyan grunted, gulped the wine, and held out the cup for more. It was odd, he thought, standing here and discussing the woman in the garden. His mind slid dizzily around the picture, and he tried to recall how she had appeared kneeling in the cold.

But he hadn't seen her. Not really. It was too high, from this chamber, to see anyone who might be walking in the garden below. But Reynarth had seen. He was farseeing, the mage. He could see where others could not.

He had seen that Gweneth would die. He had seen that the child would live. Fenyan knew this to be true, for why else would the mage have let the Elvish witch try her healing potions?

The Elvish witch. It was an epithet that had become like a title in his mind. The Elvish Witch. And Reynarth knew that the Elvish witch was carrying a child before anyone else had known.

"Reynarth, what was in the potion that the Elvish witch used on my wife?"

Reynarth watched him carefully now. "Simple herbs, my lord, and wine."

"Aye? Good Elvish wine?"

"I don't know for sure, my lord."

"Hadn't you tried healing potions before?"

"I had, my lord."

"And they didn't help her."

"I am sorry. They didn't."

"Neither did they kill her."

Reynarth held his silence for a moment, letting the implied accusation linger between them, before he spoke. "You don't think that the healing potion that the Princess Nikia used was responsible for your lady wife's death, do you?"

Fenyan laughed a little, coughed, and shook his head. He reached behind him to refill his goblet yet another time. Holding it in an unsteady hand, he watched the mage above its rim. In truth, it was easier to think Gweneth magic-killed than to remember that he hadn't bid her farewell, that he hadn't so much as thanked her for his son.

He'd not loved her, not ever. But she had loved him. That should have counted for something, should have earned her a grateful word, a small good-bye. It hadn't, in the end, earned her so much as a thought. Fenyan hadn't known his wife was dead until the women had entered the bedchamber.

"I can think anything I wish to think, mage."

Reynarth strove for a look of shocked surprise. They had come to an edge, an edge between the prince's dislike of the Elvish princess and a budding fear and hatred. It would not do now for Reynarth to accuse the witch openly. Fenyan must do that on his own. And when he did, when he voiced his charge, or even his suspicion, no matter how unfounded, the concerted opinion of the Citadel would fall in behind him.

"I am certain that the Princess Nikia was only trying to help," Reynarth replied.

"Aye, surely," Fenyan mocked. He wondered if he truly believed the thoughts that were peeping through the wine fog in his mind. Did he really believe that Nikia's potion had killed his wife? It hadn't been long since he'd spoken words of thanks to his brother's wife. He was too confused to think.

"What spell did she use, Reynarth?"

"Spell, my lord?"

Fenyan squinted and shook his head. "Spell, mage. What spell did she use?"

"I don't know that she used any spell." Reynarth kept the lie smooth and believable.

"Of course she did."

"She may have. I'm not familiar with Elvish magic, my Lord."

"I do not want her near the child."

Reynarth held his peace, composing his face into an expression of questioning and mild puzzlement.

"I mean what I say, Reynarth. I don't want her near my son."

"You'll find it hard to convince your father of a reason for that decree, my lord."

"I can handle my father."

Reynarth nodded. "As you say. But you must retire now. There will be a lot to do in the morning."

"Aye, there will. Tomorrow I will spend the day with my son." Fenyan grinned wide and loose, a drunken tribute to his happiness.

"And tomorrow you will bury your wife."

Fenyan nodded. He felt agreeable, confident, happy. There was no thread of wondering in his mind now. "And that, too."

And tomorrow, Reynarth thought, sipping his wine, I'll give thought to your wishes, my lord, that the Princess Nikia be kept away from the child. Seeds of fear, of mistrust, could be sown in this fertile ground, he realized. And if the physical symbol of the treaty between Mannish and Elvish falls into disrepute, can the alliance itself stand strong?

Reynarth smiled and finished the wine.

* * * * *

Nikia went to her bed with the dragging steps of one who cares little where she rests. She crept into Garth's arms, buried her face against his shoulder, and found more tears to weep.

He comforted her wordlessly. She'd always seemed a child to him, a pretty, silver-haired girl with star-colored eyes. Though willing and always happy to please, she'd seemed till now to need no one. When he was with her she was glad. When he was gone . . . he did not know. Tonight she knew a woman's grief, the loss of a friend, of one whom she had named "Sister." Tonight she wept for that loss.

He didn't know that she also wept because the whispering invasion was renewed again.

In the morning, she awoke fevered, and before the end of the day Nikia miscarried her child.

PART TWO

I know I am but summer to your heart,
And not the full four seasons of the year.

—Edna St. Vincent Millay

CHAPTER 13

The ghosts of winter did not flee with the coming of spring, but continued to haunt. They were the ghosts of Gweneth and Nikia's tiny never-born child. Dail saw them daily in Nikia's eyes, once as bright as starlight, now the color of misty morning fog.

In the winter, the bard had feared that he was falling in love with his cousin's wife. Now, in the spring, he wished for nothing so much as for Garth to get her with child again, to light those empty eyes with hope and renewal.

Anything, he would think as he watched her wander through her long, sad days, anything to banish the fog and bring back the starlight. Even another man's son. That much did he love her.

And yet no promise of a child would lay to rest the other, darker ghosts roaming the Citadel: the whispers, suspicions, and fears.

In shadowed corners, pages murmured questions. Servants nodded fearfully, and the ladies of the court drew away from

Nikia as though from a carrier of plague. More and more, Dail heard the muttered references to "Garth's witch," "the Elvish sorceress," and once, horribly, "Gweneth's slayer."

Like an illness traveling on the air, suspicion and mistrust of Nikia spread through the Citadel. Yet, try as he did, Dail could find no source for the epithets, no spring from which these foul waters welled.

Often now at night, alone in his chambers, his fingers played along the fine leather tooling of his dagger's sheath rather than the strings of his beloved harp. He yearned to use that dagger for Nikia's sake, but ghosts and whispers are no target for steel.

* * * * *

The young elf rode with no consideration for his horse, and only little hope that he would safely reach the camp of the Mannish scouts. Ice touched the night; the winds blew hard and bitter in the Kevarth Mountains. Even so, he felt nothing of the cold. Need and fear warmed him.

"Faster!" he cried, lashing his horse. "Faster!"

The wind caught his words and whisked them away. The elf felt the surge of powerful muscles as his mount leaped a fallen tree. He tried to move in concert, but cold and fear made him clumsy. The horse nearly stumbled.

Would they believe him? If he could find the Mannish scouts, would they believe his tale? Carnach Bay had been black with sails, the shore writhing with the disembarking armies.

The elf groaned aloud. Armies, aye, but armies of what? Mannish? No. And certainly not Elvish.

He prayed to his hunting gods that he would find the proper words to describe what he had seen, words that would not make him seem a madman.

* * * * *

Yvanda watched, smiling, as the elf took his horse over the blowdown. He was tiny in the globe, but she felt his fear.

"Let him through."

Yvanda glanced over her shoulder. "Indeed? He will warn them."

The Sorcerer shrugged. His changeable eyes were clear now with amusement. "It matters not at all whether he warns them. Let him. Let them get word to Damris." He laughed. "Let the little kings know what they are up against." He moved away.

Yvanda smiled again. Arrogant, she thought, but not without cause. "Where are you going?"

"To the sea cave. Don't do anything to prevent him from reaching his destination."

"As you say." She turned back to her globe and watched as the horse died under the elf. She watched, smiling, as the messenger resumed his long journey, on foot now, through the dark to the small encampment of Mannish scouts.

* * * * *

Fenyan stood silently in the shadows of the corridor. He watched, keeping his breathing still, as Nikia left the nursery. He did not misread the look of sadness and longing in her eyes. She had been to see his son.

He'd wondered when she would finally find her way to the nursery. It had taken her nearly five weeks.

Sadness and longing, he thought. She who has lost her own child now comes to see my own little Ybro. Yet why now, after so long a time?

He would never have thought that it was not Ybro Nikia sought, but Gweneth. He, who long ago ceased to miss his wife, could not have imagined that Nikia found comfort in the babe's eyes, gray like his mother's, in his calm smile, and even in the very shape of his face.

Nikia was only an arm's length away from where he stood when he spoke. "Good morning, Nikia."

Nikia gasped, caught her hand to her throat, and smiled in recognition when she saw who it was who had so startled her. "Good morning, Fenyan. I've been to see your son. He's a lovely boy. You must be proud."

"I am. Thank you." They did not speak for an awkward

moment. Nikia glanced at him and tried make her voice easy, light.

"I . . . have been ill, of course. I am sorry that I have taken so long to visit." She was suddenly uneasy. He watched her so carefully! Surely he had known of her illness. Did he think her jealous? Nikia spoke quickly. "He is a beautiful child."

"Aye, so he is." Fenyan paused again before he spoke. "I hope you will excuse me. I want to look in on him myself."

"Of course. I give you good morning, Fenyan."

He nodded curtly and watched her go. She was not the same woman he had known these past months. She was thinner now, her eyes sharper. She appeared nervous and less sure of herself.

Could it be as the mage says? he wondered. Is she jealous of the child, she who has lost her own?

"They are not like us," Reynarth had said only recently. "Women form a stronger attachment to their children. Oh, aye, I doubt not that you love the little prince, my lord." Reynarth sighed. "But women are different. They view a child as a possession. 'From my body,' they will claim"—here he laughed—"as though a man had no part in the child's making at all! But it makes them different. And when a woman loses a child, well, who can say how she will react? Some despair and weaken and pine. Others become strange and secretive.

"And the Princess Nikia? My lord, I find our own women strange enough to predict. An Elvish woman? The gods only know how she will take her loss."

Fenyan stood in the silent corridor, empty now that Nikia was gone. Who indeed could tell how an Elvish witch would react? His lips a thin, hard line, he entered the nursery.

Whispers and doubts trailed after Nikia now, like the soft gray smoke of a hidden fire. Even her loyal bards were not quite as enthusiastic about their lady as they had been.

Fenyan would ask the nurse to have a care.

* * * * *

"How could they navigate Carnach?" Liam asked. "It is still choked with ice!"

"No, my lord. It is not."

"But it must be! It never clears this soon!"

The scout shook his head. "My lord, there is one who has seen them."

"Who?"

"An Elvish hunter."

"Where is he?"

The scout moved restlessly, as though considering carefully his reply. When he finally did speak, it was not to Liam but to Alain.

"Your Grace, the Elven is dead, but he gave us his message before he died. The northern hordes have put in at Carnach Bay. He saw them, Your Grace. They move against us even now."

Alain nodded slowly. "I believe you. It is time."

Silence fell on the chamber. In his place at the council table, Garth let his eyes wander from his father to his brother. The war for which they had prepared all winter was upon them. He clenched his hands and rose slowly. In his mind's eye, he saw ruined farms and an empty cradle. The latter image caught hard at his heart. He didn't know whether the cradle in his mind was the one in the cottage at Harvest Run or one that might have been for his own child, never born.

"Father," he said, "my army will ride to Dekar."

* * * * *

The courtyard was filled with the stamping of horses, the harsh voices of officers, and the clash of spears and swords. The very air was alive with the sound and presence of Alain's armies. Banners waved on the soft spring breeze—Garth's own green and gold, and blue and silver, the colors of the Royal House, raised for Fenyan.

Bright morning light flashed from Garth's mail and shield. His hands were gauntleted, and he had to work to control the taut prancing of his great war-horse. He was going to join with Dekar's armies to defend the mountain passes. Fenyan's army would meet the enemy at Carnach Bay and strive to keep them from the rich farmlands of Raeth in the north.

This was no enhancement of the border patrols now. This was the first foray of war.

Nikia walked slowly down the broad steps of the Citadel. Her gown was summer green, her hair piled high, like some silversmith's winsome confection. Thin her face was, and as pale as moonlight. In the crowd of ladies gathered to bid their men farewell, she moved in a little sea of loneliness.

An ache, like the long, cool mourning of wind, drifted through Garth. Though Nikia was alone, she moved bravely, her head high, her steps confident.

Throughout the long winter, he, too, had heard the dark murmuring of the Citadel's folk and, though he tried, he had found no source for them. He felt a sudden stab of pain for Nikia, who had not earned what she now endured.

I am abandoning her, he thought, wrestling his impatient mount to stillness, and I am leaving her friendless.

Across the courtyard, Darun Lord Calmis called something to a groom, then caught Garth's eye and flashed him a smile. Garth grinned back. Not entirely friendless, he realized. There is Darun, and of course her Lizbet. And Dail will keep her busy now that we have reduced the numbers of his bards.

Nikia came to stand as close as she could to the huge, restless destrier. Garth thought that something of the stars had returned to her eyes. He did not see that the brightness was caused by tears, barely checked.

"Love," he said, kissing the hand she held up to him. "Have a care." It was his familiar phrase of parting.

"You are the one who must have a care, Garth." She smiled, for she would not send him away with tears.

The horse stamped and snorted. Garth brought him under control with a sharp word. Swiftly he leaned down again and kissed her. "Don't fear for me, Nikia. I will be fine." His voice was bright and confident. "I will give your love to your father."

Tears were dangerously close to spilling now. The princess swallowed hard and nodded.

I love her, he thought, and he was surprised. The words had been said before between them, but often they were offered as a thanks, a tribute to the pleasure she gave him. Lately he had spoken them as comfort. Here, in the bright light of the morning, on the edge of war, he thought them and meant them. He loved her courage, her determination that he not see the pain she felt. Yes, he loved her.

But before he could speak again, the war-horse jerked and pranced away. Behind him, Fenyan called out, and dozens of voices were raised in concerted farewell.

"I love you!" he called. She might have heard him, for a soft bloom of color brightened her cheeks and her lips parted as though in surprise.

She called something back, and when she waved to him, she looked for a moment like the girl she had been in the autumn and not the haunted woman she had become. The breeze caught a stray wisp of her silvery hair as she rose on tiptoe to see him sweep away on the tide of war.

* * * * *

Nikia stopped just inside the door of the Great Hall. The memory of her parting with Garth was still fresh. Dail stood at the head of the long table, his bards and bardings seated close around him.

"Good morning, lady."

The group was a sadly reduced one. Nikia counted only four bardings, the newest and youngest lads, and five bards. Dail had sent the others to ride with the troops. On these men would rest the responsibility of recording, in song and tale, the deeds of the warriors. Through their eyes, the story of the defense of the Two Kingdoms would come alive.

Nikia caught her lip between her teeth. Who among her bards and bardings would not return from this war? She shook her head, as though to shake away the thought. "Good moring, Dail."

Dail watched her slow progress, but he was the only one. The others remained still, seated where they were. Not one of them looked around.

Here, too? she wondered with a sharp pain. Here, too, will I encounter the whispering, the sly looks, the badly hidden gesture against evil?

Nikia glanced at Dail. The smile he gave her was not as bright as usual.

"To work, lady," he murmured.

"Aye, to work, master, and perhaps we can craft such songs this day as will ring above the sounds of war."

But the song-crafting did not go well. Tunes would not fit words. Stories and tales were raised, then abandoned as unfit. By the time the fire in the hearth had burned low, and then, untended, fell to ashes, Nikia was weary.

The sun shone warmly on the city, flowing like sweet honey into the gardens of the Citadel as it roused them to life again. But it did not penetrate the Citadel itself. Garth had once told Nikia that, in the heat of the summer, the folk of the Citadel would flock to the Great Hall to pass a cool evening. But that was in the heat of the summer. Now the Great Hall was still chilled throughout the day. Fires were yet lighted in its hearths at night if there was to be a feasting.

Dail rose, rubbing cold hands together, and started toward the hearth. "I can't credit that spring has come when I spend too much time in the hall."

Someone in Dail's group murmured. Nikia didn't hear the comment, but she heard someone else chuckle.

Nikia looked around to see who the speaker was, but she couldn't tell. Dail knew, however. He did not return to his seat but came to stand beside Nikia. He looked over his group of bards, his eyes resting on Yfr, seated farthest away.

"I didn't hear you, Yfr."

"I made no comment, master."

Yfr's eyes were dark, unreadable. His face, a lean angular one pocked by some childhood illness, was still. His eyes, however, moved slightly away from Dail's.

"Odd," the chief bard said softly, as though speaking to himself. "I could swear I heard your voice."

Again there was soft laughter. Dail's eyes swung away from Yfr. He went down on his heels beside Nikia, his arms knotted with tension, his fists clenched. "Does something amuse you, Jac?"

"No, master."

"You lie!"

The words cracked like a whip. Yfr might have been able to stand that hard blue regard of his master's, but Jac could not. He flushed, turned his eyes away, and shuffled his feet.

"Well?"

Jac swallowed. "I—I meant no disrespect, master."

"Disrespect? How?" Dail was not going to let the matter go. Nikia looked away from Jac, squirming under his master's disapproval, to Yfr, who had gone white. Both bards looked at Dail. Then their eyes slid away from him to Nikia.

She understood suddenly what kind of a remark had been passed.

Biting her lip, Nikia rose to her feet. She placed a hand on Dail's shoulder. Suddenly, like a white tide rising, anger surged through her. She felt cold to the tips of her fingers. All the weariness and fears of the winter fell away, as though they were but the fears of a child who does not understand that shadows are merely the play of light on a wall and not lurking demons.

She was tired of the whispering, tired of the innuendo and the sly suggestion that she was the dark, magical cause every time something went wrong, from the spoiling of a meal or the unruliness of a horse or dog to a page's stubbed toe.

She had endured the loss of a friend, the loss of a child, the loss of her own confidence. The face, pinched and frightened, that looked back at her from the mirror each day was not one she recognized as her own.

Nikia shivered. I have lost even myself, she thought. But no more.

She would not go about the Citadel like some captured animal, some fey child, ashamed and afraid. Her magic, small as it was, was the song to which her blood moved, as much a part of her as the pulse in her veins, the air she breathed. It was her heritage, and one that she had tried to deny for the sake of those who now whispered that she was an evil witch.

She would be a victim of those whispers no more. At her father's hall, she would call on the bright silver lines of her magic to light a hearth fire as casually as anyone here would reach for a tinderbox. Now she would do so here as well.

She looked again at Yfr. If possible, his face had become even whiter. The hall itself seemed to be holding its breath. "Am I correct, Yfr, in assuming that you think that I might light the fire in the hearth more efficiently than Master Dail?"

Dail's shoulder under her hand tensed, and she felt his muscles jump as though he would reach up to restrain her. But he did not.

Yfr swallowed hard. She read fear in his eyes. "Have you an answer for me, Yfr?"

The bard remained silent. Dail leaned a little forward. "The Princess Nikia has asked you a question, Yfr. I suggest that you answer her."

Yfr's voice was a hoarse whisper. He bobbed his head once, then again. Oddly, in that moment, Nikia felt a stirring of pity for him. "Yes, lady."

"Well," she said, striving to keep her voice even, "you are correct." She lifted her hand, saw him flinch, and shook her head. "You need not fear, Yfr. Come here."

Nikia had never seen a man look more like a creature in a trap than did Yfr. He looked about him, jerking his head from one to another of his companions. When he found no help there, he turned his eyes toward Dail.

His master remained silent. "Come here, Yfr," Nikia repeated quietly.

Yfr rose slowly to his feet and came, with halting steps, to the dais. He stood below Nikia, not meeting her eyes.

"Come with me," she said, her voice still quiet. She took his arm and felt him flinch.

Nikia guided the bard to the hearth. She placed him to one side, feeling all the time the fear and the terror that emanated from him. In that moment, she felt truly sorry for him, but she had no wish to spare him.

"You are correct, Yfr. I can light the fire quicker and more efficiently than Master Dail can. In fact, I am quite skilled at such things. Since you are so curious about this little talent with which I have been blessed—aye, blessed, Yfr—I'll give you a demonstration."

The bard made a low moan of fear deep in his throat.

"Hush, Yfr," she said, her voice gentle now. She didn't wish to frighten him to death. "You will break my concentration."

Whatever it must have taken to silence his terror, Yfr applied it. He remained quiet.

Nikia commanded the fire. Flames leapt suddenly to life in the hearth as warmth and light replaced the cold embers. Had she not been holding Yfr's arm tightly, he would have crumpled to the floor at her feet.

"You are correct, Yfr. It is more efficient."

Eyes wide, he nodded. It was all that he could do.

"I can extinguish the fire, too, Yfr. Shall I show you?"

"No!" His voice was a gasp of terror. His hands, hanging at his sides, twitched. Nikia knew what it was that made them move so.

"You seem to wish to make the sign against evil."

He was silent. Nikia could see that he was convinced that she would shortly blast the life from him with her magic. She almost wanted to laugh, and she might have, had she not felt so sorry for him.

"Go ahead, Yfr. It won't hurt more than my feelings, and it might make you feel better."

His hands moved then, forming the simple gesture. Nikia saw in his eyes that he did not will them to move. They simply moved.

"Lady—lady," he stammered.

"Go back to your place, Yfr." He went, backing away from her until he came to the steps of the dais. He stumbled once, righted himself, and, panting hard, resumed his place. It took a certain amount of courage, Nikia thought, not to flee the room screaming.

She went to stand beside Dail, who had not moved through the whole demonstration. She looked out over the silent group. There was fear on some faces; others she could not read. She turned to Dail.

"Master, I am sorry to have interrupted our work. It seems to me that this curiosity—and I name it far more gently than it deserves—needed answering."

Dail nodded grimly, but his eyes were bright with approval. "Aye, lady. You're right."

"Thank you for that, master. However, this morning's labor has taken the heart out of me for work." She bent swiftly and took up her little harp. "I hope that your bards will excuse me."

Dail moved as though he would stop her from leaving, but before he did, he saw the look of grim determination in her eyes. "Aye, lady. But perhaps it is not you who should apply for excuse."

"I agree. Good morning, master."

"Good morning, lady," Dail said gently. He watched her leave, marking her proud, straight back and her carefully lifted head. When she was gone, he turned abruptly toward the little group before him. His first thought was to dismiss them all, but he bit back his curt words and took up Dashlaftholeh.

"We have work still," he said, keeping his voice even. "Let's not waste any more time."

All his songs that day were about courage.

CHAPTER 14

"You want us to bury them, my lord?"

Garth shivered in the cold night. "Aye, Captain. Bury them."

A gray fog of disapproval, his lords' muttering, eddied around him. Garth took their meaning easily enough. He gestured dismissal to the young captain and turned to the lords who awaited his orders.

They were four, each a man who had dominion over a province of the northern lands. Garth had picked these lords himself to form his council and to provide troops for his army, although Fenyan had advised against it.

"Take men you know well, brother," he had said. "Take men who have known you all their lives, as I will."

But Garth had disagreed. It was, in his view, more reasonable to take with him men who would be defending their own lands and homes.

"My lords," Garth said now, "will you await me in my tent?"

"But you'll waste the energies of our men in burying enemy dead!" It was Lorm who spoke. He was older than Garth, nearly of an age with the king. His blue eyes were sharp and hard, his expression full of distaste and disapproval.

Garth smiled bitterly. "Aye, Lorm, I will expend the energy needed for mass graves, and judge it well spent. Better that than that the vile carcasses lie unburied, fouling water and soil alike."

Lorm looked as though he was about to make another comment, but when he caught the bitter light in the prince's eyes, he remained silent.

"Will there be anything else, my lords?" Garth asked quietly.

No one spoke.

"Well, then, await me in my tent. We'll confer shortly."

Alone, Garth drew his cloak tighter about him. It had been raining since morning. The battle had been fought—aye, and won after a fashion—in the icy spring rain. Fully half of the Elvish who had come with him were dead. Nearly as many Mannish warriors had fallen. The army was badly tattered.

Screams and cursing had filled the day, as well as fear and sometimes triumph.

Ultimately, he thought, there had been triumph. But at such cost!

The memory of terror, like a weakness, snaked through Garth's stomach as he remembered the fiercest part of the battle. It seemed to him that the warriors of the enemy, wretched creatures from some vile netherworld, would never stop coming against his army.

How is it that we won? he wondered. The land was wracked by the passage of the battle. Sweet, fallow fields that should have been prepared for planting lay torn and shattered. Death had passed over the land with hooves of steel, plowing for its own seed.

Garth shivered. He saw no beauty in victory. His heart ached with the thought. No symmetry, no pattern, no bright picture for the victor to see. Only this—death and ruin.

Torches flickered far out over the fields. Men carried them

on their search for their fallen comrades. There would be mass burials for both sides, but no Mannish warrior would consign a brother to the same pit as an enemy. The Elvish did not return their dead to the earth, as did the Mannish. The Elvish captains had come to him earlier, cloaked in grave courtesy and asking his permission for funeral pyres.

Garth had refused. The flames would call attention to their camp and light a possible midnight raid.

"But, Prince Garth," the leader of the captains had reasoned, "the enemy has fallen back. They won't attack again tonight."

"Perhaps, and perhaps not, *Halthe*. I grieve with you for the loss of your comrades, but there will be no pyres tonight. Is there something else that you can do for your fallen brothers?"

The captain had looked grim. "No, Prince, there is nothing else that we can do."

"Then you must bury them with the rest of our men. We'll give them all the honor that they deserve." Garth met the elf's hard silver eyes and held them. "And that is much, *Halthe*."

"Aye." The elf had left, surrounded by the ghosts of his comrades, who would be buried in cold earth, honored by strangers, rather than sent, in flaming glory, to the gods.

Now, in the night silence, cries rose high and fell abruptly, sometimes far and sometimes near. Garth drew a long, thin breath. His men were not only seeking the dead, but also dispatching those who could not benefit from the healers' attentions. Among warriors, this was called the Final Salute; among healers, it was known as mercy.

"My lord!" Garth turned toward the sound of the cry. He saw a young man, a bard, he thought, running across the camp. His clothes were soaked and muddied, fouled with the blood of battle. In a face slick with rain, his eyes were rimmed red with fatigue.

"Baro," the bard introduced himself, making a sketchy bow. "Good even, my lord. There is a rider come. He's Elvish, and from the look of him, he's a hunter-scout."

"Where is he?"

"In your tent, my lord."

Heavy with weariness, hungry and wet, Garth drew a long breath and let it out in a sigh. "I'll be there momentarily."

* * * * *

The elf was a tall hunter-defender, late in his middle years. His hair, hanging lank and dripping with rain, was not the characteristic silver of the young of his kind, but turning iron gray. His face, lined and haggard, spoke of one who had spent much time in the open. Standing apart from Garth's gathered council, the elf maintained the distance a wary mountain panther would keep from a tangle of snakes.

Garth took a goblet from the small camp table and handed it to the elf.

"Thank you, *Halthe*." Fully half the warm wine in the goblet was drained before the hunter-defender spoke again. "I'm Kairn, *Halthe*, of the king's scouts. The enemy army, such as is left of it, moves north and west. They're moving fast toward your sea town on the Carnach peninsula."

"Seuro?"

"Aye, *Halthe*, that's it. Seuro."

Lorm muttered sourly, his voice rough and touched with doubt. He had not taken well to working and fighting alongside the elves. The skill of their warriors in battle, the patience and cunning of the Elvish hunter-defenders, did little to promote his trust. Lorm had considered them enemies for too many years.

Lorm felt he was caught between two evils: one before him and one within his camp. Garth heard a grunt of agreement from another of the lords. It must be Childe, he realized. He and Lorm were of a like mind about the Elvish allies.

"My lords . . ." Garth turned then but did not step toward his men. Instead he moved so that he stood nearer to the elf. "Have you questions for Kairn?"

Lorm's eyes narrowed. "Questions? Aye, my lord." He tilted his head back and regarded the elf through slitted eyes. "How do you come by so particular a piece of information, hunter?"

Again Childe murmured. Garth let his glance pass over Childe to rest on the two lords who had remained silent. Juro watched carefully. Baile, as was his habit, betrayed his feelings by neither word nor expression.

Kairn placed the half-emptied goblet back on the small table and stood at ease, his hands loose at his sides. It did not escape Garth's attention that the elf's right hand hung near the hilt of his dagger.

"It's my job to provide *Halthe* Garth with such particular information." Kairn watched the northern lord for a long moment, then allowed a smile to touch his lips. There was no mirth in the expression. "Do you wish to congratulate me? Well, there will be no need of that. A task assigned is a task performed."

"You're an arrogant one, aren't you, Elf?"

"No," Kairn said, his voice soft and dangerous. "Only confident." He dismissed Lorm with a contemptuous look and turned to Garth. "*Halthe*, our party was made up of four Elvish hunter-defenders. Two came close to the enemy's camp only an hour after the battle, and they learned of the enemy's plans. They stayed only long enough to confirm this news before they returned to me. I stayed only long enough to hear their finding before I rode to you."

Garth guessed that the elf had ridden half the night. He looked exhausted. "Thank you, Kairn. Find some food and dry clothes now. The bard who has his tent near to mine will help you. His name is Baro."

"Thank you, *Halthe*, but my scouts are waiting for me."

"As you will." Kairn made his bow for Garth's sake. His leave-taking of the others consisted of an ironic glance as he ducked out of the tent.

Garth was angry. It had been a weary day, filled with death and fighting. It seemed, now, that the fighting was not over.

"My lords!" He lifted his eyes to take them all in. "You will do well to remember that Kairn and his scouts, Dekar's warriors, are our allies. You'd better start treating them as such."

Lorm's eyes darkened. He glanced at the others, but saw no sign of assistance. Even Childe was now silent.

"My lord, it's no easy thing for a man to transform an enemy into a friend."

Garth smiled grimly. "You need not transform them. They have done that themselves." He let the smile fall from his lips then, to be replaced by a hard, stern look. "You will accept my thinking on this matter, Lorm."

It was not a question but a command. Lorm nodded once, but he could not hide his reluctance. "Aye, my lord. Of course."

"Good." Garth gestured toward the low camping stools that furnished the small tent. "Sit, then, my lords, and we'll lay our plans for tomorrow."

* * * * *

The council lasted long into the night. Plans were made for a day of rest for the warriors who had survived the battle. This was against Juro's advice. He preferred to pursue the weakened enemy at first light, on the principle that a retreating army is physically and emotionally on the defensive, but Garth's thinking prevailed. A rested army would make better fighters.

Deep irony colored Garth's words. "We've fought long and hard for this Ford of Tillane. We might as well rest here while we can. I expect a messenger from Fenyan. We'll give him the day, and we'll give that day to our warriors as well. We know where the army of the enemy is headng. Kairn's scouts are dogging them every step of the way, and we'll be kept aware of their movements."

It was not a hard point to press. The other lords did not take his view, so Juro, privately grateful for an opportunity to rest, soon gave his own assent.

* * * * *

In the silence of the deep night, Garth lay restless and far from sleep. Exhaustion made his bones seem as heavy as lead, his muscles as thin and weak as a spider's weaving.

So many dead! So many final salutes . . . warriors had gone bravely against an army peopled by creatures which could only have been spawned by some foul sorcery. These were neither the sons of men nor elves that they fought. These were sorcerer-bred creatures who fought with unnatural strength.

Garth had prevailed this day. Would he be able to again?

He didn't know. Drawing a long, tired breath, he moved uncomfortably in his blankets and closed his eyes.

In the hunter-defender Kairn, he had seen something of Nikia—the proud lift of his head, the starlight gleam in his eyes. Far to the south, she slept, her hair all tumbled, a lonely princess in a lonely bed. She fought her own battles there in Damris and fought them with courage.

The little thrill of surprise he had felt in the Citadel's courtyard so many days ago again trickled through him. "I love you, Elvish lady," he whispered to the night.

* * * * *

"The devastation of the farmland between Raeth and Seuro breaks my heart to see. Brother, I move on to Seuro. The seaport is under siege. The defenders, many of them the Elvish troops first sent by your wife's father, have sent appeals for aid.

"Brother, meet me there. From my position on the seacoast, I can be sure that I will reach Seuro a day, perhaps more, before you do.

"I will count on your aid, Brother, and together we will be able to defend this city. I remind you that this city is the key to the North. If it is captured, from there an enemy can entrench and send out his armies with ease to maraud the South."

Garth folded the parchment, placed it on the table, and glanced around the tent.

"You've heard my brother's message, my lords. We ride to meet him tomorrow. By that time, the burial details will have finished their work.

"Prepare your captains and have your warriors advised. We will meet here again in my tent after the evening meal."

Garth rose to his feet, nodding to the four departing lords. "Good day, my lords."

Alone, he resumed his seat and surveyed once more the maps that were strewn about the table. Their journey would require careful planning if he was to arrive at Seuro in time to bolster Fenyan's efforts. Garth fired the oil lamp that held down the corner of the largest map, and by its light he studied late into the day.

That evening he met with the four lords of his council. Together they laid their plans for the movement of the army west and north with great care. The council ended late, and each lord sought his bed with little delay. The march that would begin tomorrow would be a long and hard one. Men and elves alike would be asked to cover distances in a day that might have been deemed impossible.

* * * * *

Dawn splashed red across the riven fields. Garth's army was two days gone, and there was little left behind to show that an army had camped at the Ford of Tillane. Little, that is, but the five pits that were the mass graves of the fallen.

Three of those pits were covered, as best as possible from the stones at hand, by low cairns to protect the honored fallen from the depredations of scavengers. Two others were long, broad trenches, filled in hastily, covered only because it had been the will of the prince. Beside the trench that had been dug farthest from the encampment of the army ran a smaller, thinner trench. Here Garth's warriors, with fell humor, had made their privies.

Here, before any creature of the day was stirring and after the night creatures had returned to their sleeping places, a movement disturbed the calm.

It was simply the skittering of dirt and pebbles, a small tumbling of the clods that covered the farthest trench. The dawn breeze stirred, touched with a chill unwonted even in this northern spring. The breeze sighed, cold and soft. As the last star of night faded from the dawn-washed sky, a small moan rose and drifted across the day.

"*Rise now, rise,*" the breeze said. "*Rise now, sleepers, and turn your faces to the sky.*"

The voice spoke softly but not gently. It had a deep timbre, and a faint trace of amusement touched its sighing chant. "*Rise now, rise.*"

The skittering became a thrusting. The displaced earth

rolled quickly away down the sides of the trench, splashing here and there in the puddles of the previous day's rain, sliding into the privies.

"*Rise now, rise,*" the breeze coaxed. "*Rise to touch the air. Rise to see the day.*"

Something humped upward, lifting earth and shrugging into the light. It became a shoulder, an arm, a hand. It moved, twisting and rising, shedding darkness and earth as it stood.

"*Rise,*" the whispering song continued. "*Rise, and take your companions with you.*"

The thing rising from the burial trench had a face dark with mud, crusted with thick, black blood. It moved in a chilling parody of a man stretching after a long night's sleep, turning its eyes to the sun and letting its mouth fall open.

"Rise!" the thing cried, taking up the song of the breeze. "Rise! Touch the air! See the day!"

Movement snaked along the trench as the earth undulated from the exertions of what was buried beneath. In this manner, the fallen warriors of the Sorcerer rose again, earth-covered and cold, animated by the command Yvanda had sent on the chill dawn breeze.

Along the cairns, stone tumbled to earth, and man and elf rose, animate but dead. A sigh ran among the risen, running in counterpoint to the song of the breeze.

Cloaked in evil, covered with the stench of death as though it was the cloth of the grave, the fallen warriors of both armies chanted their filthy *Laudes*.

CHAPTER 15

. . . the colors of the fall, fire guards them all . . .

The bards had been faced, and Yfr's affront defeated, but Nikia had no sense of victory. The grim, dark whispering that seemed to have become permanently lodged in her mind persisted. It followed her, ghostly and malign, from one end of her day to the other, lying in wait for her in the darkness of the night, pouncing like a cat who licks his lips before torturing his prey.

She knew now whose voice it was. Likely she had known all along. It took this new, wounded Nikia to face the truth.

Wounded, she thought now. Yes, I'm wounded, and I'll not be hurt again. Not by the whisper of rumor and not by the cruel torment of this invisible voice.

The invisible voice was not the voice of nightmare, not the fey imaginings of a pregnant woman, nor the murmurings one hears when ill. It was the voice of the only one in the Citadel who could speak to her in magic. It was Reynarth's voice, and none of her own magic could keep the whispering at bay.

As insidious as fog, it slipped through every barrier she raised and confronted her, amused, with deadly persistence. It was a little war they fought, mage and elf, and if Reynarth had won the first battle, Nikia had not yet fallen to defeat.

She was aware, now, of her own core of steel and stubbornness, and he could go hoarse with his whispering before she would let him see that she even heard the ceaseless murmuring.

She longed, each night in a bed empty of all but deadly whispering, for Garth and the comfort he could bring, and for his love.

More and more often now she found herself wanting to know what it was he thought, how he felt. She had seen the surprise in his eyes the moment before he left her, and she recognized it for what it was—a sudden, and perhaps overwhelming, knowledge that he loved her. And she, though there was not even an instant to let him know, had risen to that knowledge as a swimmer rises to light and air.

"I love you!" he had called, and Nikia had known at once that though he'd used the words before, he had never meant them as he understood them then. Nor had she. And now a war and half a kingdom lay between them.

From time to time the military dispatches Garth sent to the king were supplemented by letters. These came directly to Nikia's hand from the messengers. The news was no fresher, no better, no more kindly put than in the dispatches, but it was directed to her, a word from Garth's own hand.

These letters became like maps, guides to the landscape of his hopes and his fears. And, too, they became almost talismanic. When she read the letters, she heard his voice. And when she heard his voice, she did not hear Reynarth's dark throaty whispers, haunting like low thunder growling in the far reaches of the sky.

Love, Garth wrote. Nikia settled more comfortably on her bed, tucked her feet beneath her, and held the letter in hands trembling slightly, waiting for the whispering to fade. *We have taken Seuro. The city can feed us for a long siege, and I think we can defend it. We have lost many men, but I expect that*

*Fenyan's troops will soon rejoin us, which will make our
defense stronger.*

Nikia paused, searched her memory for information about
Fenyan's activities, and placed the writing of this letter shortly
after the time that the two armies had joined to secure the seaport city against the Sorcerer's warriors.

The last dispatch, received two days ago, had been from
Fenyan. It told of the battle for Seuro, of his plans to leave
Garth's army to defend the city while his own warriors set up
lines of defense against raids from the sea that surrounded the
peninsula. She returned to Garth's letter.

*We have heard rumor of my brother in the city, and that
rumor tells me that he has been successful in defending the
naked seaside around Seuro. I await his messenger, but up to
now, none has come.*

*Your father's warriors fight like demons—no, I won't use
that word even in admiration. But never have I been so grateful to have Elvish warriors beside me instead of across the battlefield from me.*

*These are raids no longer, Nikia. These are battlefields, and
we are at war. Who do we fight? I don't know—I know only
that they are demons in truth. Their warriors are huge creatures. My hand is reluctant to put the name "men" to them,
although men they must have been at one time. Each fights
with the fierceness and strength of two of our warriors, and
death seems to hold no fear for them. By all standards, they are
ugly and fearsome to behold. Every rumor that fouled our taverns in the autumn was true: They are demons.*

*But they do not make up the whole of the enemy forces.
There are men, and more of them than the fell creatures I
describe. They are the light-haired men of the northlands,
grown bold and fearless in the company of these witch-spawn.*

*Witch-spawn. Here in the North, they speak of the Sorcerer
more than we do in Damris. Here he is an intimate fear, a reality. Here they have had a year to become accustomed to the fact
that he is once more a very real enemy.*

*To you in the South, Nikia, he is still the stuff of legend, but
you have not seen his work of late, only heard the rumors of it.*

If the rumors were frightening, Love, the reality is a nightmare.

But as much as he is held in fear, there is another who commands an equal fear, and she is his witch-mistress. Your people call her Yvanda, the Dark Lady. Our folk only call her the witch-mistress. I am certain that she does not care by which name she is called, as long as that name inspires fear.

Nikia let the letter fall from her hands. She took a long, slow breath to still the pounding of her heart. Garth's words were frightening, but most frightening of all was seeing the name of the witch-mistress: Yvanda. Dark Lady. She shivered. Dark Lady. . . .

Nikia rose quickly to her feet and paced to the window, as though by leaving the letter behind, she might leave behind the fear it engendered as well.

But fear was not so easily banished. It lingered in the shadows, whispered in her mind. Below, in the Queen's Garden, the early summer sun shone along the circular paths, touching the herbs and plantings with bright light. There were many duties that needed her attention, but Nikia suddenly felt that the balm for her fear would be the sunlight.

Her resolution firm, Nikia rang for Riche.

"Madam?" The page's smile was his usual bright one. "How may I serve you?"

"Have you seen the Lady Lizbet this morning, Riche?"

"Aye, lady. She and the Lord Calmis have gone to the stable. I believe that they spoke of a morning ride."

"Find them, Riche, if they haven't left yet, and ask them if they would do me the kindness of waiting for me."

* * * * *

The warm sunlight of afternoon lay across the blue slate floor of the council chamber, spilled like gold across the backs of the assembled council. From the open windows drifted a breeze sweetened by its journey across the Queen's Garden. Reynarth dropped his eyes from the king's hard regard. He masked his face carefully with an expression of regret.

"It is a magic stronger than I can fight, Your Grace. I can

only beg your forgiveness and that of the council."

"Your weather skills?" Alain questioned. His voice was low and hard.

"They've been countered at every turn, Your Grace. I feel the power of something—nay, someone—far stronger than I. Each time I try to turn the rain, each time I try to call the sun, another commands who is stronger."

It was a lie. Reynarth had made no attempt at all to aid their armies with his weather skills. It was he, with his magic and spells, who had called the hard spring rains on the armies of the Two Kingdoms. It was he, aided by the power he now denounced, who had guided the storms in from the sea, washing the coast until it was a mire that bogged down the horses of Fenyan's army. No sign of that lie showed now on Reynarth's face, however. The king and his council saw only regret and disappointment.

Alain spoke again. "Have you been able to observe the battle, Reynarth?" He leaned forward on his elbows. "Have you been able to see its progress?"

"No, Your Grace. I know no more about it than you do."

"The Sorcerer."

Reynarth nodded grimly. "Aye, Your Grace. His magic clouds the North. I can't see through it."

"We had hoped, Reynarth, for your aid. We had counted on your skills to bolster our armies."

There was, Reynarth thought, a little bitterness in the king's tone. Was it blame? He dared not raise his eyes to see. He must preserve as carefully as possible this charade of regret and failure. There must be no question in Alain's mind that his mage had tried but failed.

"My skills, Your Grace, can't compare to the Sorcerer's. And—there is another."

Murmurs whispered about the room as the council members drew their breaths in surprise.

"What other?" Liam asked. He glanced from Alain to the mage.

"The witch-mistress." The murmuring grew, swelled by an undercurrent of fear.

The king met his mage's eyes and held them. "Garth has spoken of this witch-mistress. Tell me what you know, Reynarth."

Reynarth was careful not to let his satisfaction show. The fear he had hoped to engender could be breathed in the very air.

"She is the mistress of our enemy, Your Grace."

"How do you know this?"

"Rumors, of course. And something else." He let his words work their effect before he spoke again. "It's something I felt as I tried to reach the princes' armies and aid them. There's another power, one nearly as great as that of the Sorcerer. This is the power of a woman."

"And how do you know that?" It was Celedon, his voice hard and full of doubt.

Reynarth glanced toward Lord Celedon, met his eyes, and smiled grimly. "One knows who is versed in magic, my lord. It's easy enough for me to tell the magic of a man from that of a woman. Why, I would know the Princess Nikia's magic for a woman's skill had I never seen her before. There is a touch, a voice within the magic, that tells the seasoned user whether a man or a woman is at work."

"The princess?" Celedon shook his head. "Hers are but small magicks, if they are magicks at all."

"Oh, aye, they are magicks, my lord. Be assured of that. The princess is a skilled—" he paused as though seeking the proper word to describe Nikia—"a skilled witch."

"Witch!"

Reynarth spread his hands. "It's just an expression, my lord."

"A vile term, and one I would not hear applied to the wife of our prince."

Reynarth dropped his gaze again. He presented an expression of contrition, of sadness. Privately, he smiled. He'd turned the direction of questioning away from his lack of assistance and toward the princess. "I beg pardon, my Lord Celedon. I offer no offense to the princess."

Celedon snorted and was about to speak further, but Alain

stopped him with a gesture. "Enough of that. We're not here to discuss the Princess Nikia."

"But, Your Grace," Celedon said, his face flushed with anger. "Insult has been brought against the princess!"

"It is not insult to name her what she is," Reynarth murmured.

Celedon glared across the table at the king's mage. "The term you use is insulting, Reynarth."

"Enough!" Alain shouted.

The room fell silent. The lords of the council cast their eyes about the table, meeting each other's gaze, then looking away.

"Your Grace?" Reynarth rose from his place. "I offer my apology. I meant only to use the princess as an illustration. I agree. Let's try to forget the painful matter of her magic and begin again to plan our tactics, for we must plan them without counting on my skills."

Alain cast his gaze around the room, taking and holding the attention of the members of his council. The loss of Reynarth's magic was a heavy blow. They'd hoped, with his previous assurances, that he would be able to give them fair weather or call foul weather down on their enemies. They hadn't foreseen going against the Sorcerer undefended against his enchantments.

Wearily Alain asked Liam for a count of the new troops raised. Yet, although he listened, and although he participated in the discussions, Alain was distracted. He didn't like the talk of Nikia's magic or the thought that some among them considered her a witch.

Small magicks, aye, he thought. She has those. But what other skills? Doubt crept into his mind, a doubt fed by the fear that his kingdom would soon be overpowered. Reynarth's magic had failed. There was no one to defend them now against the enemy's sorcery.

And in his Citadel lived an Elvish woman who served to remind his people that their own Mannish strength could not hold out against the vile magic of their northern opponents.

* * * * *

The Great Hall was empty when Reynarth paused near the opened door. He was pleased with the direction the council meeting had taken, and he was pleased that his own skills of misdirection had sown not only seeds of mistrust against the Elvish witch, but also seeds of fear among Alain and his lords. The strategies they now planned were born of uncertainty and doubt.

The mage smiled slowly, his green eyes lighting with the anticipation of prey at hand. He glanced down the length of the empty hall. If I do this well, he mused, there will be little cause to feast here in days to come.

As he turned to leave, the brightly colored beauty of the Ylin tapestry caught his eye.

Alain had ordered the tapestry hung in a place of honor at winter's end. Refurbished by the loving hands of women who had held the Princess Gweneth in affection, the Ylin tapestry occupied the wall behind the dais. Some said it was as though the queen herself presided over the hall.

For his part, Reynarth had never seen any beauty in the old-fashioned thing. It reminded him of the foolish and childish nursery songs that had so fascinated the bards all winter. The designs were bright and skillfully crafted, from the jeweled halter of the woman's pony to the intricate embroidery of her own gown.

There's something about that gown, he thought. Frowning, he entered the Great Hall, old nursery songs whispering in his memory.

The border of the gown, he realized suddenly, was not simply the random pattern he had once thought it. Reynarth drew a sharp breath and stopped where he could best see the whole design of the gown's border. The symbols seemed familiar. He had seen them before, and he knew them now for what they were—runes.

"Gebo," he whispered, picking that rune's symbol in the rich design. "Uruz, Inguz, Wunjo, and Berkhana."

Reynarth took a step closer to the tapestry. He repeated the names of the runes, searching his memory, checking the names against names heard once before in the Great Hall. The first time those names had been spoken here had been at Nikia's wedding feast.

"Partnership, Strength, Fertility . . ." Here he stopped and smiled. Nikia may have been fertile, but that fertility had come to nothing after the first conception. "Joy and Growth."

The runes that decorated the wedding cup Nikia had presented to Garth those many months ago were the same runes he checked now. They were the very runes embellishing the border of the gown worn by the woman in the Ylin tapestry.

How odd, he thought, that Ylin's gown should bear the exact runes that appear on an Elvish wedding cup.

"*These the colors of the fall,*" he whispered. "*Fire guards them all. Red as blood, spilt in war.* . . . And what of the other song? *The jewels are the shades of the fall.*"

His breath caught in his throat. There were clues here!

If there were clues, then what was the puzzle? What was the riddle? Color and runes. Color repeating in patterns easily discernible in children's songs . . . and runes that appear on the gown of the great Mannish queen Ylin and on the traditional wedding cup of the Elvish.

These were answers, but to what questions? Reynarth squinted at the tapestry, taking in its every detail—the pony and its dazzling bridle, the runes bordering the richly colored gown of the queen.

Runes, he thought, on the gown and on the cup. Colors in songs, and colors on the bridle. Reynarth's eyes flicked quickly to the bridle again. Colored jewels! Emeralds, sapphires, diamonds . . . no! He stepped closer still, until the fabric of the tapestry touched his shoulder, until his face was so close to it that he could smell its musty fragrance.

No! Not emeralds, but *one* emerald. And one diamond, a single sapphire, a ruby, and a topaz.

"*These the colors of the fall* . . ." His voice was nearly a chant now, his words soft and puzzled. "*Red as blood spilt in war*: the ruby. *Green as summer growing*: the emerald. *Blue as sky above us all*: the sapphire, of course. *White as water flowing*: the diamond!" The topaz, he realized, must represent fire.

He knew that answers were not given to puzzles that did not exist. There must be a riddle somewhere to fit these answers.

Reynarth laughed softly. It was ironic that he found himself in possession of answers and now sought the questions.

Ruby . . . emerald . . . sapphire . . . diamond . . . topaz. Precious stones adorning a pony's bridle. And Elvish runes decorating a Mannish queen's gown.

Reynarth squinted at the tapestry, digging deeper into his mind for the question that fit the answers.

Ruby, emerald, sapphire, diamond, topaz. Ruby—

"Ruby!" The word leapt from his lips in a crow of triumph. The Great Hall's emptiness caught it and sent it echoing down the lengths of the chamber.

The Ruby of Guyaire?

The jewel was a symbol of the Elvish king's right to rule his folk.

Then quickly, almost without his own volition, the words of the nagging little nursery song came back to Reynarth's mind. He knew at once what the virtue of the Ruby of Guyaire was.

And he knew at once that he must have it!

CHAPTER 16

Nikia and Lizbet went laughing along the corridor to their chambers. It had been a fine day, a glorious ride. Though the outing had not served to decrease her fears, Nikia felt better able to control them for having left them, for a short time at least, behind.

Still, even now, they crowded back. She shook her head and thrust the fears aside, glancing at her companion. Nikia smiled to see the vibrancy of Lizbet's eyes, the color touching her cheeks.

Oh, Darun! Nikia thought. If I did not so like you for yourself, I would love you for what you have done for my dear Lizbet!

Lizbet paused at the door, her hand still on the jamb, her head lifted. Nikia stopped behind her, and for some reason that she did not understand, she felt her heart start to beat in little erratic rhythms.

Lizbet turned from the door, her face pale, and took Nikia's arm. "Come away, *Halda*." Nikia could barely hear her words.

"But, Lizbet—what is it?"

A stirring from within, the smallest of sounds, caught Nikia's attention. Someone was inside her chamber! Before Lizbet could stop her, Nikia pulled away and opened the door.

He stood cat-still in the doorway between the reception chamber and Nikia's bedroom. His eyes glittering, green and sharp, showed him caught between apprehension and anger.

"Reynarth!" Nikia whispered. Behind her Lizbet gasped.

"Good day, lady," he murmured. A smile, soft and silky, did nothing to cool the anger in his eyes. "I've been looking for you."

"Aye . . . and waiting?" Nikia crossed the little chamber, and the mage moved slightly, so that he blocked the view of her bedchamber. "Surely my page told you that I was riding," she said evenly.

Reynarth shrugged. "I didn't see the lad."

Though fear as cold as a winter wind chilled her heart, Nikia refused to tremble, refused to feel anything but anger. How dare he enter her chambers without her permission! Hatred and loathing curling in his eyes like smoke or snakes, he watched her carefully. He almost laughed. Darkly, so that only she could hear, he whispered in her mind with the dry, haunting voice of winter.

Have a care now! The game has become dangerous, and I don't think you've the skill to play, elfling.

Elfling! So he thinks me a child! Aye, well, we shall see! She lifted her head and eyed him coolly. "Well, I am here now, Reynarth. What is it you want?"

The cat-green eyes shuttered, the hatred dimmed, and the mage moved away, drawing her eyes toward him. "Only a moment of your time, lady. But you must be tired. The matter will hold." *For now.* He took a brief bow and turned on his heel. When he passed Lizbet, she shivered as though a ghostly breeze had touched her.

"Good day, ladies," the mage said evenly. "No doubt I'll see you both at evening meal."

Very little of Lizbet's fear left with the mage, and Nikia's anger only flared higher. She went to her bedchamber.

By some instinct, or perhaps because it was the most valuable thing that she possessed, she went directly to her dressing table to seek the ruby. It was there on the table, encased in its crystal box. Nikia stopped, reached out for it, and then withdrew her hand. Was this where she had left it?

She sent her mind back to the night before. She had worn the ruby to a dinner honoring a deputation of Mannish lords from the northern provinces. When Nikia had returned to her chambers, she had been tired and had simply removed the ruby from her neck and placed it in its little crystal resting place, leaving it out on the dressing table. Nothing at that hour seemed more important than finding her bed with the greatest speed.

And here it was. But Nikia thought that it had not been so close to the edge of the table. She had placed it nearer to the mirror, she was sure.

Was she sure? Might not Lizbet have moved it this morning while rummaging for a brooch or hair comb? Of course, but still . . .

"Lizbet, did you move the ruby this morning?"

Lizbet's expression was puzzled for a moment. A little frown brought lines between her eyes. "Aye, *Halda*."

Nikia relaxed, but Lizbet's next words sent a thrill of fear skittering through her.

"But you have taken it out again."

Nikia stopped where she stood, her fingers still on the crystal case. "Taken it out?"

"Aye, *Halda*. I put it away this morning when I was getting the combs for your hair. I know I should have put it away last night, but the hour was late. . . ." Her explanation dwindled away and her frown deepened.

"Lizbet, I found it right here on the dressing table."

"I swear to you, *Halda*, I put it away this morning. I made certain to."

They were both silent for a long moment.

"Lizbet, we've found out what so attracted the mage that he felt free to enter my chamber unbidden."

In Lizbet's eyes, it was sacrilege. There was no other word for it. The ruby was an heirloom so ancient and so bound up with the power of the Elvish rulers that she could not conceive of alien hands even touching it. There was a look in her eyes akin to superstitious dread.

"*Halda*, you must go directly to the king!"

"No, Lizbet. It is all right now. How can I go to Alain and tell him that I think someone has been at my jewels?"

"You do not think, *Halda*, you *know*! And you know who it was. We saw him."

"We did not exactly see him, did we?"

"*Halda*, why else would he be here?"

"Why?" Nikia shrugged. "I don't know. I think you're right, Lizbet, but what evidence can I bring? The ruby is here, unharmed, and we didn't actually see Reynarth in my bedchamber. No, Lizbet, I think I'll deal with this in my own manner."

"But what will you do?"

"I will think, Lizbet." She smiled gently. "I haven't been doing that too much lately. It's about time that I did."

* * * * *

Nikia did not think for long. As Gweneth had said of the Ylin tapestry so many months ago, treasure often seemed to be found lying out in plain sight.

There is a kind of puzzle that her father's mages made for the amusement and instruction of their students. These pictures, drawn with such skill as to seem only simple lines, could be first one thing and then another, depending on the angle from which they were viewed. Trees became deer, deer were also fishes, and fishes were clouds.

"What you see," those canny old mages would tell their bemused students, "is not always what is. And what is, is not always what you see."

As a child, Nikia had delighted in trying to find all the angles, trying to number every apparition in the deceiving lines. It was simply a matter of adjusting the angle of one's view, stepping back, and clearing away the persistent idea that these pictures were simply sketchy lines.

She did this now, mentally moving the pieces of the puzzle a little, readjusting her own angle. The picture fell into place with little thought or effort on her part. Nikia shivered. The picture wasn't completely clear. She couldn't tell whether it was a sketch of hope or nightmare, but she knew that she needed a friend to help her decipher it, someone she could trust.

Nikia went at once to Dail.

* * * * *

Nikia stared at the Ylin tapestry, hardly breathing. Her eyes went immediately to the jewel-studded bridle that the little horse wore. Emerald, sapphire, diamond, ruby, topaz . . . Ruby!

The Ruby of Guyaire glowed gently in her hand. Even now, with no firelight on it, no sunlight to bring out its glow, it still seemed to pulse, to breathe light. Nikia raised the gem and let it dangle from its silver chain.

"What do you see, Dail?"

Puzzled, the bard looked from the princess to the Ruby of Guyaire, then to the tapestry. Nikia saw his blue eyes fix on the jeweled halter, then snap quickly back to the ruby in her hand.

"The shape," he said softly.

Nikia nodded.

"It's not a classic one, lady, that I know. It's unusual, both in the cut and in the facets. It's shaped like the jewel in the tapestry."

With quiet triumph in her voice, Nikia said, "They are the same jewel."

Dail shook his head. "No, lady. This is Ylin, a Mannish queen. What would she be doing with the Ruby of Guyaire?"

Nikia smiled and placed the ruby back in its crystal case. The snapping lid seemed loud in the silent hall. "Ylin, you say? I give her another name."

Dail did not speak. He would not have interrupted Nikia's speech now for anything. He only nodded once for her to continue.

"I name her Aeylin."

"I don't understand."

Nikia laughed. Even in her eagerness, she took pleasure in bemusing the chief bard. "Listen to a little song, then, Master Dail."

She sang without harp accompaniment, but her voice was true enough on the old tune.

> "Ah, hands of beauty, slim and fair
> fingers skipping, touching.
> Ah, lady bold, how came you there
> in caverns dark and drear?
> What paths you followed in your toil,
> dim and full of danger,
> To kneel before the ancient spoil
> in caverns low and cold?
> Ah, eyes so bright and full of light!
> ah, heart so full and hoping!
> Reach now and take them for the fight,
> from caverns dark and drear."

It was a fragment of a song, a little bit of ancient rhyme that somehow had become lost and found again. The Elvish folk had preserved their oral tradition for many generations, but still, some of the oldest, most ancient songs were lost, leaving only these ragged traces of tune and verse. This song, now called "Queen's Bane" by Nikia's people, was among the most ancient.

Dail nodded his appreciation, and Nikia could see that he had already committed the words and melody to memory. No song escaped his cataloging, and Nikia wondered when this little bit of ancient ballad would appear, polished and cleaned and slipping gracefully from Dail's harp.

"It reminds me of an old piece . . . but that one was about our Ylin, something about the lady's jeweled weapon, secret-wielded. . . ." Comprehension settled like a cloak around Dail's shoulders. "They *are* the same! Nikia, what are you saying?" He used no 'lady' now, for his excitement swept away his courtly address.

Nikia laughed again. "They were the same woman."

"How? The woman pictured here is one of my own people."

Nikia glanced again at the tapestry. But he was wrong. He was wrong, and she was amazed afresh that she had not noticed it before.

"Look at her dress. See the little symbols that adorn her gown? You've not seen them before, but members of this court have, and not so long ago. They're the very runes that decorate the wedding cup I presented to Garth at our marriage feast.

"Their old names are Gebo, Uruz, Inguz, Wunjo, and Berkhana. Today we call them Partnership, Strength, Fertility, Joy, and Growth. See?" Nikia traced the decorations on the gown's edging, her fingers touching the bright yarn lightly. "These are the same."

Dail drew a long breath of surprise. "Her gown, then, is . . ."

Nikia supplied the words. "A wedding gown."

"Aeylin. Ylin. Aeylin." Dail repeated the names to himself, his voice finding a natural cadence, and Nikia knew that somewhere, whether or not he was aware of it now, he was writing a song.

"The same woman," she said softly. "Do you know what those jewels are that adorn the horse's halter?"

Dail shook his head.

Nikia held up the crystal case. There, in her hand, was the only surviving jewel of the set. "They are the lost Jewels of Elvish."

"The *what?*"

Nikia sighed, then laughed. "My father used to wish for them, then mock himself for wishing for a legend. The stories say that the jewels conferred powers to the rulers of Elvish over the five elements, four natural and one which is the province of humanity. The emerald gives power over nature and growing things. Who wields the sapphire controls the air, the diamond controls the waters, and the topaz controls fire. The ruby gives the bearer power in war.

"But every Elvish king knows there is no sense wishing for a legend. The jewels vanished centuries ago!"

All the little songs with all their little clues were whirling around in Nikia's mind now. She looked at the tapestry again.

"Dail, I don't think they vanished. I think they went with this lady as a wedding gift."

"A marriage? To whom?"

"To one of your folk."

"And neither people remembered? It seems as if such a gift would be hard to forget."

Nikia shrugged. "Who remembered the name of the lady in the tapestry until now? But, no, I don't think both people completely forgot. We composed songs about it, both of our peoples. What we forgot was what the songs meant. Time does that. And wars happen. Old allies become enemies again, and old gifts are lost." She looked at the ruby again, then at the tapestry.

"Dail, I think the last time our people plighted their faith and made a marriage alliance, the ruby came back to Elvish. And it's been there ever since."

"Until now," Dail whispered.

Nikia shivered. "Aye, until now." She had known all her life that the Ruby of Guyaire was a talisman of power. But it seemed to her, and surely to her father and his own fathers, that the power it contained was the bearer's right to rule over Elvish. Never had it been used for military might. She could not imagine that any among her people living now would know what use to make of the ruby. It was a magic thing—her mind shied from the word *sorcerous*, although she knew it must be—and a thing that required skills beyond the Elvish folk's present knowledge.

But someone must know what use to make of it. Someone did know, or hoped to know. He was Reynarth. And that was why she was here.

They moved to the dais and took their familiar seats on the steps. Nikia placed the ruby between them.

"Listen to me, Dail. There's something I have to tell you. I wish—" She paused, for never had she wished that Garth were with her more than she did now. "I wish that my husband was here, for he, I think, would have the patience to listen to this tale. It is strange and seemingly full of a woman's fancies. He has seen most of the effects of what I am going to tell you, although it is true that he never knew the cause. Until today, neither did I. But please listen."

It was not an easy tale for Nikia to tell, but she told it from the time that she first heard the whispers to the time when she at last understood from where they had come. Finally she told of Reynarth's attempt to steal the ruby.

"Dail, even as he tormented me, he must have been putting the clues together in some part of his mind. And he's made it clear today that he wants the ruby. Lizbet and I happened upon him at his theft, or surely the ruby would be in his hands right now."

"You accuse Reynarth of treachery, my lady?"

Nikia was silent for a long moment before she met the bard's eyes. "Aye, Dail, I accuse him of treachery. If he believed that he had discovered the jewel's history, then he believed that he had discovered a valuable talisman, and were he an honest man, wouldn't he have come to me with his knowledge?"

"It seems that an honest man would. But what will you do now, lady? Will you go to Alain?"

Nikia had been thinking about that for many hours. She should, of course, but what use would Alain make of the ruby? She said as much, and again Dail agreed.

"But, lady, why would Reynarth want it if not because he could use it?"

"Perhaps he does believe that he can use it. But if that was his belief, and if he wished to use it for the good of the Two Kingdoms, why did he not approach the king? No, Reynarth wants the ruby for his own use."

Nikia looked down at the ruby in its case. It had always been a thing of beauty to her, a symbol of her people and the power of her father's house. Now it had taken on a different aspect. It was a treasure far greater than they had ever thought.

"Dail, he can't have it. I'm taking it to the king." She rose and smiled faintly. "And I could use a friend with me now."

"You'll have me, Nikia."

She thanked him. Nikia hoped the bard's support would lend her the credibility she'd need when her story began to sound like a nursery tale.

CHAPTER 17

Had the servants been wailing in the halls, weeping in the corridors, and moaning in the kitchens, Nikia could have had no clearer sense that something was terribly wrong than she did when she left the Great Hall with Dail.

There were folk about, but they were all strangely silent. They went about their duties with heads down, eyes averted, and shoulders hunched, as if in some kind of pain. The lad who crossed their path with oil for the torches in the corridor moved in a shuffling, quiet gait. He was normally a quick-stepping young fellow, and there was ever a whistling song on his lips. He was silent now, his eyes cast down, the pots of oil sagging from his arms as though they were twice the weight he was accustomed to carry.

Nikia glanced over her shoulder at him, but his back was to her and she could determine nothing. They passed a maid on the stairs. Ducking the princess a curtsy, she, too, kept her eyes lowered.

Dail stopped on the stair and waited for Nikia. The look in

his eyes told the princess that he, too, sensed something amiss.

Fear crept into Nikia's heart, a little tug of something that presaged pain. She thought of the winter and the loss of her child. The feeling that overtook her now was related, in some way, to the feeling she had then.

She would let her thoughts go no further.

* * * * *

Alain's face was white, haggard, drawn. He looked, for the first time since Nikia had known him, like the aging man that he was. His eyes avoided Nikia's when she entered the council chamber. Instead, they went past her, and she sensed that they went past Dail, behind her, as well. Nikia had no idea what the king was looking at, or for.

Robes whispered as men turned to stare at her. And then there was complete silence. Ominous silence.

"Father." Nikia stopped halfway across the room to stand next to where Lord Celedon was seated. She felt the lord look around at her as she spoke. His eyes were the eyes of the little lad in the corridor, of the maid on the stairs.

"Nikia," Alain said softly.

Nikia began to tremble. There was a hollowness in his voice, a strain that spoke of great effort. "Father," she said again, and this time the address was not ceremonial. She tried to understand the pain she saw in his eyes and, trying, knew that it was shortly to become hers.

Celedon rose from his seat and took her arm gently. His big, rough hand was calloused from much riding. Nikia's mind skipped away to a night many months ago when he had proudly announced his wedding gift to Garth and his new bride—fifteen mares and three stallions, the best of his herd. The best in the kingdom, for no lord bred swifter or more beautiful horses than Celedon.

Nikia glanced over her shoulder to see where Dail was. She found him standing a few steps behind her. He knows or he guesses, she thought. She could guess, too, but she would not.

Celedon led the princess slowly along the length of the chamber. She went with him like a woman going to the edge of a precipice from which she might not return.

"Father?" Alain looked away from her then and made some gesture to those who sat behind them. The silence was punctuated by the sound of men rising from their places and leaving the room. There was no sound of voices at all.

Nikia allowed the king to seat her in the chair closest to his. She placed the ruby absently on her lap. "Father, what is it?"

Alain took up a parchment and handed it to her. Folded and weather-stained, it still smelled of leather from its journey in the messenger's pouch. Nikia understood that she was to read it.

My King— Nikia took a small breath, steadied her shaking hands, and continued to read. *My King, my message is brief, for there is little that I can say. Prince Fenyan has not returned to Seuro, and that city is lost. Seuro lost! I cannot credit it even now. The battle that we waged was fierce, horrible. There came against the defenders of Seuro an army filled with demons and filled, my King, with men I know myself to have been killed at the Tillane Ford! Credit me, my King, for it is true! We have twice killed the same foes, and yet we come against them again. But even worse, we see now our own dead filling the enemy's ranks! The battle was hopeless. Seuro lies in the hands of the enemy, and demons walk the streets by day and night.*

There remains not a Mannish or Elvish warrior free and alive in the city. Who did not die in the fighting was killed out of hand by the forces of the Sorcerer when they overran the city. Or worse. Pray, my King, for those who were not killed.

Of those who survived, I know nothing except for my own little band of warriors who have fled to the mountains. We are few, a mere seven Elvish warriors and ten Mannish.

My King, I have had no word of Prince Garth.

A sound escaped Nikia's lips then, a small sound, like a sob or a moan. Her hands grew nerveless. She had to clutch at the message to keep it from falling to the table.

"*I have had no word of Prince Garth.*" She was not aware that she had spoken the words aloud until she heard the king clear his throat. Nikia looked up.

"He—he is dead?" she whispered.

Alain shook his head. "I don't know, Nikia. I don't know."

Nikia's eyes went back to the dispatch. Dispatch! It was hardly that. It was the knelling of a death bell; it was a great empty space in her, a cry of fear that would soon echo across the Two Kingdoms.

"Perhaps—" she began falteringly, her voice so low that she could not imagine how Alain heard it. "Perhaps he still lives."

"No! Please the gods, no!"

Alain's words frightened Nikia. There was terror in his voice. There was something as strong as the scent of fear in it, and she recalled the messenger's words: *Who did not die in the fighting was killed out of hand by the forces of the Sorcerer. Or worse. Pray, my King, for those who were not killed.* And still she prayed that he was alive.

"Nikia . . . child." Alain rose from his place and came to stand beside his son's wife. He placed a hand on her arm, and she could feel it trembling. She could also feel strength, for even in the king's grief there was still strength. "Shall I call your waiting woman?"

Nikia shook her head, not trusting herself to speak. Please, let him be alive! she prayed. *Pray, my King, for those who were not killed. . . .*

Nikia clenched her fists in her lap and was surprised to discover something hard and warm in her right hand. She had forgotten about the ruby. She had forgotten all that had happened before this moment. Slowly she looked down at the little crystal case in her hand. The case had been a gift from Garth, a gift to celebrate the news that she bore his child. Nikia shuddered. The child was never born, and now Garth . . . She looked up again and met the king's eyes.

"Why didn't Fenyan go to his brother's aid?"

Alain's eyes narrowed at the accusation in her voice. "I don't know. His last message told of his plans to join with Garth's armies and hold Seuro. I have had no word since."

Another son missing.

Nikia clenched the ruby in her hand harder. Her throat thickened with pain and tears, her eyes burned. It was a labor to breathe. Again she sought the king's eyes and saw his fear. If both his sons were lost, his only heir was an infant, the sweet-tempered son of Gweneth and Fenyan.

Only this tiny heir, Nikia thought, only this fragile child. No! That was admission that Garth was dead. She wasn't ready to admit that. He *must* be alive.

Nikia's breath caught in her throat. He might have escaped! The man who'd sent the message didn't know what had happened to Garth. But she knew that for a weak hope. Had Garth escaped, wouldn't he have found a way to send word to his father?

Slowly, as though of their own accord, tears began to roll down her cheeks. She sobbed once, then again. And then she wept uncontrollably.

* * * * *

Laughter both triumphant and derisive filled Reynarth's mind, casting a dark and fearsome shadow on his heart. He lowered his eyes and let his gaze fall away from the face that filled the globe.

He hadn't hoped to hide the discovery of the ruby's talismanic power. He knew better than to hope that he could hide anything, any thought, from the Dark Mistress. She could pluck knowledge from him as easily as plucking fruit from the vine.

The little princess has been guarding this treasure all this time?

"I don't think she knows what the Ruby of Guyaire is, mistress, or surely it would have been used before now."

Has she gone to Alain? The question was sharp, hard, snapped in a tone that demanded instant response.

"No. She can't have had time. She only learned today that Garth is missing." Reynarth swallowed hard, took a long, steadying breath, and raised his eyes to the globe again. "Mistress," he asked, his voice soft, his tone servile, "can you tell me the fate of the prince?"

Again there was laughter, again the perfect scorn that flayed his soul. *Can I? Yes, mage, I can. I can tell you the fate of both princes, for it is my fate that lies on them now.*

She played a game concocted to remind him where the power lay. Reynarth nodded once. "Mistress, will you tell me?"

I will tell you this: Both princes yet live, but one will be dead ere long. She smiled, this time forbearing to laugh. Reynarth saw challenge in the smile, but he did not accept it.

It would have been good to know which of the king's sons was to die, but he had pressed her. She was impatient for answers now, and he would press no more.

I want the ruby. Get it for me.

"I can't. Not now."

You cannot? Why not?

He would have answered, with his words couched in care, but he wasn't given the chance. She entered him, filling his mind, plucking among his memories, searching the hidden places, and left him, ragged and gasping.

You are a fool! Damnation filled her voice. *Your clumsy attempt to steal the ruby has cost us!*

"Mistress! Forgive me!"

I do not forgive, mage, nor do I forget. I want the ruby, and you will get it for me. It must be done quickly, before she goes to Alain with her knowledge. Then, as swift as lightning dancing on a dark horizon, her thought changed. *Will she go to Alain?*

"At some time, she must."

Or will she go to her father?

"Dekar?" It was a new thought. But why would she go to Dekar?

Yvanda picked up his thought and tossed it back at him. *Why? Only because she has been cautioned by Dekar with regard to her childish little magicks. Only because there is little trust of her in the Citadel now. And because her father will soon summon her back to his kingdom.*

"Call her away?" Pain and loss, anger and fear coursed through him now. Nightmare and dream, terror and longing, all filled him until he fell before the storm within. "But I want her!"

The need was torn from him, the words wailed forth before he could stop them. Exposed and vulnerable, he cowered before the globe.

The witch-mistress watched her captive carefully. *You will have her, and it will be more quickly if she goes.*

"How can that be?"

Listen, mage, for I have crafted a plan. It is one that will get us both what we want. She paused again, laughing softly. Evil was couched in that softness. *Listen and play your part well, and you will be rewarded.*

Reynarth listened, and soon he understood. The plan was simple, the more beautiful for its simplicity and the more workable for it. He smiled as he listened, for he knew that this plan would not fail, and he knew that the Ruby of Guyaire and the Princess Nikia would soon fall into his hands.

Do you understand?

"Aye, mistress. I understand."

See that you play your part well and with patience. The little princess will soon be yours. What use you make of her then, I care not. The ruby will soon be mine, and what use I will make of it, you will learn soon enough.

She was gone, leaving fear and confusion in her place. Reynarth turned away from the globe and pulled himself stiffly to his feet. He had nothing now but Yvanda's plan and the promise of desire fulfilled. Shivering in the warm night air, he smiled.

CHAPTER 18

"You haven't been to the king?" Dail spoke carefully, watching for the reaction his words would bring. There was no reaction to see.

"No, Dail, I haven't."

"He must be told."

Nikia smiled bitterly, saluting the double edge of her dilemma. She should go to Alain with her knowledge of the ruby, but what use could he make of it? How could he, a Mannish king, one who mistrusts and avoids magic, make use of the ruby?

Indeed, she thought, what use would Dekar make of it? Her father had no knowledge of the ruby's true powers. To him, it was only a symbol, if a precious one.

"Lady?"

"Aye, Dail, I heard you. Someone must be told."

"I don't mean to plague you, lady."

"Still, you do. I just don't know what to do with the accursed thing!" She heard tears in her voice, turned her back

on the bard, and paced the length of her reception chamber.
"I only know that Alain won't know what use to make of the
ruby—and neither will my father."

"I don't know where else the ruby should go, lady, but to
your father. You have to take it out of the Citadel if you want to
protect it from Reynarth. And where else but among your people can you hope to find out how to use the thing?"

Nikia glanced around, sought Dail's eyes, and held them.
"Some people might call what you just said treason."

"Treason?" Dail smiled. "Aye, I imagine some might think
of it that way. But they'd be wrong. Alain won't know the use
of this talisman. Would I see it fall into Reynarth's hands? No,
that, lady, would surely be treason."

"Truly you'd help me?"

"I'd help you, Nikia."

"You are a good friend, Dail."

"Do you think so? Well, perhaps I am." And perhaps I am
not, he thought bitterly. Perhaps I am instead a poor friend
who seeks to gain favor and one who doesn't know what to
hope today. For if Garth is dead, then you, lady, are free.

The thought sickened him, even as it lighted a faint spark of
hope. Dail got to his feet. "Lady, you must be tired. I'll leave
you to rest."

She watched him leave, sighing for the secret she kept from
him. Nikia crossed the chamber to retrieve the small parchment which she had carefully folded and tucked inside one of
the log books that morning.

Messages, smelling of leather and ink, of dry parchment,
full of command and question. Nikia had been turned this
way and that by such messages for what seemed most of her
life.

She took up her father's message again to read it. Dekar's
words were solicitous, filled with sympathy for her. But Nikia
knew her father well, and she knew that there was more to the
words than fatherly sympathy.

*Word has reached me of the fall of Seuro and of your hus-
band's heroic deeds there. I know, Daughter, of your uncertain*

status at the Court of Alain. I make no judgment as to the well-being of your husband, for who can know whether he is alive or dead? While I hope for his safety, Daughter, and while I pray our gods that he will return to you, I write now to ask you to come home. I cannot command you, for you are no longer mine to command, but I ask you to return to me and to the folk of your father.

I have sent a like message to Alain, requesting that you be given proper escort. I have not said to him, and I do not say to you, that you are a widow now, that your proper place is among your kin. We cannot know if this is so. I only ask Alain that you be escorted to my hall to rest for a time with your folk of the forest.

The message closed with his loving regards and said no more. And yet it said so much!

Dekar was a cautious man, and a wily one. The ruby was among foreign folk, allied though they were, and he wanted it back with the Elvish now that Nikia's status among the Mannish was in doubt.

He was wily indeed, for he knew full well that Nikia would not leave it behind in the ordinary course of things, but she would travel with it. And he knew well that there was no better way to rock the alliance that was so crucial to both kingdoms now than by asking for its return.

Nikia wondered if Alain would be willing to let her take the ruby. It was now the only tangible symbol of the alliance. She smiled bitterly.

And she? What did she wish to do? Nikia had no answer. Her wishes were confused, her needs were confused, and her allegiances, for the first time since she had left her father's hall, were no longer clear.

Part of her yearned for the cool comfort, the lovely familiarity of her father's hall. Another part needed to remain here, in Garth's home, waiting for word of him. It had been nearly two days since the messenger had arrived with the news that Garth was lost. She thought every hour that another courier would come clattering into the courtyard, brandishing his message pouch and shouting the glad news that the prince had been found safe.

Nikia could not admit that he was dead, not yet. And wouldn't leaving the Citadel be such an admission? But to go home, she thought with wistful longing, ah, that would be peace indeed. At least for a time.

The Elvish captain who had ridden to Damris with Dekar's message had been attended only by a squire. There was no escort of Elvish warriors, and it appeared that Dekar would truly fall in with his daughter's wishes.

Or did he seek to judge Alain's sincerity by his actions?

She might have resented this manipulation, for she recognized it at once for what it was, but she did not. Nikia had been raised a princess, in the full understanding that often in matters of state her own wishes would not be consulted.

The intent of her father's message was clear to her: He wanted the ruby with the Elvish again in this time of doubt, and he wanted to obtain it in such a way that the alliance between the Elvish and Mannish kingdoms was not injured.

Nikia wondered for a moment if Dekar would be as pleased if she contrived a way in which to return the ruby to him and still remain behind at Damris. It was a bitter thought, and it lasted only a moment. Her duties were the price she paid for her privilege, and only a child would protest and cry "unfair."

"Well, Father," she said aloud, folding the parchment carefully and tucking it back into the book. "I will try to convince Alain that I must go home for a time."

Her mind made up on that question, she found that she could form a resolve on another. "And I will bring you the ruby, as you so subtly asked. But, ah, Father! I'm bringing you more than a symbol of our house."

* * * * *

There were reasons why Dekar had regarded Alain as a respected enemy in the days before the alliance. Nikia had heard those reasons from her father's lips often enough. And often enough, those reasons had been accompanied by heartfelt curses in the Old Elvish tongue. Not the least of the reasons was Alain's ability to judge a situation aptly and accurately, and to make the best decision on it that he could.

Nikia's ability to convince her father-in-law that she wished to "rest for a time with her folk of the forest" was certainly not the deciding factor in Alain's decision to finally agree to let her go.

She could see, all the while she was talking to him, that Alain's first inclination was to deny her father's request. He did not like letting the ruby, a physical warrant of the treaty, go from his possession. Neither did he want to let her go.

But in the end, after much persuasion on her part, Nikia received Alain's guarded blessing. He knew, as Nikia had known, that it would appear belligerent on his part to refuse to let her visit her own people in her time of sorrow. At the same time, it would appear belligerent on his part to create the impression that he desired to keep the ruby with him.

Alain was a wise man, and Nikia could not help but respect him for it, but he did not let her go easily. He ordered an armed troop as escort and commanded that Nikia be accompanied by Darun Lord Calmis and by the chief bard.

Nikia hid her smile when she heard who was to make up her escort. She understood quite well that Alain was sending with her the two who would most easily be able to persuade her to return to the Citadel.

We are treaty warrants, this ruby and I, she thought ruefully, and my father is in no position to cast aside this treaty now!

* * * * *

"She goes." Reynarth drew a long, satisfied breath. He laughed, and it was a bitter, triumphant sound. "Let her go, then."

He watched Nikia's small image in the globe and settled back comfortably on his bed. "Let her go, and let her herself take the first step of the plan."

He watched for a moment longer, lingering over the little scenes playing out before him. Nikia's would not be the only leave-taking. His own possessions, the few he deemed necessary, had already been made ready for a journey.

CHAPTER 19

Death stood at Fenyan's shoulder, and he knew full well that this dark enemy might have him before the day was out.

His hand dropped to the scabbarded sword at his saddle. He stroked the fine, cool metal of the grip and let his fingers caress the intricate design adorning the jeweled hilt. The sword had been his since he was old enough, and strong enough, to wield it. It had been a gift from his father, a treasure from Alain's coffers, beautifully crafted and inscribed along its broad length with words of courage and strength. "Kingward," it had been called in older times.

"You are well and aptly named, good sword," Fenyan murmured as his hand came again to rest on Kingward's hilt. He took a grip on his mount's rein to still the war-horse's restive prancing. The beast scented battle and was eager for it.

"And you, my friend, rest easy awhile. There'll be work for you soon enough."

As though taking patience from his rider's words, the horse subsided, snorted once, and stilled.

Fenyan's army stretched behind him, two thousand strong, veterans who were as restless as Fenyan's great war-horse. Watery sunlight fell on them, dully gleaming on their light armor, dancing along the lengths of bared weapons. Fenyan picked out his captains, met the eyes of each one, and nodded.

Gravin, nearest to the prince, raised a fisted hand. "My lord, we are ready on your word!"

Fenyan nodded once more and turned back to face the battlefield. It had been crimsoned with blood many times before now. He knew the lay of the land well. His army had fought for these fields before. Many of them had died, and more, he knew, would die today.

Seuro must be reclaimed. This precious port city had become the key to his father's kingdom. In the hands of enemies, it would open the north and east coasts and provide a broad corridor for the Sorcerer's armies to enter and take the kingdom.

Seuro was presently in the hands of the enemy. If he could retake the city, secure it with the warriors who even now waited for his word, Fenyan knew he could hold it where Garth's smaller force had not been able to.

Fenyan shifted his weight in the saddle, narrowed his eyes, and searched across the wide plain separating him from the bone-white walls of Seuro. The plain was deserted. Not even a stray breeze moved on it. Yet even as he watched, the air, pregnant with the threat of rain, stirred, wavered, then shifted. The sky grew dark with clouds rolling in from the sea behind the walled city.

His heart sinking, Fenyan knew the clouds would wait until they'd scudded well past Seuro before they dropped their threatening burden of rain. It was a ploy he'd fought against before: weather magic.

And you, Reynarth, he thought, what have you done for us? Where are your magical counters to these ploys? Fenyan drew a steadying breath. There could be only one answer to the question, and that answer was one he dared not contemplate. If Reynarth's skills were no match for the enemy's, then this army must stand alone.

And stand it will, he vowed, until the last man has fallen.

He watched as a curtain of dark rain swept in from the east, turning the plain to mud, falling insidiously between the city and Fenyan's army.

"What matter?" the prince murmured. "We must fight or drown." He smiled a twisted smile. "Either way, we die."

And what wages Death had claimed for his work! Fenyan did not doubt that Garth was dead. Puppy-bright, someone had once called Garth. Fenyan had never heard a more apt description. Deadly with a sword, incisive and canny in his strategies, still Garth had never been at heart a warrior. Garth should have been born in peaceful times to raise hounds and horses and babies. Even, Fenyan thought grudgingly, elflings, if such made sense to him.

How empty his brother's eyes had been that winter night when Nikia's child came never-born! He'd wept bitterly, the puppy-bright prince, and his grief and tears had seemed alien to Fenyan, who had wept for no one since the death of a mother only he, of the two, remembered.

Now Garth was dead. Fenyan's scouts had told him, with great certainty, that few Mannish or Elvish warriors remained alive in Seuro. There had been rumors, the stuff of nightmares, about the survivors. Fenyan stroked the length of the scabbarded sword.

"Kingward, stand by me well this day. Do me honor, and I will return that honor. Drink your fill today, Kingward, and toast the brother I avenge!"

He tested the swiftness of the scabbard's release. Satisfied with the smoothness of Kingward's glide, Fenyan raised his right hand, lifted his eyes to the rain-weary sky, and cried, "Forward!"

It took only the pressure of his knees to send the great war-horse leaping forward. Behind him, Fenyan heard the voice of the thousands who were his army. Before him, rising as though from the rain, he heard the dull roar of those who defended Seuro.

* * * * *

Curses poured from Fenyan's lips like blood from a dying man. Kingward leapt about him, drinking in great bloody drafts. Still, it didn't matter. The rain, ever present and never slackening, poured on the bloody battlefield, turning to mire the ground beneath the two armies.

Overbalanced, horses slid and fell with crushing weight on their riders. Foot soldiers struggled and fell, unable to defend themselves against the dark warriors who surged against them. It was not that the rain and mud had no affect on the army of the enemy, it was only that there were so many of them that it did not matter. Where one fell, five more came to take his place.

Bellowing orders and wielding Kingward as though it were the bloody right arm of Death, Fenyan saw the line of his army falter, break, and shatter.

"Stand!" he cried, spurring his horse forward, slashing his way to the front of his army. "Stand and fight!"

It might be that they would have, if they could have. But there was nothing on which to stand but the treacherous mud, and no way to gauge the attacks of the enemy through the dark curtain of the rain. Men fell screaming and dying. Horses, riderless and wounded, bolted among the foot combatants, trampling the fallen in their terror.

"Captains! Regroup!"

There was no way that the captains, reduced now to the common lot of their own foot soldiers, could have obeyed his orders. Fenyan dropped the reins of his horse and gripped his sword with two hands, hewing the witch-spawned warriors who came against him. They rose, inhumanly large, on either side of him. He could feel the clawing of their hands as they groped for him from behind.

"Kingward! Drink!" It was a battle cry newly born this day. Fenyan screamed the command each time his sword sliced at an enemy warrior, each time a limb, a head, fell sickeningly to the mud beneath his horse's feet. "Kingward! Drink!"

But there was too much for Kingward to drink. Weary and hoarse with his battle cries, Fenyan looked up to find that he was surrounded, six warriors deep, by the enemy.

Cold hands reached out for him; dead eyes laughed in triumph. A gray-skinned, three-legged creature standing near his right shoulder began to howl, a high, gibbering cry of horrible victory.

The war-horse reared and struck out with steel-shod hooves. It didn't matter. Any enemies who fell were replaced by other, more horrible creatures.

A clawed hand grasped at Fenyan's left arm, another at his right. With a cry of furious despair, he felt Kingward fall from his grip. Naked now, undefended, he was pulled from the back of his horse. His booted feet slid in the blood-gouted mud, and he went down sharply on his knees.

One of his captors, the howling creature, danced and gibbered senselessly. Fenyan jerked his head around and saw that he was far from the rest of his men.

Fear rose in him then, and terror. He did not cry out, for he could not. A roughly scaled hand clamped tightly across his mouth. A jagged-edged knife blade danced before his eyes, dull silver in the rain. Fenyan had never seen anything with more clarity. The blade's tip touched the large vein beneath his ear and paused there for a moment.

Seuro is lost! It was that reality, and not fear of death, that struck Fenyan cold to the heart. He had no more time for thought, not even to pray. The knife moved again, tracing a bloody path across Fenyan's throat.

For a brief instant, Fenyan felt his own blood, hot and thick, cascade down his neck, but the warm flood of life passed from him quickly. He was dead before his body dropped to the mud.

* * * * *

Gravin brought the news to Alain that his heir was dead. "He fought bravely, Your Grace. He was a banner before his men."

Mourning filled the Citadel and the city of Damris, and the king wept for another son.

* * * * *

"Do you trust this mage?"

Yvanda smiled and stretched beneath the soft bedclothes. She moved closer to her dark bed partner and laid her head on his shoulder so that her dark hair flowed over them both, covering his withered arm. It had long ceased to bother her, this useless arm. Yvanda smiled again and turned her face to the Sorcerer.

"My lord, of course I trust him. I know his price, and I can pay it out."

"Ah!" His smile was lazy and thoughtful, his eyes shaded from green to brown. "One does well to gauge a buying price correctly."

She knew that he did not refer to the mage Reynarth but to herself. But that didn't matter. She'd not only gauged Reynarth's price.

Each of us, she thought, accepting the Sorcerer's caress, each of us has a price. And, my lord, I have gauged your own as carefully as the mage's.

She hid that thought quickly and moved her hand to touch him with the intimacy that years had taught her. "My plan goes well enough. Those I have sent to join Reynarth will be waiting for him when he arrives at the meeting place. They will do his bidding—rather, my own bidding, from his lips—and he will continue on to Seuro."

"And once there?"

"He knows this place, my lord. He knows that his reward will be brought to him, and ours to us."

"And you have taken care that his price, the Elvish princess, will be turned over to him unharmed?"

Yvanda laughed, moving her hands more skillfully now, and let her lips brush against his. "Aye, my lord, I have. What good the reward if it is damaged?"

"And the use of this ruby? Who knows it?"

"None, my lord."

He eyed her carefully. "Not even you?"

"There are ways to discover its use. We will learn them in good time."

"Aye?" He rose above her, tangling his hands in the rich

lengths of her hair, and held her still beneath him. "Let it only be as useful as you, Dark Lady, and I will be satisfied."

Softly Yvanda laughed. She must be careful now. She must foster trust on two fronts with all the skill she possessed.

The abandoned child of the gods moved in concert with him she called her lord and reviewed the plots she had crafted. When he was done and had fallen back from her to seek sleep, she was satisfied that all would be well.

CHAPTER 20

Nikia made the journey to her father's hall on the day Fenyan died. Her party left Damris with little ceremony, for Alain thought it best not to announce the fact that the princess was leaving the city. Because of this caution, they departed from the Citadel in the predawn gray of what would prove to be a fine summer morning.

There was no sign in the pearly sky that rains fell with horrible vengeance in the North. Nikia's leave-taking was under far different circumstances than her arrival at Damris had been only a few seasons ago. It left her sad, and longing for home.

Nikia pondered that word "home" for much of her journey. When the A'Damran was left behind, she barely noticed the greening of the meadows, the bright sheen and sparkle of sunlight on the five lakes in the Diamond Chain. At the close of the third day of their journey, the smoky green crests of the forested mountains bordering Elvish rose before them. "The Elvish Ramparts," Calmis called them. It had the sound of a phrase newly minted, but Nikia only smiled absently and murmured, "The tail of the Kevarth Mountains." She was engrossed in the intricacies of the word "home" and could not take the delight her companions did in this lovely borderland between the kingdoms.

For many weeks after her arrival at the Citadel, Nikia had found that she had to make a conscious effort to think of that place as her home. When the word was spoken, it would call up memories of the forests and the mountains, of the Elvish folk. She would see herself sitting with her father of an evening, talking and listening to the songs of the bards or riding out into sun-dazzled woods on her strong mare with Lizbet and the young nobles of the hall. Now when she thought of home, Nikia could call up no clear picture of where that place might be.

The images were confused ones: she and Garth sitting before the hearth in their chambers; riding with Lizbet and Calmis over the fields and meadows that surrounded Damris. Then, chasing quickly after those images, came visions of the thick green forests of her father's kingdom, the hospitality of Verdant Hall, open to the river breezes and filled with the soft sound of Elvish voices murmuring and singing in the long, sweet evening of summer.

It did not escape Nikia that the pictures she recalled now of the Elvish lands did not include herself in them. Caught between two homes, balanced between two longings, Nikia knew the bittersweet taste of a homesickness that had no ready remedy.

A remedy there would be, she thought, swaying to the easy rhythm of her mount's gentle gait, if only my child had not been never-born. If only my husband yet lives.

* * * * *

"This child has chosen his mistress and will not leave her." Dekar leaned down to gently brush Riche's hair from his cheek, being careful not to disturb the lad who had fallen asleep at his daughter's feet.

Nikia smiled. "It's not the way among the Mannish to do without servants," she said wryly. "But you're right, it's almost as though he chose me instead of being chosen for me."

"You have been well, Daughter?"

"Aye, well enough."

"And you are happy to be home?"

Nikia sighed. She was happy, but still haunted by a strange homesickness. She glanced across the room that was her father's private reception chamber to Dail, who sat near the window, his hands still and silent on Dashlaftholeh. The bard, like Riche, was constantly in attendance. Nikia wondered if her father would remark wryly about that as well. She sensed that there was only wary trust between the two.

They are different men, she thought, reaching for her wine goblet. And yet, in ways, they are similar. Each knows well how to use courtesy to cloak his thoughts.

Her fingers went idly to the ruby. Dekar had listened with cautious speculation to the news that Nikia and Dail brought. There was hope, Nikia thought, in those silvery eyes she knew so well, and something else. A seeking after power? She did not know. She knew only that it made her uncomfortable. It had not been an easy task to convince her father that the ruby must remain with her even here, even in its home.

Looking back toward her father, Nikia was not sure that she had convinced him. "You do know, Father, that I'm only here on a visit." Her voice was gentle but firm.

Across the room, she heard Dail stir, followed by the soft sigh of Dashlaftholeh being set down. Nikia did not have to look to know that the bard was listening, ready to lend support if he was needed.

Dekar's eyes narrowed. He looked at the bard, then watched his daughter carefully. Though he was surprised that such strength and firmness bolstered her words, he did not show it. This was not the sweetly compliant daughter he had sent to warrant a treaty so many months before. There was determination and, aye, even stubbornness in her expression now. He recognized the firm lift of her chin from earlier times, but never had he experienced that determination turned against his own wishes.

"Daughter," he said, careful to keep his tone soft and reasonable, "there is much studying to be done if we are ever going to learn the use of the ruby. Surely you will not deny us its use."

"No, Father, I won't. Once its use is discovered, once we have learned the way of it, I'll hand it over to you gladly. But now it is still a treaty warrant, much as I am, and so it will stay with me."

Silvery eyes met and gauged each other. Father and daughter were silent across the hearth where they sat.

"You are not the same child I sent to Damris."

"I'm not a child anymore, Father."

"I see that. You have become something else—a political creature."

Dail rose from his place at the window. "I hope you will excuse me, Your Grace, if my presence is awkward here."

Dekar regarded the Mannish bard carefully. "I could not think the presence of a friend of my daughter an intrusion, Master Dail."

Dail dropped to a seat on the floor beside the sleeping Riche. Around them the woodland sounds mingled with the quiet passage of Elvish folk in the corridors and the sigh of breezes off the River Altha. So close were the river and the forest, creeping up to the very edges of the hall, that Dail could close his eyes and almost think he sat beneath the broad pines. In the courtyards and gardens, he was never quite certain where the forest ended and the hall began.

Nikia sipped her wine and placed the goblet back on the little table. "You call me a political creature, Father. I was that when I went first to Damris. You must not fault me for learning my place too well."

"So. And you no longer respect my wishes?"

"Aye, Father, I do. But your wishes run contrary these days, and I have difficulty choosing among them. What am I, Father?"

"You are my daughter."

"Aye, and Garth's wife, and a treaty warrant. And above all those things, I am a princess. I will abide by the promise my own word has made."

"And that promise is? . . ."

Nikia sensed that both Dekar and Dail awaited her answer with considerable interest. "Surely you know it, Father, for it was you who had it of me. I am wed to Prince Garth. I am his wife, and I am, along with the ruby, a treaty guarantee. I've given my word, my heart, and my body to this. Don't ask me to forsake that now. I won't."

She is no pawn, Dekar thought, and the thought brought with it a peculiar sense of loss along with pride. She is a woman grown.

"What do you think of this stubborn daughter I have sired, Master Dail?"

Dail closed his eyes and smiled. "You should be proud of her, Your Grace."

"Aye?" Dekar said. "Well, I am. And I'm happy to see that she's won so steadfast a friend in her short time at Damris."

Are you? Dail thought. Then why do you watch me so closely, King? What is it you seek to learn from me? He lifted his eyes to the king's and saw that Dekar had apparently learned what he wished to learn.

More than a friend, the old king's eyes said. Have a care, master bard!

Dekar drew a soft sigh and shook his head. "As you will, Nikia, for now. We'll see what our mages and bards learn, and then we'll have this conversation again.

"Think about this, though, Nikia: You assume that your husband is not dead. You've given your heart to this Mannish prince. It's a wife's heart, which tells you to hope for him. But what if he is dead?"

Nikia was silent for a long moment. When at last she answered, her voice was low and controlled. "When word comes to me that he is dead, Father, we can talk again about my place."

In the silence that fell between them, Dail rose gracefully to his feet. "My lady," he said, bowing slightly to Nikia, "if you don't need me, I will pack this lad off to a better sleeping place."

"Aye, thank you, Dail."

"Your permission, Your Grace?" Dail bowed to the king, who smiled coolly.

"So," Dekar murmured after the bard had left. "You have made some good friends among the Mannish."

"Master Dail? Aye, Father, a good friend."

"And you trust this bard?"

"I do, and I have."

"Interesting. His own king might not take a kindly view toward the man who allowed so powerful a talisman to be taken from his country."

"We've discussed that."

"They are crafty men, bards. They often seem to know the hearts of others as well as they know their own. But this one . . ."

Nikia's eyes narrowed. "Aye? This one?"

Dekar smiled. "It only seems to me that this one knows his own heart best, and that it's there where his motives lie."

"His motives lie with mine, Father." Nikia sat straighter, feeling the need to defend her friend.

"Oh," Dekar agreed, "I am sure they do, Daughter." But he spoke from a knowledge that Nikia did not yet have.

* * * * *

The storm broke shortly after Nikia had left her father and slipped into the comfortable bed of the chamber that had been hers for most of her life. She lay trying to ignore the advance of a headache, truly pleased to be sleeping back among familiar surroundings again. But the ever-present ache of Garth's loss was never far from her. There was seldom a moment when she was not brought to sharp awareness of it. It was no easier to bear here than at Damris.

So sharp was her grief, so new and dark, that she hardly noticed that for the first time in many nights, she slept unaccompanied by Reynarth's whisperings. One torment exchanged for another, she thought wearily.

Nikia lay quietly, listening to the thunder crashing above the roof of the hall, smelling the scented wind, and hearing the drumming of the rain. It was a lovely sound, the rhythm starting with a gentle patter, increasing to a passionate staccato beating, and subsiding again to softness. She loved the smell of it, the wet green scent of earth absorbing moisture, the musty scent of the woodcrafted hall itself in the dampness.

Then, as suddenly as it had come crashing overhead, lighting the corners of her chamber with its brilliant flashes, the storm was gone. It did not drift away, for early summer storms seldom do. They leave all abruptly. With it, as though the wind had swept into the chamber and carried it off, went Nikia's headache.

She went quickly to sleep.

* * * * *

What had awakened her? Nikia could not say. A sound, perhaps, or a strange, unfamiliar smell, lingering in the room like the last wisps of a dream. Perhaps.

No fog of sleep confused her. She felt no lingering doubt, that familiar doubt a sleeper feels when startled awake. She was alert and fully aware of her surroundings. And something was wrong.

Nikia sat up, brushing her hair back from her face and letting the coverlet slide down from her shoulders. The air was cool with the pleasant night chill one enjoys in the first days of summer. Her room was dark, a place of shadow and pools of blackness.

Blinking, she slid to the edge of the bed, groping for the robe that should have been lying nearby. It did not come to hand, and Nikia got to her feet, snatching up the first clothing she could find, a hunting outfit she had worn that afternoon.

Unthinking, Nikia slipped into the fine leather breeches. Her shift was a short one, appropriate for summer nights, and this she tucked into the waistband of the breeches. Eyes on the clear-paned glass of the door that led to the terrace outside her room, Nikia made her way silently, on bare feet, to the door.

The terrace, too, was dark. There was only dim starlight to see by. She considered rounding her hand to call the blue witch-light, but she did not.

Nikia listened but heard nothing. Yet something had disturbed her. Not a sound, but something that felt, or smelled, wrong. A swampy scent. Dull and dead, like the scent one turns from in the marshes, the scent that warns that something has died here, and not long ago.

Someone was on the terrace. Nikia slipped back into her chamber, snatched up the boots that had been abandoned with the hunting outfit the afternoon before, and pulled them on. Her hand strayed downward, slipping along her right thigh where the little skinning knife lay in the sheath pocket of the breeches.

Swinging around, Nikia felt for the first time the weight of the ruby depending from its chain around her neck. It was, as it had been since she had left the Citadel, tucked inside her shift. Day or night, despite her father's request to place it in his care, the ruby stayed with her.

She slipped across the golden parquet floor, soundlessly undid the latch of the door to the terrace, and glided out into the night.

The scent was stronger here, a smell of wrongness, of death. The fingers of her right hand went again to the knife in its sheath and tapped on the chased silver hilt in restless rhythm. Nikia surveyed the terrace, giving her eyes no time to adjust to the dimness.

She stepped to the polished wooden railing that edged the terrace, from which she could see the sloping drop of the river-banks. Listening, she heard nothing but the lap and sigh of the river.

Nikia turned to survey the terrace again. East of her own chambers, in line with them, were the guest chambers. There Calmis and Dail were quartered. No light or sound came from those rooms. The sense and scent of evil increased. She began to shiver.

Nikia stood for a long moment, thinking that she must return inside, that she must call someone. A sound, a slight scuff of booted feet, brought her up short.

A long pool of shadow, like the thick web of a night cob, separated itself from the blackness near the occupied guest chamber.

Nikia sighed gratefully. "Darun?"

"Aye, my lady."

Nikia started toward him, almost running. "I thought I heard something out here."

"I did, too. And smelled something foul."

Then she had not been imagining it! Nikia looked up at his face and saw it formed into lines so grim that she might not have recognized him. "Darun, what is it?"

Calmis shook his head. "I don't know, but Dail sensed it, too."

"Where is he?"

Calmis gestured toward the terrace rail with a sharp jerk of his head. "Below, my lady . . . looking."

"Call him back." Nikia shivered as fear crawled along her spine. Memories came back to her, memories of the thing that the fisherman had found on the banks of this very river in the autumn. "Darun, call him now."

"But—"

"I command it!" Nikia hardly recognized the harshness of her own voice.

Calmis gave her a quick, puzzled look, but he obeyed. He stepped to the edge of the terrace and whistled once, low and clearly, into the night. Another whistle, faint and speaking of distance, followed on his, and then a second.

Calmis turned sharply. "Lady, please go inside." His voice was hard, his expression unyielding. This was not the Darun Nikia had come to know. There was nothing of the polished, gentle diplomat here. This was a lord, with a lord's commanding ways. "Inside, my lady. Now."

He grasped her elbow. There was such strength in his grip that Nikia wondered briefly if she would find bruises. It was the wrong tactic, and he knew it at once when she drew up and pulled her arm from his hand.

"Take your hand from me, Lord Calmis. You may not command me."

"My lady . . ." He tried to gentle his voice, but strain and something close to anger hid just under the surface. "Please return to your chambers."

"No. Whatever Dail has found is of interest to me. I'm going with you."

Fool! Little fool!

Nikia saw the words in his eyes. Turning from her with a sound of mingled anger and impatience, Calmis made for the flight of stairs at the far east end of the terrace. Nikia, checking her anger and fear, followed.

The steps were damp, slippery from the recent rain and the newly rising dew. The scent of the river drifted up to them as they made their way down to the banks, and the scent that had pulled Nikia from sleep and out into the night grew stronger. Once she stopped, gagging, and swallowing a bitter sickness that threatened to leave her retching. Calmis, bent on joining Dail, did not stop for her.

They joined Dail at the river's edge, Nikia coming up just a moment after Calmis. Looking up from where he was crouched in the muddy verge that separated the green banks from the water, Dail caught his breath in a sound that clearly spoke his surprise. He rose to his feet, his blue eyes pale in the dim light. "Darun, did you wake the whole hall?"

"Aye, it seems so, my friend," Lord Calmis growled.

Nikia knew that the anger was for her, and she thinned her lips and stepped forward. "Calmis didn't wake me, Dail. I was wakened by the same thing you were."

The scent, faint but foul only moments ago on the terrace, almost overwhelmed her here. Nikia cast about for the source of it, but saw only the river and the dipping and bobbing of the fishing boats far down in the cove.

"You shouldn't be here, lady," Dail said, again glaring at Calmis.

"It is a done thing, Dail. What have you found?"

The bard shrugged, passing over his anger and surprise, and went back down on his heels as they had first seen him.

As one, Calmis and Nikia crouched down beside him. It was clear to them both that the source of the stench, the place from which it emanated, was there in the mud.

The light was bad, and Nikia moved her hand absently, cupping her fingers and filling her palm with cool, blue witch-light. Calmis gasped, but Dail motioned her closer. There, dimly seen in the mud, were prints.

She could not tell if they were footprints, for she had never seen such feet as these, and there were not two marks but three.

"What—what are they, Dail?"

The bard ran a hand through his dark, disheveled hair. "Footprints—of a sort."

Calmis spoke then, leaning closer and wrinkling his nose. "But there are three, Dail. Two creatures?"

"No. One, I think."

Nikia got to her feet then, stepping away. What kind of creature would have three feet? Two, aye, and four, and even the six-legged night cob. But three? The hair raised on her neck and arms.

As though called from her thoughts, there was a small scrambling in the long grass at the river's edge. Dark and round, its many eyes gleaming redly in the blue light, a night cob scuttled out of the grass into the mud.

Nikia jumped back, startled at the sight of it. It was only half as large as her fist and completely harmless. Startled, frozen in its place, the night cob stared, all its eyes whirling in every direction. Dail laughed softly, a sound that told Nikia that he had been nearly as startled as she.

"A night cob," he said. "And small for one, at that."

The cob scuttled away from the grass, scrambling across the toe of Nikia's boot and over the place where the three-footed prints were.

The cob stopped, frozen again, standing in the very center of the tracks. It writhed, and if night cobs could scream, Nikia knew that this one would have sent up a cry of pain so piercing as to wake the hall.

The cob twisted, jerked, and then collapsed onto its side. A little breeze off the river caught it, tumbling its body again until it was well out of the tracks and into the shadows beyond Nikia's light.

Nikia moaned in horror and, letting her light die, turned away, burying her face in Calmis's shoulder. The six legs of the night cob had been burned to the last joint. Where its dark, furry body had touched the prints, there was nothing of skin, only gaping raw wounds.

As though the night cob's death was simply a prelude, Nikia was caught in a sudden whirl of terror.

There was a soft cry from behind them. Over Calmis's shoulder, Nikia saw the steps leading from the east end of the terrace, and there, bathed in the light of another blue sphere, stood a figure robed in white, followed closely by a smaller one, clattering down the steps, heedless of any noise. Lizbet and Riche, Nikia thought, even as Calmis tightened his arm about her.

"Riche—" But her words were cut off, as well as her breath, by Calmis's hand. A cry sounded from upriver, low and fearsome. Nikia struggled against Calmis's hand, trying to look in the direction of the cry. Something was wrong, but what?

There were no fishing boats in the cove! But there had been, for she had noticed them only moments before. Another cry sounded from behind them. Nikia caught the flash of Calmis's blade.

"Darun!" Nikia could barely gasp his name, so hard did he hold her. She twisted in his grasp, looking for Dail.

Like creatures from some dark nightmare, six figures, hunched and thin, swarmed up from the river's bank. Starlight danced on naked steel but did not reflect from their flat, black eyes. They saw Dail, and one of them hissed and pointed.

Nikia screamed. "Dail! Oh, Darun, help him!" But Calmis could do nothing with Nikia in his grasp, and he knew that he must not let her go, even as he watched Dail go down under the attack of the small, dark creatures.

Crushed against Calmis, Nikia barely heard the cries behind her, all low and all speaking of triumph. Before she could take another breath, sharp-clawed hands dragged her from Calmis's arms and hauled her toward the river. A hand, stinking and foul with dirt and blood, clamped over her mouth. Nikia jerked her head back and bit hard. Her captor's hand was rough and scaled and so vile that she gagged.

Calmis loomed for a moment in her sight. She felt his hand

suddenly on her shoulder, then grasping her wrist. Nikia saw it, for it was all that she could see, held immobile by the strength of her captor's grip about her neck and mouth.

There was a ring on Calmis's hand, an amethyst, flashing in the starlight. And then the ring vanished, covered in a rush of blood.

Nikia was jerked backward, gagging and retching against the vile hand clamped over her mouth. Behind her, Calmis cursed, then cried out in pain. Someone—Lizbet?—screamed in horror.

Nikia struggled, then felt her stomach go weak with the knowledge that her struggling was useless. The pressure of the arm about her neck grew stronger. The edges of her sight blackened, and her breath whistled in her lungs. Then there was only the long fall into darkness.

CHAPTER 21

"There are no princes in the Mannish kingdom." Reynarth smiled as he took up a comfortable position in the richly upholstered chair. He nodded to the creature standing before the broad, map-littered table. "And Alain displays his grief with abandon."

The creature did not move, did not acknowledge his words. This was a Darkling, animate yet dead. Her golden hair fell across her face, and she made no move to brush it aside. If it irritated her, she gave no sign. She responded to nothing but Reynarth's command.

"Wait for me within."

The Darkling moved then, slowly, carefully, turning to leave him, neither looking back nor forward. She knew where to go, and she went there.

Reynarth watched her for a long moment. She was one of the least bizarre inhabitants of the keep of Seuro. A Darkling—dead but able to move, able to move but incapable of emotion or thought. She existed by command and functioned by command. She was, he thought with a cold smile, useful enough.

He rose to his feet, dropped his hand to the short sword that hung scabbarded at his side, and gestured to the two guards who stood at the door of the large chamber. One took up a torch, and the other fell in behind.

They, too, moved without comment, not because they were incapable of word or thought, as the Darkling was, but because they were warriors, remanded to his command. Neither men nor elves, they were a breed apart, creatures who, like the Darklings, had their origins not in the loins of men and the wombs of women, but in the fell power of the Sorcerer's witch-mistress.

It had taken Reynarth some time to become used to the look of them. Their slanted heads, rangy limbs, and overlarge hands and feet sickened him at first. The gray skin and slitted eyes still made his skin shiver. But they were tools for his use. He realized that a tool needn't be lovely to be appreciated, but simply efficient. These warrior-things were that if nothing else.

The oily smoke of the torch ran before them. Reynarth coughed once, but not from the smoke. Ancient stenches haunted the place. Light seldom came here, and the air was foul and filled with the odor of lingering hopelessness and death. No hope survived in the dungeon beneath the keep of Seuro.

By the light of the guard's torch, Reynarth made his way to the last cell in the second block. The dungeon rang with the moans of men and elves who had long ago given up their hopes.

Reynarth shook his head. Interesting, the layers of hope imprisoned men could build. First the hope of ransom. When that died, there came the hope of escape. That, more than all others, faded fast. No one escaped from the dungeon of the keep. Its walls were stone the thickness of a man's height. The door of each cell fronted a narrow corridor manned by guards stationed at each end. No window to the outside world relieved the noisome darkness.

And when that hope died, as it always did, the last hope was born: the hope for death. That one, unlike the others, eventually would be realized.

"Here, my lord." The guard stopped before a cell he knew well. He set the torch in a cresset high on the wall and stepped away from the thick wooden door.

Reynarth moved closer, and the keys at his belt jangled, danced a little, and fell silent. It was enough of a sound to rouse the prisoner within.

"Good day," Reynarth said, his voice soft and wry. "And it is a good day, I assure you."

The prisoner didn't speak. He merely turned his head to see his visitor. His face was paler than Reynarth had ever known it to be. His chin was covered by a dirty and unkempt beard, grown straggly and filthy.

It had not pleased Reynarth at first to learn that this particular prisoner was part of the keep's doomed population. He would sooner have known this captive was dead. But Reynarth was a man who quickly recognized the possibilities of any situation. He smiled now, a cold smile of anticipation and satisfaction. This situation held many possibilities indeed.

"What? No greeting?"

The prisoner lifted his head, moved his lips slowly, and narrowed his eyes. He spat, with poor aim, but laughed bitterly just the same.

"I see. Well, it appears that you won't need the day's water ration."

The prisoner spoke then, his voice cracked and weak, dry and barely heard. "Save it, then, traitor. When you rot in the desert of the seven underworlds, you'll need it."

Reynarth laughed. The bravado of the man in chains amused him. He gestured toward the guard, who retrieved the torch.

"Brave words, my friend. A pity you can't eat them, for you will hunger because of your loose tongue."

Reynarth turned to leave then, taking the light that had so pained the prisoner's eyes. Still, the darkness was harder. Alone and chained in his cell, Garth was left again with only the rustling of vermin and the damp rotting rags of the clothing which remained to him.

* * * * *

Nikia couldn't remember much of the journey south. Hot summer sun glared on the River Altha, turning it to a burning silver stream; brazen blue skies rocked over the swiftly moving boat. Though clouds of insects hovered at the edges of the river's banks, they did not trouble those in the boats.

It seemed strange to her, in her few moments of lucidity, that they were going south.

There were three boats, swift and slim, from the fishing craft that had been moored in the cove near Verdant Hall. The single sail had been removed from each. The boats were powered by the paddling of two creatures, one in the front and one in the rear. In each boat, two more creatures, foul-smelling and three-legged, sat amidships as guards.

The boat in which Nikia lay held only her and Calmis. Darun! she thought each time she glanced his way. Is he dead? But, no, why would they bring a dead man along? He must be alive. Yet never once did Nikia see him move during any of the time she remembered of the journey.

Each time she woke from restless sleep to raise her head to look about, a guard would scurry down to where she lay in the center of the boat. Something foul-tasting would be forced between her lips. Then she'd taste the salt tang of the leather flask, the bitter vileness of the liquid it contained. Before Nikia could think to spit it out, before she could even swallow the whole of it, she would drop away into a bad and broken sleep that never refreshed.

* * * * *

After a time, Nikia's scattered perceptions filled with dampness, darkness, and shadows. She lay on a rock floor, chilled and shivering, huddled among other unmoving bodies.

Once, in the dark and dampness, she woke. No light of fire relieved this darkness, ever. But some light leaked inward from the outside. She lay in a cave. They must be in the southern part of her father's kingdom, near the seacoast. The scent of salt air reached her on stray breezes. Nikia did not move. She wanted no more of the foul sleeping draft. She glanced about her as much as she could without moving her head.

She lay facing the cave's mouth. There were two guards there, wakeful and murmuring among themselves. Trembling, Nikia shifted her gaze, and it fell again on Calmis.

He lay with his back to her, but she recognized him. She thought she saw a thin rising and falling of his shoulders. He was breathing.

Close by, Nikia saw the dim white glow of cloth—Lizbet's robe. Beneath that robe, partly covered by a mud-stained hem, lay Lizbet's foot, bare and white.

And the others? She thought she sensed breathing behind her, but Nikia did not dare turn to see. She tried to determine if it was the breathing of one other, or of two. She could not tell.

Weeping silently, afraid to wipe the warm tears from her cheeks, Nikia closed her eyes again and slept.

* * * * *

The princess didn't know how many mornings had passed since the capture. She recognized the graying dawn light and the clean, new smell of sea breezes at daybreak. There would be sunlight soon.

She'd no sooner placed the time and drawn a cautious breath of the sweet dawn air than rough, clawed hands grabbed her arms and dragged her to her feet. Reeling with dizziness, she staggered against the arm of the guard who held her. Stumbling, her cheek brushed against its shoulder. The feel of the scaled, foul-smelling skin against her face brought Nikia back to her feet, her heart racing painfully.

She gasped and the creature laughed. Nikia had never heard such a sound—a rough, grating noise—but she knew it for laughter.

She looked about her then, free to move at least her head, and placed the others. Calmis stood unaided, his right hand bound in a filthy bandage that had the look of not having been replaced for days. Bruises darkened his face, and blood matted his tawny hair above his right ear. One eye was swollen shut.

Behind Calmis stood Lizbet. Nikia wouldn't have recognized her had she not recognized the robe her friend had been wearing the night of their capture. Her hair was unbound, tangled and dirty. As Nikia's eyes fell on her, as she was holding back a cry of pity, Lizbet turned. At the sight of Nikia, her face crumpled and she began to weep silently.

Nikia's heart burned with pity. At that moment, an anger rose up within her. It burned hotter than fear.

Two of the creatures held Dail. His face was as battered as Calmis's, and blood caked over a cut that scored the bard's face from temple to cheek. Riche, small and almost unnoticed, stood within easy reach of only one guard.

Their eyes appeared startlingly similar to Nikia in that vile dawn. Boy and man, they looked sick and haunted, and each bore the look of one who had failed at some vital task.

Nikia spoke to neither. She gave Dail a small, shrugging smile, bitter and hurt, to tell him that she was well enough. Riche, raising his brown eyes to meet hers, stilled the trembling of his lips manfully, straightened his shoulders, and lifted his chin. Nikia loved the child in that moment.

That day they began their shipboard journey, bound for northern lands, and there was nothing any of them could do to stop it. A large ship had put into the little bay Nikia knew as Lan Leich. It bore three small sails, and Nikia noted places for ten oarsmen on each side. The ship should make good speed.

The captives' hands were bound before them with thick chains. The chains joined a single thick length from the cuffs on their wrists to a weighty metal collar fastened about their throats.

Though it had been days since she'd eaten, Nikia realized that she wasn't hungry. The bitter draft gave strength as well as sleep, but Nikia's stomach churned at the memory of its vile taste.

The ship rocked beneath their feet as they boarded. When Nikia stumbled, she was dragged roughly forward. They were taken into the ship's dark hold, where the chains connecting one to the other were removed. Their wrist chains remained.

There was no port to admit light, and the fetid stuffiness of the hold was complete once the hatch was closed.

* * * * *

Nikia stood still in the darkness. The soft sound of a sob came from her left. She knew that this was Lizbet. She heard a murmur, a childish voice, and by it she placed Riche.

Lifting her head, widening her stance for balance in the stinking darkness of the hold, Nikia spoke for the first time in many days. "Dail?" Her voice was rough and hoarse. "Dail, where are you?"

Nikia heard scuffling, and then the sound of Dail's voice in the blackness. "Lady?"

"Is there any water?"

The question seemed to catch him off balance, and it was a moment before Dail answered. "I don't know."

"Find some." It was not a request but a command. The steel in her voice startled Nikia.

"Aye, lady." The bard's tone showed no surprise, only willingness. Nikia heard him moving about in the dark, scuffling here and there, and at last heard a small murmur that indicated satisfaction.

"Water?"

"Aye, but stale."

"It will have to do." She took a few steps to her left, groping outward with her bound hands. "Lizbet? Lizbet!"

The soft weeping halted. Nikia sensed that her waiting woman was standing near.

"Lizbet, listen. I need your help. Darun needs tending. Darun?"

"Here, lady."

"Is Riche with you?"

Riche himself answered. "Here, lady. I'm here."

"Good. We will do the best we can to clean your wound, Darun."

They moved awkwardly. As her eyes adjusted to a darkness relieved only by a sliver of light outlining the hatch, Nikia saw her friends as dim forms. "Lizbet, can you tear the hem of your gown to make a bandage?"

Lizbet nodded in the darkness. Then, realizing that Nikia could not see her, she said softly, "Of course, *Halda*."

Dail grabbed the bucket filled with sour water and dragged it forward. Calmis went down on his heels, then sat, groaning softly. Blindly reaching for his wounded hand, Nikia removed the dirty, blood-caked wrapping.

"Ah, for light!" Dail whispered. "Lady? Can you call forth your blue fire?"

Nikia wanted to, but she dared not risk the light. She would have to do the best she could in the dark. She took Calmis's hand gently. He'd lost a finger.

She shuddered, remembering the sight of the amethyst ring vanishing in a gush of blood. How long, she wondered, has the hand been untended? Has it festered?

She did not know, but she didn't smell the foulness of a rotting wound. It smelled sour, aye, but not festered. Nikia felt the heat of infection as she laid her hand under his, holding it while Dail scooped water from the bucket with his cupped hands.

"Wash it as best as you can, Dail."

The water was warm and oily. Nikia wondered then if they might be doing the infected hand more harm than good. Calmis's sigh of relief was enough to encourage her to go on. She let Dail rinse the hand, feeling the water trickle through Calmis's fingers and down her own arm. Beside her, she heard ripping sounds. Lizbet pressed a length of cloth into Nikia's free hand.

It was difficult, in the dark, to wrap the wound. Nikia felt Calmis flinching away from her touch, and once his arm jerked, the sudden motion setting her off balance. She reached down with bound hands and touched the wooden deck of the hold for balance. It was slimy beneath her fingers. Nikia recoiled at once.

"Riche, steady him, please."

Nikia heard the lad murmur small phrases of encouragement and hope to Calmis. She worked as quickly as she could.

Finally, content that she had bound the cleaned wound as best she could, she sat back on her heels.

"There, Darun, it's clean at least."

Calmis was silent for a long moment. Only his labored breathing could be heard. When he spoke at last, his voice was cracked with pain. "I've lost a finger, haven't I?"

"Aye, my friend," Nikia said gently. "You have. And never can I repay you that debt."

He leaned forward, touching his manacled hands to her own. "You owe me nothing, lady." The bitterness of failure haunted his voice.

Nikia held his hands in her own for a moment, choking against the pain of tears.

In the darkness of the hold, Nikia heard the catch of a sob in Lizbet's voice. "Let me help you, Darun. Come with me."

Nikia listened to their shuffling movements, followed by another—Riche's no doubt—and sat still where she was.

"Lady?"

"Aye, Dail?"

"There's a pile of leathers at the far end of the hold. Come with me and you can rest."

Nikia doubted that she would ever rest again. Still, she got to her feet and allowed Dail to take her bound hands in his own and lead her across the hold.

The leathers were old and no longer soft, but cracked and harsh from exposure to the salt air. It didn't matter to Nikia. She ached for light and air.

When he had settled her down, Dail dropped beside her, his back against the curve of the ship's hull.

"We're under way," he said after a time. "Have they taken the ruby?"

Though it was a question, Nikia realized that he knew, or guessed, the answer. Snatching at her shift, she moaned softly when her fingers did not touch the ruby. Horror touched the edge of her soul: The ruby was gone! Nikia shuddered to think that the filthy scaled hands of her captors had touched her, searching for the treasure.

She reached out in the darkness, her hands clasped in prisoner's prayer, and touched Dail's booted leg. "They have it, Dail. The ruby's gone."

"And yet," the bard said softly, "we're still alive."

Nikia looked up then. She tried to see Dail in the blackness but saw only shadow. "Dail, why are they burdening themselves with prisoners when a swift raid and escape would have been far easier?"

Dail let his breath out in a puzzled sound. "I don't know. They must be following someone's orders."

"But whose?" Nikia recognized that as a foolish question as soon as she spoke it. She knew whose, just as clearly as she knew, by its rocking and creaking, that the ship was out of the bay and into the open sea.

"These can only be the Sorcerer's creatures. The orders must be his."

"It must be so, lady."

"But—how would he know about the ruby?"

"Reynarth."

"*Maeg he sawol hwidre!*" Nikia spoke the curse in her ancient tongue, the words hissing from her lips like burning steam. "May his soul whither! Wretched traitor!"

"Traitor, aye, yet I'll wager that we live because of him. By my reckoning, we have been five days captive."

"Five days!" Five days in the hands of these witch-spawn! Nikia's mind skittered here and there. She thought of her father, wondering if he had parties of warriors out searching for her. And she thought of Alain at Damris. The Ruby of Guyaire, that precious and clueless weapon, was no longer in possession of the alliance.

Five days. . . . How did the war progress? Had there been some news of Garth? Had word finally come to his father that he lived? Or that he had died?

Nikia moaned at that thought and turned her face to the wall. She lay there for some time, sobbing, for now she could weep and now she did.

Dail slipped his arms around her, holding her to him in his bound embrace. Her tears were hot on his neck and so salty they stung. They were not the worst pain.

CHAPTER 22

Nikia was never so aware of the stink of her body than when she and her companions were finally taken topside. Clouds, slaty and thick with the promise of rain, hid the sun. Still, Nikia's eyes ached with the glare of daylight. Her legs trembled beneath her.

Two guards stood on either side of her, though neither touched her. Nikia looked about, trying to place her companions. She moaned aloud at the sight of them.

They were filthy, pasty-faced, and thin. Lizbet, her lovely Lizbet, was a wraith in a foul white bedrobe. Her hair hung about her face and shoulders, matted and lank. Her hands, those lovely white hands, looked more like claws, scabbed and dirty.

Nikia went to her. The guards followed but made no protest. She embraced Lizbet gently. Over her shoulder, Nikia could see Dail where he stood, twice guarded as she was. His shirt—she remembered that it had been of finest linen—was gray with dirt. His beard had started to grow silver-chased.

And Calmis. If Nikia had thought him dead on the river journey, what must she think of him now? He could not stand under his own power, but had to lean against the wall of a cabin enclosure, bracing against the gentle roll of the ship. It was a mark of his deterioration that he was left unguarded. Riche, a mere ghost of a child, stood near him, holding him steady.

Beneath her filthy hunting leathers, hidden away inside her unwashed flesh, beat a heart that was filled with murder.

Even then, after all this time a prisoner, Nikia's hand slid down the side of her breeches, reaching for her little skinning knife. She didn't expect to find it. She'd long ago discovered that it was gone. Still, her hand strayed to the place where it should be.

She would gladly have killed with it. And so, with a murderous heart, Nikia stood in the heat of a storm-threatening summer day, holding Lizbet close to her and dreaming of killing.

Like a cold wind, she saw sudden anger, then fear, in Dail's blue eyes. The look was warning enough to prepare her for the touch on her wrist. Nikia's flesh crawled with disgust beneath that scaled hand.

The creature, one of the guards, spoke and pulled her roughly away from Lizbet. Nikia didn't recognize a word of the creature's guttural language, but she understood well enough that she was to go with it.

She cast one look over her shoulder at her companions, saw Dail move as though to accompany her, and saw him jerked roughly to his knees by his own guards.

"Stay," Nikia called, as though he had a choice and would choose to obey her wishes.

Dail raised his head and moved as though to speak, but he was too tightly held by his guards to do even that. His look of mingled fear and anger chilled Nikia.

She was jerked along behind her guard, aware, even over her own body's odor, of the foulness of its smell. She went where it led, stumbling along in its wake, her legs unsure and still too weak to serve her well.

They went behind the cabin structure against which Calmis

had been leaning. Nikia saw a short flight of stairs leading steeply down, so narrow and so low that she had to duck her head to enter.

The three-legged creature pushed her inside a cabin. Nikia's eyes, affronted first by the light, now took several seconds to adjust to the cabin's dimness. When they did, she wished that they had not.

She knew what the thing was. She remembered the story that the tavern folk had told at Damris. It was taller than any man or elf, cloaked in black, swathed from neck to throat, hooded even in this summer heat. Nikia could not see its face, but she heard its breathing.

When it moved from its place behind the low table at the far side of the cabin, Nikia caught the gleam of finely polished black boots.

The guard twisted her arm sharply, yanking downward. Though her knees hit the deck hard, she made no sound to acknowledge the pain. For a long moment, she heard no sound in the cabin but the harsh sibilant of the black thing's breathing. Then it spoke.

"Ah, my lady." Its voice was the voice of the wind moaning about the gates of the burial yard at Damris, thin and high and wailing. Nikia wanted to scream, but she bit hard on her lip so that no sound would escape her. She thought of murder in her heart, called back to her mind the pictures of her companions and the heart-wrenching sounds of Riche sobbing in the night. She called hatred up to defend herself, and it served her well for a time. She made no sound.

"Let her rise, Jek." The guard dragged Nikia to her feet. "Let her go, Jek." The thing that was her guard let go, and Nikia caught her arm close to her, chafing it absently, trying to find the courage to bring her eyes up to meet those of the black thing.

"I am Carah," it said in its graveyard voice. It made a motion with its black-gloved hand toward its throat and the ebony clasp of its cloak. "There is something I want to show you."

Nikia raised her eyes to its face for the first time, but she could see nothing of its features and had only the vaguest sense that there was indeed a face within that hood. She sensed, too, that it was smiling. Still she did not speak.

Fingers moved on the black clasp, deftly undoing the brooch without having to look. The cloak fell away to show fine silk livery, black as all its other raiment and relieved only by the thing which lay on a silver chain at its breast.

The Ruby of Guyaire!

Then Nikia did make a sound, a sound like a growl, a sound she would never had thought herself capable of making. She moved instinctively, outrage giving strength to limbs weak with lack of food and exercise. She leaped, and her leap was cut short. She was thrown to the deck by the weight of her guard, Jek.

Panting and gasping under its foul weight, Nikia struggled helplessly. Carah laughed aloud this time.

Nikia screamed and clapped her hands to her ears. She would go mad from the sound of that laughter! Her soul would shrivel and blacken and finally die if she had to hear that dreadful sound again. Still, she heard it. She heard it through her hands and through her cries.

"Father!" she screamed, almost mindlessly. "Father!" She cried out to him, to Dekar, so far away. "Garth!" She screamed for her husband, feared dead, and to her gods, to anything and anyone in whom she had even the slightest faith. Carah continued to laugh.

There was nothing—the ruby, her heart, her life, her soul— Nikia would not have surrendered for that sound to stop. After what seemed hours to Nikia in her terror, the black thing finally stopped laughing.

She heard boots thud on the wooden deck as Carah approached her. It spoke to her guard, its voice a cold and heartless wind-cry. Behind her, the door opened and then closed.

Whimpering, Nikia flinched away from Carah's nailed grip. She was pulled to her feet. Stumbling, her knees too weak to hold her, she sagged and was righted.

Through the curtain of her filthy hair, Nikia peered up at Carah. Two red pinpoints glared from within the hood. It breathed in reptilian sibilants, chuckling faintly like the last rumble of an earthquake.

Nikia moaned aloud.

Carah pulled her to her feet and drew her closer. It was like being drawn toward ice. The hair on her neck and arms bristled. With its gloved left hand, it touched her face.

Nausea churned within her belly. Bile rose in acid heat, searing Nikia's throat. The thing's hand lingered a moment on her face as its red, glowing eyes seemed to grow larger. Then the hand moved, tracing a path with two fingers down the side of her cheek, resting a moment on her jaw, and then traveling along her neck.

Nikia moaned and sagged again.

"Come, stand firm, lady." She could only whimper. Carah's hand rested, two fingers, in the hollow of her throat.

"Here," it said, its voice dropping to a whisper. "Here is where the silver chain hung." The fingers traced the place where the ruby's chain had depended.

"Yes," it said, its voice soft as a snake hissing. "Quite a prize—if you were clean." The cold leather of the glove left an icy trail as Carah's two fingers slipped inside Nikia's shift. "And here. . . ." Ice touched the place between her breasts. She had no voice left, for it was snatched away by horror. "Here is where I found a treasure."

The hand lingered. Blood pounded in her temples, and the room grew dark. Nikia knew that she had not the strength to resist. Carah knew it, too, for the red points of its eyes were as bright as evil stars.

If she had had a voice with which to do it, Nikia would have begged, pleaded, screamed, but she could only stand, mute and beyond movement.

It held her thus for a long moment. Suddenly she was spun away, freed of its grasp, and flung to the floor.

"But the prize is not for me." The laughter, abominable, death-filled, started again, and Nikia gratefully let the blackness claim her.

* * * * *

Nikia slept that night between Lizbet and Dail, seeking but never finding warmth. In all the places where the black thing had touched her—arm, face, neck, and breast—her skin was seared with the white of frost burn.

She slept at times, but those times were worse than when she did not. Nightmares filled her sleep, dark memories of Carah. When she lay awake, she spoke to no one. She could not respond to the anxious questions of her friends, nor could she offer Lizbet the assurances that she needed when the cold burn marks were discovered on her body. Did Lizbet think she had been raped?

Possibly she did. Nikia could offer nothing to reassure her, for in her heart, if not in her body, she had been. And yet she had no strength for words, no wit to make the distinction. She could only huddle closer to Lizbet on one side and to Dail on the other, and silently ride the nightmare.

In the morning, they reached Seuro and the end of their voyage.

* * * * *

The great keep of Seuro was like and unlike the Citadel of Damris. As were most of the constructions of the Mannish, the keep had been built of hewn stone. The native light-colored rock gleamed white in the summer sun. The keep stood wider at its base than at the top. What windows breeched the walls were really ports—narrow, deep slits from which defenders could fire arrows down on an invading army. Nothing about the keep of Seuro suggested that folk other than warriors had ever lived there.

The keep was no seat of familial power as was the Citadel at Damris, but a hard, cold place for warriors, a place of defense, a place to greet with death any who wanted to challenge the safety of Alain's gateway city.

In the summer light, harsh from the reflection of the sea, whitened by the bite of salt air, the keep of Seuro gleamed like naked bone. It stood at the far tip of the peninsula; from it all roads began, and to it all roads returned.

The city of Seuro existed to support its keep. In history's

dark, far reaches, the keep had sprung up bone-white as though constructed of skulls and not limestone, to defend the seacoast and fertile Raeth from the light-eyed, golden-haired Northmen and the Elvish. This farthest outpost of the Mannish served for countless years as a barracks and stronghold.

In the peaceful times had come women and merchants, shippers and sailors. Of such people are cities made.

Soon there were markets and homes among the barracks and forges and stables, all crowding at the skirts of the keep as bear cubs play at their mother's flanks. And that mother, that hard and deadly she-bear, rose above the commerce and dwellings, huge and white. Seuro became a wealthy merchant city, but she never forgot her origins, she never became soft.

From her barracks came the hardest and most deadly of Mannish warriors, men nurtured on the briny sea air and proud legends of their unconquered fathers. No man was assigned from another province to Seuro's keep. Only the sons of Seuro served there, as though by right. Never in all the long history of the Mannish had this rich warrior city been defeated—until now.

It was to this city, empty and conquered, that Nikia and her friends were brought.

Gulls cried in the bay, sharp and hungry noises at once plaintive and demanding. The city of Seuro rose before Nikia, silent and grim. The day shone clear, and the docks sulked at the edge of the water, empty and forsaken.

There should have been men filling those docks, running here and there, workers preparing to load and unload ships. There should have been noise and singing and the chattering babble of the many folk who inhabited a seaport town like Seuro. Soldiers should have been drilling in the keep, patrolling the docks, their shields and spears glinting in the sunlight, their hard, bright raptor's laughter ringing above the bustle of the city. And there should have been ships.

But only the gulls sang; only the hot, lonely wind stirred.

Under guard, much as they had been the day before, the prisoners saw no ship but their own in the harbor. The ghostly silence was broken only by the gulls' cries and the patient lap-ping of water against the wooden piles of the docks. Nikia stood in the shadow of the cabin structure, shivering with shock and fear.

High summer lay on the city. The breeze, hot and salt-tanged, set the sails of the prison ship slapping and spanking. The three-legged creatures who manned the ship sweated and gleamed all over their filthy scaled bodies.

Filthy and ragged, Nikia and her companions entered the city of Seuro, the richest city of Alain's kingdom. She remembered a passage from one of Garth's letters to her. It was one of the last she had received from him, in the spring, and it told a little about Seuro, a city she had never seen: *This city can feed us for a long siege, and I think we can defend it. It is a rich and lovely city, Nikia, and I hope someday that you will see it in peace and the full bloom of its beauty.*

They had not defended it successfully, and now it lay, silent and lifeless, in the hands of an enemy.

What, they had wondered all those weeks ago, could have accounted for the fall of Seuro? What could have breached the harbor defenses and conquered those strong-hearted folk whose greatest pride was to act as buffer in the North?

Nikia thought about it, in a wild and frightened way, as they were marched through the silent cobbled streets. She looked everywhere, searching for life, for movement, for some sign that there were others in the city besides the prisoners and the guards. She saw nothing.

She heard little but the echoes of the gulls crying behind her and the skittering and startled cries of rats, unseen as they fled the prisoners' approach. What caused those fat, bold marauders, the rats, to run in fear?

She saw no people. The buildings of Seuro, warehouses and shipping offices down by the wharfs, then shops and homes as they progressed through the city, loomed still and empty. No hand or face appeared at any window, no sign of cautious curiosity.

Wind whistled, forlorn and mourning, down the streets and alleys of the city, marking the prisoners' passage and announcing it to no one. Their footfalls, shuffling and nearly sound-

less, echoed dully. Nikia would have had no difficulty believing that they, the prisoners and their guards, were the only
creatures living in Seuro.

When they arrived at the keep, the impression vanished.
The captives were led through corridors, up steps, and down
others. Along their way, they gained, through quick, almost
unconscious impressions, a picture of the keep.

There were guards, many like the three-legged wretches that
escorted them now, ranged at intervals along every corridor. At
the foot of every broad, white stone staircase, sentries stood
watch. These bore little resemblance to the creatures that herd-
ed them through the keep's interior.

Tall, lean, rangy things, their skulls were long and slanted,
giving them the appearance of forever cocking their heads to
listen. Their eyes were mere slits, dark gashes in their gray-
skinned faces. Massive hands bore three spatulate fingers.
These sentries never looked at the prisoners when they passed,
nor did they acknowledge their shorter fellows who conducted
the captives.

Riche breathed in a ragged pant of fear. Nikia heard Dail
snarl something that might have been a prayer or a curse. For
her part, she was reminded of Garth's phrase "witch-spawn."

The legends of men and elves often deal with folk unlike
themselves. Nikia had learned tales in childhood that told of
the doings of dwarves, gobold, and coblynau. As a child, she
had even thought such folk to be real, to have existed, to have
had life in the farthest reaches of ancient times. But she'd never imagined creatures as foul and warped as these real-life ones
she was seeing now.

She went where she was led, trying not to see the torn and
burned tapestries lying in scattered heaps against the high
walls, the shattered furnishings, the piles of filth from which,
horribly, bones protruded. And always she remembered that
this was the place Garth had defended. This was the place he
had lost. Had he died here?

Near the top of the keep, the captives were jerked to a halt.
A guard stepped forward to speak with one of the tall sentries
stationed at the entrance to the only chamber that they could

see on this floor. The creature listened, nodded its tilting head, and disappeared within.

Lizbet was silent beside Nikia. Riche and Dail stood beside Calmis, as close as their chains would permit. None spoke. The guards watched them carefully, their hands lying near the daggers at their belts.

The sentry returned and spoke to the guards, and they moved among the prisoners, freeing Nikia from Riche, then fastening his chain to Calmis's collar so that they were all attached in an awkward circle. Freed from her friends, Nikia felt suddenly alone and more vulnerable than ever.

A hand clamped on her elbow, and Nikia was led forward. She looked back once, met Dail's eyes, and said in a broken whisper, "Take care of them; take care of them."

"Lady—" Dail could say no more. Immediately he was dragged away, and the door, guarded by the sentry, opened.

Nikia followed silently where she was led, gathering the little strength of mind and body that she had left. The anger that had buoyed her on the journey to Seuro was banked and nearly dead. She had nothing but hunger and thirst, fear and pain. The collar around her neck chafed, tearing raw flesh with every move. Her manacles tightened steadily with the swelling of her hands.

Behind her, the thick wooden door closed with a dark, hard sound. The chamber was still, silent, and cool. Square and spacious, it was outfitted as a study or library. A large rectangular table stood at the far side, placed before a hearth now cold and unused in this season. Papers and scrolls lay scattered on the table. On the three remaining walls were places for hundreds more scrolls.

From behind a small door in the west wall, Nikia heard a voice, then another, and sudden, harsh laughter. With a thrill of fear, Nikia recognized the laughter.

The laughter stopped abruptly. The second voice, a woman's, Nikia thought, murmured again, and then the door opened.

Reynarth's cat-green eyes glittered as they met Nikia's. A smile stretched his thin lips as he crossed the chamber. "The

Princess Nikia," he murmured. Nikia smelled wine heavy on his breath. She was reminded suddenly and painfully of her own thirst.

She lifted her chin, for she could not lift her head without tightening the manacles on her wrists. Reynarth lifted his hand and motioned to the guard. "Release her hands, Gal."

Nikia shuddered when the guard's fingers scrabbled on the manacles and her flesh. The rush of blood returning to her swollen hands was both relief and pain. She stepped back from the mage.

Reynarth nodded to the guard. "Leave me."

Alone in the chamber with the mage, Nikia wanted nothing more than to flee, but she held herself still and silent.

"You've changed, lady," Reynarth said, his voice still quiet. His glance took in her filthy hunting leathers, the stained and stinking nightshift, her tangled and dirty hair. "You will, no doubt, wish a bath and a change of clothing."

Nikia wished for them fervently, and good food, and most of all something to drink. Still, she remained silent.

"Come, Nikia, you haven't lost your voice as well as your beauty, have you?"

"I will have nothing from you, Reynarth, until I know why we have been brought here and what is to become of my people."

The mage laughed again, an echo of her winter nightmares. Nikia shuddered but forced herself to remain still.

"Your pardon, Nikia, but you sounded quite regal, and in this setting, and from one who appears nothing more than a gutter slut, it amuses me greatly."

Nikia raised her chin more firmly and gazed pointedly at a place beyond Reynarth's shoulder. She had little dignity left, but what little she possessed, she gathered about her like a tattered cloak. That cloak was as ragged as rotting silk. It could do her no good, but it comforted her a little.

"Well, Nikia," he said finally, "you may be content to stand proud and stinking like a garderobe, but I find it offensive. I'll tell you what's to become of you and your companions, if only to get you to bathe."

He might have had his servants toss her into a tub of water at any time he wished, or simply have her removed from the chamber if she so offended him. But he chose instead to mock Nikia's helplessness, playing the game of prerogative. She hated him, and something of her hatred must have shown on her face, for suddenly his laughter ceased. The light in his eyes damped.

Reynarth's hand lashed out with the suddenness of a striking snake. It struck Nikia's face with a crack, and its force sent her spinning to the floor. She hit the flags hard, bruising her hip and knee, her teeth rattling in her head.

Stunned, unable to move, Nikia lay gasping in surprise. She clenched her teeth against threatening tears.

"Get up." Nikia did not move because she could not.

"Get up!" He clamped his hand on her arm and jerked her roughly to her feet. Fury blazed in his eyes, and hatred twisted his face. Reynarth had never loved her, but until now Nikia had never seen the true degree of his loathing.

"I tire of you, wench. I tire of your foolish pride and childish regality. You are no more than an Elvish bitch, spawned from Elvish dogs! What will happen to you? I could tell you, but instead I'll show you."

Reynarth jerked her hard across the room, kicked open the door of the little chamber beyond, and thrust her inside. Staggering with the force of his thrust, Nikia stumbled a few steps and caught her balance before she fell again.

The chamber was small and square. Fine hangings graced the white stone walls, tapestries and silks. On a dais in the center of the room stood a bed, richly dressed and rumpled with recent use. A woman sat silently in the center of the bed. She was tall, golden-haired, and pale-skinned. Nikia saw the slim tapering of her ears. She was Elvish.

The woman looked up at a word from Reynarth. She turned her face toward them, and Nikia gasped. The woman had the tall, pale beauty of the folk of Dekar's northern borders. Those folk, like the Mannish, were marked by blue eyes. In the Elvish, the color was not so deep as in the Mannish, but still, the silver was touched with blue, making the woman's eyes the color of pale dawn skies. A slackness of expression, a dullness of eye, marred the clean beauty of her face. In repose, that lovely face had no expression at all.

At Reynarth's word, she rose from the bed. When the coverlets fell away, she stood on the dais, splendid in her beauty and naked in the hot summer light.

"This is Rhia," Reynarth said to Nikia. The woman didn't move. She stood like a well-trained beast, awaiting the command to move. Her eyes never met Nikia's, nor did they seek Reynarth's. Instead, they rested someplace in the middle ground between them.

Nikia drew a shivering breath. Who was she? A northern hunter girl, captured in a raid? A forester's daughter, snatched from a border camp? Her face was childlike, her body slim, tall, and womanly. Nikia was surprised by a sudden stab of pity for the woman whose vacant eyes held nothing but shadows and night.

"Aye"—Reynarth's voice was a satisfied growl—"she is lovely. She'll stay here with me, for a time at least. And when I no longer find her entertaining, she'll fill a place somewhere else."

Again Nikia shivered, her mind skipping, horrified, around the borders of her imagination, trying not to see into that land of terror to the places that Rhia might go. She swallowed and looked back at the woman.

Rhia stood straight and lovely in a shaft of sunlight. Suddenly Nikia realized that, although Rhia's mouth hung slightly open and although she had moved on Reynarth's command, Rhia didn't breathe!

That knowledge went through her like a cold shock. Nikia stared harder, her gaze shifting from those shadowy eyes to the creamy white breasts that didn't rise, even slightly, with the movement of life.

"Ah, you've noticed. But surely you know that the dead don't breathe? Rhia, come."

Rhia stepped down from the dais and crossed the room with graceful, measured steps until she came to stand before the mage.

Reynarth touched Rhia's silky white shoulder. His fingers traced a path down her arm, caressing and slow, until they reached her hand. This he took in his own and raised it slowly, until Rhia's fingers were near Nikia's face.

Rhia's fingers touched Nikia's cheek, feeling like the cool that drifts out of subterranean chambers. When Reynarth took his hand away, the arm fell with a sudden, muscleless drop to her side.

Moaning, Nikia stepped back, and stepped back again until her shoulders dug into the stone wall of the chamber.

Rhia was dead, and yet she moved. She walked and she stood, and those shadow-filled eyes lifted and dropped, and looked and saw. But she was dead!

"Rhia," Reynarth said, his voice sounding muffled and far away to Nikia. "Give Nikia a bath."

"No," Nikia gasped. "No! Don't let her touch me again!"

Reynarth laughed, a harsh, pitiless sound. "Oh, yes, Rhia," he said, ignoring Nikia's plea. "Give this filthy little princess a bath. I can't stand the stink of her any longer."

Nikia pressed her back to the wall, breathing in hard, painful gasps. Rhia moved toward her, reaching out her cold, dead hand to touch Nikia's.

Nikia screamed, then dropped to her knees, her back still against the white stone wall, her hands before her face, her fingers tangling in the matted nest of her hair. She screamed, and winding in and out, through the throat-tearing sound of her horror, she heard Reynarth's laughter bellowing.

CHAPTER 23

Reynarth nodded to the guard who stood at the entrance to the cell. "Open the door."

The door swung wide on screaming hinges, and the mage entered the cell. He watched Garth carefully. "Your brother is dead."

Garth raised his head and narrowed his eyes. "You lie."

"No, he's dead, all right. He has been for some time. Haven't you wondered why your father's armies haven't been able to win back Seuro?"

Garth had wondered. He had hoped, and at last he had despaired. The thought that Fenyan might be dead haunted his sleep. It was the one thing that might account for the fact that there had, lately, been no battles outside the city's southern walls. He had been able to hear those battles from his prison cell. He had been able to hear the clash of armies, the thunder of war, each time Fenyan's forces came against the city.

And yet, in the last seven days, he'd heard no such sounds. The keep, or at least its dungeons, had settled down to a grim

parody of peace. In his dark cell at night, listening to the constant trickle of dampness edging down the walls, and huddling
in the fouled straw that was his bedding, Garth had wondered
what had become of his brother's army.

But he would admit none of this to Reynarth. "You lie."

"You are stubborn, Garth."

"Why should it matter whether I believe you or not?"

Reynarth smiled slowly. "I don't care whether you believe or
disbelieve me. What you believe doesn't change the truth."
He shrugged. "I just thought you'd like to know."

Garth drew a long, slow breath, steadied his thoughts, and
closed his eyes. He refused to deal with the thought of his
brother's death here before this traitor. "If it doesn't matter,"
he said, his words slow and deliberate, "then you won't mind
if I don't believe you."

"As you wish." Reynarth lifted his hand to the neck of his
robes. Casually, as though toying with an ornament there, he
smiled. "But there is something that I know you will believe.
Someone you know has come to Seuro."

He let his hand fall away from the thing at his neck. The
Ruby of Guyaire dropped to the length of its silver chain,
blood red and glowing against the dark background of his
robe. "Surely you recognize this little bauble."

"The Ruby—" The words came from his lips in a moan, a
soft sound of despair. "The Ruby of Guyaire."

"Beautiful, isn't it?"

"How did you come by it?"

But Garth knew how. He knew that the ruby was never far
from Nikia. He knew that it would not be here unless his wife
had been taken with it. Or might it have? Hope leaped, a small
flame in his heart. Couldn't Reynarth have stolen it?

"Thief!" He spat the accusation.

Again Reynarth smiled. "No, not at all. Well," he said, his
smile becoming self-deprecating, "perhaps, in your eyes. But I
assure you that I came by the ruby directly from the hands of
your wife."

"Where—where is she?" Garth's mind was awash with fear,
flashing him quick and violent pictures, casting every horror

vividly before him. He jerked his hands against his manacles, ignoring the pain of his raw wrists. "If she is harmed, I swear she'll be avenged!"

Reynarth's lips twisted in a scornful smile. "By you? Hardly, my young prince."

"If not by me, then by her father, traitor. And by mine."

"I'm not worried about the vengeance of two old men. But rest easy. She is here and even now being made comfortable."

"Why?"

"Oh, she'll have her uses." Reynarth lifted his hand to the ruby again and rubbed his thumb over the red facets of the jewel. "Which do you think is the more valuable, Garth, the ruby or the princess?"

Reynarth nodded to the guard, turned quickly, and left Garth alone in the dark with the dull thud of the closing cell door.

"Nikia!" Garth whispered. He closed his eyes and tried to control the fear and despair that welled in his heart. Nikia! Here in the keep? But where? And how?

Garth leaned his head against the damp stone wall of his cell and took a long, steadying breath. Was the mage lying? Garth didn't think that he was. How else could he have come by the ruby?

For a moment, he gave credence to the idea that Reynarth had stolen the ruby. But that seemed a dull and flat answer. Why steal it? Aside from its value as a precious jewel and its value as a symbol, why steal it?

It didn't matter why the mage had the ruby now. What mattered was that he had, in his traitor's keep, the heirs of both kingdoms.

But, no. Not Alain's heir. There was Fenyan's son. Garth laughed bitterly at that thought. Aye, and a fine heir that babe will make. Of what use is a child in the nursery? At best a rallying point, a symbol. Should anything happen to Alain, the kingdom would be lost. Embattled, it could not survive the reign of an infant king and a council that would surely split into factions.

Who would act as regent? By right, it was his place to hold

the regency for the babe. Yet he knew that there could not be a man in the whole kingdom who believed that he was still alive. What did that leave but a struggle for the regency and a war lost, if it was not lost even now?

The rough edges of the stone wall cut into the back of his head, sending small darts of pain down his neck. Garth didn't know for certain that the war was lost. As long as his father and Dekar remained safe in the South, there was still a chance.

Fear tightened his heart again. How could Nikia have been taken from the Citadel under the very hand of his father? How could she have been captured? Did this mean that the Citadel had come under attack? But that way lay the dangerous thought that his father was dead, that the Citadel had not survived an attack.

"Ah, gods!" he cried, his voice ragged. Trapped within the labyrinth of fear that Reynarth had created for him, Garth clenched his hands into pitiless fists, his nails grinding blood from his palms.

* * * * *

Reynarth was gone. There was only Rhia, standing where she had been when he left her, waiting with unearthly patience. She didn't look toward Nikia, didn't bend to offer comfort, but only waited with lifeless, eternal patience.

When Nikia moved, Rhia reached down her hand, closed it over Nikia's wrist and lifted her to her feet. "Come," Rhia said, her voice as thin as a sound heard from another room.

Her flesh crawling where Rhia touched her, Nikia rose to her feet, standing unsteadily against the wall. "Let go," she whispered. "Don't touch me."

Rhia's hand dropped. She stood, waiting. "Make my bath," Nikia said dully.

And Rhia, naked still, padded across the floor to a curtained recess. When she had drawn the curtains aside, she turned back to Nikia. "The water will be brought," she said and returned to the bed, taking up the place she had occupied when Nikia first entered the chamber.

In moments, the water, steaming buckets of it, were

brought by the twisted, three-legged things that Nikia had encountered on the prison ship.

These, however, wore livery of black and silver. Three of them went back and forth with the buckets. Each, as it passed, paused with its burden of water to balance on its three legs and stare, eyes wide and fanged mouths agape, at the naked woman on the bed. They rolled their eyes, made wet, guttural sounds in their throats, and laughed as they passed.

Pity moved Nikia's heart for the poor creature who saw these looks and could not even cover herself without command. Looking about her, Nikia found a robe. She snatched it up and tossed it to Rhia.

The robe lay where it fell, half covering her legs. Rhia didn't move, not even to look at Nikia.

"Rhia?" The Darkling looked around then, bringing her head up and turning her cold, lovely face to Nikia's.

"Rhia, cover yourself. Put on the robe."

Rhia obeyed, slipping her arms into the sleeves of rich silk, rising on her knees to pull it around her. Then she sat back, cross-legged, in the center of the bed, awaiting another command.

"Rhia," Nikia said again, testing her voice and her ability to command her, "find me soap."

Her eyes still dark, Rhia rose, fetched the soap, and returned to Nikia. The bath was hot, and as Nikia stepped into it, the thought of her companions came back to her. She considered Reynarth's words when she had asked what was to become of them. He had not answered but only shown her Rhia. Was that the answer? Would Reynarth and his fiends have done to them what had been done to Rhia? Would she next see them lifeless but somehow animate? Would she find them motionless until commanded, with no life, no thought, no soul left for Nikia to recognize?

And what about her? Nikia understood Reynarth's intent clearly: She was to replace Rhia in the mage's bed.

Nikia moaned at the thought and slid deeper into the tub of hot water. Her mind skittered frantically off on tangents, but it always returned to one overriding question, as though it were a solution: How could she change her fate?

It was a hard thought, coming from no place in her mind that she recognized. It was the kind of thought she had never entertained before. She had spoken with Dail about the reason for their capture. Yet never during the voyage in the prison ship, nor during this whole day, had Nikia once thought that she might affect the loss that the Two Kingdoms had suffered when the ruby had been taken.

Now, clean and feeling the aches in her body ease, Nikia dared to wonder if she could reverse that loss.

Shivering despite the warmth of the day, she rose, and the water sloughed off her body in little rills. "Rhia."

The Darkling looked up from her place on the bed.

"Bring me clothing."

Again Rhia moved about the room from cupboard to cupboard until she had collected a full set of clothing. She brought Nikia small clothes of the finest linen, a light blue summer gown of patterned cotton. The slippers she found were too small. Nikia put them aside.

As she dressed, Nikia could not help but see, still white and glaring, the scars of frost burn on her neck and arms and breasts where Carah's hand had touched her. Would they be with her always? she wondered. There were other cuts, on her neck and wrists, but these looked as if they would heal with care and time. There were bruises uncounted.

Still, clean and dressed, Nikia felt stronger. She didn't know what she would do, or could do, prisoner that she was. She didn't know what was planned for her, beyond Reynarth's threat. Neither did she know what the mage had done with her companions. But it was certain that the ruby was by now in his hands, and it was certain that he knew, or suspected, its power. That power could wreak a havoc on the Two Kingdoms that might never be repaired.

Yet, if I am to die, and I am sure that he will not keep me longer than it takes to have his pleasure and tire of it, then I will die trying to regain the ruby.

* * * * *

In the fading light of evening, colored shadows spilled from the Ruby of Guyaire onto the yellowing parchment. Scattered around the parchment, covering nearly every bit of the surface of the long table, lay other scrolls, some rolling back into their original form, others held open by whatever object had come most quickly to Reynarth's hand.

Yet none of these scrolls, none of the parchments, dry and aged so that they rustled and crackled beneath the mage's hand, yielded what he most sought. There was no real clue to the ruby's use, no word or spell to be found among these ancient writings that would unlock the jewel's power.

Squeezing his eyes closed against the scene of his failed search, Reynarth cursed softly. Time was passing, time that had become empty of promise. He opened his eyes again, his attention drawn back to the reflection of the jewel's beauty on the parchments. There must be an answer!

He lifted his eyes to the ruby itself, surrendering to the insistent call of its power. Oh, aye, he realized bitterly, the power is there. He felt it, strong and pulsing within the heart of the jewel. His own heart rose to the call it exercised, heard the soft martial song. But this power lay outside his reach. Reynarth cursed again.

There were clues, of a sort. He had found them through painstaking searches among the old scrolls. He knew from his studies that the ruby was indeed what he had hoped it would be. It was a power stone, a gathering place for the strength of the one who wielded it, and it was even more, for it possessed a power of its own. Captured by its scintillating beauty, the mage let his mind touch the edges of the ruby's magic.

Scarlet light filled his eyes, touched his mind, and danced around the borders of his soul. It was the kind of power stone that would require the wielder's total surrender. There must be no self brought to the use of the stone, only need, only courage, and above all, only the ability to survive the wild strength that the Ruby of Guyaire would impart.

He possessed the need, and he would find the courage. Could he survive the strength of the ruby's power? He didn't know, for he didn't have the key to obtain it. He was a rat trapped in a scarlet maze, scurrying, twitching, striving to find entrance to a place of power. But there was no key and there was no door; there were only impassable scarlet walls.

And there was something else. Reynarth stirred, but he didn't take his mind away from the ruby. Somewhere within the sweet song of power that the ruby was humming in his brain was another song, a more familiar one, crooned by a well-known voice. It was the voice of his Dark Mistress, singing in deep counterpoint to the ruby's martial song.

"Mistress?" He spoke the word out loud, in a soft, hoarse whisper.

Mage.

"Through the ruby?"

Aye, though it is not easy, nor is it comfortable. Break away.

Break away? he thought. But that wasn't easy, nor was it comfortable. There was an alluring attraction to the deep-breathed song of the ruby's power—the sound of booted feet marching, the thunder of armies moving, the rumbling progress of power.

Break away! Now!

With a wrenching jerk, Reynarth broke the spell of the ruby's song. His mind aching, his vision skewing wildly, he fell back against the arm of his chair, gasping once, and shut his eyes against the red pain throbbing behind them, turning sightless darkness to scarlet agony.

Almost of its own accord, his hand moved across the parchment-scattered table until his fingers touched the base of the clear globe which had been used to hold down the edge of a very old, crumbling scroll. The clarity of the globe aided the return of lucidity.

Reynarth drew a long, hard breath, but that lucidity was short-lived, battered down by a numbing rush of emotion, a violent vortex filled with need and desire. Mist engulfed the globe.

So you play. Yvanda's words were heavy with scorn. *So you peer and poke and play with this power stone? What have you learned?*

Reynarth's lips twisted in a bitter smile of self-recrimination. "Only that the ruby is a way, mistress, which leads to no door." He heard the despair in his own words and shivered. "But, mistress, I have found something."

And that is?

"It's an old jewel, mistress, and not of Elvish making."

How came you by this knowledge?

"By my readings . . . by my searching here among the scrolls and parchments. This keep is the oldest among the Mannish, and it holds a great library of scrolls. Some of the oldest of these touch on the first settlings of the Mannish and Elvish folk in this land. The ruby, I think, is neither of Mannish nor Elvish make. It was crafted by an older race."

A Dwarven stone.

Reynarth started. He had never heard wonder in her voice before.

A Dwarven stone! Aye, it would fit. There was power, of a kind, in the old Dwarvish folk. Aye, it would fit.

"Do you know the way of these ancients, mistress?"

Her silence spoke of cool consideration. When she spoke, Reynarth heard her smile. *Anything can be learned. What says your Elvish princess?*

"Little enough yet, mistress."

She spent some time in her father's hall—time enough for her to tell him of her find. How closely have you questioned her, mage?

"That remains to be done."

See that it is done subtly. She may hold knowledge that has yet no meaning to her. She may hold keys to puzzles she does not yet know exist.

"As you say, mistress." Confidence returned, lightening the fear of failure that had up to now darkened the mage's mind. If Nikia held answers, he held the keys that would unlock her cooperation. Those keys languished even now in the dungeons far below the keep.

Time grows short, mage. I grow impatient, as does another. The wars go well enough, but I—we—would have this jewel to cement our gains.

The threat implicit in her words clouded Reynarth's mind.

He shivered and swallowed back his fear. "Aye, mistress. There must be a key."

I trust that you will find it, mage. Her words were cool, as hard as the bleached stone girding the keep of Seuro, harder than loss.

Reynarth drew a long, shuddering breath to speak. Even as he did, Yvanda was gone, the globe clear and unreflecting. Reynarth shivered at the touch of cold sweat tracing down his ribs.

With the recession of fear, the mage began to finely tune his plan to extract the information he needed so desperately from Nikia. There were needs working within him which would make the cruelty of the plan a pleasure for him, a balm for the wounds inflicted by fear. He sat back in his chair and steadied his breathing.

* * * * *

Night claimed the city of Seuro and covered the keep with its black wings. Reynarth rose, and with a careless gesture, he lighted candles about the room, bringing forth the little flames that fed on the wax and wick.

Returning to the table, he took the globe in his hands, closed his eyes to concentrate, and caressed the globe with easy, regular strokes. Behind his closed eyes, he knew that the ruby was still where he had left it, glowing softly and calling to him with its insistent power song. He made a determined effort to banish the thought of the jewel.

After much concentration, he succeeded. In its place, he called up another picture, working with easy skill until he had it clearly in his mind. Carefully, with the relish of an artist bringing forth a picture from stark canvas, he painted the nightmare that would be the first part of his work for that night.

* * * * *

Wolves howled songs of bloody defiance around the edges of Garth's sleep. Mist, gray and damp, chilled the peace of dreamlessness and made his mind shiver. He moaned and stirred, trying to move away from the thing that had invaded sleep. Insidious fingers of nightmare crept into his soul, twisting things that were once beautiful.

Through the mist and howling, he saw a face, fair and lovely, framed by the beauty of silver hair touched gently with the moon's light as it lay on a familiar pillow.

Nikia! In his sleep, Garth took a long breath. Hope and love stirred in him. "Nikia!" He cried her name in his dream, and his lips formed it, breathing her name into the foul silence of the dungeon's night.

She stirred, his dream-wife, and moved her arm from beneath her body. Then she turned her face, so that it was bathed fully in the moonlight.

"Ah, love!" he whispered in his dream. "Nikia!"

Her silver hair fell, a curtain now, across her face, hiding it from his view.

"Nikia?" She stirred again, awake, and rose on one elbow. But for the gossamer length of her hair, she was naked. The smooth gleaming curtain of her hair flowed over her shoulder, running like a moon-silvered river past her breasts, ending at the swell of her hip.

"Nikia!" As though responding to his voice, she turned. Her eyes lighted with welcome, and yet Garth knew with sudden, cold certainty that she wasn't seeing him, wasn't welcoming him.

There was a harlot's gleam in her eyes. His wife's lips parted, moist and deep red in the moonlight. Wanton laughter filled Garth's dream. He had heard her laugh as she had in their love-play, but this was something different. This was not the pleased laughter of a woman who found joy in receiving and giving, but instead the laughter of demand, of lust ungentled by love.

She stood beside the bed in the chamber that they had shared, arms wide, tossing her head so that the silvery hair fell away from the beauty of her body.

"What payment?" she asked, her voice harsh with anticipation. "Show me your fee, for I have shown you your purchase."

A hand moved into Garth's field of vision, and he moaned

aloud, the sound dying in the forlorn, empty night. It was a long, gnarled hand, with fingers spatulate and misshapen. On its palm rested a small trinket of shoddy make, a wretched bauble worth nothing for its craftsmanship and less for the sum of its parts.

"It is enough for now," Nikia said, laughing. "Be quick."

But it was not quick. Garth watched, struggling to escape the dream, as his wife raised her graceful white arms in the moonlight to embrace her hideous lover, one of the guards who kept watch in the dungeons. He watched in disgust as the creature's hands touched her breasts, groaned aloud as the sweet, clean-limbed Elvish body that he loved so well entwined with the rough, unhuman guard. She sported and laughed in the bed they had shared as husband and wife, serving the guard's needs in a manner that was horrible to watch.

And when she was done, she cast the creature from her bed, laughing and tossing aside the little trinket that she had claimed as her harlot's pay. "Where are the others?" Her voice was lazy and soft now.

The sated guard shook its long, slanted head. For the first time, Garth heard its voice, low and rough, speaking in a guttural language he should not have understood but did.

"There are no others but one. He is here."

Reynarth stood at the foot of the bed, his face hidden in the depths of his robe's cowl. As Garth watched, numb with horror, his wife opened her arms, climbed to her knees, and welcomed the traitor to her bed.

Their voices mingled in mystic chanting; lights of magic, argent and golden, filled the room. Garth's dream's vision skewed. He caught his breath, stunned by the violent change in perception as he saw the scene in the chamber through eyes other than his own. He heard a voice laughing, crying encouragement, and realized that it was through the guard's eyes, still present in the chamber, that he saw his wife and the mage.

Fire coursed through veins that were his and not his. A body, his own and yet not, responded to the scene in the bed. Sweat sheened him now, and anticipation caused him to fill with a lust that must have its release or burn him from within.

Wanton cries filled the bedchamber, filled Garth's dreaming mind. Livid light exploded behind his eyes. He woke, weeping to find a shameful evidence of his participation in the dream.

He screamed once, a cry of terror and denial, and listened numbly to the echoes his scream awakened among the other, unseen captives who shared his dungeon.

He dared sleep no more that night. Still, it hardly mattered. Day and night, waking or asleep, images of his wife's vile treachery haunted his mind and poisoned his heart.

Madness crept into his soul, but he did not recognize it when it came.

CHAPTER 24

The wind moaned through the winding passages of the cavern like a tortured thing, mingling with the howl of creatures damned. Yvanda drew closer to the central chamber.

She drew a long, testing breath, filling her lungs with the scent of sea and brimstone. Light painted crimson shadows on the roughly hewn walls of the cave. Beneath her feet, hard and damp through her light slippers, she felt the downward slope of the floor. These last passages, leading from the sea gate into the deep heart of Souless, were chill and moist. She shivered, not from the chill but from the nearness of a power she still respected.

The red-stained walls grew broader, farther apart. The ceiling, low before, rose, sweeping high over her head to form the final arch of entrance to the sea cave. Shadows darkened from red to black. Yvanda paused at the entryway.

The sea cavern was larger than any hall in the palace above. Its walls and ceiling, hewn by time and the sea, swept upward, their peaks hidden in shadow. In the three walls of the cavern yawned three smaller arches. These led into the deeper warrens beneath the palace of Souless. From the east wall, one accessed the dungeons. To the west, the breeding dens lay, foul with the stenches and wretched cries of the Sorcerer's captives. Here, through the agencies of her magic, those captured in battle, the luckless creatures swept up in the bloody nets of war, were mated, body and spirit, with the dead. In this place, the hideous minions of the Sorcerer's army, twisted bodies housing blighted souls, were born.

The arch in the northern wall was gated with steel. None who passed that way came back alive. None, she thought, but the Sorcerer.

"My lord?"

A flame-rimmed pit dominated the sea cavern. Silhouetted dark against the bloody light of his magic, the Sorcerer paused and lifted his head. His eyes this day matched the flare of his sorcery. "I have been waiting."

Impatience tightened his voice. Yvanda tried to assuage it at once. "I know that, my lord, and I am sorry to have caused a delay, but I trust the news I bring will be counted worth it."

He gestured absently for her to enter and turned his attention back to the pit. Yvanda took her place beside her master.

Heat rushed up from the blood-colored gulf as liquid fire boiled and gurgled in its depths. The pit itself was the length of several tall men. Flames, like fire ghosts, danced along its rim as though they possessed life of their own. Scarlet light writhed out from the confines of the abyss and played across their feet, licking upward to change the colors of their garments to a bloody hue.

"How goes the campaign, my lord?"

The Sorcerer laughed deep in this throat, a deadly, satisfied sound. His magic fire limned his cold, expressionless face. As handsome as a deadly raptor, as cold as a snake, never through all the ages had he changed. Lifting his arm, he extended it over the pit, careless of the flames leaping suddenly higher from the edge. "See?"

Yvanda heard the soft breath he took, listened to the whispered words of magic that he spoke. They were alluring words,

words that would create pictures of what was passing in the south. The seeing globes had been fired from this pit. Here they were infused with their powerful far-seeing ability. This, though, was but a small part of the power that surged from the pit.

The Sorcerer's soft words dwindled, faded, trailed away. The liquid fire of the pit darkened, stilled. Steaming clouds rose up from the depths of the abyss, blinding sight for a trembling moment.

When she could see again, Yvanda made a small sound of approval and delight. "Wonderful!"

"The act or the sight?"

She took a small step forward, coming as close to the edge of the pit as she dared. Before her, as before a queen who stands on her highest battlement, stretched the Two Kingdoms. The circumference of the pit could not possibly, in nature, have held all that she saw. But aided by the Sorcerer's expanding magic, it did.

The Citadel rose at the far edge of the pit. The A'Damran flowed across a countryside rich and green with summer's touch to join the River Altha at the Ford of Tillane. The Diamond Chain, gleaming, interlocked lakes, and the Landbound Sea lay like jewels on the living map. To the east, the Kevarth Mountains trickled up from the south, broadening as they crept north and sprawling up against the Strait of Carnach. Dekar's forests splashed darkly against the edge of the glittering sea.

To the north and west, perched on the shores of the sea, with the despoiled farmlands at its southern skirt, lay the keep of Seuro and its silent, damned city.

"Wonderful," she whispered. "And see, my lord, how the keep of Seuro acts as our gate?"

"Aye, a gate it is." He lifted his arm again and moved his hand across the image of the Two Kingdoms. Steam rose, took solid form, and settled on the landscape at her feet.

The lands within the pit twisted. Battles raged, small and dim. As though from a great distance, Yvanda heard the sounds of killing and death, the sounds of victory. The armies of the defenders fell, and falling, gave up more and more of the southern territory to the invaders who poured out from the keep of Seuro. To the west and north, fierce battles were waged in the mountains. And here Yvanda saw the Elvish armies, companies of hunters and warriors, go down in defeat against the living and the undead, the Sorcerer's forces.

She laughed, and hers was a full and complacent amusement. "Lovely to see, my lord, lovely. But still, it is a vast land to hold."

"It will be held easily enough once it is won."

"Easier, perhaps, than you think, my lord. And it can be won more quickly than this."

He looked up sharply then and turned away from the map which so engrossed him. "How, then?"

"The ruby."

His eyes narrowed, but it was not with the expression of interest she had looked for. "You have found its key?"

"Not yet, my lord, but it is near at hand."

"Aye, so you say, and so you have said often before."

"It is, I assure you. It is in the mage's hand, and the key must come soon enough."

"To his hand?"

Yvanda shrugged. "It matters not whether it comes to his hand. He will not have the power to use it when it does." She shook her head. "He is a rustic, a mere dabbler in magic from the southlands. He has neither the courage nor the skill to use what he learns."

"And so you let him do your searching for you?"

"Of course."

"What do you know of it so far?"

"That it is a Dwarven stone, made by the olden people."

"A Dwarven stone." He shrugged away that information. "And what use is that knowledge? There are none of the Dwarven race alive to tell its secrets."

"The mage is confident that the Elvish princess has the knowledge of its use."

"Pah! Is he? And if she had this knowledge, why then hasn't she used it before now?" He turned back to his living map, watching with a cruel smile as Elvish warriors fell before his own armies. "She would have used it long before this had she the knowledge."

"So it would seem. But still, he thinks she hides this knowledge. And would not you or I, my lord, if such a weapon had fallen into enemy hands? If she has the knowledge, he will get it from her, and the ruby will be ours."

"My armies are sweeping the puny defenders before them. In the space of a month, they will have forced their enemies into the sea. This ruby, this talisman, will do little, I think, that my own sorcery is not accomplishing."

"But, my lord—" She had not expected this. She had hoped instead for praise and his satisfaction. Yvanda thought quickly, recovered her poise, and shrugged. "But, my lord," she repeated, taking care to make her voice softer, more humble, "this ruby will hold in thrall all that you have won. I do not think any resistance can survive the will of the ruby."

"Aye, it may be so. But I will not wait for the riddle of an ancient legend to be solved. The war goes well enough, but it is not won yet. You have been too much away from your duties here. The dens are empty, and the last of our warriors will soon go forth. More must be bred if we are to hold the land that we have taken.

"It is enough! You have spent too much of your attention on this quest that would be better attempted when leisure is won. I want you here, Yvanda, to do the work that you do best. Forget this ruby now and spend your skills in better endeavors."

"But—"

"I command it!"

There was no way to gainsay the command. There was no way to change the Sorcerer's thinking now. Yvanda lowered her eyes and turned her face away. "Aye, my lord," she said softly.

In her heart, laid out before her as clearly as the pit showed the war's campaign, Yvanda saw his sorcery withering before her might, the Ruby of Guyaire resting in crimson glory on her breast, spilling its bloody light across the Two Kingdoms. She spoke no word of this thought but turned from him.

"Please excuse me, my lord, and I will attend to the tasks that you have said I have forgotten."

He watched her leave the pit, his eyes narrow and gauging. He knew, as he saw her enter the arch in the western wall, that she would bear watching once the key to the ruby's power was unlocked.

* * * * *

Rhia left Reynarth's bedchamber, at the command of a Darkling guard, about the time the sun cast its setting light across the room. Alone in the chamber with the growing night, listening to the guards in the corridor, Nikia took up a seat at the window and watched the silent, empty streets far below.

The cooler breezes of the night wandered though streets which were bereft of activity. Once she saw the changing of the guard far below. These were the only things moving, and they, she thought bitterly, imparted no life to the starkly darkening scene below her window.

As she watched and waited, Nikia tested her hope that she might be able to regain the ruby. The Elvish said that the gods will not grant the tools to create unless they are prepared to also give the opportunity.

She smiled bitterly. And what tools have I? I have but little hope and much need.

Behind her, the door opened, its ancient hinges creaking protest in the darkness. "You are summoned." The Darkling's voice was like the crack of ice in a frozen river.

Nikia rose slowly to her feet and breathed deeply to still the trembling in her knees. She crossed the room and passed the guard, feeling the chill of his touch as she left the room.

* * * * *

Reynarth was dressed coolly, as the warm night dictated. The white stone walls of the keep trapped and held the day's heat. The mage wore only a loose, belted robe of black that reached to his knees.

Nikia thought again that he was not, feature for feature, an ugly man. Yet she would ever remember him as hideous.

She stood silently for many moments before Reynarth finally chose to look up. When he did, she could only stand and stare: he wore on his breast, depending from its perfect silver chain, the Ruby of Guyaire.

It was a mark of his scorn that Reynarth had not ordered Nikia chained. She raised her hands now and clenched her fists so tight that her nails bit into her palms. "You are an obscenity, Reynarth!"

He smiled as one would over the actions of a rude child of whom one was marginally fond. "Come, Nikia, you must learn to accept what can't be changed." He raised his hand to the ruby, cupping it in his palm, and lifted it as though offering it for appraisal. "Lovely, isn't it?"

Nikia remained still and met his eyes coldly.

"Come here." She went reluctantly, seeing no gain in refusing. She stood before the table, close enough to reach out and snatch the ruby from him. A dagger lay on the table, holding down a corner of a parchment. The blade was closer to Reynarth's hand than to hers.

"Do you know what this is?" He nodded toward the parchment. Nikia looked down at it and saw that it was a map. Even from where she stood, she saw that it depicted the Two Kingdoms. There was no key, but she could readily see that it illustrated the enemy's campaigns. Nikia had been away from news of the war for too long not to try to study the map in earnest. What she saw left her cold.

Her eyes went first to the city of Seuro. It and much of its surrounding lands were shaded in red. The red, a sign of the Sorcerer's dominance, extended south for many miles, reaching nearly to Raeth.

Raeth . . . the province of Gweneth's father. Nikia's heart squeezed with pain, sharp and hard. She remembered Gweneth and her kindness, and the friendship that had sprung up between them. So much had happened since those days when Gweneth's willing friendship had eased the loneliness of a child thrust suddenly into a world of strangers. Ah, Gweneth! See what has become of us now! You are gone and I am lost. . . .

"Reynarth, you killed Gweneth, didn't you?"

Green light flickered in the mage's eyes. "I think you could say that I did."

"Why? Why have you betrayed your own people?"

The green light flared, and Reynarth's face twisted into lines of grief and sorrow, then settled into the stone of anger. "Because they've betrayed me, witch! There was a girl, a child still . . . but she would have grown to be my wife. She was killed by Elvish soldiers. Alain calls you allies now, but I know better."

Nikia heard his pain, saw it in the cold light gleaming in his eyes. She looked away from his eyes, away from the pain. She couldn't afford to see his grief as anything but an explanation of his actions. She wouldn't let herself think about anything but the present danger. She turned her attention back to the map.

The poisonous red of the Sorcerer's hand extended east and west, full to each coastline. He had taken much of Alain's kingdom under his sway, and nearly a third of her father's lands. Nikia needed no further explanation to know that the war was going badly for the Two Kingdoms. Slowly she raised her eyes to meet the mage's once again. She tried not to let any feeling show on her face, but she knew at once she had not succeeded.

Reynarth's smile was catlike. He'd recovered the mask of smooth hatred. "The war goes well, as you see."

Nikia did not reply.

"It will be ended soon enough, Nikia," he murmured, cupping the ruby in his palm again. His thumb traced the perfect facets with absent possession. "And you have provided the weapon."

There was something in his eyes, in his tone, which showed Nikia that, while she may have provided the weapon, he lacked the knowledge to use it yet. His steady regard hinted at questions. Did Nikia know how to use the ruby? Clearly he didn't.

Nikia thought quickly. Was this the tool the gods would provide, and the opportunity as well? Could she convince Reynarth that she did indeed know how to use the ruby?

When she spoke, it was lightly, feigning a confidence that she did not feel. "You surprise me, Reynarth."

His eyes were alert and sharp.

"Indeed," Nikia continued. "You have this weapon, and you choose to wear it on a chain as though it were the merest trinket."

"It will be used when the time is right."

Nikia's words came fast on her rapid thought. "I am sure that you have the right folk at hand to ignite its power." She spoke nonsense, bait in a tenuous trap.

"Aye," he said, lying, "I do."

"And your master?"

This was a stroke. Reynarth's green eyes flinched slightly. He recovered quickly, however, and masked the fear with a bland expression. "What can you know of my master?"

"Nothing, of course. His presence has been hinted at, and his actions have been suspected from the beginning, of course. But I don't know anything about him. Nor," she added softly, "do I know much of the one they call the Dark Lady. Do you?"

"I have nothing to do with her," he said quickly.

"Ah, then you're wise. They say the Sorcerer is jealous of his power, Reynarth."

Fear flickered once more in the mage's eyes. He let the ruby drop from his hand, and it fell, swinging on its silver chain, catching the light, sending bloody reflections across the map.

Nikia watched the slow dance of scarlet shadow across the map of the Two Kingdoms, shading all the lands for which blood was even now being spilled. It was a mesmerizing dance, a fascinating play.

She heard a distant and heartless song that had no words but instead the sound of the clash of battle, of warriors marching. The ruby promised bolder anthems than this for the one who could turn the jewel to his own use. Or to hers.

Nikia lifted her head with a great effort and put aside all thought of the ruby's dangerous promise. "What do you summon me for, Reynarth? Surely not to discuss your war campaigns."

"No," he said, all fear gone from his eyes. "No, not for that. You know, I think, the reason why you have been summoned."

Ah, gods! Everything she had thought to be a gain since entering the library fled from her. Everything that she had thought to use as strength failed her. She knew very well, now, why she had been summoned.

The mage's eyes reminded Nikia more strongly than ever of a stalking cat. "You won't be joining your friends tonight." Reynarth moved his hand, the one that had fondled the ruby, in dismissal.

"Go back within, Nikia, and I will join you." His voice was calm, his expression mild. There was nothing in him that admitted doubt. He knew that there was little Nikia could do to resist.

And whispering in her mind came memories of those who depended on her, of her friends, who lay imprisoned below in Reynarth's dungeons, chained in filthy cells and unable to help themselves. Nevertheless, what Reynarth now intended gave, if only faintly, the hope of some freedom for Nikia.

He'd watch her constantly, but no chains yet bound her. The ruby, that precious treasure which wore now its ancient guise of weapon, would be close at hand as long as she remained here.

It was that hope which condemned her now. Nikia realized that she had been wrong, only a short time ago, when she thought that her hands were not bound. Steel did not hold them. They were chained now by hope.

Trembling, Nikia left the chamber.

* * * * *

There were no songs in Dail's heart now. The tunes that had always played comfortingly in the back of his mind were gone, driven out by fear. He'd been a day and a night in this place, and fear for Nikia grew with each hour's passing. He shifted his back against the damp stone and pulled again at the thick chain that held him to the wall.

"It's useless, Dail. Why waste your strength?" Calmis's voice was dull and heavy in the darkness.

"What should I save it for, my friend?" Dail tugged again

steadily, yanking close to the place where the chain was fastened to the broad iron ring mortared into the dungeon wall. He heard, with a rising of hope, the soft sound of ancient mortar crumbling, the grating of stone and iron. "I think this ring is coming loose." Dail tugged again, and again he felt the soft drift of dried mortar on his wrist. "Can you help me?"

Calmis rose, shuffling in the foul bedding straw, taking the few steps that his own chain would permit. They did not bring him near enough to help. "This is as far as I can go." Dail's chain clanked. "Dail! Keep it quiet. The guard will hear you!"

Dail laughed bitterly. "And what if he does? He won't know this from the sounds of all the others."

Calmis realized that the bard was right. The dungeon groaned with the voices of prisoners who cried aloud for water, food, mercy, who slammed their binding chains against stone walls in frustration or madness.

"Darun, how are Riche and Lizbet?" Dail got to his knees and began to twist the ring.

Calmis moved closer to the cell door, thick and wooden, ancient but strong. Gray light reached them from a small barred window high in the wall. "My lady? Lady Lizbet?"

Lizbet didn't answer. His heart darkened with fear. She had been so silent when he had last seen her, dumb with exhaustion and terror. Neither she nor Riche had answered their calls before this.

"Riche!"

"My lord?" The boy's voice was a small, familiar sound, and Calmis drew a tight breath. At least Riche was well enough to answer!

"Are you all right? How is the lady?"

"She's sleeping, my lord. She's well enough, I suppose."

Calmis heard the boy's movements, soft rustlings in the straw, but heard no sound of chains.

"Riche, aren't you chained?"

"The manacles were too large for my wrists."

Calmis turned from the window. "Dail?"

"I heard. We can't afford to call any attention to him now. Break it off, Darun."

Riche, hearing Dail's whisper, sighed. Calmis heard the rustling of the boy leaving the door of his cell. Then he heard the soft murmuring of Riche's voice and Lizbet's reply. He wanted to call out again, to speak with her, but he didn't dare.

Riche was free! Calmis tried, with stern logic, to put down the small spark of hope that flared suddenly within him, but it would not die. Dail's chain was loose, and the lad across the corridor was free.

What could that do to gain them freedom? Nothing, he knew. There were still chains binding his own wrists and Lizbet's. And there were still thick walls and iron doors to keep them in.

CHAPTER 25

Elvish hunting captains say to a woman who would join their bands, "You are joining a company of hunters who must become warriors when the borders need defending. Are you prepared to fight?"

The woman answers, "I am."

The hunting captain places the woman's left hand on his own heart. He gives her a father's kiss. "There is one thing you might be forced to endure," he says, "that your companions who are men will not. Are you prepared?"

In ritual, the woman answers, "This thing is of no value unless it is freely given. Taken from me, it is only a ghost."

"Join us, then, and increase our ranks by one more hunter-defender."

Hunter-defender: scout, warrior, provisioner, ranger. They are the hard folk who spend their lives on the Elvish borders, the deadly pride of Dekar's armies. They are archers who can shoot the eye out of a hawk in midflight. Silent trackers, they can trail a rabbit through the stoniest waste. As provisioners, they have fed armies on the scant provender of a drought-starved woodland, found water where none could hope to. As warriors and rangers, they have no equal in ferocity.

If an enemy makes the mistake of thinking that a woman of these bands is less deadly than a man, he does not live to make that mistake again. They are the daughters of foresters who have grown to adulthood with only the sky and forest for a roof, the soft leathers of animal skins for clothing, the bounty of the woodland at their fires.

They live as neighbors to the gods and walk the forests in grace. And they have a core of strength, Nikia thought now, that I don't.

The thought washed dimly across her mind, making little imprint on the wrack of pain and humiliation Reynarth left behind. He had taken her in rape that first night, and again in the day and night that followed. She had not been able to defend herself with physical strength, nor with her small magicks. In all things, Reynarth had been the stronger.

Alone now, the room empty of his laughter, her body empty of his triumphant taking, Nikia struggled to distance her mind from her physical pain, fought to keep gibbering thoughts of horror from overwhelming her. She lay still and used, unmoving on his bed.

She lay that way for a long time, long enough for the shadows of night to color with the rose of imminent dawn as they crept across the floor to touch the edges of the dais. She never moved once.

Her hair lay tangled and damp on the pillows. Her hands and fingers relaxed their clench not once.

Thoughts of death came stealing on her with the day, thoughts of murder and thoughts of suicide. Her imagination flashed her pictures, like scenes from tortured plays, pictures of herself flying to freedom from the window not far from the bed, her hair billowing out behind her, her skin shining in the rosy new light of the day, her arms outstretched to embrace freedom. Then, shifting suddenly, with no help from her, the scenes changed to pictures of blood-washed murder.

Nikia smelled the blood she saw in her mind. She saw it in

her imagination as it pooled on the library's stone floor—blood welling from a dagger wound, rising and bubbling, a spring of red to wash the scarlet ruby resting on Reynarth's breast. A hunter-defender's dream of vengeance.

Nikia shivered then and finally moved. In the night, Reynarth had worn the ruby. Its hard-edged facets had bruised her skin. Bleeding scarlet color, the ruby had spilled its shadows across her flesh, turning her breasts faintly red where it lay between them. The mage didn't care that it would leave bruises behind.

Nikia wished she could cry, but tears never came. They never burst out of the pain grasping at her throat. They never cooled her burning eyes. She had been raped to the sound of Reynarth's laughter, and silence was all that was left to her.

Were she a hunter-defender, a woman of the northern bands, she wouldn't be lying here wishing for tears that would not come. Her wishes would be for vengeance. Her plans, deadly and dark, would be carried out through the agency of a dagger's cool, gleaming blade.

Hunter-defender, her thoughts murmured repeatedly, hunter-defender, hunter-defender. . . . She listened to the words in her mind until they gradually became a definition, a title.

Hunter-Defender. Nikia, Hunter-Defender. In her mind, she saw herself not as the familiar, richly robed Princess of Elvish. She saw instead a young woman dressed in rough hunter's garb—soft leather breeches, high, sturdy boots, and a blouse of hunter's rust. A knife was housed in a simple sheath at her belt, and a long bow slung across her back.

Nikia: Hunter-Defender. She liked the picture, she who had spent all her days in a king's hall, who had hunted only for pleasure. Identity skewed, and she could no longer call up the picture of the troubled but willing child that she had been.

I am not who I was. I am nothing now. Nikia laughed bitterly. The sound fell into the silence and startled her. She was something—a prisoner who lived by Reynarth's whim. He could end her life at any time.

Aye, spoke the quiet voice of her thought, but before he

does, you have this still: that you do live. Choose, and be what you will.

Hurt in her body, bruised in her soul, she imagined that she could feel the bone grip of the dagger in her palm, hear the song of an arrow released in flight. Somewhere, deep in the center of her, she imagined what it would be like to feel as strong as a hunter-defender, as graceful, as easy with killing.

She could move then.

Gathering her tired limbs under her, Nikia rose to her feet. She was unsteady, tired, and aching. She spotted a robe on one of the steps of the dais. She recognized it as the one Rhia had used. Remembering her pity for the Darkling, Nikia put it on and gathered it close about her.

"I *will* choose," she whispered, "and though no captain has initiated me, I will be a hunter-defender. I choose to live!"

She found a jug of warm water in the alcove, which had previously held a tub for bathing. She cleaned herself as best she could, wrapping herself in the robe again when she was done.

Nikia prowled the little chamber, feeling the cool flags against her bare feet. She stopped at the window to bid her never taken flight to freedom farewell. She looked down at the ghostly city as the sun rose. Those plans for death had been the plans of a child. She was no longer a child. She was, now more than ever before, a princess. And something else: She was one who, in her heart, roamed with the deadly hunter-defenders.

She would find a way to avenge herself. And she would defend her friends. These things she would do until the last of her strength was gone. A long ache drifted through her. It might be—aye, likely it was—that what vengeance she would deal would not be only for herself but for her husband as well.

"Garth!" she whispered, but the sound was an empty ache. She tried to call up his face and found that she couldn't do it. He is long of face, she told herself, and his hair is reddish brown. His eyes, she thought, the color of a deer's coat, sparkle with merriment.

But still no picture of him came to her. Garth, her husband of so short a time, had left her with little memory of himself, and Nikia felt that it was not his fault but her own. She felt a pang of guilt. Did he live? That question, a constant anthem of pain in weeks past, had flown from her heart in recent days.

If he lived, what would he be like now? Would he be like Rhia? Would she find him wrapped in that otherworldly cold, animate but dead? Would he stand motionless, vacant, waiting for command?

And suddenly, unbidden, came the memory of another man, tall, blue-eyed, and with nimble hands that brought from the simplest harp music sweet and dancing. "Dail." She wondered how those friendly blue eyes had leapt so clearly into memory. Nikia shook her head. "Oh, gods," she whispered, hardly knowing why, "help me, I beg you!"

* * * * *

"I would give much for a light." Dail flexed his aching arms as best as he could and squeezed his eyes shut against the burning of skin rubbed raw by the iron bracelet of his manacles.

Calmis moved to the length of his own chain and strained his eyes in the gray, dim light to see. "Better to wish for a hammer and chisel than light, my friend."

"Aye, and better still to wish for our chains to be struck off and the doors opened to set us free," Dail muttered bitterly. "Instead I have this—a loose ring that will loosen no more."

The bard was silent for a long moment, resting his aching arms and shoulders. He was almost glad for the ache. When it tore along his muscles, as it did now, it dimmed another pain, the gnawing fear for Nikia.

Oh, lady, he thought. Lady!

The little litany of dread, of longing, whispered in his heart as it had for all the uncountable hours of his captivity. He gritted his teeth and twisted the chain again.

Mortar slithered, a whisper, from the hole. When he spoke again, there was the soft breath of renewed hope in his words. "Darun, I need your help. The water bucket . . . is it nearby?"

"Aye." Calmis reached for the leaky wooden bucket. "What good will this do?"

"The carrying strap . . . how is it attached to the bucket?"

Calmis felt with his hands in the dim light, bringing the

bucket closer to his face for examination. "It's not a strap, Dail. It's a light chain." He grimaced. "I've no doubt that wooden handles or leather straps rot fast here. The slats of the bucket are fouled with slime."

"Is the chain fastened to the wood with bolts?"

"Aye, two . . . one on each side."

"Remove one of those bolts for me, Darun."

Calmis braced the bucket against his knees with his injured hand, then began to work at the rotting wood with the other. The foul water that remained in the bucket sloshed over the sides, spilling onto the straw. "Hah! I've just lost our water ration for the day."

"We won't be here to miss it. Have you freed one?"

"A moment. . . ." The wood, coated with scum, slipped from his grip. Calmis's wounded hand began to throb and ache again. He clamped his back teeth against the pain and continued working at the bolt, pulling with his fingers and pounding it with the heel of his hand. "Ah! There, I've got it!"

Dail ran his fingers over the rusty bolt. It was small, barely large enough to fasten the chain to the wooden bucket, but he thought it would serve his purpose.

"Now," he said, satisfaction warming his voice, "take up your listening post again, my friend. It will go faster now."

Calmis wedged himself into the corner between the door and the wall. The dungeon sounds had become familiar, a woeful song for which he would never find words. Chains and manacles rattled against stone as the harsh voices of the hideous guards rose and fell. Through these sounds wandered the moans of unseen prisoners. The moaning, a low, dark dirge of many voices, would rise to gibbering screams at the passage of anyone along the stone-floored corridor. Once, while peering out from the tiny window of his own cell, Calmis had seen hands scrabbling and grabbing, thrusting out from filthy cells. Sore-scabbed arms would grope, reach, and fall away as the guards passed by. After his first sight of this wretched dance of arms, Calmis had never looked again.

Now the dungeon was, by comparison, fairly quiet. Prisoners' moans twined with the sigh of damp breezes. Far down the corridor, a guard's voice soared in raucous laughter. And soft, hesitant, and furtive, he heard Dail chipping away at the weakened stone that held the bolt of his chain.

Dampness from the weeping stone wall crept down Calmis's back, reaching with cold fingers beneath his shirt. Outside it was high summer. Here it was always winter, a bleak winter in which bodies rotted and souls died. Calmis shook his head against his grim thoughts.

"Dail, have you given thought to how you will escape once you have loosened the bolt?"

"Aye," Dail's reply was low and preoccupied. "Ah!"

"Loose?"

"Looser."

Calmis bit back a sigh of impatience. "Where will you go? This place is well guarded, Dail."

"We, Darun."

"We?"

"We." Dail's voice was rough with effort. "All go or none goes."

Calmis laughed bitterly. "You didn't tell me you had a key to these cells."

"Easy, my friend. I have no key, but I have a plan. Quiet now and listen for me."

Calmis subsided, and Dail chipped, eagerly and silently, at the stubborn stone. Nursing his throbbing hand, Calmis wondered what plan the bard had conceived that would free all of them.

* * * * *

Reynarth balanced between two fears. Somewhere between them was triumph, if he could only grasp it. He hoped he'd found what might be a Dwarven answer to an Elvish puzzle.

He knew, now, that he would never give over the ruby to Yvanda.

Fear rushed on him like waves crashing on the beaches of Seuro. The power of the ruby was far greater than he had hoped. Better, he thought behind closed eyes, had I dreaded than hoped. But in that direction lay despair. Struggling within himself, gauging his strength and daring again to hope, Reynarth thrust aside his fear and found a place to think. His thoughts were colored by old words and ancient worlds.

Blood: Ignite the power that I crave. Power: Move in strength to my need. Strength: Fill with courage this ready heart. Courage: Guide the bloodstone to my need.

The rhythms and patterns of the words were Elvish. The history of the ruby had been gleaned from an ancient scroll, penned by a long-dead scribe who called himself "Darvat."

No Elvish name that, and certainly not Mannish. The harsh, crabbed handwriting on the faded scroll lacked the flowing art of the Elvish style and did not have the brief, economic strokes of Mannish lettering.

All this Reynarth set aside as underpinning for the scribe's first words: "I am Darvat of the First People."

The mage remembered the four lines of the spell Darvat had copied into the scroll, speaking of Blood, Power, Strength, and Courage. These were the elements to be used in the spellcasting. Try as he might, his own magic would not move in response to the lines. This was an Elvish spell and would heed only the call of Elvish magic. It needed the touch of an Elvish mind.

Reynarth sat back, opened his eyes, and let all effort drain away. The ruby, where it lay on the table, was dull and unresponsive. He had an elf available to touch the ruby. She could never control the ruby's might. She could, however, unlock the spell for him. She was cowed and broken, but he would take no chances. If persuasion was needed, he would use the lives of her friends and her husband as threats. If that didn't work, he would hold up reign and power at his side—gifts he did not believe she had the strength to claim.

Satisfied that once the spell was put into effect, once the ruby's power was unlocked, he could move it to his own will, Reynarth smiled.

He played a dangerous game, a deadly treachery. He was well aware of this. He wouldn't give the ruby to Yvanda. But with the jewel's power behind him, there was no need to fear.

* * * * *

Nikia paced the room, watching the day color the sky, listening to the sound of seabirds borne on the breeze. She realized that this was the only sound she had heard in the hour that she had been prowling the chamber. Curious, restless, she opened the door separating the two chambers and found the library empty.

Leaving the door of the bedchamber open behind her, Nikia silently crossed to the table. She studied the map, still on the table where she had last seen it. The red stain had crept farther southward. She wondered what battles were being fought today. How many warriors, Elvish and Mannish, were left to the Two Kingdoms? How many of those precious warriors would die today?

And where in all this place were her friends? Nikia wondered again if Garth were here as well. If he lived, and that hope was growing dimmer, was he held someplace in the vast dungeons under the keep?

Silently, moving on bare feet, Nikia stepped around the table and stood where Reynarth had been seated the day before. The table was empty but for a small, clear globe. It would fit neatly into an adult's palm or the two cupped hands of a child.

Nikia moved her hand toward the globe, then away. She looked up quickly, listening. She heard nothing but the distant cry of seabirds, the soft breath of the breeze, and the sound of footsteps passing in the corridor outside. Startled, Nikia stepped back, away from the table. The steps passed, paused a little farther on, and then continued.

Reassured, she returned to the globe. She was fascinated by the thing, had never seen anything like it before. Nikia leaned forward, touching it lightly with the fingertips of her left hand. Then suddenly, as though the room were set alight by torches, the shadows leapt back, careening away from the walls. Light sprang up from beneath her fingers.

Nikia leapt back. Stumbling against the large chair, she fell into its seat. She caught her breath in a frightened gasp and snatched her hands to her lips.

Had anyone heard? Had anyone seen? That flash must have had the strength to carry beyond the room, both from the window and under the cracks of the door. Nikia listened again, trying to hear any sound over the thudding of her heart.

There was no sound. She realized then that there must be no guards posted outside the door. Nikia smiled bitterly. How could the mage imagine that the weary and broken woman he had left only a few hours ago would have the strength of heart to attempt an escape?

Satisfied that the flash had not been detected, Nikia leaned forward again. This time she did not touch the sphere but held her fingers slightly above it. She closed her eyes, cleared her mind, and called into play senses that had long gone unused.

Breathing softly, Nikia moved her magic within her. She felt a calm begin to settle on her heart and mind. This was indeed familiar territory. She extended her senses carefully, closing the distance between her mind and the globe.

Magic surrounded the globe with an almost palpable aura. Carefully, with an explorer's patience, Nikia brought her mind closer to the globe's magic. The stamp of Reynarth's use was all over it, dark and strong. Whispers of words spoken in hours and days past washed through her mind.

With a suddenness that rocked her, she realized a strong presence that was not the mage's. Female and ancient, dark and powerful, the presence grew clearer, closer. Nikia pulled back. She opened her eyes and turned away from the globe. The presence had been growing nearer, stronger. Nikia knew with certainty that, had she remained in touch with the globe, she would have been drawn into contact with the being.

But who? Who is it that speaks with Reynarth in the globe? Certainty settled in her mind as a dark cloud settles across the sun. Yvanda.

Almost of its own accord, her hand crept toward the globe again. She held it steady against the trembling of fear, closed her eyes, and held her breath. She was afraid and confused, and in her fear, her thoughts went back to where they had been before she had touched the stone with her magic. As a talisman, a protection, she called up thoughts of Garth.

Garth! Love, look where we have come to!

When she opened her eyes, Nikia's glance fell again on the little sphere. The clarity of the glass faded, grayed, and then pulsed with light and life. And it was not empty.

The image was small, but clear in every detail. The color was crisp, like a view seen through the clearest spring air. The walls of a dungeon wept with moisture. She could almost smell the prison's fouled air.

Light, dim and gray, seeped in through a high barred window. Holding her breath and listening with all her magic skills, Nikia searched the cell until she found its occupant crouched in a black, shadowed corner. His head was bent over drawn-up knees and his clothes were only rags. But she knew him. It was Garth.

He stirred, moving his shoulders as though twitching under the touch of a dream. But he did not lift his head or wake.

Garth! Again he twitched, again he moved as though in restless sleep. Nikia thought she heard a soft, groaning protest.

Garth? Love, can you hear me?

He sighed, his breath shuddering in her mind. He lifted his head, still asleep, and let it fall back against the wall. Even the bite of the rough stone did not wake him.

Gray light fell across a face familiar and yet not. It was thinner than she had known it, drawn and white with more than lack of sun. Lines, like the seams of scars, were etched around his mouth and eyes. Even as she watched, his lips, cracked and bruised, pulled away from his teeth as though baring in some angry snarl.

Images, like mist from a swamp, swirled and twisted in his mind, drifting into hers. Nikia gasped in horror. The images were ugly, loathsome pictures of betrayal. Something or someone was filling his mind, his soul, with the sights and sounds of a betrayal that had not been.

Reynarth! This had the stamp of his handiwork. Nikia raised trembling hands to her face and pressed them hard to her cheeks, forcing herself to remain calm.

Can I reach him? Can I show him that his dreams are lies? Ah, gods, what has been done to him?

Tentatively, and with great caution, she returned her hands to the globe, touched it gently, lightly, reaching for her husband's mind. The globe, she knew, would send what images she wished to Garth, if only she could find the skill to do it. She had never done this before, never reached into the mind of another.

Garth, she whispered. *Love, these are lies! Listen to the truth now, remember the truth!*

The Queen's Garden, rich with the scents of sweet thyme, lemon balm, and basil in their autumn bloom, warm with the last full sun before winter, filled her mind. She remembered the hunting bitch, Misty Morning, bounding through the wooden gate, Garth close on its heels. It had been their first meeting.

Her memory skipped away from the scene to others, more private and filled with an unfolding knowledge that would become love if cultivated. Laughter, discovery, and contentment colored her thoughts, even as tears of loss traced silver paths down her cheeks.

Does he feel this now? Can I give him back these memories, unstained by the foul things he dreams?

Garth? Love? Her mental voice sought him gently, insistently, calling him from tainted dreams. *Husband, do you hear me?*

She could not be sure that he had, but he moved again, still caught in the grasp of sleep. He lifted his head away from the wall, and once again gray light fell across his face. The lines were still deeply etched in his face, lines of pain, but Nikia thought she saw a lessening of his torment.

He sighed again, and this time the sound she heard in her mind was less wrenching and more the sound of a man drifting back into sleep after departing nightmares. Trembling, Nikia withdrew from the scene of her husband's imprisonment.

Her mind racing, still moving within the globe's power, she found the scene changing with sudden swiftness. Indistinct images swirled in the globe and in her mind, following her scattered thoughts. Dizzy with their flow and rush, Nikia squeezed her eyes shut and instinctively groped her way toward the others she knew to be imprisoned in the keep's dungeons.

When she opened her eyes again, she thought for a panicked moment that she'd lost control of the globe. The little sphere still showed a prison cell, she still sensed damp, foul air, still heard the rustling of vermin in straw that had not been removed from wet stone floors in far too long.

She heard a voice, and that voice was so familiar that Nikia's heart leapt with hope.

Darun, she whispered in her mind. She saw him stir and lift his head. Though he moved only a little, Nikia knew that he moved in response to her whisper. *Darun*, she ventured again. *Can you hear me?*

With mounting excitement, Nikia saw her friend's eyes narrow, saw him gather his legs under him and rise to his feet.

"My lady?"

Yes! Darun, listen to me!

"My lady? No, how can this be—?"

Hush now and listen to me!

"Am I mad? What is this?"

Nikia worked quickly to dispel his doubts and fear, sending confidence and assurance through the globe's channel in swift images. *Do you see? I am well, and it is truly Nikia who speaks to you. There is no time to explain now, Darun!*

He caught her urgency and stilled his mind. She told him swiftly where she was and that she was well. If Calmis caught any mental picture of what she had suffered in the night and day before, it was from unguarded memory. He did not acknowledge it.

I've seen Garth. He's alive, Darun. He's in a cell like yours. But I couldn't tell if he's near you.

"Lady, Dail thinks that he can free himself, and he says that he can free the rest of us."

Lizbet and Riche? Are they nearby?

"Only across the corridor."

Darun, search for Garth. Find him. He has been—I don't know what the word is, Darun—tortured? It is as though his thoughts are not his own, as though his will has been swept away and his mind filled with something vile and horrible.

She could not bring herself to detail the things she had seen writhing in Garth's mind, but she could see by the expression in Calmis's eyes that he understood. Some stray memory had drifted from her mind to his.

"It will be done, lady."

Yet Nikia could see in his mind that Calmis had not the first idea how he would accomplish the task. She shivered, not liking this ability to see into another's most private places.

Thank you, Darun. If I can reach you again, I will. Have care, and have faith!

Doubt wavered in Calmis's mind, but he hurriedly covered it. Nikia smiled. Fast learner! she thought.

I must go now, Darun. I have been at this too long, and I do not know when— But even as she spoke, Nikia heard the sound of voices in the corridor. Not taking the time to think, she leaped to her feet, severing her connection with the seeing-stone.

Her head pounded with the pain of the abrupt breaking of the link as she ran soundlessly across the room to where the door of the bedchamber stood open. Blessing the chance that had caused her not to close it, Nikia ducked inside, shutting it silently even as she heard the door of the outer chamber open. In the library, Reynarth bade a guard to wait for him. He entered the bedchamber, his eyes sharp and green, his smile sardonic.

"Good morning, Nikia," he said smoothly, quietly amused. Did he know, she wondered, that she had been within and discovered, all unknowingly, the secret of the little globe?

His face was as calm and smooth as his voice had been. She saw only satisfaction there, and Nikia imagined that it had to do with the fact that she was immediately accessible to him and powerless. Not so powerless as before, though, she thought.

Reynarth crossed the little chamber, came to stand before the bed, and regarded her with a faint smile. "I trust that you found an opportunity to sleep while I was gone?"

Nikia nodded sullenly. That she did not have to force. But there was hope now, and her courage had been bolstered from an unexpected source. She must not jeopardize that hope by misplaying her role.

Reynarth chose not to note her silence. "Come with me."

He did not look at her again, nor did he wait for a reply. Turning abruptly, as one who has business elsewhere, Reynarth left the bedchamber.

As Nikia made her way through the library chamber, she took care to keep her eyes down, unable to meet the glance of the guard waiting there. She remembered the looks cast at Rhia, the leering grins.

She could not let her gaze go even once to the table where the little globe stood. She saw it, clear and inviting, out of the corners of her eyes, but she would not let even her thoughts dwell on it.

Quietly Nikia followed Reynarth from the chamber.

CHAPTER 26

"I tell you I heard her!"

Dail shook his head. "I don't doubt you, Darun. I just want to know how. My lady has skills in magic, but you, my friend, are distinctly unmagical."

Calmis ran his fingers along the chain of his manacles. He had no answer, and for now he didn't care. "She's here, and she's alive. That must mean something to you, Dail."

It meant everything. It meant that he could hope again. And even if his hope was unnamed, still, it lived. His fear for her had been like a constant nausea churning in his belly. It had run, like a keening wind, beneath his thoughts since she'd been taken away.

"Take care of them," she'd told him. Dail rubbed the knuckles of his manacled hand across his rough, bearded jaw. She'd laid that charge on him as though she believed it was something he could do. As though, he thought now, she were still able to issue charges and was not a half-starved prisoner going to meet some terrible fate of her own.

He shivered in the cell's damp and chill. "Starflower," he'd always thought her. Lately images of ruined gardens had haunted him. Now at least he knew that she was alive.

And so was Garth. Something flickered and died far back in Dail's mind. Hopes were rising and falling, and he dared not acknowledge the death of the particular hope that was dimmed now by Nikia's news that her husband lived.

It had been a traitor's hope, and one Dail banished now as unworthy. His cousin lived, and Dail would not permit himself to acknowledge that some secret place in him might have wished otherwise. As much as he loved Nikia, he didn't want to hate himself. She had charged them with Garth's rescue, and he knew that he must attempt it, and succeed if he could.

"Dail?" The bard looked around and met Calmis's steady, level gaze. He saw sympathy in his friend's eyes, and understanding.

He's known, Dail realized. He's known for some time. What could be more transparent than a bard in love? He answered the question bitterly, as though it were the denouement of some cruel joke: a bard in love with a woman who can't be his.

"Aye, my friend, it means much to me. It means that all of us—Garth, the princess, and us, her friends—yet live. And our mission is more than escape."

"I don't understand," Calmis said.

Dail shifted his position so that the feeble light straggling into the cell was over his shoulder. Freedom—his own, at least—from the shackles that bound him to the wall was a given. The bolt was nearly loose.

"Darun, listen to me. This is a strange story."

Working all the while, Dail told the tale of the discovery of the Ylin tapestry and the clues it had supplied to the mystery of the ruby's history. If he remembered that he had admitted to himself then that no woman's beauty, no woman's spirit, could move him as Nikia's did, he didn't let it show. He was, after all, a skilled bard, and one who could school his voice to evoke any mood, any emotion.

Calmis, caught by the tale, frowned. "I didn't know there

was a mystery connected with the ruby. It seemed to me that the Elvish had always held it as a symbol of kingship, nothing else."

"So it was. Even Dekar didn't know what a powerful talisman he passed on to his daughter."

"But Reynarth knew."

"Not all along. I think he discovered the ruby's true nature only a short time before the princess did. It was then that the news of Garth's disappearance came to Damris, and as you know, few of us had time to think about anything else. Reynarth made an attempt to steal the ruby in the Citadel then, but he failed."

Calmis scowled. "Aye, well enough, but he has the ruby now. Does he know the use of it, I wonder?"

Dail shrugged, moved again to catch the poor light, and continued to work at the bolt. "I don't think so, or he would have used it."

"How do you know that he hasn't?"

"How? We're still alive, aren't we? It is in his mind, I think, that the princess knows the way of the ruby. I think we're being held hostage against her cooperation."

"And does the princess have the knowledge he seeks?"

Dail shook his head. "No, and neither does Dekar, or he wouldn't have let the thing go."

"Aye, that's true enough." Calmis paused, watching his friend in his work. "Dail, what good will this thing do anyone if it can't be used?"

"Oh, it can be used. One must only know the way of it."

"And Reynarth hopes to discover that and rise up against his master?"

"The Sorcerer. Aye, I imagine so. All points that way, else the ruby would be in the Northlands and we and the princess would be long dead, wouldn't we?"

"Twice a traitor, and still he hopes to live?" Calmis laughed bitterly. "He plays a dangerous game."

"I don't think he has the skill to win, my friend."

"How are you doing?"

Dail grinned and stepped into the center of the cell. The

chain was dangling free and trailed after him in the straw. "How is this?"

Calmis laughed. "Well enough! Now what scheme have you laid to free the rest of us?"

"A simple one. Listen now . . ." Then quickly, in a hushed whisper, he told Calmis what he planned.

It was easy enough, Calmis agreed, and there should be a good chance to carry it off. It required only patience and waiting. That, he knew, would not be the difficult part. The difficult part would be finding Garth in this rat's maze of dungeons.

* * * * *

"It's a simple enough spell, Nikia," Reynarth said as he led her deeper into the belly of the keep.

Nikia swallowed the bitter words of anger that rose to her lips. If he had discovered the spell, it would only be a short time before he acted on it.

Her limbs were as heavy as stone as she forced herself to follow him. They went down long corridors, lightless but for the torches borne by the two guards. As they descended into the keep's lower regions, the air grew foul and damp. They were on the seaward side of the keep. The air smelled salty beneath the moldy stench of long unused corridors. Pale, ugly growths slicked the stone of the floor. Nikia walked carefully, picking her way in the wavering torchlight.

"You're quiet, Nikia. Doesn't it amuse you to think that this fabulous ruby, this symbol of Elvish rule, was but one of many trinkets crafted by the Dwarven kind in times too ancient to recall?"

"How should that amuse me?" she asked, her voice low, but still tumbling back in echoes from the stone walls that lined their way.

"How? There is amusement to be found in irony, don't you think?" Reynarth was confident that the powers of the ruby would soon be his. "A trinket of the ancient Dwarven folk becomes the symbol of the rulers of Elvish. Their merest toy finds a place of honor and worship in these times."

"How have you come by this knowledge? None among the Elvish know this, or indeed anything about a Dwarven kind."

"You doubt me? Well, it hardly matters."

Nikia slipped on the slick stones and righted herself. *No, he lies. He has no understanding of how to use the stone or he would have used it before now.*

"Your master will be pleased to know this, Reynarth," she said softly.

His back and shoulders stiffened. Nikia didn't miss it. *He plans treachery again!* "Won't he be pleased? Or should I say 'she'?" Nikia recalled the female presence that surrounded the seeing-stone. She was certain now that it was Yvanda, the Sorcerer's witch-mistress, with whom Reynarth had been plotting. "I imagine she'll reward you richly for finding such a powerful talisman."

Reynarth's smile was as brittle as ice. "She already has."

* * * * *

The light in the cavern pierced Garth's eyes, stabbing in fiery shafts. His filthy rags clung to limbs almost too weak to support him. Were it not that two guards held his arms, he would have sunk to his knees. He hadn't eaten in three days.

At first he'd tried not to sleep. But each night sleep eventually came. And with it came nightmares so frightening, so painful that he no longer knew sleep from waking, dream from reality.

How could you have trusted her? his dreams asked. Night and day, they questioned and mocked. *How could you have thought her to be faithful, in love with you, a simple man? What were you to her but a toy, something to amuse herself with, something to be petted when it pleased her and forgotten when you were gone? Magic speaks to magic, the Elvish say. And if you have no magic, to what can she speak? To nothing, and nothing is what she considers you.*

She is a witch, and a witch who is tired of the simpering role of faithful wife, dutiful daughter, simple child. But that is gone now. She sports and revels with magic and the things magic has created.

But did she? Was she the traitor his fearful dreams portrayed? Garth didn't know. His memories were being poisoned. He had only one left, and even that was dying.

The scent of an herb-filled garden, warm and fresh in autumn sunlight, drifted as pale as a shadow among the damp stenches of nightmare.

Aching limbs eased, if only a little, and Garth's bruised heart lifted as other memories sighed among the dark shadows of his remembered nightmares. Silver hair and silver eyes . . . a smile filled with hope and a sweet, ingenuous willingness to love. . . .

Was this truth?

* * * * *

Nikia fought to control rising nausea. The tiny picture the globe had presented her could not ever compare with the reality of Garth's condition. His limbs were thin and trembling, his clothing, remnants of his fine breeches only, was filthy and crawling with vermin. Matted hair, and a beard so tangled and rough with dirt that it must hurt him, hid his face.

"Garth!" His name passed her lips as the sound of pain. "Dear gods! Oh, my husband—"

"Witch," he muttered. "Witch! Filthy traitorous bitch!"

"Oh, gods, Garth—you can't believe that!" Had her gently placed memories done nothing to ease his torment? Nikia's hands began to shake, and a cold, trickling sweat traced icy paths down her neck.

"Whore! Elvish whore . . ." But there was no conviction in the accusation this time, and his words trailed away.

Nikia took a step toward her husband, then another. Garth's dark eyes screamed his confusion and of a battle being waged within.

No! his eyes cried. I don't believe this! I know it is a lie! I know it's some artifice of magic. . . .

The words seemed to hang, trembling, on his lips, yet he couldn't speak. Reynarth's hold on him was still strong. But it was enough for Nikia to see that faith and love struggled with doubt and pain. It will win, she thought. He will win!

As though to justify her own faith, Garth stood away from his guards, shrugging off their hands with an expression reminiscent of the princely prerogative he had once enjoyed. He stood for a long moment, wavering on legs too weak and unsteady to hold him long. Something else wavered in his eyes. For one long moment, Nikia thought that he would continue his reviling epithets.

"Nikia, love . . ." His voice broke, low and lost, the sound of a child wandering too long after dark.

"Garth, you must believe that I love you—"

Moving swiftly, Reynarth snatched at Nikia's arm and dragged her back. "Take him away!"

"Reynarth," she whispered, "what have you done to him?"

"I?" The mage shrugged. "Nothing." He watched as Garth was hustled out of the cavern. "Nightmares, I suppose. They work on a man, whittling away at his hope until only a husk remains. Luckily husks," he said softly, "can be refilled."

Aye, Nikia thought numbly, refilled with poison, hatred, and fear. "Why have you brought me here?"

"Why, to reunite you with your husband, of course. But it would seem that he wants nothing to do with you."

Nikia wrapped her arms around herself, for she felt colder than she had ever been. She had to cling to the memory of the recognition of love that she had seen in Garth's eyes. "Why have you done this?"

Reynarth dropped all semblance of pretense. "Listen well, Nikia. Your husband isn't the only one I hold. The lives of four others depend on you.

"I didn't lie when I said that I had discovered the history of the ruby. Nor did I lie when I said that I had found the spell to unlock its use. But there is something I need from you, little princess, and I will have it, or your friends will suffer such torments as to make your husband look a happy man. Do you understand me?"

Nikia gasped with pain. "I hear you."

"I'm glad you do. Now come with me, and remember what you have seen here. This will be as nothing compared to what will be done to your friends if you don't cooperate."

But what does he want? she thought wildly. What knowledge do I have that he doesn't possess? Ah, gods, you must help me now!

* * * * *

Yvanda was drained. She had little strength and less magic. She had spent days at her task of creating warriors for the endless, greedy maw of the war. Engendering life in the dead, pulling foul and twisted creatures from the steaming Pits of Creation that lay far beneath Souless, all this she had done. And now she was weary beyond telling.

"You have done well," the Sorcerer said. But even his words of praise fell on her unnoticed.

"How goes the war, my lord?" she asked from habit, as she had asked many times in these past days. The war had not been going well. She lifted her eyes to meet his then and gauged his silence. It was not going well now.

"These warriors you have given us will turn the tide. That and our skills together."

They stood before the large pit in the sea cavern. The map, created by the Sorcerer's magic, told a tale of doubt. The Two Kingdoms rose stronger now, retaking lost ground and pushing closer and closer to Seuro.

What accounted for their sudden resurgence? Yvanda thought it was a last spurt of strength born of fear. They were outnumbered, even now, even before the new armies could join the battles.

As though his thought had followed hers, the Sorcerer spoke. "They are fighting for their lives. It is a final gasp of strength." But doubt shaded his words, and Yvanda heard it clearly.

"What else, my lord? A last push, a last desperate struggle."

He was silent, his darkly handsome face no more responsive than chiseled ice. Yvanda watched the living map again, watched as battles were played out before them, observed with stilled breathing the renewed thrust of the armies of the Two Kingdoms.

"And what of the Ruby of Guyaire?" He put the question

casually, but Yvanda didn't fail to hear the real interest in the
Sorcerer's words. She met his eyes, careful to match his manner.

"I know not, my lord. At your command, I have been at
other tasks. It rests still with the mage in Seuro while he seeks
its key."

"I want it here now."

Indeed, she thought, her eyes going back to the pit, where
life and death were being played out before her. I would have
had it here long before this! She covered her thought hastily.
In itself, it was no testimony to the treachery she planned. But
she knew her master well enough to know that he could read
not only thought but intent as well.

"Will you send for it now, my lord?"

"Aye, and I would have it brought here quickly. They come
close to Seuro. They battle fiercely, and although I know that
they will not prevail, I want the ruby far from their reach all the
same."

"Shall I go for it, my lord?"

She saw the light of the pit in his eyes, flickering red in the
darkness of the sea cavern. She felt the sharp probe of his
thought. She dared not move. It would not do for him to sense
her thoughts. There must be something within her for him to
read.

She held her regard steady and filled her mind with
thoughts of the war raging without. She tinted her thoughts
with a slight fear and with deeper hues of confidence.

His eyes drew hers as the flame draws a moth. He smiled.
"Yes, go for the ruby. If need be, bring back the mage as well.
He can complete his work here. I will not have the talisman so
near to the armies of the Two Kingdoms any longer than it
must be now."

"Aye." Her word came on a soft breath; she would not let
relief be heard in it. "Aye, my lord. It will not take long. There
must be a ship ready in the bay."

"You will advise me when you have arrived."

"Aye, my lord." She glanced over her shoulder at the living
map once more. Soundless battle still raged there. When she

returned her eyes to his, she was calm. "You may expect to hear word from me tomorrow, my lord."

He watched her leave, his eyes sharp with new understanding. He'd tasted treachery in her thoughts. It amused him to think that she believed herself undetected.

When she was gone, he laid plans of his own, brief and efficient; plans to rid him of the danger of her treachery.

* * * * *

The salt-tanged winds of the strait blew fresh and clean. Yvanda filled her lungs as though breathing air for the first time since she'd left the sea cavern. Gulls wheeled and screamed above the little ship, dipping and sliding on the air currents. Yvanda wrapped her light cloak about her as protection from the salt spray. The sun shone full and warm on her face. She smiled as she felt the whip of the wind in her long dark hair. Power once again surged through her as strength returned. The slap of the sails above sounded like music to her ears.

She didn't turn to watch the receding lines of the shore, nor did she once think to bid farewell to the place that had been her home for so long. Solace it had once been; Souless it was now. She had dwelt there since the gods had fathered her. She didn't plan to return.

She felt no remorse, no sense of leave-taking. She was going onward, and she bent all her thoughts to the keep of Seuro and the Ruby of Guyaire. That talisman was her key to freedom and more power than she had ever hoped to gain.

The ship rose and fell beneath her feet. She braced herself instinctively against the gentle motion. The sea hissed and foamed around the ship's hull, rushing toward a shore that was only a dim gray line on the horizon. Yvanda laughed aloud, and then caught the laughter back.

A low voice growled against the wind. A chill of fear, something she hadn't felt in many long years, crawled along Yvanda's spine. She knew that voice; it was the Sorcerer's. She'd heard it snarling in anger, sliding smoothly over the making of deadly plans, laughing, laughing, for too many years.

She turned quickly, looking for the ship's captain. Standing on the deck, he seemed to hear nothing but his crew and the gulls' screaming. One seaman scrambled up into the rigging, while another ran along the ship's stern, making ready to bank the sails to catch the quickening wind.

Suddenly the smooth growling words vanished as though they had never been. Yvanda heard nothing but the sea's rumbling mutter, the sound of betrayal.

"No!" she cried.

Inside herself, where the magic lay, she reached and groped, trying to find the strength to resist what she knew was about to happen. But all her dark strength seemed to have fled from her, to have gone into some silent and unreachable place. She stood helpless before the silent vengeance of a master who had known all along that she plotted treachery, and she knew she couldn't help herself.

No storm rose to whip the waves into their killing swells, no wind bellowed, no rain fell. But the sea, responding to the Sorcerer's command, leaped and roared, its waves foaming high enough to break against the spars of the little ship's masts. In moments, the ship was swamped, her occupants drowned, dashed to their deaths in the unforgiving black waters.

The gods' child was only one among the many who died on a sunlit sea that settled, sighing, back to complacency in moments.

She knew, in her last moment, that she had been found out, caught. She knew that a child of the gods was not immortal, and deep within her rage and fury ran a light, frail thread of something that in another would have been called relief.

CHAPTER 27

I am Islief of the First People.

The things of which I write are things most sacred, things most holy. And I write of hope, always keeping in mind the sin which was committed in the name of hope. Old I am, old and old.

The crown is lost, and lost again. The jewels are broken and scattered. The gods were right. The crown should never have gone from us.

I will wait a long time, and waiting, I will hope that the crown will be found again.

By these elements will it be known: Ruby, Emerald, Sapphire, Diamond, Topaz. Each had its place in the crown and each its power.

Ruby: Mistress of War. Emerald: Ruler of Nature. Sapphire: King of Air. Diamond: Prince of Water. Topaz: Thane of Fire.

I gave these things to the Second People in hope, and though the crown is broken, still I hope that trust has not been misused.

* * * * *

Nikia closed her eyes and took a long breath. She'd read these words over and over during the long day and knew them as well as though she herself had penned them. They were a last testimony from the hand of a member of a race who had, over long years, become lost and forgotten.

Drifting through her thoughts came a gentle voice from memory: *Legends speak of the small folk called dwarves, who delved in your northern mountains for jewels to make rich treasures. Should I stop to see if I can find their hidden treasure houses?*

Those had been Garth's words. They had been spoken in jest. What jest would ever pass his lips again?

Tears pricked at Nikia's eyes, and she turned her head. She heard the soft, even breathing of the mage, who sat across the table from her.

She studied the scrolls at her own insistence. His threat of death or worse to Garth and her friends kept her here delving among old parchments and the words of a people long dead. And there was something else: hope. She almost laughed aloud. What hope, Nikia?

"It's a strange phrase."

Nikia started. Reynarth's words jerked her back to grim reality. "Which?" she asked wearily.

"The Second People. Who are they?"

Nikia's lips twisted into a bitter smile. "Surely you've gleaned that much from the scrolls."

Reynarth regarded her carefully. Did hopelessness make her careless of her words? Or was it some certainty that she still was held in value?

No matter, he decided. She was a wretched thing, a shadow of the princess she had been. Thinner now, with a face shaped by pain and fear, there was nothing of the regal girl who had ridden into the city of Damris nearly a year ago. That pretty child was gone, replaced by a hard-eyed, pale-skinned woman who dressed in whatever castoffs he gave her.

No childish roundness graced her cheeks and body now. Only hard angles and harder eyes. He had carved away most of that beauty, but he was not displeased with the woman who remained. She was, after all, his creature. He had created her. He owned her. She would do the work he needed done. There could be no threat from this cowed, bitter-tongued woman.

"Who are these Second People?"

"They are us, Reynarth."

"The Elvish?"

Nikia laughed, a dry, mocking sound. "No. They are us, Mannish and Elvish. We were one folk in ancient times."

"A groundless insult."

"You think it an insult. Aye, perhaps you do. Well, it doesn't matter. There is truth in what I say. There are clues in ancient songs, and the Ylin tapestry that hangs in the Great Hall of the Citadel at Damris bears me out. Ylin and Aeylin are the same woman. We were once the same people."

"Who is this Aeylin?"

"Do you want a history lesson? I thought you wanted something else."

"Tell me."

Nikia shrugged, glad to rest her weary eyes. "Ylin you know, I am sure. Your ancient queen. Through clues laid in song and legend, Dail and I learned that she was the same woman as the Elvish Queen Aeylin, who took the five fabled Jewels of Elvish as a wedding gift to her husband. Likely he was the head of a separatist faction who later became the father of the Mannish people. So you see, Reynarth, my own marriage wasn't unprecedented, although none alive today knew it."

"That can't be. There are no magic-users common among my people."

"Not common, no. But where do you think your ability to learn magic comes from? Oh, I know, it is a craft you had to learn from childhood. But ability is the key to learning that craft, as any other. For that ability, you may thank ancestors we each have in common."

"This is foolishness."

"Think so if you will. I can't see how it matters now, anyway. You have done your best to see that there will be no continuing of what the ancients called the Second People. We'll live as slaves now, if your master lets us live at all. Were there to be a history to survive us, Reynarth, it would curse you."

"Enough!"

It was enough. She had let her bitterness and anger overwhelm her sense. She didn't want to distract him from the search they both shared.

"What of the spell?"

Nikia sighed wearily. "It is a simple enough spell, to be sure."

"Why can't you work it?"

"There is more to an Elvish spell than simply mouthing words, Reynarth. Spells passed down from one to another are learned easily enough. But only the creator of a spell knows the intent of his work.

"If I don't learn the spell-maker's intent, it will work no better for me than for you."

"You're stalling."

She was, but she shook her head. "No." Nikia tried carefully to let her denial show some truth. "No, I'm not. This isn't a spell I want to see go awry, Reynarth. You know the danger of that."

He did indeed. A miscast spell had taken Gweneth's life, had set his plans wavering months ago. He could take no such risk now.

"If you toy with me, Nikia, you'll spend each day of a long life regretting your game." His voice was dark and filled with the promise of pain.

Nikia swallowed and reached for the spell scroll. "Let me study in peace, Reynarth. You do neither of us any good now with your threats."

His eyes narrowed. He watched her as she bent again to her perusal of the scroll. He sensed danger, but he didn't know how to turn back. He knew he wouldn't be able to cast this spell, the key to the ruby's powers. She was his tool; she was the key to the key. Reynarth summoned patience and watched Nikia carefully, as a cat watches its cornered prey.

* * * * *

Black blood fouled the wet straw. Dail stepped out of the way of the vile flow and watched as it hissed against the stone. The stench of the blood was powerful, sharp and putrid. The misshapen creature, their guard, was dead. Dail dropped to his knees and searched among the keys at the thing's belt. "Damn! I can't tell which is the right one! What do you hear, Darun?"

"Nothing . . . nothing yet. Hurry!"

Dail fumbled with the keys, choosing one and then another. After a moment, he found the key that unlocked Calmis's manacles.

"Take what weapons you can find from this piece of carrion," Dail muttered, working on his own bonds. When he was free, he accepted a dagger from his friend. "What about you?"

Calmis hefted a short sword. "This will do me well enough. I have the reach of you, my friend. I'll make good use of it. What now?"

"Cover this thing with straw and wait near the door. I'll free the others." He let the chain drop near the fallen guard. It had crushed the side of the unwary guard's skull when the creature stepped inside the cell to deliver the foul water and crusts of moldy bread for their meal. "Cover the chain, too. It won't do to let them discover just how it was overcome yet."

Dail crept to the open door and peered cautiously up and down the corridor. The whimpers and cries of the other prisoners would be good cover for whatever noise they made in escaping.

Sure that he was unobserved, Dail stepped across the stone-floored corridor and tried first one key and then another before he got the door of the cell that held Riche and Lizbet open.

"My lord!" Riche gasped.

"Aye, lad, aye. Lady Lizbet?"

"Here, Master Dail." Dail heard more heart in her weak voice than he'd expected. "How—how is it that you're free?"

"No time to explain now, my lady." Dail undid her chain swiftly and ushered them both out before him. The corridors were still clear. "Darun?"

"Here." Calmis appeared in the door of their cell, the short sword in his good hand. "What now?"

"A quick run, my friend, or nothing. Two of us have weapons, and two do not. My lady and the boy must stay behind us."

Lizbet nodded, shepherding Riche before her, keeping him safely between her and Dail. Calmis, the best defended, would run ahead.

"Take a deep breath, friends," Dail murmured. "We get only one chance."

And Calmis was gone, running softly down the corridor, never once checking over his shoulder to see if the others were behind him. He knew they would be.

He saw only one guard at the brazier at the end of the corridor. The others must all be about delivering the slop that passed as food to the prisoners in the other cell blocks. Calmis moved silently.

The guard stood with its back to him as it tried to ward off the dungeon's chill before the brazier's coals. Calmis slipped in closer to the guard. He gathered a silent breath and touched the creature's shoulder lightly. The guard stiffened and jerked around. Calmis lunged to bury the short sword between its ribs.

The sword thrust was blunted on the creature's mail. Calmis stepped back, recovered, and thrust his weapon upward and into the guard's unprotected throat.

Dail caught the dead thing before it dropped and eased it silently to the floor, its black blood hissing. "Don't step in it!" he whispered to Lizbet and Riche.

Calmis wiped his sword on the guard's tunic and snatched up another short sword and dagger. The sword he gave to Dail, and the daggers went to the others. "Where to now?"

The bard shook his head. "Upward. I remember something about how we got here. There's a guard's room at the end of the second corridor above here. If it's not empty, we'll move on until we can find a place to stop and recount."

Breathlessly they pressed on.

* * * * *

I am Islief of the First People.

So the ancient chronicler began each scroll, as though he hoped, by this simple device, to impart some memory of himself and his kindred.

Nikia was weary of the words. Her back ached from leaning over the scrolls; her eyes throbbed dully in her head. She knew the way of the old spell now.

The words were simple enough, graceful even in their leading way: One element begets another.

Blood: Ignite the power that I crave. Power: Move in strength to my need. Strength: Fill with courage this ready heart. Courage: Guide the bloodstone to my need.

She did no more than recall them now, afraid to reach out with her magic for their power. Yet even as she held the words firmly in her mind, Nikia felt their strength. It would be so easy to lose herself in their will, to feel the rapid surge of scarlet power flash though her!

But, no, not yet. She glanced covertly at Reynarth. The ruby lay on the table between them, shimmering with light and promise. Or did it threaten?

She couldn't tell. It seemed foreign to her now, no longer a part of her life. This lovely gem, this blood-red jewel, was no longer the symbol of her father's house. It was instead a remnant of an ancient people, a doorway to great power.

"Nikia!" His voice rough with strain and waiting, edged with suspicion, Reynarth leaned across the table and closed his long hand around her wrist. "You've played this game long enough, Nikia. You're not reading those words. You haven't been for an hour."

In defense, she spoke the simple truth. "I'm afraid of this thing, Reynarth."

"I don't care what you're afraid of. Your task is merely to unlock the power. Mine is to control it."

"Do you know what you ask? Do you know what this talisman will do?"

"I know." But he didn't. He only hoped to control the power he would unlock. He didn't know that he had the strength to work the ruby to his will. It was a weak link in his plan, but one that he was willing to risk now.

Viselike, his hand tightened around Nikia's wrist until she grimaced with the pain. "It is time, Nikia."

She drew a long breath and was not surprised to feel it shuddering in her breast. "I don't have the strength yet, Reynarth. I am weary from long hours of study and work. I have to rest."

"Bah!" He threw her hand from him and turned away. "More delay!"

"No—yes, yes, it is a delay, but would you risk all in a miscast spell? Would you truly throw away your game on an ill-chosen chance?"

There was only one answer. He was not in a position to risk a poorly cast spell. The magic the ruby would unleash would be felt across the Two Kingdoms, even to the castle of Souless. He would get no second chance if the spell went awry. That warning would herald him as a traitor to his masters.

Reynarth's eyes narrowed. He was gauging his moves, but he knew that Nikia was right. "Get from here, then, and sleep. I'll not disturb your sleep tonight. But when I come for you again, be ready."

Nikia rose slowly to her feet. She had purchased more time, but to what end? She was only delaying the final reckoning, the inevitable use of the ruby. Shaking her head, she left him and closed the door quietly behind her.

Sleep came easily enough, for she was exhausted. She had not lied in that. But it was filled with scarlet dreams.

* * * * *

Dail peered out into the shadows of the corridor. He willed his thoughts to be still, forced his mind to grasp and order them. Luck had brought them this far, to the second level above the dungeon and safely past two sentries. It was well enough to trust to fortune in the first panic of escape, but now there must be a plan if they were to find Garth in this rat's maze of a dungeon.

He glanced at his companions and smiled briefly. Lizbet stood within the encircling embrace of Calmis's arms. What discretion had marked their attentions to each other at the Citadel was lost now in the fear of the keep. Calmis held her gently, but there was a strength in his brown eyes and an expression that bespoke of his determination that no harm would come to the Elven while he breathed.

Riche crouched in a corner of the small room that had once held two guards. His eyes were wide as he stared at the rapidly stiffening corpses of the overpowered sentries.

Poor lad! Dail reached out and stroked the boy's matted hair. "You've made a brave run with us, Riche."

Riche rose slowly to his feet. He stepped gingerly over the bodies of the sentries, careful not to tread in the dark blood that stained the stone floor.

"Master," he said, his voice a soft whisper, "do you know where the prince is being held?"

Dail shook his head. He scouted the shadows again, afraid that even these whispered words might be overheard. But the corridor was empty, and no sound came down its shadowed length. Nevertheless, he knew that they couldn't stay here long.

"I don't know where he is—only that he's here somewhere and that he's alive." He gestured to Calmis. "Tell them what you heard."

It was a strange tale to Riche, only half understood and only accepted because it brought hope.

Lizbet sighed. "Nikia's well! She must be if she's spoken to you this way." Her eyes lifted to Calmis's in a smile. "Thank the gods, Nikia is well and strong!"

Strong at least, Dail thought. We can only pray that she is well.

He drew a long breath and checked the corridor again. It was still dark and silent. "I don't know much about this keep, Darun. Do you know anything about it?"

Calmis smiled bitterly. "The last time I came here, it was to a better welcome than we've had lately. I know my way well enough in the upper chambers." He frowned, trying to recall what little he knew about the keep's lower regions. "There's a cave below these dungeons. It opens onto the sea. It was used, in better times, to unload cargoes bound for the keep. Any of those storage places could be converted into cells. It would be a good place to keep a valuable prisoner secure. It wouldn't be the usual place to look for someone."

He thought, too, that hiding a valuable prisoner in plain sight among the wretched occupants of the dungeons would be a clever ploy as well. He mentioned it reluctantly.

"It would suit Reynarth's evil humor," Dail agreed, "but I don't think he has time for humor now. If I were him, I'd have Garth in the last place anyone would look for him. How far are we from this cave, Darun?"

"If I knew where we were, I could answer that, my friend." Riche spoke up, his voice hesitant. "My lords?"

Calmis glanced at him. "Aye, lad?"

"We are three levels down from the entrance floor, my lord. We were five levels down in our cells." He shrugged when they looked surprised. "I counted."

Dail grinned and clapped the boy's shoulder. "I'm glad someone thought to! Good lad! Darun, does that tell you anything?"

"It tells me enough. What is it, then? The cave?"

"We'll give it a try."

And if he would rather have been searching for Nikia, Dail let nothing of his feelings show. He told himself that he was afraid that her peril was the greater, that Garth in his cell was in less danger than she. He dared not explore his reluctance further than that.

* * * * *

Voices, as hollow as cavern depths, followed Nikia through her dreams. Light, red as blood, brighter than the sun, cast black shadows before her and behind. She couldn't hear her own frightened thinking over the booming voice.

I am Islief . . .

The light flared. Shadows leapt around her. Nikia stumbled on the rough flooring, and stone bit into her knees and hands.

. . . of the First People!

A mighty anthem of war surrounded the words and couched them in terror. Nikia held her hands up to her eyes, trying to shade them from the scarlet brilliance. Through her hands, rendered translucent by the blaze of light, she could see the blood running in the veins of her fingers and pick out the black outline of her bones.

Blood: Ignite the power that I crave!

A great trembling gripped Nikia. She staggered to her feet but fell again, her legs shaking too hard to hold her steady.

Power: Move in strength to my need!

The stone-walled world about Nikia began to rumble and thrum with a power mightier than earthquakes.

Strength: Fill with courage this ready heart!

Whimpering, the sound lost in the rumbling of the earth's depths, hidden by the booming voice of Islief of the First People, Nikia gasped and found the air hot enough to burn her throat. Above and around her came the stamp of booted feet, the clash of sword and shield, the martial anthems of war.

Courage: Guide the bloodstone to my need!

Tiny she was, a mere scrap of life writhing in the infinite fire of war unleashed. Her screams, raw and piercing, were the mewlings of some insignificant creature swept into a holocaust.

Blood . . . Power . . . Strength . . . Courage!

Wailing, Nikia fell on her face, her arms outthrust, her fingers scrabbling and clawing at the unyielding stone of the earth's womb.

Then suddenly, though Islief's voice still boomed, though the bloody light of war still flared around her, Nikia heard her own cry rise, taking flight to the vaulted heights. It rose, fluttering and weak, and found a shadowy echo. And she heard that echo and rose up on her knees, braced against the shuddering stone.

"Blood!" she screamed, and found the strength to rise, wavering, to her feet.

"Power!" And her voice was stronger, firmer than before.

"Strength!" Her heart ceased its quaking, staggering falter.

"Courage!" Nikia raised a clenched fist to the unseen roof of the earth's chamber, reaching, grasping, clutching, as her legs strengthened, as her heart rose.

She opened her fist and lifted her hand high as though in offering.

Her hand was empty. A wail, piteous and lost, the sound of a wraith turned away from its barrow, drifted through the suddenly silent chamber. Nikia fell again to her knees.

* * * * *

The wail still echoed in her ears, her fists ached with clenching, and her heart trembled and tripped.

Nikia was alone and in a familiar place, huddled in the center of Reynarth's bed. Nothing remained of her dream but her burning throat and quaking heart.

Even as she drew a breath, wincing at the gentle passage of air in her throat, another wail arose and took flight. Nikia started, swung off the bed, and staggered to the little window.

The sound came from outdoors, a cry of despair and hopeless worship. Streets that had been empty before ran and flowed with activity and motion as creatures, the same kind as the guards plus the three-legged beasts, streamed out into the roads and byways. Their screams of despair and helplessness were met by similar wailing from within the keep.

Caught between the wailing from without and within the keep, with the memory of the dream cry that haunted her sleep, Nikia sat down heavily on the cushioned seat of the window embrasure.

"Dear gods!" she whispered. "What can this be?"

* * * * *

Calmis crouched in the shadows at the head of the short flight of stairs descending to the cavern level of the keep. From below, fresh air flowed upward, eddying through the fading stink of the dungeon levels they were leaving behind. Dail stood close at his back. Calmis heard his friend's soft breathing and the louder, more frightened breathing of Lizbet and Riche behind them.

Slowly, almost absently, Calmis ran his fingers along the edge of the short sword that lay across his knee.

"Darun." Dail's voice was more than a whisper. The bard

knew that a whisper in these echoing caverns carried faster and farther than a soft voice. "What do you see?"

"One guard, with his back to us."

Carefully silent, Calmis shifted his position. There was only one sentry that he could see, and that one's back was to the stairs. There might well be others beyond. It would be foolish to expect that the sentries would be fewer closer to the place where their master's most valuable prisoner was kept.

Calmis narrowed his eyes. He could easily take this guard. He'd worry about what lay beyond, in the cavern, later. He had seen and done much killing this day.

He was a diplomat trained, a man who had made his career soothing blows and reinterpreting meanings. He had received, as a matter of course, training as a man at arms as well. Seldom before now had he been called on to use that training. Yet he didn't begrudge the killing. If he did later, so be it. Now he was as casual at blood-letting as any hardened warrior.

"Follow me closely, Dail," he said. "I'll take this one. You'll have to take whatever waits beyond, if any."

Calmis listened while Dail passed the word of their plan on to Lizbet and Riche. Casting one glance over his shoulder, Calmis saw that Riche was now behind Dail, with Lizbet farthest behind. The lad's eyes were wide and bright, fear battling eagerness. Calmis knew that the little page would be backing Dail in any action to come.

"Ready?" Dail nodded, and the lad loosed his dagger.

Slowly and with great stealth, Calmis eased down the stairs, one at a time, pausing after each to watch the guard. The creature shifted from time to time, one foot to the other.

Keeping to the shadows against the wall, Calmis continued. One step . . . pause . . . another step . . . another pause. Three more steps and the creature would be within reach. Calmis drew a soft, long breath.

He took another step down, felt the cool press of stone against his side. Behind him, Dail barely breathed. Moving his sword to a more comfortable grip, Calmis leaned forward and took the last step. He had learned from experience that these guards wore no gorget to protect their vulnerable necks.

He reached out his left hand slowly, carefully. His fingers were nearly on the sentry's shoulder, his sword raised to strike, when the hideous wailing began.

Behind him, he heard Riche cry out and Lizbet gasp. The sentry under his hand bolted upright, stiffening. Calmis threw himself back into the shadows. Only an act of supreme willpower kept him from dropping his weapon and clapping his hands over his ears.

The wailing rose from everywhere within the keep, cascading down the corridors above them, filling the cavern below with sounds of despair . . . and with something else that Calmis couldn't identify.

He glanced back at Dail and Riche. The lad was on his knees on one of the steps, held there only by Dail's strong hand.

"Darun! Look!" Calmis jerked back toward where the guard had been, but he saw only an empty post. Above them, the clattering of booted feet ran in a weird staccato beneath the wailing song.

"It's gone!" Before he could say more, Dail's hand pulled him back hard against the wall.

"In the name of the gods, Dail, what is this?"

"I don't know!"

They ducked into the shadows as other guards from below passed them, all running upward to join the stream of their fellows flowing out of the keep.

All about them chaos reigned as the creatures of the keep ran blindly upward, trailing their wails behind them.

CHAPTER 28

"He is here!" Rage and horror flamed in the mage's eyes; Nikia couldn't tell which was dominant.

Reynarth snatched at Nikia's wrist, jerked her from her seat at the window, and hauled her to her feet.

"Reynarth! What is it? What do you mean?" The terror in his eyes sparked Nikia's own fear. Dry-mouthed, she pulled against his grasp. His hand tightened, grinding the bones of her wrist.

"The Sorcerer! Fool, that I delayed! Fool, that I listened to your feeble excuses! He is here!"

"But—I don't understand—"

Reynarth jerked Nikia, stumbling, across the chamber and thrust her into the library. She staggered, righted herself, and turned on her captor.

"Has your treachery been discovered?" She smiled, seeking to find calm. What small calm she found was shattered by Reynarth's blow across her mouth. Nikia turned on him.

"Have a care, Reynarth! You need me!"

"No more of that, Elvish witch! I have had enough of that!" He paused and lifted his head as though listening.

Throughout their exchange, the wailing had continued, flowing over and around their words, making a dirge-song that filled the air of the keep.

"Do you hear that? That is the sound of his creatures crying in helplessness at his approach. They can't help themselves; they know when their creator has come. Listen!"

She couldn't have shut out that awful sound had she tried. It seemed that now the wailing had taken on a different tone. The roar of the ocean echoed in it now, with waves rushing and hissing and more tumbling in to fill the gap.

"Every one of his creatures in this city knows of his arrival. They run to the port; they can't do else. We have time, but only a little."

"We?" Again he struck her, and again Nikia stumbled. She tasted blood in her mouth; tears stung her eyes.

"Now, Nikia! There will be no more delay! Something has gone wrong. If anyone should have come, it should have been her, Yvanda. Where is she?"

His voice was high with fear as his eyes darted around the chamber. He reminded Nikia of a frantic rat in a doorless maze. Nikia knew then, with a sudden cold chill, that he had played his game of treachery not only against the Two Kingdoms, but also with Yvanda against the Sorcerer.

He had never planned to turn the ruby over to Yvanda, either. Had there been time, Nikia would have pitied him, caught in too many webs of his own making. As it was, she could only shiver in fear.

"Take the ruby—now!—and work the spell." He clutched at the jewel where it lay on his breast. He fumbled at the clasp of the chain, couldn't work it, and tore at it, snapping the fine silver links in his fear and urgency. "Now!"

The ruby felt cool and hard in her hands. Nikia trembled. She must make it work, but where was the strength? Where would she find the power to control what she unlocked, to prevent Reynarth from snatching the power that he so desired?

"Now!"

Nikia sucked air into her lungs, fought to steady herself, and turned from the mage for a moment. When she turned back, she saw no lessening of the twin flames of horror and rage in his eyes.

He must try to master the power of the ruby now. It was his only protection against the master he had betrayed. But could he control it? Would it run rampant through him, devouring him with his own lust for it?

With cold certainty, Nikia knew that she must hold the power. Reynarth believed she was too weak to resist his will once the spell freed the ruby's crimson strength. Nikia didn't know how she could stop him. Still, she must try.

Hunter-Defender! It was the title she had taken to herself one grim morning: Hunter-Defender.

You have hunted successfully, she told herself, finding the key to this awful talisman. Now you must defend! If it meant her life and the lives of those who depended on her, the lives of all those who made up the armies of the Two Kingdoms, she must not let this talisman of power fall into Reynarth's hands! This weak and twisted mage couldn't hold it to his own desire. It was too great, too strong, too consuming. And it must not fall into the hands of the Sorcerer.

"Power," she said softly.

"Now! Do it now!" Reynarth screamed.

"I am!" Nikia's voice was a ragged scream, filled with her own fear and need. She jerked her head up, fighting for control. She met the mage's eyes across the ruby and smiled through swelling lips. "I am. You must trust me now, Reynarth. You can do nothing else."

His eyes were brittle with hatred. He knew too well that he must trust her, and he hated that he must. The wailing greetings of the Sorcerer's creatures changed again. They had seen their god, they had drunk at the fountain of their creator's power, and they were moving once more. The sound grew. They were returning to the keep, but not to posts deserted. They were returning with their god, a mob of creatures whose only will was his.

"Do it now, Nikia! Do it now!"

Within herself, Nikia groaned. O gods, help this hunter-defender. O gods, help me now!

"Power," she said again softly. Nikia closed her eyes and shut the mage away from her sight and her mind. There must be no distraction. Slowly the wailing softened in her ears, receded, and was no more.

"Come at my need." Her voice sank to a whisper as she prepared her mind and magic to exercise skills she feared she didn't have. Calm gentled her fears; assurance filled her. Behind her eyes, the light grew faintly red like the sun seen through lids lightly closed.

Nikia breathed softly, evenly, feeling her magic course within her. The first thing she must do is identify herself to the talisman.

"I am Nikia," she said aloud. In her heart, she added, I am the Hunter-Defender. She opened her eyes and gazed at the ruby in her hand. Warm red light spilled across her fingers. Softly, easily, as though slipping into a pool of warm water, Nikia stilled her breathing and slid into the crimson depths of the spell.

* * * * *

"There isn't a guard left in the place!" Calmis shook his head. "I don't understand it, but I think we'd best make use of it while we can."

Dail agreed. He glanced at Riche and Lizbet, standing terrified and silent in the gloom of the cavern's shadows. "Darun, how many places could they hide Garth here?"

"A dozen . . . more, perhaps."

"Then we'll all search. And quickly. I don't know how long this grace will last or what it means."

It wasn't, in the end, a long search. It was Riche who found the cell. His voice wavered between triumph and horror, echoing from the stone walls and ceiling as he cried, "My lords! I have found the prince!"

It was indeed Garth. But his face, shaped and sculpted by pain and despair, hunger and grief, was not a face that Dail immediately recognized. He squinted in the wavering light of abandoned torches, peering through the bars of what had once been a storage room.

His eyes appeared muddy, flat with confusion and questions. "How—how can it be?" He spoke in a dry rasp, a croak that could hardly be heard even in the silence of the cavern.

Dail grinned wryly. "I hardly know myself, my lord."

"My lord," Riche piped, "we have come to free you!"

"To free me? But how?"

Dail saw at once that answers would only glide away from his mind if they were given. Confusion reigned there now. "Later. Let us do what we've come to do first. We'll tell you what we can afterward."

The iron chains binding Garth were new and shining in the uncertain light. Dail still carried the ring of keys he had taken from the slain guard, but none would release the manacles that bound both Garth's hands to the rough stone walls.

"Move to the end of the chain, my lord, and close your eyes."

Garth did as he was told, crabbing forward as far as he could, squeezing his eyes shut. Raising his sword high above his head, Dail caught a deep breath and held it. Then, with all the strength he possessed, he brought the sword down as though it were an axe, aiming for a taut link near Garth's left hand. The ring of steel on steel echoed through the abandoned cavern. The link held fast.

Again Dail raised the sword, and again steel sang. Garth's right hand came free. He scrambled to his feet, wavered, and reached for Lizbet's supporting hand. "You wield a sword better than I thought, cousin," he said.

Dail grinned and raised a trembling hand to wipe his face. "Aye, well, a bard doesn't wander from place to place and learn nothing about swords, my lord." He drew a long breath and was not surprised to find that he was trembling. The honest admiration in the prince's brown eyes was ample thanks. At that moment, no memory of the woman he loved stood between Dail and his cousin. He clasped Garth's hand warmly. "Well met, Garth."

"Aye," Garth breathed. "But have you found Nikia?"

"Not yet. It's a strange tale, and there's no time for all of it now, but listen and we'll tell you what we can."

The darkness that had filled Garth's days, his nights, his mind and soul, seemed suddenly to be lifting. He clenched his fists to still his shaking hands. "Tell me, then. I'll need a little time to steady my legs."

Dail spoke quickly, retelling the events of the past weeks, of Reynarth's treachery and the true history of the Ruby of Guyaire. Though it was not easy, he managed to tame the bardic muse within him that protested having to tell so wild a tale in so brief a time.

Garth looked from one of them to another, as though seeking confirmation of Dail's story. The tale was true, though, and he had only to look at the fear lurking in the boy's eyes, the wavering attempt at bravery that Nikia's waiting woman made, to know it.

"And the war?" he said. "Do any of you know how the war progresses?"

Calmis sighed. "It progresses, my lord, but who can say how? It's not lost—it can't be, or none of us would be here to wonder about it."

Dail agreed. "We've little enough time to worry about it, though. I don't like this silence, this absence of guards. Something is happening, and it smells to me like an ending."

The lovely Ruby of Guyaire a talisman of war? Garth shuddered, remembering how often he had seen it, glittering and beautiful, lying on Nikia's breast.

We bargained for it so hard in the treaty negotiations, he thought, a chill spidering up his arms and neck. Who, I wonder, was the winner of that bargain?

His legs trembled under him, and he leaned back against the cold stone wall of his prison cell. There was something else they had bargained for in that treaty—someone else. Now it was she, if Dail's understanding of the situation was true, who stood between the wrath of an ancient jewel and the treachery of a traitorous mage.

And I doubted her all these horrible days and nights. . . . But it wasn't my fault. It was Reynarth's doing. . . . Garth's excuse sounded lame in his own mind.

Gardens and herbs, long sweet nights in the arms of a willing wife, a child's death. . . . Her grief, mine, ours. . . .

"I want to find my wife."

"Indeed we *must* find her, my lord," Dail said softly, "for if we find her, we will find the ruby."

"Where is she?"

"Here somewhere," Dail said. "Darun?"

Calmis shrugged. "If she's anywhere, she's with Reynarth. And he, I am sure, would have taken the best chambers in the keep for his own. Those would be at the top of the keep, the chambers of the rightful captain of the keep."

Garth nodded. "Of course." He glanced once at each of them, stood away from the wall, and reached for Calmis's sword. "I'll need this."

Though Calmis gave his weapon readily, there was doubt in his eyes. "You aren't strong yet, my lord. Perhaps—"

"I need your weapon, Darun, and thank you for it." It had been Dail, Garth knew, who commanded this little band of prisoners till now. He eyed the bard carefully and saw nothing there but concern. He stood away from the wall.

"Darun, get the boy and the Lady Lizbet to safety. I don't know where you'll find it in this place, but do it. Dail, you come with me. I think two can steal through this place better than five."

Calmis glanced quickly at Dail, then nodded. "Of course, my lord, as you say. But have a care."

Garth's smile was brittle. "Don't worry. The safety of these two is in your hands, Darun. The only thing I ask is that you pray that the gods attend us."

Dail, too, prayed. The thought of a long run through the maze of this keep with a man unsteady and weak on his legs chilled him to his bones.

* * * * *

"Blood! Ignite the power that I crave!"

Nikia touched the ruby to her bleeding lips. The jewel felt warm now in her hands. Crimson light splashed across her and, like a scarlet fountain, down to the stone-flagged floor. In her blood, Nikia felt the thrum of the magic which had reverberated in her dream.

"Power! Move in strength to my need!"

The jewel was hot, but the heat did not sear her fingers. Instead, her own blood coursed stronger, faster, filling her with undreamed-of power.

"Strength!" Nikia gasped as the ruby turned to flame in her fist. Blood-red light filled the library. She threw back her head and screamed at the consuming pain of the ruby's fire. "Strength! Fill with courage this ready heart!"

Nikia's heart quailed and trembled within her, quaking at the thought of the wild power she invoked. She was losing control of the spell and her will!

"What's wrong?" Reynarth's cry was a whisper beneath the drumming sound of the ruby. Nikia swung her head up, saw him, and gasped as she tried to ignore his words.

"What's wrong!" he cried once more.

"Be still!" she screamed, but she didn't bother to see if he obeyed. Instead, she grappled with her trembling will and wrestled it to stillness, trying to control her fear. Soon the terror ebbed and she tried again.

"Courage!" Nikia invoked, prayed, beseeched. Her trembling stopped, and control settled on her softly as though it had always been there. "Guide the bloodstone to my need!"

Then she was no longer who she had been.

* * * * *

Across the Two Kingdoms, armies faltered. Their warriors staggered and became still.

A man with his hand upraised to plunge a dagger into the throat of his undead enemy fell back, his blade clean, his enemy quiet beneath him. An Elvish warrior, his arrow nocked and aimed, his bow drawn to full tautness, let the arrow fall and stood, his eyes turned northward, his heart emptied and his will drained.

A king, bereft of sons, fell motionless back into his seat at the council table. Another king, in the act of mounting his gray war-horse to lead a battle from which he did not expect to return, felt his intent vanish. Around him, his warriors, too, stopped and all turned their eyes northward, as though seeking the place to which their resolution had flown.

In the Two Kingdoms, all war ceased. Invader and defender alike were will-bereft and could not think to even wonder why. They were as weapons placed aside, to be called for again when needed. A great silence took the land, and no creature moved but to breathe.

*   *   *   *   *

Like the crimson facets of the ruby, Death stood on her right hand, Terror on her left. Behind her, the twins Pestilence and Suffering awaited her command. She rose larger than all of them, cloaked in blood-red light, laughing with clear, pure joy.

At her laughter, mountains trembled, the earth quaked, and chasms were opened up to spill forth the fire of the world's life in great molten gouts. All this she saw, and one thing more.

She was not the only power abroad in this stilled world. There was one other, black, malevolent, and brooding. The waiting enemy.

She was jealous of her strength. She took a name to herself as though to gather this new strength to her: Hunter-Defender.

At her feet, scrabbling at the hem of her caldron gown, plucking and begging, a brown creature knelt. It had been a mage. It had been, in some other time, some far place, a source of fear and doubt. She did not laugh, but she smiled. The insect-thing at her feet cowered, fell on its face, and loosed its plucking hold on her hem.

Reynarth—that had been the creature's name. What name it held now, in this gap of time, she did not know. Were she to move, were her hand to shift with only the smallest motion, this thing would be dead. Did she want it dead? She glanced at Death, the midnight-clothed attendant on her right hand. Death did not move, made no indication. It was waiting for her will in the matter.

She chose to wait. There was another who required her attention. The Sorcerer, the Ancient Enemy, the Devouring Evil, moved now, and was within the city's walls. He would come, though he knew that a power as large as his own waited within.

Absently, almost carelessly, the Hunter-Defender placed the ruby on its silver-linked chain. She willed the chain whole, and it was. She slipped it over her head. If she remembered a time when other hands had done so, for other purposes, old hands and dear to her in that far time, she did not falter.

The Sorcerer was at the gate, and there was a thing that must be decided. The Hunter-Defender was ready. Silence filled the keep as it had filled the Two Kingdoms.

CHAPTER 29

Time was not a part of the place where Dail lay. He and Garth had made their fearful and silent run through the keep unchallenged. Their footsteps, echoing weirdly against the stone walls and vaulted ceilings, were the only sounds they'd heard. Garth had found the staircase to the captain's wing easily. Though it lay now in the hot summer sun as a carcass from which jackals had been frightened, he knew his father's proud keep well.

Rallying strength to purpose, the prince had led the way. If Garth saw or noticed the wreck of the place, the dagger-scored furniture, the once lovely tapestries now lying in fouled ruin, Dail saw no sign of it in his expression.

Something else moved him now, and there was nothing of the boyish prince about him. He'd been hurt in a way Dail could not reckon. His brown eyes were hard, his jaw set as stubbornly as dead Fenyan had ever set his. Yet across those flinty eyes, like shadows of the moon across stone, ran ghosts of dread.

Finally they'd come to the corridor outside the captain's chamber. Then everything had been sucked from them—strength, will, even fear. Pinned, like bats in the glare of an unlooked-for sun, they lay where they fell.

Garth struggled now to raise his head, to lift his hand, to rise from where he had fallen. He could not.

Brazen red light leaked out of the chamber. It stained the stone walls and floor with bloody color and cast black shadows over them both.

Dail could move, but only a little. He reached for the sword fallen from Garth's hand. "Garth . . ." His voice was a strained, hoarse whisper, forced through lips nearly paralyzed with terror. "Take up your sword!"

Garth swallowed hard, clenched his teeth, and reached for the sword. His hand made a spider's crawl toward the hilt. When his fingers fell short, bereft of effort and will, he groaned aloud. "What is this light? Dail, what is it?"

The bard shook his head. He did not know. He could not guess. Panting with the effort, he lifted his own sword, slid its point from the floor, and braced his grip with both hands.

Nikia was within. She must be. But what else was with her there? Where did this light, this bloody glare, come from?

"Garth, we must get inside!"

"Nikia can't possibly have lived through this!" Black despair, tinted bloody by the light, filled Garth's eyes.

"She has!" She must, Dail thought. There was no room in him to believe that the brave, sweet girl he had known before this horror came on them was dead. He saw her clearly in his mind, slim and straight, his proud Elvish Starflower.

What was left to Dail now if she was dead? She had been the vision that motivated all his plans since they had been brought to this wretched keep. He had made his escape for her. For her safety, all his prayers and beseeching had been offered.

He didn't fear his thoughts or longings now. He couldn't, even though her husband was here with him. Even now, in this inferno of brazen light and fear, he knew that she would never be his to claim. But she would ever be his to love. That must be enough for him now.

In a way, it was. It was enough to free his limbs somewhat from the grip of the crimson fear. He knew, his heart aching, that it would be enough to free Garth as well.

"Garth! Listen! She is in there. She needs us!"

There was both shame and defiance in the prince's dark eyes. He tried again to reach his sword. This time his fingers touched the hilt and closed around it. As he heaved it up from the stone floor, it came slowly, as though it had been embedded there.

The timbre of the light shifted, changed, grew. The vibration within the walls and floor of the keep increased until it became a drumming, rising in pitch and cadence. Dail staggered to his feet, grasped his own sword tighter in his two hands, and braced against a crimson wall for strength. "Can you come with me?"

"Go on. I'll follow."

Dail reached his hand out to the stout wooden door. Radiant light illuminated his flesh and brought the shadow of his bones leaping into view. He shivered, and his belly twisted in revulsion. He moved slowly, as a man trapped in a nightmare, and heaved the door open.

Because he saw her from eyes filled with love, Dail did not see the towering goddess of war but a different manifestation. Through his eyes, she was an idol cast in brilliant ruby stone. Her legs braced in an archer's stance, her head flung back proudly, she did not move.

Dail drew a soft breath of wonder. Her hair, once silver and as soft as moonlit clouds, was graced with scarlet highlights. Had a sculptor cast a mold from her living form and labored all the long years of a whole lifetime, this would have been the result.

She stood motionless yet living, as hard as rose marble yet breathing and real. On her breast hung the Ruby of Guyaire, a flaming jewel drawing in power and pouring light on every corner of the room.

Behind him, Dail heard Garth's soft groan of fear or of pain. The bard drew a long breath, his lungs aching with the effort. "Nikia!"

* * * * *

She knew the voice. Once she'd even loved it. The Hunter-Defender did not turn from that last thought. There had been love between them, the love of friends, and then, growing gently in him, so tenderly that it had lain unknown to her until now, a love different from that.

She turned her eyes away from the progress of her enemy and let them rest on the man at the door. It was the bard. He had filled her waking nightmares with soft songs. He had braced a faltering girl with the support of a love then unrecognized. She recognized it now.

"Bard," she said softly. He quivered at the sound of her voice, and his sword, his poor little weapon, clattered to the floor.

He was not alone. Another stood behind him, his back braced against the doorjamb as though he had no strength to stand. This one she had known more intimately. With this one, she had known love.

She saw them as though from a high plain. She could hardly distinguish between them. The one wavering in the doorway sagged. The other one turned, grasped his arm, and held him up. She felt no pity. Pity was a distraction. Still, far and deep within her, she was glad that neither stood alone.

The brown little creature, the thing that had been the mage, reared from its place at her feet, its small face ablaze with hatred. She did not turn but saw the motion just the same.

"Move," she said, her voice deadly and calm, "and there will not even be ash to mark the place of your death."

The brown creature subsided in abject fear, this being who loomed so large and dark in winter's nightmares. Now it merely whimpered, pitiful and ineffective.

"Nikia!" the bard whispered.

She recognized that name. It belonged to the girl, hardly yet a woman, who had ridden willingly to a fate determined by old men; a lost child who tried to find a niche in a Citadel too large and cold to embrace her. Yes, she remembered Nikia.

"Be still," she said to the bard. "I know you both."

There could be no distraction, not even the well-meaning

one of a friend seeking to aid her. And what was his little aid now? Well meant, aye, but too inconsequential to be counted among her powerful arsenal.

Still, she thought kindly of this bard and the one he supported. She did not wish to see them swept away in the battle that was to come.

"Nikia!"

"No. Be still. Nikia is not here. Wait, and perhaps you will see where she has gone."

Her words bowed the bard with grief. She watched as his legs refused to support him any longer in the presence of the ruby's awesome power. He sagged to the floor, pulling his companion down with him. His hands braced his slow fall, but soon even his arms would not hold him.

She turned her hand toward them and gave them what protection she had to give. She would be pleased if these two survived what was to come.

* * * * *

The Sorcerer waited at the gates of the keep. He felt, in every part of him, the swift draining of will and animation from his armies. He knew the final battle of the war must be fought here.

Red stained the white stone walls of the keep like the reflection of a hundred setting suns. Crimson power filled the broken city of Seuro with a bold will. It did not reach him, not yet, but he knew that if he did not go to meet it, it would reach him, swiftly and with immense power, and it would drag him to the place of battle. He chose instead to go and meet it.

* * * * *

There was a tiny part of Nikia left within the Hunter-Defender, an ember of what she had been in a previous, smaller life. It wondered and shivered and groaned under the strength of the ruby. She knew that she could not let that part of her, that small Elvish princess, become dominant. Not now . . . possibly not ever. It, too, would be a distraction. There must be no distractions.

The killing winds of the Sorcerer's mighty strength howled like a bloodstorm through the keep.

"Hunter-Defender!" she said aloud. "I am the Hunter-Defender!" The small Elvish princess cowered away.

It did not matter to the Hunter-Defender. It only mattered that the Ancient Enemy was advancing, sweeping through the stone corridors of the keep, bringing with him a wind of doom and reckoning.

* * * * *

"I am here." The Sorcerer's voice was the toll of a thousand death knells. Scarlet radiance shifted, drawing back from every corner of the keep. It settled within the ruby on the Hunter-Defender's breast.

The Sorcerer's eyes glittered, as red as the Hunter-Defender's flame, then blue, now green. He knew from the moment he had entered the keep that it was not the little mage, Reynarth, who had taken the ruby. Some other hand wielded it. Still, he hadn't expected to find the Elvish woman here. He smiled, a thin movement of lips which had not moved in honest pleasure in many lifetimes.

"What are you called?" he asked.

"Hunter-Defender."

"Who calls you that?"

"I do. It is enough."

It was. The Sorcerer glanced around the chamber. The little mage, Yvanda's tool, huddled in terror on his knees. That tool was broken and could never be used again. There were others there, and he recognized them as well—the Mannish prince, Garth, and the bard, Dail.

"Your creatures?" he asked.

"No one's."

"Yet your protection cloaks them."

"They are no part of this decision."

The Sorcerer shrugged. The Hunter-Defender would lift that protection if she must. He saw it in her eyes. They would offer him no advantage as hostages. He raised his hand. The Hunter-Defender braced. The ruby quickened on her breast.

"I have two challenges for you, Hunter-Defender. The first might eliminate the second."

"What is your first challenge, then?"

"Only this. Rise up and take what is your due! I can gauge the limits of your power. I know you might not survive a physical challenge from me. You know it as well as I do."

The Hunter-Defender did not answer.

"Or," he continued, unmoved by her silence, "meet this challenge. Come to me. What gain I might win after I have defeated you will be multiplied for both of us if we work together."

"No."

"Then what? Should you defeat me, your own powers must be used. You have called them, and they will not be gainsaid. You will wreak vengeance and a bloodier war on the land than any before now. What will be the gain? Instead, work with me and we will rule together."

"No. I command what I have called."

"And if you win? Will you put aside your power? Can you deny the use of what you have awakened and return to the little world you once knew? It is not the same place. It is shattered, broken between two armies. The dead are innumerable, the land in tatters.

"Will they welcome you back? Is not that creature, that broken wreck of a prince who cowers here beneath your protecting hand, typical of those who scorned your magic, sneered at your gifts, and called you 'witch'?" The Sorcerer's eyes lighted with lazy scorn. "But I misspeak. He is not typical. That one loved you once. See how easily his love turned to hatred? What of those who did not love you?"

It was true! They had scorned her and hurt her with suspicious whispers, taunting and sneering in their pitiful weakness.

And this one, this Garth, had abandoned his love quickly enough! Memories of him, standing weak and shattered in the cavern below the keep, came flooding back to her now. He had been easily filled with hatred and suspicion.

The arrogance of power rose within her, and the Hunter-

Defender turned her eyes to the two fallen men, seeing them for the first time as weak, tiny creatures, cowed by terror. How pitifully they compared with the Sorcerer, as tall and as darkly handsome as a snake is coldly beautiful. Well they might rule together—no king or queen, but god and goddess!

Crimson certainty filled her mind. Her lips parted in a slow smile. A groaning protest turned her briefly from her contemplations of godhood.

Garth moved slowly, painfully, from beneath Dail's protecting arm. Though fear was an ague that left him trembling, he tried to rise, his hand outstretched to her. "No! Nikia!"

He had heard the Sorcerer's words, his challenge and his offer. She saw in every line of his fear-ravaged face that he wondered if there was anything of his wife left to reach.

But there was something. It dwelt far down within her, however, forsaken and forgotten beneath the power rising triumphant in her.

"Nikia!"

Her ruby eyes softened and silvered. The hard lines of her marble face eased as though beneath a sculptor's smoothing hand. "Garth?" The Hunter-Defender whispered his name, and she saw that he knew Nikia was there within her, hidden and changed by the consuming desire for power.

Confusion scattered her thoughts as leaves before a hot summer wind. Nikia's spirit struggled with itself, dragging itself upward, demanding that attention be paid to it. The Hunter-Defender wavered.

"Nikia? Love, listen to me!"

The Sorcerer took a step toward her, judging rightly that any action against the Mannish prince now would only rebound against himself. "Get rid of that mewling wretch!"

The Hunter-Defender's face hardened and her back stiffened at the scorn and laughter in the Sorcerer's voice.

Garth struggled to get his legs beneath him so he could stand. He failed. "Nikia? Come back. Come back now and do what you set out to do!"

What had that been? She had wakened the ruby and had immediately been swept into a scarlet ocean of power. Nikia was close to the surface now, reaching out with soft hands to take the strength that had been denied her by the Hunter-Defender.

Listen, the Elvish princess urged within her. Listen to Garth! Hunter-Defender is what Reynarth made you! He's powerless now! You're no longer his creature! Would you become the creature of your most deadly enemy?

The Sorcerer sighed, then chuckled. It was warning enough. It was the Hunter-Defender who braced herself against the blast of strength and will seeking to overwhelm her.

White radiance flared from the Sorcerer's fingers, leaping and arcing, whistling with the wind of terror. Crimson light, screaming defiance and power, met and matched it.

"It is will that wins," the Sorcerer said softly.

Heat surrounded the Hunter-Defender, greater heat than unshielded human flesh could have withstood. She could spare no attention for the two men who lay on the stone floor under her protection. That shield would hold or it would not.

Ice surrounded the Sorcerer, frost touching his eyes. His skin took on the glittering sheen of snow under the glare of winter sun. Ice and flame met boldly and neither failed.

The Hunter-Defender moved forward a step, brandishing the flame of her power. Crimson lines of blood-hued fire arrowed from her fingers, streaking around the Sorcerer's ice-encased body. Though some glanced off, none harmed the ice sculpture that was her enemy.

She called her flaming darts back and gathered them as though gathering threads of fire. With quick, smoothing gestures, she shaped them into a ball as hot as sunfire, then hurled it, not with muscle but with will, full at his laughing face. It did not consume the ice, nor did it cause the Sorcerer to falter.

"We are two sides of the same power, you and I," the Sorcerer murmured. His frost-touched eyes sparkled with deadly cold. "Winter kills and fire consumes. What end could there be to this struggle but death?"

The sure path of ice was slow and creeping, stealing on life unaware and snuffing it slowly, seductively. It crept toward the Hunter-Defender now. The languor of her enemy's words settled around her, unmelting ice-jewels glittering in the flame.

The Hunter-Defender moved within the crimson halls of the ruby's power, searching for the cleansing strength of flame. When she found it, she gathered it into her heart and let the fire turn her blood to lava, her soul to a light as bright as the sun.

Roaring and snapping, a sheet of flame leaped from her feet to her head, a fiery cloak to fend off the ice of the Sorcerer.

Deep and far away, a familiar voice cried, the voice that had been hers when she was a princess of Elvish, light and breathless with horror: *I am Nikia!* The soul of that little creature darkened with horror, shrieked in terror, couldn't believe that its person wielded the ruby's breathtaking power.

* * * * *

Though Dail still had his senses about him, he couldn't move. Garth lay frighteningly still beside him, barely breathing. He, too, feared to breathe, for even under Nikia's protection, the air about him was scorched and burning.

Was it truly Nikia? How else could he name her? She was Nikia, somewhere far within that fire-draped persona of the Hunter-Defender. Garth had been right to name her Nikia in his plea. She *was* Nikia.

And she was also a pillar of flame facing a wall of ice. The elements were mighty, crimson and blue-white, fighting for dominance. Flame and ice! Dail felt the striving between them screaming in his bones and muscles.

"Nikia!" he groaned. He felt his lips blister as her name passed them in the terrible heat of the chamber. He was but a tiny creature, caught at the edge of a battle of powers his mind couldn't comprehend. Despair took him in dagger teeth and shook him like a rat. The bellowing of her fire didn't fully silence the ominous boom of ice moving inexorably closer.

When he was certain that his lungs were about to burn and blacken in his chest, Dail noticed the heat suddenly subsided. He gulped air raggedly, gratefully. Then swiftly, as hot as the Hunter-Defender's flame, as penetrating as the Sorcerer's ice, fear shot through him. The ice was winning! The Sorcerer took a bold step toward his opponent.

No! Dail screamed in his soul. Nikia!

* * * * *

Nikia was gone, of no concern to the Hunter-Defender who, if she heard the bard's cry at all, didn't understand it. She lived within the ruby's crimson heart now. Flame and fire raged about her, pushing before it its own powerful wind.

The Sorcerer, wielder of killing ice and bone-breaking cold, advanced boldly.

The Hunter-Defender drew a breath, marshaled her strength, and sent her fire leaping from within the ruby's blood-red depths. Flame rose, shrieking in hideous, scarlet rage. The Hunter-Defender's scream of defiance was the roar of flames fanned by remorseless wind. The chamber leaped with light and heat, and the Hunter-Defender closed with her challenger. Like striving gods they fought, breast to breast. The sounds of death roared about them.

Taller than she in his physical body, broader and stronger, the Sorcerer clasped her left wrist in his right hand, twisted, and drove his shoulder hard up under her chin. Her head snapped back and her knees buckled. Her flame cooled where he touched her, then sputtered and died as she collapsed to her knees.

The Sorcerer moved fast. He kicked out hard and leaped on her where she lay, breathless and hurt. His weight was the weight of icy mountains as he dug his knee into the small of her back. His right hand tangled in her hair and felt like the touch of Death.

Laughing, howling like wind across an ice-swept glacier, the Sorcerer got his arm around the Hunter-Defender's throat and pulled hard, not caring now whether he snapped her neck or strangled her.

Fire cooled, flame died, the cold of winter's heart seeped into the Hunter-Defender's bones, drove like glittering ice daggers deep through the red walls of the ruby's power, shattering strength like glass walls.

She bucked hard, but his weight was too much for her. She

twisted, screaming in rage and pain, and managed to free her
left hand. She knew that she'd have no other chance.

Desperately, her eyes deadly red coals, the Hunter-Defender
brought up her free hand and splayed it across the Sorcerer's
face.

It needed only that grip and the small hope it brought to
show her where to find the ruby's flame. Fire leaped out, flaring,
as she dug her fingers deep into his dark eyes, gouging as
though she would not stop until the heat of her flesh melted
through to the back of his skull.

The Sorcerer shrieked, and his scream tore around the seared
chamber and rebounded from the blackened stone walls like
deadly thunder. Blinded, he fell backward, still wailing.

The Hunter-Defender's flame rose, brighter than the sun,
consuming, destroying, and finally transforming its enemy.
Where there had been a blue-edged wall of frozen death, only
steam remained, roiling, hissing, and finally vanishing into
the air.

The mournful howl of the Sorcerer, conquered and driven
from the field of battle before the flaming banners of his enemy,
fled the chamber, a ghost banished into the eternal night
of damnation.

CHAPTER 30

She was not Nikia. Dail didn't know who she was, but he was very certain that she was not Nikia. The bard rose, for now he could, and backed, staggering, against the stone wall.

Garth lay still and silent at his feet, either dead or unconscious, Dail couldn't tell which. He leaned down, keeping his eyes on the Hunter-Defender, and rested his fingers lightly against his cousin's throat. He located a pulse, racing and thready. Relief left him almost too weak to stand. The prince had survived!

Whatever his hopes or dreams had been before this, Dail, long trained to honor the sons of Alain's house, felt nothing but gratitude now.

He regained the wall's support and looked around the chamber. Nothing lived here now but him, Garth, and the Hunter-Defender.

Dail remembered that she had told Reynarth there would not even be ash left to mark his death should she decree it. There was, though. A small stain of gray and black remained on the flags of the floor where the treacherous mage had cowered. Had Reynarth seen each of his twisted plans fall to ruin in the moment before his blood sizzled in his veins? When his bones turned to ash, was his soul replaced by empty despair?

Dail shuddered. This Hunter-Defender was not Nikia, but he didn't know how else to call her. He spoke her name cautiously, and she turned her face to him. He saw a terrible face, painted with triumph. Her eyes, once silver and lovely, shone hard and as red as the ruby she wore. He saw no softness there, no echo of the woman she had been.

"Bard, you live."

He couldn't read her intent in her comment, as once he had been able to do. "Aye, madam." He used the formal title haltingly. It did no justice to her majesty, but he knew no other way to address her short of deification. Instinct would not let him do that. "By your grace, I live, and so does Garth."

Her cool expression remained unchanged. Dail shivered despite the ovenlike temperature of the chamber. She smiled, but it was not a mortal's smile. "What song will you make of this day's work, bard?"

"None, madam. There are no words strong enough to craft this tale."

She seemed pleased. "Still, it is not done—not yet."

"Madam?"

"I would tear down the filthy castle that was his seat of power." Though she didn't name the Sorcerer, Dail knew well whom she meant.

And what then? When all challenges are done, when all opposition removed, what then? Dail dared not ask the question, for he feared the answer. The gentle Nikia was gone far away.

"Bard?" Dail looked up and met her scarlet eyes, then dropped his gaze. He couldn't gaze there long and keep his soul his own.

"There is a small globe on the table there . . . ah!" She shrugged when she saw that there was no table. Furnishing and scrolls, all but the stone that formed the chamber, were gone, consumed in the fire of her wrath.

Dail looked where she had gestured and saw the globe, small and colorless in the ashes. He went to fetch it. He couldn't have done anything else. It sat small in his hands, hardly warm at all. Some magic thing of Reynarth's, no doubt, with strength enough to survive the fury of the battle.

The Hunter-Defender took it from him. Her fingers, where they touched his hands, were cool. "Thank you, bard."

"You once called me Dail, madam."

She smiled again and looked him over carefully. Something like recognition or recollection touched her face. "So I did. There were others with you. . . ."

"Aye, madam. If they live, they wait in a place of safety."

Whispers of memory touched her hard, cold face. She lifted the globe level with her eyes. "They live. I cast no protection over them, but still they live. A lad and an Elvish woman—Lizbet, she is called—and another of your kind."

"Darun."

Her stony eyes grew wistful, as though she sought a memory long faded. She took a short breath and braced herself, visibly throwing off the attempt to remember. "Enough, now. There is still this one thing left to do."

She lifted the globe, as though she were feeling and gauging its weight. Dail knew that she was considering things other than its physical properties.

"Bard," she said almost absently, "come closer and watch this."

He moved slowly, reluctantly, until he stood beside her. Power radiated from her. Dail felt it thrumming in his own blood. It did nothing to cast away his fear.

She squeezed her eyes shut and dropped once again into the crimson heart of the ruby's flames. "Watch the globe, now, bard, and see what becomes of the Sorcerer's foul place."

The castle was small in the globe. Surrounded by the crimson light of her power, Souless rose, its tall, rocky spires thrust into the sky. The sun, as though called there by her will, hung in crimson splendor behind its most lofty tower. Carved from the northern mountains, Souless gleamed and shimmered in a bloody glare.

With a simple gesture of her hand, she sent ravening flames roaring and thundering through the globe. The castle of Souless rumbled and quaked. Stone fell from stone, magicks dispersed. What creatures that lived within it were freed of their master's ill-given life and died, buried under the stone of his defeat.

Nikia let the globe roll from her hands and watched as it fell to the floor and shattered. Shards of the magical orb scattered across the stone flags. She smiled. "Neatly done, wouldn't you agree?"

"Aye, madam," he whispered, his eyes still on the fragments of the ruined globe. The thing had survived the inferno of her fury. It couldn't survive her indifference.

"And now?"

With an effort, Dail dragged his eyes up to meet hers. "Now, madam?"

"Now what is left for me to do?"

Fear shivered through Dail like wind prowling before violent storms. She wore her power like a jeweled crown. He found nothing familiar in her ruby eyes.

"Nikia?"

She eyed him coolly. "She is gone. I do not know where, but she is gone."

"Have you killed her?"

"I? Not I!" The thought seemed to outrage her. Her eyes lighted like dangerous torches.

"Where have you sent her, then?"

"Away. I couldn't have her too near. She was weak, like you and her husband."

"*Your* husband."

"The prince, then. You were distractions I couldn't afford."

"And now, madam?" He addressed the Hunter-Defender, but he spoke to the ember of Nikia's spirit that he hoped still smoldered in this creature's soul. "Now that you've done what you've set out to do, what now?"

There is still godhood, he thought. He saw the same thought in her eyes. "Are we to exchange a master for a mistress?"

The air of the fire-ravaged chamber wavered as though in the heat of summer's glare. Something moved on the air, bodiless, sighing with ages-old weariness. A voice, barely heard, as hollow as an empty crypt, whispered *No!* and Dail went cold to his bones.

The air shivered, and the sounds of his breathing and the Hunter-Defender's became distorted echoes as Dail understood that someone he could not see stood in the library with them. He closed his eyes and took a steadying breath. He was not alone in the dark behind his eyes, not alone in his heart or soul.

Blue-silver eyes regarded him through his own confusion, as soothing as a blessing. He felt an ancient presence, a woman's. Who is it? he thought wildly. Who are you?

She said nothing, but her silence felt like a balm. Then, though he still saw the blue-silver eyes, mournful as a forsaken child's, Dail knew that they no longer saw him. What the woman saw was not the Hunter-Defender but Nikia.

No, the voice sighed, *you are not a goddess, child. You know, as I do, that you've not the strength for that. You couldn't reign long, and the short span that you did would be filled with blood and terror. That is not what you fought for, Daughter, not why you threw the Sorcerer down. Your strength is meant for other, better challenges.*

It was the thinnest voice Dail had ever heard, filled with a longing ache, a cold fear. Hot, wild and desperate, he heard the Hunter-Defender's protest.

"I have met my only challenge, and I have triumphed!"

Child, mourned the lady of the blue-silver eyes, *there is a greater thing to achieve than the defeat of the Sorcerer. Mend now, don't destroy. Mend, Daughter, as once I tried to.*

The heat cooled in the Hunter-Defender's voice. "Who are you?" She asked the question as though gauging the strength of an interloper.

The lady smiled. Dail saw it in her eyes, and it was a lovely, warm smile.

You know me, child, as do both your peoples. When she spoke her name, Dail heard it as *Ylin*.

The Hunter-Defender was silent for a long moment. Dail opened his eyes and saw her, head cocked, hard ruby eyes still. When she spoke again, there were burdens in her words. "I know you, Lady Aeylin."

It might have been Nikia, after all, who spoke, for there was more wondering in her expression than anger. Dail took quick hope and pressed the lady's advantage.

"Take your honored place in history, madam, and return our princess to us." His voice was gentle, imploring. "You have met the challenge of godhood already and won. Must you fight that temptation again? Nikia?"

The Hunter-Defender raised her hand to the ruby and caressed it slowly, as though seeking advice there.

"Nikia?"

Daughter, murmured the lady of the blue-silver eyes, *find a different strength.*

"Dail?" Her voice was different then, wispy as smoke and filled with longing.

Free her from the ruby, bard. Take it from her now.

He hesitated. He could almost feel the searing heat of the ruby where his fingers must touch the chain.

Bard, do it now or lose her!

Dail moved then without thinking. He reached out and slipped the ruby from Nikia's neck. She flinched once and raised her hand as though to prevent him, but she did not.

Slowly the silver-linked chain trailed through her hair, and slowly the burning power drained from her heart. She was once again Nikia.

Her hand trembling, her fingers nerveless, she took the ruby from Dail before fear could stop her. How cool it was now in her hand!

"Nikia, no!"

"Yes," she said, lifting her chin, trying to steady her quailing heart. "For this one more moment." She stepped away from him, moving almost blindly to the deep embrasured window. Red color ghosts reeled across the floor and walls.

I was going to fly from one of these windows, she thought. Tears stung behind her eyes, and her need to weep was an ache along her arms. She steadied her weak legs, squared her bowed shoulders.

Nikia braced against the stone embrasure and lifted the ruby high so that it hung swinging gently at the length of its chain, a blood-red star. She lifted her face to the purple sky of twilight and began to whirl the ruby above her head. Its pale red shadows of light danced across her face and filled, for one last moment, her silver eyes.

Was it pain or triumph that Dail saw there? He couldn't tell, but he thought perhaps that it was both.

Finally, with a sharp twist of her wrist, Nikia released the chain and sent the ruby arcing out into the darkening sky. Then she turned away instantly. She didn't want, for even a moment, to know where the thing had finally fallen.

Let it lie in some gutter of the city, she thought wearily. Let it be found by some poor hungry wretch made homeless by this horrible war! Let him sell it for his supper. Now let it feed instead of kill!

In her eyes was a child who had thrown away a thing of great value, and a woman who had severed a binding chain. Terror and triumph both warred inside her. Her jaw was stiff with her need not to weep, but her lips already trembled before a storm of tears.

Motionless, nearly will-less, she allowed herself to be sheltered in Dail's embrace and wept.

CHAPTER 31

Nikia set her brown wicker basket down beside the stone bench. Cicadas, singing their harsh, winding song, disturbed the afternoon peace with restless noise. The thick sunlight of late summer lay on the Queen's Garden, filling the air with the strong, musky scent of sage, the sweet perfume of basil, the pungent fragrance of rosemary. No weed invaded the planting beds. The earth was dark, freshly turned.

An oasis! she thought. An island in the devastation!

The bench was inviting, nestled into the shaded west corner opposite the solar doors. She had come here to fill her basket with cuttings for the rooting vases in her chamber, but she couldn't resist the invitation of the bench, for she was still weary from the long night before.

It had been a night of harrowing tales, told to a small audience who could hardly believe what they heard. Nikia had not been able to tell the tale of the Battle at Seuro's Keep. She left that to Dail, who exercised his bardic skill with the fervor and intensity of a passion too long stilled.

Some things he didn't tell, because some things he didn't
know. No one in that brightly lighted hall heard of her rape;
that tale would be told to the two kings much later, in private.
No one knew quite what it was that Reynarth had used to torture Garth so expertly. That, if it was to be revealed at all, was
his tale to tell. Even without these elements, those who heard
the tale knew it for a harrowing story.

Last night she had sat silently, her hand in Garth's, and listened to a recitation of events that seemed to have happened to
someone else. Evil growled behind Dail's words. He spoke,
and the kings saw the foul hold of Carah's prison ship, smelled
the stench of dungeons filled with the forsaken. He paused for
breath, and in the silence, shadows drifted across their souls,
running with the ebb and flow of fear.

Though he spoke unaccompanied by his Dashlaftholeh, it
was as though music, deep and filled with dread, groaned
behind his words. With an eloquent simplicity, he told of the
battle between the Sorcerer and the Hunter-Defender. All
saw, as though they had been there and needed only to call
back the memory, the battle between raging flame and inexo-
rable ice.

Dail said nothing about the lady of the blue-silver eyes.
That memory was his and Nikia's, and the time hadn't come
yet to share it with others.

When Dail was done, hours after he had begun, he reached
for a goblet of wine. Calmis had moved quickly to hand it to
him, but Dail's hand had trembled so badly that a few ruby
drops of wine spilled onto his fingers. Nikia had seen her
father shudder at the sight.

And yet, Nikia thought now, shivering in the sunlight
warming the Queen's Garden, that tale has not ended, much
as we would like to think so. There is still the lady's charge to
mend and heal. But how am I going to do that? The wounds
are so deep!

* * * * *

After the battle for the keep of Seuro, she had ridden with
Garth and their small party of friends to Verdant Hall. That

journey had been through Elvish lands nearly all the way. She rejoiced in the peace of the cool, pine-scented forests of the Kevarth Mountains. The meadows between the mountains' foothills and the Landbound Sea were green velvet, starred with daisies, sun globes, pink stars, hare's bells, and more.

When they reached the River Altha and Verdant Hall, Nikia had been delighted to see the catkins frothing with the first of their light, fluffy seed at Altha's edge, the fox's brush unfurling in the heat of the day, showing promise of the gray-brown plumes with which she had decorated her girlhood chambers.

The time at Verdant Hall had done them all good. In her dreams, Nikia saw the blue-silver eyes of the lady she had come to know as Aeylin, and those eyes smiled at her as though approving of her choice to stay for a time at Verdant Hall. Mend, Daughter, the lady had said. Nikia tried.

Garth's dark nightmares persisted, but Nikia was certain that they faded with each night she spent with him.

She had once thought to keep the secret of her rape. She had no wish to relive it, even in the telling, and she didn't know if the knowledge of it would injure Garth further. And yet, that first night at Verdant Hall, when he had told her, with many false starts and much renewed pain, of his torments in the dungeons at Reynarth's hands, Nikia knew that here was a man who might understand what rape was.

She didn't tell him the next, but on the third night. As she lay still in his arms, Nikia had told him of the rape, and though he had wept the first tears she had ever seen from him, he had understood.

The Hunter-Defender was a scarlet memory fading now with each day's passing. Nikia's magic no longer remembered the power that had catapulted it to godhood. Her blood no longer hummed to martial anthems. She was happy to be simply Nikia, daughter of a king, wife of a prince of Mannish.

Riche learned again to run and play. Lizbet, home among familiar surroundings, took on a plump, rosy aspect that was almost startling to see. Dail, who sang little and thought much, attributed it to the constant attention paid her by Calmis.

Nikia missed the bard's songs, and she was afraid that she knew the reason for this preoccupied silence. For all that the fearsome Hunter-Defender had been the dominant aspect of her personality during the battle with the Sorcerer, Nikia remembered what the Hunter-Defender knew about Dail's love. Impulse cried that she should speak with him about it; instinct whispered that she should hold silent.

The love was his, to declare or keep. Nikia hoped he would not offer it. In another time, had her heart not already been given, she would have welcomed it. Now she feared she was about to lose a friend.

If their time at Verdant Hall provided an interlude of grace and healing, the ride to Damris, in the company of her father and those of his court whom he deemed indispensable, had been another matter.

A day away from the Elvish border, Nikia began to notice that the land was drier, seared brown. No flowers danced in the dull gray meadows. The corpses of fish fouled the becks and streams, lying gray and putrid on the cracked, parched mud of the banks.

No bird sang; no rabbit or squirrel dashed away from their approach. The air was hot, still, and breathless, and the only creature they heard was the droning cicada. Even the black flies that normally plagued the streams and meadows at this time of summer were gone.

Once they had paused at the verge of a wide field, stilling their mounts in silent accord. Nothing moved, no breeze sighed, and the air lay on them like a hot glove. Garth, moving to control his suddenly restive mount, leaned forward to stroke the beast's neck.

Nikia had suddenly gone cold, shivering despite the heat of the brazen sun. She looked to Garth and saw the agony of the meadow reflected in his eyes, as bleak and hopeless as bleached bones.

Garth had reached for her hand. "I've seen this before. It was like this in the North nearly a year ago." His mouth twisted in a pain filled grimace. "The Sorcerer's first ploy is with us still."

In his memory, a wind mourned, as empty as the little cradle in Harvest Run. It whistled through empty cottages, groaned around the eaves of barns left abandoned, sighed in the throats of wells fouled with the Sorcerer's evil magic.

* * * * *

Now the wind, dry and hot, sent the dust swirling around the Queen's Garden. It seemed to Nikia that she could still smell the flat dry heat of that ruined meadow.

Can this be mended? Is there strength enough in the whole kingdom to heal this?

As though in answer, the cicadas droned wearily. The march of gray, dying land crept closer to Damris. Nikia wondered if there was another patch of green anywhere in the Mannish Kingdom.

I am going to root these cuttings, and pot them, and keep them against this plague. Oh, Aeylin, will it be enough?

The gate across the garden creaked. Nikia looked up to see Dail standing just inside. She raised a hand in greeting and watched as he crossed the garden to join her.

"Lady, the council is about to begin and Garth sent me to find you."

Hot sun burnished his hair, black shot with gray—more gray, Nikia thought sadly, than a year ago. A smile lighted his blue eyes, but not so brightly as it might have, for they were shadowed with the burden of a secret that was no secret to her.

He gestured toward the basket. "For your rooting vases?"

"Yes. We'll want these soon, I think."

Dail hesitated a moment, then dropped down beside her on the bench. "I can't help thinking about the farmers and the hunters and the people in the cities. What will they eat this winter, lady? There are no crops. Hunters are coming back empty-handed, and they don't know where the animals have gone."

"A way will be found to feed them. My father has already offered to provide guides for hunting parties into Elvish lands. It's one of the things Garth was assured of before we left Verdant Hall."

"That will feed them this year, but what about next year? Two kingdoms can't live off the bounty of one."

For a long moment, Nikia didn't answer. She didn't know how to answer his brooding, grim-hearted mood. The grief in his eyes wasn't all for farmers and hunters. A small voice whispered to her that now might be the moment when she would lose this friend.

She spoke, more to defer the moment than to assure him of larger matters. "We'll live next year when it happens. We'll learn what this plague is and discover how to cure it."

Dail watched her closely. She spoke, of course, of magic. In the year past, he had learned this much at least: Magic ills must be met with magic cures. And yet he shuddered to think that magic must again be used in the kingdom.

"You've had a bad lesson in magic, my friend," Nikia said gently, then laughed to see his surprise. "That wasn't magic; I didn't read your mind. I didn't have to," she said gently. "I've learned how to read your expression, Dail."

"Aye, lady, that you have." He stopped as though he were pausing at a crossroad and looked at her for direction. The love he felt seemed no longer a shadow or a burden. For that one moment, he neither apologized for it nor feared it.

Nikia knew then what it would be like to be loved by this man. His love is like his music, she thought—low, soft hymns, bright anthems, canticles, and cradle songs. And if we talk about this now, whatever gets said, I'm going to lose a friend!

She gently covered his hand with her own and spoke of the only thing she would ever ask of him. "It won't be an easy thing to cure what afflicts this land, Dail. The council won't be easily convinced that magic is the only cure. Garth and I have set ourselves that task, but we badly need friends in our camp now. It will not be easy to explain this to the people who face starvation now because of magic."

Nikia was silent for a long moment. When she looked up again, she tried hard to keep a note of pleading from her voice. "Dail, will you be one of those friends?"

He was yet at the crossroad. In his eyes, she could see his thoughts, and finally his decision. He moved his hand from beneath hers and took up her basket. Running his thumb along the smooth edge of the wicker handle, he smiled quickly.

"Lady, I have always been your friend. I don't understand why you would question that now."

Relief, like a cooling breeze, washed over her. Nikia reclaimed her basket and would have said something further, but Garth, standing at the garden's gate, called.

"Nikia, the council awaits! Come, love, there's work to be done."

Aye, Nikia thought, rising—work and mending and healing. She turned to Dail and whispered, "I will speak of Aeylin today, Dail. Will you be with me?"

"The lady of the blue-silver eyes . . ." Dail murmured. "Aye, lady, I'll be with you."

Always, he thought. He let her run a little ahead and watched her slip into Garth's quick embrace. She looked very right there, he thought, like part of a whole. He knew then that it was because she wanted to be there. He knew, with sudden certainty, that she would be happy nowhere else.

But if she had a choice? He didn't know. Dail crossed the garden, trying not to think about love or friendship. He would not dwell on those things now. As he walked, he put aside, before they were born, all the songs he would have sung for an Elvish Starflower.

But he was not song-reft. When he closed his eyes, he saw once again the blue-silver eyes of Aeylin, of Ylin, and the thought came to him with the suddenness of light shafting into a forest's dark glade that the mysterious lady desperately needed a new song. . . .

EPILOGUE

I am Islief of the First People. A hunter-defender has gone to war and come back in triumph. I have felt the spirit of Aeylin abroad in the land. Her descendants have not misused my trust. In my dreams, I see her blue-silver eyes; in my heart, I feel a tremor. The new age has shouldered hard against the womb of time.

Old am I, so old, and weary of watching and waiting! But I sense my ending now, as a fox scents home.

Ah, gods! Will you bring me, finally, home? Can you grant me now that grace?

THE AUTHOR

NANCY VARIAN BERBERICK lives in a small rural town in the west New Jersey hills with her husband, two dogs, and a computer. Her work has appeared in AMAZING® Stories; DRAGON® Magazine; all three DRAGONLANCE® *Tales* short story anthologies; a horror story anthology, *Women of Darkness*; and has been excerpted in J.N. Williamson's *How to Write Tales of Horror, Fantasy and Science Fiction*.

DRAGONLANCE® *Preludes*

Darkness and Light
Paul Thompson and Tonya Carter

Darkness and Light tells of the time Sturm and Kitiara spent traveling together before the fated meeting at the Inn of the Last Home. Accepting a ride on a gnomish flying vessel, they end up on Lunitari during a war. Eventually escaping, the two separate over ethics.

Kendermore
Mary L. Kirchoff

A bounty hunter charges Tasslehoff Burrfoot with violating the kender laws of prearranged marriage. To ensure his return, Kendermore's council has his Uncle Trapspringer prisoner. Tas meets the last woolly mammoth and an alchemist who pickles one of everything, including kender!

Brothers Majere
Kevin Stein

Much to Raistlin's irritation, Caramon accepts a job for both of them: they must solve the mystery of a village's missing cats. The search leads to murder, a thief who is not all that he appears, and a foe who is not what Caramon and Raistlin expect.

FANTASY ADVENTURE

THE MOONSHAE TRILOGY
Douglas Niles

DARKWELL

The ultimate struggle of good and evil.... At stake, the survival of the Moonshae Isles. Tristan must forge a lasting alliance between the divergent people of the Isles. Robyn must confront an evil that has infested the land itself. Together they must face the future as king and queen--or as enemies, forever separated by failure and mistrust. Available now.

1987: DARKWALKER ON MOONSHAE
Tristan Kendrick must rally the diverse people of the Isles of Moonshae to halt the spread of a relentless army of Firbolgs and dread Bloodriders.

1988: BLACK WIZARDS
An army of ogres and zombies guided by Bhaal threatens the gentle Ffolk while the puppet king acquiesces.

ARRIVAL

*Stories By Today's Hottest
Science Fiction Writers!*

Flint Dille

Abigail Irvine

M.S. Murdock

Jerry Oltion

Ulrike O'Reilly

Robert Sheckley

A.D. 1995: An American pilot flies a suicide mission against an enemy Space Defense Platform to save the world from nuclear war. Buck Rogers blasts his target and vanishes in a fiery blaze.

A.D. 2456: In the midst of this 25th century battlefield an artifact is discovered--one that is valuable enough to ignite a revolution. This artifact is none other than the perfectly preserved body of the 20th century hero, Buck Rogers.

THE MARTIAN WARS TRILOGY
M.S. Murdock

Rebellion 2456: Buck Rogers joins NEO, a group of freedom fighters dedicated to ridding Earth of the Martian megacorporation RAM. NEO's goal is to gain enough of a following to destroy RAM's Earth Space Station. The outcome of that mission will determine the success of Earth's rebellion. Available in May 1989.

Hammer of Mars: Ignoring RAM threats and riding on the wave of NEO's recent victory, Buck Rogers travels to Venus to strike an alliance. Furious, RAM makes good on its threats and sends its massive armada against a defenseless Earth. Available in August 1989.

Armageddon Off Vesta: Martian troops speed to Earth in unprecedented numbers. Earth's survival depends on Buck's negotiations with Venus. But even as Venus considers offering aid to Earth, Mercury is poised to attack Venus. Relations among the inner planets have never been worse! Available in October 1989.

New TSR™ Books

Illegal Aliens
Nick Pollotta
Phil Foglio
Hugo award-winning illustrator

A New York City street gang becomes guinea pigs for a group of weirdo aliens. Available in February 1989.

Monkey Station
Ardath Mayhar
Ron Fortier

A deadly plague sweeps the globe, causing the Macaques in the rain forests of South America to evolve faster. Available in June 1989.